Praise for the Series

"*A Drop of Magic* is a damned fun and original read, with sass, action, hot men, and a whole lot of magic."
—Diana Pharaoh Francis, author of the Diamond City Magic, Magicfall, and Horngate Witches series

"What an evocative, and at times chilling, tale featuring Fae, shifters and fanatics. I could not put it down until I was finished."
—Karen Fisher, NetGalley Reviewer on *A Drop of Magic*

"An enjoyable read to the start of a new series."
—Nicole Lippolis, NetGalley Reviewer, on *A Drop of Magic*

Other Titles
by L. R. Braden

The Magicsmith Series

A Drop of Magic, Book 1
Courting Darkness, Book 2
Faerie Forged, Book 3
Casting Shadows, Book 4
Of Mettle and Magic, Book 5
Chaos Song, Book 6
Lies and Illusion, Book 7

The Rifter Series
(set in the Magicsmith Universe)

Demon Riding Shotgun, Book 1
Personal Demons, Book 2
A Demon Faerie Tale, Book 3
Dancing with a Demon, Book 4

Courting Darkness

Book 2 of the Magicsmith Series

by

L.R. Braden

Magical Realms Press

Magical Realms Press
PO BOX 24
Broomfield, CO 80038

Print ISBN: 978-1-968414-03-0

Published in the United States of America.

First Published by Bell Bridge Books in 2019

We love to hear from readers!
Contact us at:
MagicalRealmsPress.com
LRBraden.com

Cover design: Debra Dixon
Interior design: Hank Smith
Photo/Art credits:
Woman (manipulated) © Wrangler - Dreamstime.com
Background (manipulated) © Unholyvault | Dreamstime.com

Dedication

For David, the love of my life.

Chapter 1

MY BREATH PUFFED out in angry little clouds as I shivered under the star-streaked sky that stretched above my patch of frozen mountain. Jaw clenched, I shoved a key into the lock on my front door with enough force to jerk the purse off my shoulder. It slid down, snagging at my elbow, and the shift in weight jostled the dome-covered cake balanced in my other hand.

I couldn't believe James had stood me up again. After all his promises. Twenty minutes standing outside his house. Then a quick call about unavoidable business at the gallery. Sure he'd apologized, given me his usual line about making it up to me "another time." But another time never seemed to come for James and me.

I twisted the keys. Those not in the lock dug into my palm.

Another time. If he said those words again, I was going to run him over with my Jeep.

The door stuck, swollen by moisture. I growled and pushed harder, hissing when my weight settled onto the freshly re-knit muscles of my right leg. I gave the door another shove, and it finally gave way, slamming into the adjoining wall with a *bang*, my keys still dangling from the lock.

I froze in the doorway. My living room was occupied.

I'd been looking forward to curling up with my cake and my anger. Habits formed through years of solitude were hard to break, and I still wasn't used to having roommates. Company was going to put a serious crimp in my plans.

Kai and Chase were sitting across from each other on my faded furniture, cards and poker chips on the coffee table between them. Neither seemed surprised by my dramatic entrance.

"You're home early." Kai glanced in my direction, and his eyes were swirling galaxies of color rather than the deep brown of his glamour— the human disguise he wore less and less these days. He was a fae knight from the Realm of Enchantment who'd been living in my guest room for about a month, most of which was spent saving the world from a murderer with a magic, world-eating box. He cradled a hand of cards to his chest so his opponent couldn't cheat. "Didn't think we'd see you till much later."

"Or tomorrow," added Chase without looking up.

I'd let Chase into my home when I thought he was just a cat, before I knew he was actually a fae who could change form at will. I let him stay because he saved my life. Of course, when I made that deal, the understanding was that he'd remain the gray tabby I'd taken in last summer, but he'd been spending more time with fingers than fur lately.

"Call." He dumped a handful of colorful plastic chips onto the pile already on the table.

"Yeah well . . ." I pulled my key out of the door and kicked it closed behind me. "Plans change."

Chase glanced up and raised a silver eyebrow over one luminous green eye. "You've replaced James with a cake?"

The plastic dome I hugged gave a clear view of the decadent chocolate cake I'd picked up on my way home.

"This is my consolation prize." I lifted my chin and carried the calorie-laden confection to the high counter that separated the kitchen from the living room. "Don't judge me."

"Let me guess." Chase tossed his long silver braid behind his shoulder, making his pointed, slightly furry ears twitch. "Something came up."

"Again," Kai added. He spread his cards on the table. "Two pair."

"Full house," Chase said with a grin. He scooped up his winnings.

Kai looked over at me. "It's important to know when to fold."

I'd been thinking the same thing all the long drive home. I'd done my best with James. I'd really put myself out there. But after all the excuses, and conflicting schedules, and missed dates. . . . I'd been down this road enough to know where it ended. I'd had my fill of waiting for men who never showed up. Still, I wasn't about to give Kai the satisfaction of an "I told you so."

I crossed my arms and dropped onto the couch next to Kai. "That little tip just lost you a piece of cake."

His smile went slack. Kai had the biggest sweet tooth I'd ever seen. "You'll get fat if you eat it all on your own."

I gestured to Chase, who was stacking his winnings into neat little piles. "Chase can help me."

Chase shook his head. "Cats don't eat chocolate."

"They don't normally eat pizza either, but that's never stopped you." I "accidentally" nudged the coffee table with my knee, sending Chase's carefully stacked poker chips cascading across the surface.

"Hey! Don't get pissy at me just because your old stiff couldn't follow through."

"James is *not* an old stiff," I said. "He's refined. Something you wouldn't understand."

He snorted. "Whatever you say."

I turned to Kai. "Back me up here."

"Will it earn me some cake?"

"Ha," roared Chase. "Spineless elf."

"Mangy stray," Kai shot back.

Chase took a bow and began to melt, shrinking and shifting until a gray tabby sat on the faded beige cushion of Chase's chair.

Sighing, I lifted a blue poker chip and rolled it over my knuckles. "What were you betting?"

Kai tipped his head to one side and frowned. "Little bits of colored plastic, obviously."

I rolled my eyes and tossed the chip back on the pile. "The chips are usually backed by money, but I guess you and Chase aren't exactly rolling in human cash."

"Actually, I received my first paycheck last week."

When Kai made the decision to stick around the mortal realm to instruct me in all things fae, he also started working part-time at a convenience store owned by a registered halfer who owed him a favor. The job was dull, but necessary to get a work visa from the PTF—the Paranatural Task Force that policed interactions between humans and fae—which was the only way a full-blooded fae could legally stay in the human realm.

"Congratulations."

"I've been thinking about what to do with it, though I hadn't considered rolling in it. I believe humans have a custom of paying a portion of the expense of shared living space, so I thought I might do that."

"You mean rent?"

He thrust a finger at me. "Exactly. What do I owe you?"

I lifted one shoulder. "On the house."

"Yes. What do I owe on the house?"

I rolled my eyes. "It means forget about it. I don't need your money."

"Are we not roommates?"

"Sure, but it's not like this is a permanent arrangement. We haven't even talked about what happens after my trip to court." My breath hitched, as it often did when anyone mentioned my summons to the fae

Court of Enchantment. Kai had convinced the powers-that-be— namely my long-lost great-grandfather—that I wasn't ready, hence his new job as my personal tutor. But we had no idea how long the arrangement would last. Maybe I'd never be ready for life among the fae.

He frowned. "I still feel I should contribute."

"How about groceries? Between you and Chase, the fridge is almost always empty."

"Deal." He thrust out his hand, and I shook it, trying not to laugh at his triumphant expression.

Chase, who'd been watching our exchange, perked up at the word "groceries." Once the deal was struck, he sprang into my lap and nuzzled his head against my chin.

Without thinking, I stroked his back and scratched around his ears.

"You know that's still Chase, right?" Kai watched us with a mixture of amusement and frustration. "You shouldn't treat him differently just because he looks like a cat."

I shrugged. "I can't help it."

Kai made a disgusted noise and scooped the cat out of my lap, dropping him unceremoniously to the floor. Chase gave an indignant hiss and sauntered off.

"If you can't even deal with that riffraff, how do you expect to get by at court?"

I nibbled a piece of loose cuticle and hunched deeper into the sagging couch cushion, wishing for the millionth time that life could go back to the way it was before Kai showed up at my door. Back when I thought I was human.

Most halfers—fae-human hybrids—returned to their regular lives after registering with the PTF, but that wasn't an option for me. Unlike the vast majority of fae offspring, I wasn't allergic to metal. Hell, it was how I made my living. And according to Kai, there was only one bloodline capable of producing fae that could handle iron. That was why Kai was still there, why I had to take faerie protocol lessons, and why Uncle Sol, the man who'd raised me since a car crash killed my mom, was doing his best to keep my name off the PTF registry.

I rubbed the intricate tattoo that wound its way up my right arm. Learning I was the by-blow of a fae-human love affair untold generations ago had been a hard pill to swallow. Finding out I was royal had been a kick in the head.

"I still don't see why I have to go. Your mission was a success, the killer was brought to justice, and gramps got back his magic death-box.

Why can't we just leave it at that and all go our merry ways?"

Kai pinched the bridge of his nose. "We've gone over this. There is no going back. The gift my lord gave you to boost your powers also marked you as his blood-kin. There's no hiding who you are now."

"I could hide just fine if I stayed here," I argued. "But parading around a fae court with the Lord of Enchantment is going to make me pretty damn conspicuous."

There was a time I would have been happy to have a long-lost relative come and claim me, as any orphan would, but I held no delusion that he'd found me out of kinship or caring. I was one of only three living imbuers—a rare gift. No fae would pass up his claim to an imbuer, regardless of how tenuous the connection or how weak the blood of the halfer.

Kai rolled his eyes—an expression I was pretty sure he'd picked up from me. "You're a member of the court now, like it or not. If you don't go to them they will eventually come to you, and I guarantee you would not enjoy that experience. In either case, learning our customs and traditions is the best way to protect yourself. Besides, there's no one in this world or any other who can instruct you in the art of imbuing as well as my lord."

I crossed my arms, frowning. "My abilities are fine the way they are."

Truth be told, there was a lot I still had to learn about my powers, and magic in general, but that was the one subject Kai had steadfastly refused to cover. Mostly our sessions consisted of mind-numbing etiquette and history lessons, although he'd recently begun teaching me how to fight with a sword.

"It's important for you to understand how the fae world works before you take your place in it. To that end…" He picked up an old leather-bound book from a pile on the floor and held it out. "A little light reading before bed."

"Haven't I suffered enough tonight?"

"It's the chronicle of your family tree. I thought you might be interested to see where you came from."

"I know where I come from," I snapped, but I took the proffered tome just the same.

"You know less about yourself than anyone I've ever met."

"What's that supposed to mean?"

"Never mind." He waved his hand as if wiping the words away. "I'm turning in. I have an early shift at the store tomorrow."

"How's that going, by the way?"

He shrugged. "I play tricks on the customers to entertain myself when it's slow."

My jaw dropped. "If someone reports you, your visa will be revoked. You'll be deported back to the reservation."

"Don't worry." He grinned. "Humans haven't got a clue."

I scowled. "Don't say I didn't warn you."

I WOKE FEELING sluggish and heavy, as though my bones and muscles had turned to jelly in the night. The dusty tome Kai had given me was a weight on my chest, pages crumpled from its fall. I smoothed the bent corners and pressed the cover flat, running a hand over an embossed coat of arms. A stylized flame sat at the center of an eight-pointed star, crossed with a sword and hammer.

My eyelids sagged, but a flash of silver in the pre-dawn light drew my attention. Shifting slightly, I peeked over a mound of crumpled covers to a waterfall of silver hair that stopped just shy of covering the naked butt of the man lying next to me.

"Chase!" I lurched away with a shriek, grabbing the sheets as I tumbled to the floor. Struggling to my knees, I clutched the tangled fabric to my chest and glared over the side of the bed.

With a yawn, Chase rolled onto his back and stretched from fingertips to toes.

My face became a furnace. "What the hell are you doing?"

"I *was* sleeping." He scratched a hand over his chest, across his abdomen, and—

I jerked my eyes back to his face. "Get out of my bed!"

"You seemed lonely. I thought you could use a little company. Besides, you didn't have any objections last night." He closed his eyes and seemed to doze off again.

Bunching my fists in the sheet to stop from strangling him, I counted to ten. Then I grabbed the pillow and yanked it out from under his head.

"What the—"

I swung the pillow.

"Get. Out. Of. My. Room." Each word was punctuated by a smack from the pillow as he struggled into a sitting position.

"Stop that!" He grabbed my wrist.

"Get out!"

"What's going on in here?" Kai stood in the doorway, rubbing sleep from his kaleidoscopic eyes.

I looked from Kai, dressed in a pair of Buzz Lightyear pajama pants that hung low on his skinny hips, to Chase, naked in my bed, and wondered, not for the first time, what had happened to the quiet, solitary life I'd enjoyed only a month before.

Shaking my head, I gritted my teeth and growled, "Everybody out."

Chase tugged on my wrist enough to plant a soft kiss on the inside of my arm, then let go with a laugh. He sprang off the bed before I could react, melting and shifting as he sailed through the air so it was the silent paws of a gray tabby that hit the floor at Kai's feet and bolted out of the room.

"None of my business." Kai smirked and pulled the door closed.

I let out an inarticulate scream of frustration and threw my pillow at the closed door, then I flopped onto the bed with a groan. Was it too late to revoke the offer to let them stay?

Twenty minutes later, I sipped steaming tea and watched snowflakes flit through the air from my favorite chair by the front window. Morning had brought with it a flurry of snow, filling the sky with white and blanketing the land in silence. Towering pines and the bare branches of aspens stood sentry around my property, cloaked in winter. The landscape did wonders to soothe my thoughts as the dim glow of the sun rose above the treetops to brighten the overcast sky.

Kai strolled into the living room in loose sweats and a Grateful Dead t-shirt. He headed straight for the dining table, which was covered with books and papers, and clapped his hands. "Ready to review your etiquette?"

"And I was having such a nice morning." I drained the last of my tea and took my cup to the sink. "Weren't we supposed to have sword practice today?"

Those lessons I actually enjoyed, and unlike knowing the proper depth of a bow to make to a member of the fae court depending on their rank in relation to my own, sword skills might actually be useful in the real world.

"You need to focus more on your weaker areas. You're a terrible swordsman, but you can probably manage not to die long enough for help to arrive. On the other hand, you will almost certainly insult someone important within moments of your arrival at court, and that can be just as deadly."

"I'm not that bad at the sword," I pouted.

"Not for someone with a week and a half of training," he conceded.

"But most fae have had hundreds of years to practice. By our standards, you're a toddler with a pointy stick and no motor control."

"Ouch."

He shrugged. "You know I can't lie."

"Doesn't mean you have to be so honest," I grumbled.

"Look, we—" Kai cut off mid-sentence. His head snapped around and he stared at the front door in wide-eyed horror. "Oh no."

"What is it?" I sprang to my feet, adrenaline coursing through me. I hadn't heard anything, and there were no cars in sight through the large window that overlooked the front of my property.

"Alex." He grabbed me by the shoulders, pulling me to face him. "You need to remember everything I've taught you."

"What are you—"

A sharp knock sounded against the door, and Kai practically flew across the room to open it, leaving me to stagger after him.

Chapter 2

THE WOMAN ON my porch had pale, papery skin that puckered like fruit left too long in the sun. Her lips were thin, almost invisible, and pulled down in a sharp frown. Drooping blue eyes as cold and clear as the winter sky stared from a web of wrinkles. I got the feeling those wrinkles were from perpetual scowling rather than any amount of laughter. Despite the weight of her years, she stood ramrod straight with her chin high, hands clasped lightly over the rich fabric of a dress from a Renaissance festival. Her silver-white hair was pulled back in a severe bun that left her face exposed. The telltale shimmer of a glamour surrounded her.

Refocusing my eyes, I tried to shift my perception the way Kai had taught me. Ever since I'd touched the beautiful, terrible chain that had burned itself into my flesh as an intricate tattoo, the few drops of fae blood in my veins had been amplified enough to peek through basic fae glamours, but the illusion of an old human lady remained firmly in place.

Kai had swung the door wide open and stood to the side with his eyes on the floor. From the line of his jaw and the tension in his neck it was safe to assume this was not someone he was happy to see.

"Hello," I said, taking a step forward. "Can I help you?"

The woman stepped fully into the room, leaving Kai to close the door behind her. Without even acknowledging my presence, she turned a slow circle, taking in the worn, mismatched furniture, the scratched desk in the corner where my computer sat, the cheap knick-knacks cluttering my shelves, and the half-eaten chocolate cake sitting on the counter. When her circuit was complete, her gaze settled on me, judging.

I tried not to shrink under the weight of that stare.

"Honored tutor." Kai kept his head bowed as he spoke, and some distant part of my brain registered the angle as significant. "May I present the Lady Alyssandra Katherine Blackwood."

It was the first time Kai had ever used my full name, and it made me shudder. I felt like something had been surrendered, something that should have been kept secret.

In one of our endless lessons, Kai had explained that the fae had a sort of naming ceremony when they came of age. It wasn't a specific age, but rather a stage of life—puberty for immortals. During that ceremony they went off alone to complete some kind of trial. Some children never came back from those trials, and some came back broken, but those who passed came back with a name. A secret name that only they knew, and if they were wise it stayed that way. The fae were protective of their names, as the true name of a fae was a powerful thing.

My name had been many things—a prison, an honor, a rebellion, an endearment, but it had never felt like a danger before now.

The woman bowed, a rigid stiff-backed bend that brought her forehead even with my chin. "Milady."

"Uh, hi." I gave a little finger wave.

Kai cringed, so I tried again.

Since "lady" seemed like a higher rank than "tutor," I inclined my chin by a fraction.

Whether that was the correct response or not, the tutor took it as a sign to rise from her bow. "You may address me as Hortense," she said in a voice like dust, dry and little used.

"And you can call me Alex," I said.

She pursed her lips and paced a slow circle around me. The hairs on the back of my neck began to itch, but Kai was pleading with wide eyes, so I clenched my fists and stood as still as I could while Hortense made her inspection.

When she stood in front of me again, she lifted her chin. "I have been sent by the Lord of Enchantment. The date of your court appearance has been set."

The words were a punch to the gut. I'd known this was coming, just not so soon. I took a steadying breath and let out a laugh that shook too much to sound real. "You make it sound like I'm on trial."

"An apt description. You shall attend the Winter Festival."

"That's only a few weeks away! She can't—" Kai stepped forward, but dropped his gaze when Hortense shot him a look.

She turned back to me. "I am here to assess your readiness."

"INCORRECT." HORTENSE snapped the word before I'd even finished my sentence. "Let us try an easy one. List the fae courts."

I took a deep breath and tried to concentrate. "There's Enchantment, obviously. Then there's the court of Illusions, the Aery, Shadows, um, Shifters, and Elementals. There's an underwater court, but I forget the name of that one. Oh, and the Demon Court."

"No!" She slapped her hands down on the scarred surface of my dining table. I hadn't thought her frown could get any deeper, but looking at the sharp curve of her lips made my face hurt. "Have you learned nothing?"

I snapped my mouth closed on my first response, took a deep breath, and asked, "What did I miss?"

"Aside from the fact that you forgot the name of the Undine and left the High Court out entirely? There is no Demon Court. That would imply demons are fae, which they are not. They exist entirely in a non-corporeal state in the Rift, the Realm of Chaos, unless a mortal is foolish enough to give them possession of a body. Including them in the list of fae courts is a great insult."

"Gimme a break." I pushed my hands through the frizz of my unbrushed hair. "I didn't know there was going to be a quiz today, and we've already been at it for nearly three hours."

My ass was numb, my back was stiff, and I hadn't gotten my shower. I stretched my arms overhead and my shoulders popped in testimony to my discomfort. "I need to get ready for work soon. How many more questions have you got?"

Hortense scowled. "Your impatience is unbecoming of a Lady of the Court. It draws attention to your very mortal sensibilities and shortcomings."

I bristled at the way she said mortal, like what she really wanted to say was disgusting or pathetic. "I don't consider being on time to my prior commitments a shortcoming. If you wanted my undivided attention, you should have made an appointment."

She pulled her shoulders back and seemed to grow an extra inch despite her already perfect posture. "You are outspoken, impatient, and ignorant."

"You're pompous, stuck-up, and condescending," I countered. Then I closed my eyes, wishing I could take the words back. Despite the way her holier-than-thou attitude set my teeth on edge, pissing off my grandfather's messenger was counterproductive.

Kai groaned behind me. Hortense had insisted he remain in the room, but outside my field of vision. Guess she didn't want him sneaking me the answers to her endless questions.

So far, I'd been asked to recite the lineage of all the major families of the Court of Enchantment; name the fae realms, the lords that ruled them, and the species most often found there; the meaning behind every type of flower and their herbal properties; the differences in the schools of magic; and the traditional ceremonies for a number of special occasions ranging from solstices to coronations. After nearly three hours of falling short on every one of her questions, I was tired, cranky, and ready to kick her out on her arrogant butt.

Looking over my head, Hortense addressed Kai directly for the first time since she'd ordered him to bring in her bags. "This child is in no way prepared for life at court. You have failed your mission."

"Lay off." I set my palms flat on the table and stood. "It's not Kai's fault I'm a lousy student."

"It's all right, Alex." Kai touched my arm. "The tutor is right. I have failed you."

I shook my head. "No, she isn't. You're doing fine. No one could have taught me all that stuff in such a short amount of time."

"I will report my findings to the lord," Hortense continued. "Given the circumstances, I should be very surprised if you are allowed to remain at your current post."

"I understand." Kai bowed his head.

Growling at the way Kai groveled to this jerk, I smacked him on the arm, hard. "Knock it off." He flinched, but didn't straighten.

Hortense cleared her throat. "These are for you." She pointed to the trunk Kai had carried in. The inside was full of books, scrolls, and piles of loose papers. "You will memorize the information stored here before I return."

I looked at her blankly. "You're coming back?"

"Of course," she said. "Someone must ensure you are prepared for court."

"That's Kai's job."

"It was." She straightened a few papers strewn across the table and took a sip from the water Kai had set out when we moved into the dining area. "I shouldn't be surprised if the lord redeploys me as soon as he receives my report. You obviously require firmer guidance than this knight is capable of providing."

My fingers curled. "You have no right to show up out of the blue and make judgments like that."

She set her glass down. "I have every right, and if the knight had done his duty you would already be aware of that. I don't know how he convinced the lord to let him try in the first place, but he is in no way capable of filling the role of tutor."

I crossed my arms. "If you think I'm going to let you take his place, you're dead wrong."

The tutor's brow furrowed. "Why would you refuse the service of those most qualified to assist you?"

"I don't like you."

She blinked. "What has that to do with it?"

"Just make sure that when you give your report, you tell him I'm against having anyone else sent here. If Gramps wants me trained, Kai is the man for the job."

She tilted her head like a bird eying a worm. "Even if it costs you your life?"

"I trust him. Which is more than I can say about you."

Hortense was quiet for a moment. Then she said, "Very well," turned, and walked out of the house.

I stomped over and slammed the door on the swirl of frost that blew across my empty porch and the unbroken field of snow beyond.

"You shouldn't have done that." Kai plucked at the hem of his Guardians of the Galaxy shirt. "You'd be better off with a real tutor."

"What's with you? You really think I want to spend time with that jerk?"

He ran his hands through his hair, and the frustration and anger he'd been keeping in check all morning came bubbling to the surface. "That's not the point."

"I'm sorry I failed her test, but I wasn't ready for it."

"That's the problem, Alex."

The disappointment in his voice twisted my insides. Disappointment, and something else. He believed what Hortense had said—he thought he was a failure—but I'd been the one to fail.

He shook his head. "The point is moot anyway. The decision is out of our hands."

I swallowed the dry lump in my throat. "Do you think Gramps will fire you?"

He gave a weak smile. "I don't know."

I bit my lower lip. I was just starting to get used to having Kai around. Sure it was weird having someone in my space, but it was also kinda nice to have someone besides myself to talk to.

"The tutor will certainly argue for my dismissal," he said. "But you gave her a pretty interesting message to deliver. I honestly don't know how the lord will take it."

"You think she'll actually tell him what I said?"

"Of course. She's duty-bound to do so."

"What do you mean?"

"While instructing or testing you as a tutor to a pupil she is afforded special privileges. However, you are a Lady of the Court. Your station is above hers. She would not dare ignore or circumvent your order. She'll deliver the message exactly as you phrased it."

I pictured Hortense repeating my words verbatim to a regal old fae on a throne, and frowned. Not the most eloquent speech, but done was done, nothing I could do about it now.

"So when exactly is the Winter Festival?" I asked.

"Sooner than I'd like." Kai rubbed a hand over the back of his neck. "The festival corresponds roughly with the winter solstice here in the mortal realm, but since time moves a little differently in the fae realms, it's not a perfect match."

In one of our endless lessons, Kai had mentioned that each realm had a slightly different time flow. If I remembered correctly, Enchantment's was a little slower than Earth's, so more time passed here than there.

"Now." Kai started pulling books and scrolls out of Hortense's trunk. "Shall we see what she's left you?"

I eyed the seat I'd spent most of the morning squirming in, and the aches in my back and neck flared. The last thing I wanted was another hour in that chair while Kai tried to jam more faerie knowledge into my head. But I had two hours before I was due at the bookstore, and with my meeting with the Lord of Enchantment looming over me, I didn't have time to waste. Sighing, I settled back at the table and reached for the first book.

Chapter 3

SINCE MY WORLD had gotten so much stranger lately, I'd come to appreciate the normalcy my job at the bookstore provided. Even my metalsmithing, which had always been a haven for me, had taken on a new dimension since learning of my imbuing abilities. If I wasn't careful when I created a piece of art, whether forging, casting, or whatever, my emotions seeped in on a trickle of magic, twisting otherwise beautiful sculptures into scrap. I could control it, sort of, but it was exhausting, frustrating, and a little scary. Working at Magpie Books was the one aspect of my life that remained blessedly normal.

I parked in the alley that ran behind the bookstore. There were three security doors in the plain brick wall of the building. Two belonged to the deli and fitness center that bracketed Magpie Books. I headed for the middle one. The back room was filled with its usual clutter of cardboard boxes, shelves of backlog, and stacks of paperwork. The front of the store, however, had been transformed.

Like most retail shops, Magpie's decorations jumped from holiday to holiday. With Halloween behind us, paper snowflakes had been hooked into ceiling tiles, tinsel was strung along the shelves, and the front windows were filled with gift ideas. A small Christmas tree, barely a foot tall, sat on one side of the register counter, tiny ornaments dangling from its branches like colorful jewels. I looked away, trying not to imagine the red gems as drops of blood. Behind the register, seven mismatched stockings hung at a rakish angle above the reserved books shelf. My name was embroidered on the third.

Maggie Hawthorne, owner and proprietor of Magpie Books, and one of my best friends from college, was leaning across the register to kiss her husband. The two made a sweet, if oddly contradictory couple. Maggie was slim, brown, and radiated energy, while Charlie was pale, chubby, and had the kind of calm temperament that was perfect for soothing others. They couldn't have been more different, and I honestly hadn't thought it would work out between them when they'd first hooked up, but they'd been together for years and it was heart-warming to see them still so very much in love.

My thoughts turned to James, and the day grew colder. Lifting my chin, I pushed my worries aside and crossed the remaining distance to the register. If James didn't have time for me, I needn't waste time on him.

I cleared my throat and rested my elbows on the counter. "Am I interrupting?"

Charlie pulled back first, cheeks blazing red, and stared at his feet. Maggie, on the other hand, just laughed. "Not at all. Now that you're here, Charlie and I can go snog in private."

I lifted my hands to ward off her statement. "Way more than I needed to know."

Turning to Charlie, I asked, "You have the day off?" Charlie was an engineer at an architectural firm across town. He was usually so busy with clients and meetings that he worked about sixty hours a week, and lunches were prime schmoozing time.

He scratched one jiggly jowl and cast a side-long glance at Maggie. "I was on this side of town for a meeting and my lunch appointment canceled. Since Maggie's shift was just about over, I thought I'd have a meal with my wife for a change."

"Speaking of meals," Maggie said. "The offer still stands for Thanksgiving."

I shook my head. With James out of the picture, which seemed a safe bet, my plans for Thanksgiving were a frozen lasagna, a blanket, and a good book—the perfect evening. "Thanks, Mags, but I'm good. You two enjoy your family time."

Charlie smiled. "You're always welcome," he said. Then he nodded goodbye and headed for the door.

Maggie looped her arm through mine and tugged me along as she trailed behind her husband. "That Marc fellow is here again." She tilted her chin covertly toward the café, where Marcus Howard sat sipping a coffee and reading the *Denver Post*. From the suit, I guessed he was on break from the nearby investment firm where he worked. The broad line of his shoulders stretched the fabric of his jacket.

"So? He comes in plenty."

"He's been coming more often lately, and he's hardly ever in when you're not scheduled." Maggie had a mischievous glint in her eye that I knew all too well. Playing matchmaker was one of her favorite pastimes, and I'd been her primary source of entertainment for years.

I pulled my arm back, bringing her up short. "You're imagining things. And even if he was interested, which he isn't, I'm dating James." The words snagged in my throat and rang hollow in my ears. Perhaps it was time to look at other options. But—I eyed the leader of the local werewolf pack—not here. The last thing I needed was another set of paranatural rules to learn.

"Of course, luv, of course. And James is a fine bloke. Still, you never know what the future holds." Her chocolate eyes skittered away from my gaze, and she gave a small shrug. "Just remember, you've got options."

Maggie's behavior was odd, even for her. After so many years trying to get me to settle on a guy, any guy, why would she suddenly suggest I keep my options open? But before I could press her for more information, she gave me a peck on the cheek and headed after her husband, calling over her shoulder, "Kayla should be back from her lunch break any minute."

I smiled. Kayla had started at the bookstore around the same time my life went to hell. She was a pixie halfer who grew up on the reservation, dressed like a Sunday school teacher, and had the features of a Precious Moments doll. Despite all that, we'd hit it off right away.

I took a moment to wander the shop and make sure no one needed help, but the handful of shoppers browsing the aisles seemed to have everything well in hand. Then I headed over to the coffee counter where Emma had just served the last person waiting in line.

"Hey girl." She beamed when I stepped up to the counter. "You want your regular?"

I nodded.

Emma spun away to make my drink, and I took in her new look as she bustled around behind the counter. Emma was one of those people who changed her appearance the way other people changed their clothes. Last week she'd been all about polka dots. This week's theme looked to be glitter.

She'd let her hair grow out, so it bobbed around her ears in loose curls of black, sliver, and light and dark blue with probably an industrial-sized bottle of silver glitter teased through it. She had on bright blue eyeshadow streaked with silver that jumped out above the heavy liner and mascara she always wore. Her lipstick was a darker shade of blue, almost navy, that contrasted sharply with her coppery skin.

I tipped my head sideways and squinted. Emma was always bubbly, but today she was practically vibrating. "What's up?"

She bounced on the balls of her feet. "I've got some big news."

It didn't take much to get Emma excited, but the way she was grinning from ear to ear had me smiling too. I leaned on the counter. "What is it?"

She set my coffee on the counter and opened her mouth—and the front bell rang. A couple college-age kids wandered in and took up position behind me. Emma's curls bounced as she swung her head from side to side. "I'm off in an hour, I'll tell you then."

She waved to the newcomers. "Next please."

Grabbing my coffee, I moved out of the way and strolled over to where Marc was sitting. Maggie's prompting aside, I had a question for the alpha werewolf.

As I walked up I said, "You know, most people don't consider coffee an actual meal."

Marc leaned back in his chair, filling the space with an aura of power and ownership that made me stop before reaching his table. He lounged with a grace few men could claim and looked at me through curls of chestnut hair. His eyes were starbursts of gold across a green field. "I'm not most people."

"No kidding," I muttered. "Mind if I join you?"

He sat up straighter and gestured for me to take the seat opposite. "What's on your mind?"

I glanced at the people scattered around the shop and pitched my voice so low only Marc's superior hearing would allow him to pick the words out over the ambient chatter. "How's Sophie?"

Before I'd known about werewolves, when I still thought the woods around my house were safe, I'd taken my friend on a hike through a moonlit field. Saying her name aloud brought back memories of that night—mud and blood and matted fur, snapping teeth and tearing claws.

I shuddered. A new, packless, hungry werewolf is not something you want to see in the woods at night. It's not something I wanted to see ever again, no matter the circumstances. It had taken a powerful practitioner to stitch me back together, and I had a lace of fine white scars from elbow to wrist on my left arm to remind me how lucky I was to be alive.

Sophie wasn't quite so lucky.

There were only two outcomes to a werewolf attack on a human—a corpse or a new werewolf. My smattering of fae blood kept me from turning, and Luke, the practitioner Marc called in, kept me alive. Sophie was human through and through. So while Luke managed to keep her heart beating, my very human friend wasn't human anymore. I knew, better than most, what a shock that could be.

Marc moved closer, placing his arms on the table in front of him and leaning in. I did likewise.

"She's improving," he said. "Slowly, but definitely improving. Her will is strong, which makes the necessary control easier. She's even been out in public a few times."

I reached out and gripped his hand, practically bouncing in my seat. "That's great."

"Yes." He looked down at our joined hands. "It is."

"Sorry." I pulled my hands back and placed them self-consciously in my lap.

Marc cleared his throat. "Her control is good, but she's having trouble making some of the necessary mental adjustments. For example, she can't seem to overcome her dislike for meat, but she needs that protein to keep up with her faster metabolism. As a result, she's lost quite a bit of weight."

Before the attack Sophie had been a dedicated vegetarian. It had been years since she'd touched a piece of meat, and I couldn't see her changing that despite turning into a ravenous carnivore. "She was always saying she wanted to drop a few pounds." I laughed halfheartedly, but stopped at the flat look in his eyes.

"It's more than a few pounds. If she doesn't get over her aversion soon it's going to cause physical problems."

"I thought you guys could heal from just about anything."

"How do you think we do that?" he countered. "Healing takes an immense amount of energy, and that energy has to come from somewhere." He shifted his legs and ran a hand through his messy curls. "She's also having trouble coping with the strict social structure of the pack. She really doesn't like taking orders from men."

I smiled. "Yeah, I could see that."

He crossed his arms. "These are issues she needs to deal with if she wants to survive this."

I was quiet for a while. I had some idea what Sophie was going through thanks to my own recent revelations, but I'd at least been able to maintain some semblance of normalcy. Sophie couldn't go back to her old life. It could be months before she had the control to interact with people on a regular basis. Until then, she was in quarantine.

I rested my fingers on Marc's wrist and gave it a squeeze. "Thanks for the update, and for everything you're doing for her."

He offered a small smile. "You're a good friend for her to have.

Hopefully you'll be able to see her soon."

The bell behind me jingled again, and I twisted around, ready to jump into action if someone actually wanted to buy a book, but it was just Kayla, returning from her break. I lifted a hand in greeting, and she returned the gesture.

"So." Marc covered my hand with his, sandwiching my fingers against his wrist. "How are you doing?"

"Hmm?" I turned back to Marc.

His starburst eyes shifted away. "I was sorry to hear about James's predicament."

I frowned. "Predicament?"

Marc raised an eyebrow, then released my hand so he could turn his newspaper. There was a picture of James under the headline, *Gallery Overdose*.

Grabbing the paper, I flattened it on the table and read:

> Local law enforcement responded to an anonymous call Tuesday night that led to the discovery of a dead woman in the apartment above the Souled Art Gallery in Boulder. The woman's death, caused by a fatal dose of heroine, was deemed accidental by the coroner's office, but information uncovered during the investigation has police scrutinizing the part the gallery's owner, James Abernathy, may have played in providing the drugs that led to the woman's tragic end . . .

I trailed off, unable to focus on the words. Tuesday night . . . our botched date . . . James had called it "unavoidable business at the gallery." Translation, *I'm being detained for questioning about the dead girl in my apartment.*

I tried to swallow, but my mouth was too dry.

Marc pressed his lips into a tight frown, then said, "I thought you and he were . . ."

I nodded, numb, the implication heavy between us. If I was dating him, I should have known.

This cast Maggie's comments in a whole new light. She must have seen the article, or one like it. She wanted me to keep my options open in case James turned out to be a criminal.

But she was wrong. The police were wrong. James might be an inconsiderate ass sometimes, but he wasn't a killer or drug dealer.

I finally managed to swallow. "James would never do something like that."

"You know that for a fact?" Marc was looking at me intently, as if searching for some secret.

"Of course." I lifted my chin. "We may not have been dating long, but I've known James for years. He'd never hurt anyone."

Marc opened his mouth, then snapped it closed with a shake of his head. A muscle jumped in his jaw. "People aren't always what they seem."

"You'd know."

He flinched at my jab, and I bit my lip. I was being childish, and I hated it. Hurt brought out the worst in me. And James's silence hurt.

"Excuse me," I said, pushing to my feet. "I need to make a phone call."

Marc nodded. "And I should be getting back to work. Take care of yourself, Alex."

As he walked out the front door, I tried to ease the pressure in my temples that signaled the approach of a massive headache. James might have had a good reason for his silence, but the cat was out of the bag now. I deserved an explanation. At the very least, as a friend if nothing else, I needed to make sure he was okay.

Snagging my coffee, I headed past Kayla with a quick comment about making a phone call and settled in the relative privacy of the back room with my phone. James was on speed dial—wishful thinking about our relationship status—and I smashed my thumb into the picture of his face.

I drummed my fingers on the cluttered desk, flinching each time the phone rang without answer. Finally, his voice mail recording picked up. I ended the call.

Scrolling through my contacts, I found the entry for Joe. He was James's right hand man, his personal assistant, and director of operations at the gallery. If something had happened there, he was sure to know about it.

Again the phone rang in my ear. Again my fingers drummed. And again the robotic voice of a mail service dashed my hopes for an explanation.

I squeezed the phone, resisting the urge to hurl it across the room.

David. I found David Nolan in my contact list and pressed the call icon under his goofy smile.

David was a good friend. He also ran the security company that covered the gallery. If there'd been a crime, he would have been questioned, the footage pulled. He'd know what was going on.

He answered mid-ring. "You better not be calling to cancel."

I sighed in relief, then frowned. "What?"

"Our plans for tomorrow. You, me, learning to shoot."

Shooting lessons, right, cuz I didn't have enough on my plate. I pinched the bridge of my nose. "That's not why I called. But now that you mention it—"

"You're not canceling. You promised. And after everything that's happened, I'll feel better knowing you've got protection."

"I assume you know why I'm actually calling."

"You mean aside from my charming personality, razor wit, and unparalleled conversation skills?"

"Obviously."

He sighed. "Then I suppose it must be to get all the juicy details about the incident at the gallery last night."

"What do you know?"

"Only bits and pieces. What did James have to say about it?"

I gritted my teeth. "I wouldn't know."

"Sore subject?"

"What happened?"

"The cops came by to review footage from the gallery security cameras. Most was what you'd expect. James and Joe making rounds of the gallery, schmoozing patrons, working on their laptops. Then, just before six, a woman walked into the parking garage and rode the elevator up to the gallery. James got on, and they both went up to the apartment."

A flicker of jealousy fluttered through me.

"Ten minutes later, James left through the parking garage, alone."

I frowned. "So James let a friend stay in the apartment. What's the big deal?"

"The big deal, Alex, is that the woman on the camera was found dead half an hour later."

For a moment, the world seemed to stop while my brain wrestled with David's words. It was a sad commentary on my life that my initial reaction was not sorrow for the poor dead woman or horror that such a tragedy could happen, but simply, *not again.*

"Alex? You there?"

"Mmm."

"The police found the woman in James's apartment after getting an anonymous call. The coroner deemed it a drug overdose, but the police are still investigating."

Raised voices filtered through the door to the store, and I pressed a hand over my free ear to block them out.

"Who was she?" Again the faint pinch of jealousy tightened my chest, but I tamped it down. James had plenty of female acquaintances, just like I was friends with plenty of guys. It didn't mean anything.

"I don't know, Alex. The police don't share details they don't have to."

"What about the drugs? Do you know why the police think he was involved?"

"Apparently they have a witness who saw James make an exchange with the dead woman through the apartment windows."

I frowned. One whole side of James's apartment was floor-to-ceiling windows looking out over the flatirons. "From that distance, he can't have known what they were exchanging. It could have been anything."

"That's all I know."

"Do you think it's possible?"

"That James is dealing drugs?" Silence stretched on the line, and the voices from the front of the shop hammered against my attention. "I don't know, Alex. James plays his cards pretty close. He's definitely got secrets, but he's not stupid. If he was involved with drugs, and I'm not saying he is, I don't think he'd get caught."

"That's not exactly a vote of confidence."

"It's the truth."

"It—" The shouts were getting louder. I recognized one of the voices as Emma's. "David, I have to go."

Ending the call, I shoved the phone in my locker and pushed through the door to see what all the commotion was about.

Chapter 4

EMMA WAS STILL at her post. On the other side of the glass counter, hands on hips, stood her mother. Aside from the Polynesian tan they shared, Emma and her mother couldn't have looked more different. In an ankle-length skirt, button-up blouse, and a tightly twisted bun, Loni Yamada was every bit as conservative as her eldest daughter was radical.

Sitting at a table behind Loni was May, Emma's eleven-year-old sister. May had the same coppery skin as her mother and sister, but she'd inherited a flatter nose and narrower eyes from her father. She scribbled notes on a sheet of music, completely ignoring the argument.

Circling the Yamada family was Kayla. She hovered around the perimeter, flapping her hands in what I guessed was supposed to be a calming gesture but looked more like fanning a flame. "Please, please, don't shout. You're disturbing the other customers."

I glanced behind me. Sure enough, the few other faces in the store were all turned toward the spectacle, though I wasn't sure "disturbed" was the right word. Most stared with the open curiosity of drivers passing a wreck.

Taking a deep breath, I put on my "person in charge" face and walked into the fray. "What's going on here?"

Silence rang through the store as everyone turned toward me.

Then Emma, Loni, and Kayla started babbling again, and I was slapped in the face by a solid wall of noise.

I raised my hands, palms out, and shouted, "Quiet!"

All three women snapped their mouths shut.

With a sharp nod, I turned to Emma. Whatever was going on, she'd be at the center of it.

"Oh Alex, it's so exciting." She bounced up and down on the balls of her feet, the chains on her belt jingling. "I passed the practitioner test. I'm going to be Luke's apprentice!"

"As if that's something to be proud of," Loni hissed. "It's bad enough the way you dress, now you go and do *this* without even thinking how it affects your family. Poor May will be marked forever because of your foolishness."

"I don't mind, Mama," May piped up, eyes never leaving her work. "I think it's cool Emma can use magic."

Loni threw her arms up. "You see? You see what you've done?"

"Stop being so dramatic, Mama. It's not like I've joined a cult or anything."

"That's exactly what it's like." She shoved one knobby finger into Emma's face. "Except you've drawn your whole family into it. Your sister and your children and her children, you'll all be marked as demon spawn."

Loni turned pleading eyes on me. "Tell her. Make her understand."

I'd known Loni was conservative, but I'd never considered her a Purist. Like my father, Loni's husband was lost during the war. Unlike my father, they'd gotten a body back for the funeral. I could understand her hating the fae for what they took from her, but Purists were against all forms of magic, even those practiced by their own people on their behalf.

Frowning, I shook my head. I'd experienced firsthand what Luke could do thanks to my encounter with the werewolves, and I had nothing but respect and gratitude for his magical aptitude. It was the only thing that had kept me alive. "I don't think there's anything wrong with Emma learning magic."

Loni swiveled her finger at me, its calloused tip hovering inches from my face. "You are a bad influence, Alex Blackwood."

The bell on the front door chimed, and Lucas Miller, local practitioner, stepped inside.

"You!" Loni swung her finger around to point squarely at Luke.

He took a step back, hands raised in surrender. His chocolate brown eyes were wide with surprise, and his thick, dark lips turned down at the corners. "Uh, am I interrupting something?"

Like most practitioners, Luke was a pacifist. Guess you got paranoid when the PTF threatened to lock you in a windowless room for any show of aggressive behavior.

"Leave him alone, Mom." Emma ran around the counter to plant herself between her mother and her new mentor.

"You stay away from my daughter, you . . . you demon." Spitting on the floor, Loni grabbed May's wrist and stormed out of the store. The willowy girl barely managed to grab her notebook before she was dragged away. Emma followed them to the door, but stopped on the threshold, wringing her hands.

Luke ran one dark, thin-fingered hand over his bristly, black hair and pushed his glasses a little higher on his nose. "Do I even want to know what that was about?"

"She's pissed about Emma becoming your apprentice." As I spoke, Emma flailed her arms wildly behind Luke's back in an attempt to get my attention.

I furrowed my brow and mouthed, "What?" Then I saw my own confusion mirrored in Luke's face.

Emma laughed weakly and cleared her throat. "Um, I heard you complaining when you were in here the other day that you had too much work and you needed some help, and I passed my practitioner test, so I thought, well—" She shrugged, a look of hopeful apology on her face.

Luke hooked a thumb toward the door. "That was your mother?"

"She's just mad I took the test without asking first."

Flannel-clad arms folded over Luke's loose Star Wars t-shirt, blocking the lower half of Yoda's face. "That's not what it sounded like to me."

"She'll come around. She's not really a Purist, she just doesn't like being reminded of magic. She's been that way since dad died. But she needs to stop living in the past. Being a practitioner is special; not many people can do it. Once she sees what I can do, I'm sure she'll understand."

"A lot of people hate practitioners, especially those who lost loved ones in the war. If you plan on pursuing this, you'll need to get used to it." He stepped up to the register and said, "I'm here to pick up a special order."

Kayla darted behind the counter, eager to have something she could handle. She searched for a moment, then thunked a six-inch-thick tome on the counter and rang up the sale with a smile.

Luke turned to go, but paused with his back to us. "You need to make peace with your family before you pursue your studies. If not, you may lose the opportunity, and you'll regret it for the rest of your life. Trust me."

Slowly, the store returned to its regular rhythms. Kayla thanked me for helping diffuse the situation, though I wasn't sure how much help I'd actually been. The customers who'd been watching the morning's impromptu entertainment went back to browsing the shelves, and Emma resumed her station at the café, a crestfallen look on her face. I trailed after her.

"Want to talk?"

She shook her head. "He didn't say he'd teach me," she whispered.

"He didn't say he wouldn't." I patted her arm. "Sounds like he wants to give you space to handle this issue with your mom first."

She nodded.

"What are you gonna do?"

"I don't know." She chewed at the cuticle of one blue-glazed fingernail. "Sometimes Mom drives me insane. I mean, I'm twenty-three years old. I can make my own decisions about what I want to do with my life. I don't want to work at a coffee shop forever, and I've got zero interest in taking over the bakery. Do you have any idea what kind of hours we have to keep over there to make sure everything is fresh in the morning? It's a nightmare."

"I get that you don't want to take over the family business, but why take the practitioner test?" I asked.

"Are you kidding? Who wouldn't want to have magic if they could? Haven't you always dreamed of being able to just wave your hand and make something happen?"

I thought about Kai's endless lectures about the history and structure of magic, its challenges and dangers. Practitioner magic was different than fae magic, but the basic principles were probably similar. "I don't think that's quite how it works."

She wasn't listening. She was off in some magical place in her head where all her problems could be flicked away with the swish of a magic wand. She was going to get a very nasty wake-up call if Luke really did agree to train her.

We all had to grow up someday.

I left her to her fantasy and went to talk to Kayla.

"Do you think Emma will become a practitioner?" Kayla's voice was soft.

I shrugged. "Technically, I think she already did."

"She should stay away from magic." Her whisper dropped another decibel. "She probably thinks it will bring her happiness, but that's not true. Magic always comes with a price."

I drummed my fingers on the counter, considering Kayla's words. Magic certainly hadn't brought me any happiness. A lost father, a dead friend, another that turned furry once a month. Plus a secret that would get me arrested and used as a guinea pig if the PTF found out. The most I could say about magic was that it kept things interesting.

Sighing, I rubbed little soothing circles over my temples. Every new concern was an icepick drilling into my brain.

Kayla set a hand against my arm. "Are you okay?"

"Just a headache," I said. "Stress."

She frowned, a littler pucker creasing her forehead. "Would you like to relax?"

I snorted. "Of course, but that's not how stress works. You can't just will it away."

"What if you could?"

I frowned. "What do you mean?"

She tipped her head toward the back room.

Curious, I followed her through the door marked "employees only." She stopped in the middle of the sorting area, reached behind her, and tugged at the zipper on her dress.

"Whoa, whoa! What are you doing?" I grabbed her arm to stop the zipper getting any lower. "Not that I'm not flattered, but I think you've got the wrong idea about me."

Kayla turned her big brown eyes on me. "I'm just going to give you something to help you relax."

"Something that requires taking off your dress?" I shook my head. "No thanks."

Her eyebrows pulled together. "If my body offends you, you don't have to look."

"What exactly are you proposing here?"

"Pixie dust."

I released her and took a step back. "Pixie dust?"

She finished unzipping her dress and the fabric slid to the floor. The thin, milky skin I'd expected to see was draped in what looked like a second, iridescent dress that wrapped over her shoulders and down her back. The colors peeled away from her skin, and a pair of cellophane- thin wings lifted off her back.

"Wow." My fingertips drifted toward the translucent wings, but I pulled back, afraid to damage them. "Can you fly?"

"If I need to," she said. "But what I wanted to give you," she ran a hand over the edge of one of her wings, "is this."

A layer of shimmering gold dust coated her palm.

"You know the old myth that pixie dust and a happy thought can make a mortal fly?"

I nodded.

"Pixie dust makes mortals euphoric."

"Oh. *That* kind of flying." I shook my head. "No thanks."

Pulling open her purse with her free hand, she took out a tiny vial and scraped the glittery dust into it. Then she pushed a cork in the end and handed it to me. "In case you change your mind, just dip your pinky and lick."

I took the vial and held it up to the light. The finest glitter imaginable sparkled inside. "So your wings produce drugs for mortals?"

Her wings folded back around her body, pressing tight to her skin, and she pulled her dress back on.

"Guess that explains the high collars and long skirts," I said.

She nodded. "The dust works on halfers and fae too, but requires a higher dosage."

I froze. Why tell me that unless. . . . No. There was no way Kayla knew about me. How could she? I pushed my paranoia aside. She'd only shared the information as a bit of trivia, nothing more.

I tucked the vial in my jacket pocket, thinking of the allegations against James. "I appreciate the gesture, but I don't think drugs are the answer."

"Then what is?"

I shook my head. "Wish I knew."

Chapter 5

SUNLIGHT WARMED my skin as I sat on the living room floor in a pair of stretchy pants and a tank top. I'd woken early—the worries flooding my thoughts worked better than an alarm clock. Scenes from Emma's argument with Loni kept popping into my mind. She'd seemed so proud of becoming a practitioner, excited despite her mother's disapproval. But then, she'd had a choice. In my imagination, my father and I took their places and I tried to explain that I hadn't wanted to be fae. I couldn't help it. But there was no changing what I was, and no point trying to justify that to a dead man.

Taking a deep breath, I rolled my head from side to side, trying to alleviate some of the tension in my neck and shoulders. I'd already run through all my usual poses—Triangle, Warrior, Downward Dog, Plank, Cobra. I was as loose as I could get, but my muscles were still a jumble of knots and cords. I took another long, slow breath, closed my eyes, and tried again to clear my mind.

This time it was James who floated to the surface of my thoughts. I'd left him a message after work. He hadn't called me back. Not to apologize, not to explain, not even to let me know he was okay. My jaw tightened. That last part irked me the most. I understood he had a lot on his plate, that long explanations and romantic complications were out of the question, but complete silence? Forget significant other, that wasn't even friend behavior. He'd cut me out entirely the moment I became inconvenient.

Forcing my jaw to relax, I pushed those thoughts to the back of my mind, but Hortense took their place, counting down the seconds till my fated court date like the hands of a doomsday clock.

"Sleeping works better lying down." Kai bumped my shoulder as he passed.

"I'm not sleeping, I'm breathing."

"So am I," he said. "Funny thing about breathing, you can do it while you move. Come on."

My breath came out as a sigh and I opened my eyes. "Where are we moving to?"

He peeled back the wrapper on a Snickers bar and bit off the top. "The yard. I may not be the best tutor, but I can teach you the sword. Considering your performance yesterday, I think you're going to need it." Two more bites and the candy bar was gone.

"You're going to get diabetes if you keep eating like that."

He opened another Snickers.

I stood up and shook out my knees. Meditation had been a bust, but maybe a more physical activity would refocus my mind. I was going to go crazy if I spent the rest of my day obsessing about things I couldn't control. I gave the phone on the end table a scathing look.

"Still hasn't called?"

I pressed my lips tight.

"Maybe you're better off."

"Don't start."

Kai and James knew each other from way before either of them knew me. Neither was willing to elaborate on their previous encounter, but both were adamant I should not trust the other. James disapproved of Kai living with me, and Kai disapproved of me dating James. I'd ignored both their warnings, but I was starting to think Kai had the right of it. Still, I made my own decisions thank you very much, and I didn't need a backseat driver pointing out the folly of my attempted romance.

Kai headed outside, and I went into the bedroom to retrieve the tooled scabbard and belt he'd given me. Once it was secure, I tugged the sword free, checking it didn't snag, and looked down its mirror length. Like most fae weapons, it was forged from a silver alloy. Not the strongest metal, but necessary since so few fae could handle steel. The double-edged blade was two and a half feet long and tapered to a wicked point. The hilt was carefully wrapped in red, black, and gold leather that fit comfortably into the palm of my hand. There were small engravings near the crossbar that Kai said were marks of ownership. The sword had come from the Lord of Enchantment's personal collection, another gift.

Along with practical lessons, Kai had taught me a lot about the different weapons used among the fae. My sword was the type generally worn at court by those still in training and wasn't used much outside of duels, a fae tradition he assured me was still very much in favor. It was also traditional for court fae to have at least one knife hidden on their body at all times, though most would have three or four.

Sheathing the sword, I pulled on my hiking boots and joined Kai in the clearing that spanned the gap between my house and studio. Breath billowed around my face, puffing out to join wisps of fog tucked between trees. To the north, across the basin of Caribou Ranch, the Peak to Peak Highway snaked up a distant ridge, asphalt flashing through green and brown trees in the morning light.

Five minutes of practicing forms, and I was drenched in sweat. The sun had melted the night's frost, and my movements turned the ground into a muddy mess that made my footing slippery. Focusing on the prearranged patterns, I did my best to ignore the slush seeping into my boots.

"Good." Kai lifted the wooden sword he used for my lessons. "Now let's try some actual combat."

My silver blade connected with the thick wood of Kai's practice sword time and again, sending vibrations down my already tired arms. A lifetime working the forge had made me strong, but I'd lost a lot of muscle mass after my run-in with a feral werewolf and I wasn't back to full strength yet.

After fifteen minutes, my arms were heavy and slow.

At twenty minutes, Kai effortlessly flipped the sword from my numb fingers and pointed his stick at my throat. "You're dead."

"Agreed," I panted, bracing against my knees.

"You're definitely improving, but we need to work on your stamina."

"How often does a duel last more than twenty minutes?" I argued.

"There have been duels that lasted days. Regardless, you would not have survived twenty minutes if this had been real."

I lifted my head just enough to see him. "Days? You're joking, right?"

"I can't lie."

"Yeah, but days? That's impossible."

"I assure you, it's not."

With a groan, I let my head drop. "Just kill me now."

"Tempting, but no. I will, however, release you from further humiliation this morning. Don't forget to clean your sword before you put it away." Kai swished his stick in a fancy salute, then sauntered off toward the house.

I stayed where I was until the sweat on my skin turned cold. Then I heaved myself straight and trudged across the muddy field to where my sword was stuck point-first in the frozen ground. Resting one sweaty palm against the hilt, I convinced my tired fingers to close and pulled it free. The blade was splattered with mud.

"We could both do with a bath," I told it, and carried it back to the house.

"STOP LOOKING AT me like I'm a pimple on a demon's ass." I crossed my arms and sank lower in the uncomfortable dining room chair. As soon as I was clean and dressed, Kai had started in on the next set of lessons. And while these didn't leave any noticeable bruises, they hurt just as much as our sword practice.

"Demons don't get pimples, and they don't have asses." Kai slammed his book closed.

"Well excuse me for missing that little tidbit in *Faerie Races for Dummies.*"

"They're not a race of fae." He dropped the book on the table and ran both hands through his hair so hard the skin on his face pulled tight. "Do you even listen when I speak?"

"I'm listening. There's just so much . . ." I gestured to the piles of books and manuscripts scattered over the table. "Stuff."

"That *stuff* is going to keep you alive at court. Considering how bad you are at dueling, you don't want to give anyone a reason to challenge you."

"You make it sound like everyone at court is just looking for an excuse to fight me."

"They are." He planted his hands on the table and leaned forward. "Most of the fae at court would love nothing better than to cut your heart out. All that's stopping them is fear of reprisal. If you give them an excuse to duel, you'll be one "accident" away from your grave. You either need to get infinitely better at fighting, or avoid it altogether."

He flopped back in his chair with a huff.

My mouth was hanging open, so I snapped it shut. Kai had said from the beginning these lessons were supposed to keep me alive at court, but I hadn't thought he meant it so literally. I'd considered my preparation more as an attempt to avoid the political suicide of embarrassing my granddad.

Swallowing hard, I asked, "Why do they want to kill me? I'm nobody."

Kai let out a long sigh. "You're not nobody. You may not care about being acknowledged by the Lord of Enchantment, but they do, and there are plenty of fae that resent your effortless acceptance at court when they've had to struggle and prove themselves. That aside, duels are one of the fastest ways to increase standing in the fae hierarchy. Since you have a high standing without the ability to back it up, you're an easy target."

"Great." I sank even lower, practically laying down in my seat.

"There are also fae who seek to weaken the lord's position by undermining his choice to acknowledge you. Remember, Alex, fae live a very long time. Most of that time is occupied with scheming, politics, and outright war."

"I could care less if I make him look stupid. I didn't ask him to acknowledge me, and if I'd known what it meant I would have told you to take his stupid gift and shove it." I thumped my head against the chair back. "I wish he could just undo it. At this rate, I'm gonna get killed over a title I don't even want."

"It's not that simple."

"It never is with—"

"Shh." Kai lifted a hand.

I sat up a little straighter. "Don't you shush me."

"No, really, Alex, stop talking," he whispered. "Someone's here."

A moment later, there was a knock at the door.

I moved to the window and peeked past the curtains.

Two police officers stood on my porch. One was a man with thinning black hair swept back with gel, and a frown that looked permanently etched on his face. The other was Officer Sarah Nazari. Her black hair was pulled into a tight braid, exposing her severe features. Rather than a uniform, she wore black cargo pants and a half-zipped leather jacket over a simple blue shirt.

I took a step back and breathed out as quietly as I could. Not that it would matter. With her werewolf sense of smell, chances were she already knew Kai and I were in the house.

The only other time we'd met, Sarah helped me because she wanted to see justice done. That didn't make us friends. The fact that I knew she was a werewolf made her see me as a threat, and no amount of promises would convince her otherwise. For my part . . . it was hard to feel comfortable around someone who'd wanted me dead less than a month ago. Especially after experiencing what a werewolf could do firsthand.

I rubbed my arm, feeling the lace of scars that ran from elbow to wrist.

If the police wanted to talk to me, it had to be about James. Taking a deep breath, I straightened my shoulders and opened the door.

"Good afternoon, Ms. Blackwood," Sarah said. "I'm detective Nazari." She gestured to the man beside her. "This is detective Herrera. May we come in?"

Guess we were pretending to be strangers. Fine by me. I moved to the side and gestured for them to pass. "What's this about?"

The two cops stepped inside, and Herrera's attention shifted to Kai, who was standing in front of the dining table, arms crossed.

"And you are?" Herrera had a much higher voice than I expected, like he just took a hit of helium.

"Her roommate," Kai answered.

"Of course," Herrera said. "Sorry for the inconvenience, but we'd like to speak with Ms. Blackwood in private."

I met Kai's eye, and nodded.

He scooped up the lesson materials scattered across the table, tucked them away in Hortense's trunk, and moved toward the door. "I could use some fresh air."

Sarah gave Kai a wide berth as he passed. Then she closed the door behind him and the three of us took up positions around the vacated dining table. She and Herrera each pulled out a notebook and pen.

"I assume you're aware of the body found at the Souled Art Gallery?" she asked.

I nodded.

"Where were you Tuesday night between five and six p.m.?"

"Getting ready for a date."

"Can anyone verify that?"

"My friend, Maggie, helped me get ready."

Sarah passed her notebook and pen to me. "Could you write down her contact information?"

I jotted down Maggie's name, number, and address, then passed the notebook back.

Herrera leaned over to peek at the notebook. He pursed his lips, and scribbled a note in his own. "When did you leave your friend's house?"

"Around five-thirty."

"And then?"

"I went to James's house."

"Did you see Mr. Abernathy?"

"No. He called to cancel shortly after I got to his house."

Herrera scratched his pen into his hair. His scalp was red and a little swollen. Either he spent way too much time in the sun without a hat, or he'd recently patched a bald spot. "What time was that?"

I shrugged. "A little after six."

Herrera nodded to Sarah, who placed a photograph on the table in front of me. "Have you ever seen this woman before?"

The woman in the photo had long blond hair that fell over her shoulders in a golden waterfall, full red lips, and a figure most women couldn't achieve without surgery. Her eyes were huge and blue, and somehow sad. Despite the smile on her face, I got the impression she was about to cry.

I shook my head. "I've never seen her before. Is that the woman you found at the gallery?"

"Yes," said Sarah. "And it wasn't the first time she'd been there."

"Was she a friend of James's?" My heart constricted in sympathy. Not long ago, one of my close friends had died. No one should go through something like that alone, which made James's silence sting all the more. Wherever he was seeking comfort, it wasn't with me.

"I guess you could say that." Herrera leaned back in his seat, watching me. "According to the escort service she worked for, James requested her on a regular basis."

"Escort . . . service?" A rushing sound filled my ears. It was suddenly hard to breathe, hard to think. Surely I'd heard wrong?

"Mr. Abernathy's been engaging her services for a while now. Good tipper by all accounts."

My fingers turned to claws under the table, digging into the meat on my thighs. A hooker? That's who he was with before our date? Was she the reason he'd missed so many others?

Sarah tapped a finger on the table between us, and my attention snapped to her as she said, "I take it you didn't know?"

"There has to be some other explanation." I cringed at the hope that crept into my voice, turning it into the plea of a victim who couldn't accept the truth. I cleared my throat. "Just because he was seeing her doesn't mean he was . . ."

"No," agreed Sarah. "But he admitted to . . . being with her the night she died."

"Tell me, Ms. Blackwood," Herrera interjected, "Do you have access to the gallery's apartment?"

I frowned. "Yes."

"When were you last there?"

I glanced at the ceiling and counted back in my head. "Two weeks ago, I guess."

Herrera rubbed his pen against his irritated scalp, setting loose a flurry of little white flakes that drifted like snow onto his shoulder. "You haven't been there since?"

I shook my head, staring at the tiny blizzard.

Herrera jotted something down. "Is there anyone else who might have visited the apartment that night?"

I shrugged. "None that I can think of."

"What about Mr. Abernathy's employees?"

"Elsa, his housekeeper, goes there sometimes to clean up and stock the fridge. Joe sometimes works late at the gallery, but he usually stays on the main floor."

More note-taking. "Joe would be Joseph Carmichael, Mr. Abernathy's personal assistant?"

"He prefers the term attaché, but yeah."

"How well do you know Mr. Carmichael?"

I drummed my fingers on the table. "Joe was a fixture at the gallery long before I showed up. He handles most of the day-to-day stuff. He's . . ." Pompous, self-important, insufferable. "Meticulous."

Sarah rubbed one hand over her chin. "Has Mr. Abernathy been acting strange lately? Any undue stress? New people coming around?"

My mind flashed back to a dark night a few weeks ago, when a man I'd never seen before dangled me like a rag doll to get me to deliver a message. *James Abernathy has been a very naughty boy.*

James said the negotiations with that sicko Bryce's master were well in hand. He promised everything was fine. But Bryce had made a promise too, whispered in my ear that night. *We'll bring his world down around him.*

I shuddered and rubbed my neck where Bryce's tongue had tasted my skin.

"Ms. Blackwood?" Sarah's gaze was intent, searching.

"Not that I've noticed." The lie tasted like ash in my mouth, but I'd promised James I wouldn't report the incident. "Honestly, if you want to know more about what he's been up to or with whom, your best bet is Joe. He handles James's scheduling and whatnot."

Joe was James's go-to-guy, the one James called when he was in trouble. I was just the wannabe-girlfriend who didn't know he was sleeping with a hooker when he was supposed to be with me; who he didn't trust with the name of the businessman who'd threatened me to get James to a meeting; who didn't seem to know one goddamn thing about the man she was involved with. I laced my fingers together to keep my hands from tightening to fists.

"That's enough for now." Sarah pushed back from the table and set her business card on the polished wood. "If you think of anything, give us a call."

I walked them to the door. Herrera headed for the black SUV parked out front, but Sarah stopped on the threshold and grumbled in a low voice, "If you're smart, you'll forget James Abernathy. Too many secrets." That was ironic, coming from a werewolf in cop's clothing, but I nodded and shut the door softly behind them.

Chapter 6

SINCE KAI WAS still gone, I decided to take advantage of my reprieve from lessons and headed to my studio—an oversized shed that sat a little way from the house. Dedicated to creativity and exploration, the studio was a place separate from the rest of my life; a place where I could get lost in my work and forget all the worries that plagued me in the real world. At least, it used to be.

Ever since learning I had the ability to magically imbue my art, the process of creation that used to come so naturally to me now took effort. Instead of feeling relaxed and rejuvenated after working in the studio, I was more often drained and frustrated when I left the shed.

Kai said it was because I was consciously tapping into my fae abilities, drawing more from them than I had in the past. James said it was because I was over-analyzing my ability and worrying about what it meant to my art. Whatever the reason, playing with metal wasn't as fun as it used to be.

I ran my fingers over the handles of my hammers, each nestled in its assigned place on my pegboard. Uncle Sol's half-finished Christmas present waited at one end of my work bench—two sets of incomplete chess armies facing off. One side sported hard, geometric angles, while the other was all curves and contours. Both had wax figures mixed in their ranks, waiting to be cast. To one side lay a collection of rough metal soldiers, casualties awaiting triage, eager to have their sprues cut so they could rejoin their brethren. A steel cylinder of investment hid more wax figures, ready for casting, but I hadn't prepped for a burnout today. The kilns were cold.

I turned instead to a project I'd started the week before. It was full of abstract shapes made from cast or forged silver and bronze. I was making a hanging Zen garden where a person could sit in the middle and have the elements move around them. They could also walk through the garden along a number of paths that wound throughout the sculpture. I'd arranged with the Denver Botanic Garden to do a special installation in the spring. That gave me three months to finish, assuming I survived my trip to the fae court.

I crossed my arms and sighed, assessing the pile of shapes I'd already made, trying to decide what came next. The sculpture was supposed to give the viewer a sense of peace and tranquility, two emotions I definitely wasn't feeling at the moment. I was going to have to work hard to keep my magic in check.

After annealing a strip of thick silver wire, I sat down at my anvil with my favorite hammer. I closed my eyes and took a deep breath, trying to clear my mind as Kai had taught me. Then I began to work the metal, and as I worked I pictured the glassy smooth surface of still water; a cloudless blue sky that stretched from horizon to horizon; the warm, safe feeling of being a child wrapped in my mother's arms.

Then I thought of James's arms wrapped around me, and an entirely different warmth spread through me. The heat turned cold as doubt and anger crept in at the edges of my mind, fracturing my concentration.

My hammer stuttered then stilled.

I looked at the twisted metal on my anvil. The wire was just beginning to take shape, but I could already see it was a lost cause. There was no peace, just frustration.

Tossing the piece onto the scrap pile, I set my hammer back in its cradle on the pegboard and rubbed my temples. I didn't have the internal calm to pull the project off. Not today.

I stepped out of the studio and breathed in until my lungs strained. Then I blew out a noisy sigh. The final wisps of fog had burned off, and my breath no longer condensed in the air, but a chill remained, waiting to surge back with the coming night. The sun hung heavy in the sky, scraping its belly on the horizon. The days were growing short.

I took three steps across the muddy field where clumps of soil and decomposing pine cones turned the remaining snow a dirty brown, then froze. My front door was open. Streaks of brown and white and scattered pine needles marked a trail over my porch. Something large had entered my house.

My muscles hummed with adrenaline, but I stayed rooted to the spot, straining my senses to discover what was waiting inside.

The needles of a blue spruce shook in the breeze, sending down a cascade of glittering powder. Strands of dry moss swayed gently from the leaning trunk of a dead pine that would need to be cut out before next summer. The twitter of a wood thrush drifted through the trees.

Nothing else moved in the forest. Nothing moved in the house.

Was Kai still out on his walk, or had he been caught off guard by whatever—I shook my head. Kai was fine. He was a Knight of the Realm. He could handle himself. And there were no sounds of conflict.

Moving slow to reduce the crunch of ice and gravel under my boots, I inched forward. Goosebumps sprang out under the layers of my winter clothes. Then a thump and a curse from inside broke the silence.

I sprinted the last few steps to the threshold. My sword was tucked away in my bedroom, but I hadn't been taking Aikido for nothing. I sprang through the doorway with a yell and braced for a fight.

Kai stared at me with wide eyes and an open mouth. He blinked and sputtered, "What are you doing?" around a mouthful of laughter.

Glaring at my perfectly alive, perfectly annoying roommate, I gestured to the space behind me. "I saw the open door, and the tracks across the porch, and—" I took in the trunk of a small pine tree resting in his hands, swallowed a hard lump in my throat, and pointed. "What is that?"

Kai looked down at the trail of green needles he'd tracked across the living room, then back to me. "A tree."

I gritted my teeth. "I can see that. What's it doing in my house?"

Kai's brow furrowed like I'd just asked him to explain the meaning of life. "Isn't this what mortals do for Christmas? Decorate their homes with jewel-encrusted trees under which they collect gifts?"

Shaking my head, I placed my hands on my hips to keep from balling them into fists. He didn't know. How could he? We'd met barely a month ago. There was no way he could know that Christmas trees hadn't been welcome in my house since. . . . I shook my head again, this time to clear an image of Mom, lying in a hospital bed, a long gash across her temple.

"That *is* what people traditionally do, but—"

"Oh good!" Kai sagged in relief. "I've never been in the mortal realm for this particular holiday. We fae have the Winter Festival, but that doesn't involve trees or presents."

I swallowed the lump in my throat, looking anywhere but at the Christmas tree. "Christmas is *after* our trip to Enchantment. Why decorate now?"

He frowned. "Remember how I said time moves differently in the realms?"

I nodded.

"Well, chances are you're going to miss Christmas. I know you've been chafing under your fae obligations, so I wanted to help you celebrate this human holiday before we left." Kai's face was all worry lines, puckering his forehead and outlining his mouth.

I sighed. He was just trying to be nice.

My gaze dropped, finally settling on the tree. For a second, I imagined it as a battered mess of scattered needles and broken limbs draped over the crumpled hood of my Mom's old Corolla, dangling by the single rope that hadn't snapped on impact. Twinkling lights sparkled in its branches, red and blue strobes of the ambulance that took my mother away.

Pressure burned behind my eyes. I couldn't get a deep enough breath, my chest was too tight. But this wasn't the last tree my mother bought, the one I'd badgered her to get even though she'd worked late and she was tired. This was a peace offering. A gift from a friend.

Beware fae gifts. They come with a price.

It seemed the price of this gift was a resurgence of memories I'd tried to forget. I pinched the bridge of my nose, fighting back tears.

I wasn't against Christmas itself. I wasn't a total Scrooge. I still exchanged gifts with my friends and Uncle Sol. I just didn't do the tree anymore.

Kai propped his tree in the corner, branches shedding yet more needles. It filled the house with the scent of pine and sap, and the mingled memories of joy and loss. The tree was barely four feet tall, the branches were lopsided, and it had two tops. It wasn't the kind of tree you would buy on a lot, not something you'd see in a store or on display in the public areas around town. It was a Charlie Brown sort of tree, sparse and sagging, and it made me want to smile.

There hadn't been a Christmas tree in my house in eleven years. Maybe it was time to move on.

Kai's frown deepened. "If you don't like the tree, I can—"

"It's fine." My voice cracked, and I coughed to clear it. "The tree's fine. I just—" The damage was done. Making a fuss now wouldn't accomplish anything other than making Kai feel bad. But I needed to clear my head. I was already raw from Hortense, and James, and Emma, and my whole life being turned upside down. I could feel the walls of my self-control slipping, but I didn't want to break down in front of Kai. I needed space. "I've got some errands to run."

He looked from me to the tree and back again. "Don't you want to help decorate it?"

I shook my head. "Surprise me."

"What about your lessons?"

Shaking my head again, I grabbed my wallet and keys, and my coat off the rack, and headed out the still-open door.

A layer of frost obscured my Jeep's blue paint and rust spots, and the black cover that would come off in the summer to open the top. After cranking the heater to full blast, I chipped the ice off my windshield and blew into my cupped hands until the cab warmed up.

My chest ached. The pressure behind my eyes increased. I rubbed the small scar under my jaw, where the skin was slightly puckered.

I was seventeen years old, waiting in yet another new place for my mom to come home. The school I'd be transferring to was already out on winter break, so I'd spent the day unpacking boxes, trying to make the new apartment feel a little less empty. I found the Christmas decorations near the bottom of the pile and sorted through the ornaments, each one the receptacle of a memory. Mom had promised to pick up a tree after work to make the place feel more like home.

But when the door opened, all that arrived was a tired woman wearing my mom's face. She dropped her keys into the little ceramic bowl I'd set on the table by the door. She didn't even seem to register the addition. Her eyes drooped. Her feet dragged.

"Where's the tree?"

"I had to work late. I'll get one tomorrow."

I set the box of ornaments aside. "But you promised."

She made a placating gesture. "Tomorrow."

I crossed my arms. "You're always breaking your promises. Like when you said we could stay at the last place till I graduated. And now I have to start all over in this stupid town where I don't know anyone just for half a year of school."

Her eyes slid closed and she let out a long sigh. "Okay, sweetie." She lifted her keys from the bowl. "Let's go get a tree."

I wrapped my fingers around the steering wheel. Had Mom's hands been too cold to grip the wheel properly when she hit the ice that night? My knuckles turned white. The plastic groaned under my grip.

I didn't really have errands to run, I just needed to get away from the house for a while. Away from lessons, and roommates, and my own thoughts. Since that last one wasn't possible, the next best option was to drown them out. I put the Jeep in gear, and drove to the noisiest place I knew.

PEARL STREET WAS a walking district with shops of every kind lining the sides, and vendors with carts dotted throughout. Tinsel twisted up lampposts and patio railings, wreaths hung in windows, and an overwhelming scent of cinnamon and artificial pine saturated the air.

Throngs of people walked the mall's length, bundled against the cold or ignoring it entirely. Salvation Army volunteers stood on every other corner, ringing their bells at the crush of holiday shoppers. A group of roving carolers, wearing Victorian outfits for no apparent reason, competed with the music piped through the stores. A contortionist in purple spandex prepared for her show, and a group of monks in yellow and red robes ate ice cream cones and pointed to the rainbow kites on display in a nearby window.

I stopped at a small cart selling every kind of hat imaginable. Standing in front of a mirror, I tried on a Viking helmet complete with braids, a pirate hat with a big floppy feather, and a red-and-white striped "Cat in the Hat" hat that slid down over my eyes. When I left the hat stall, I knew my hair was a frizzy mess, but my heart felt a little lighter.

Two blocks later, I paused at the edge of a crowd to enjoy the music of a busker playing guitar. The guy was good, the space around him was filled with people, and interspersed throughout the crowd I caught the familiar shimmer of fae glamours. I tried not to look, to just relax and lose myself in the music, but my eyes kept drifting back to those spots of "not-quite-right." Giving in, I refocused my eyes and studied the fae around me.

Despite what that stuck-up tutor thought, I'd learned a lot since Kai had come to stay with me. I knew the three-foot-nothing man to my left with the big, drooping ears was a gnome. The bright red feathers on the woman across from me meant she was from one of the aery races, probably a harpy or sylph. To her right was a man that, try as I might, I couldn't bring into focus, which meant the glamour he'd cast was strong enough to block other fae. At least, fae as weak as I was.

The tinkle of bells pulled my attention to the shop behind me.

No, not bells.

I stepped up to the door of a spice shop, the mixed aroma of their wares seeping through the glass enough to make my nose itch. Meat rubs and curries vied for dominance as I leaned in to inspect the curtain of beads in front of the door. I trailed a single strand over my palm, thumbing the metal orbs.

No one could enter this shop without passing through a curtain of iron beads.

My mouth went dry as my eyes lit upon a sticker in the window. A silhouette with pointed ears had a big red line drawn through it. The words circling the image proclaimed, PROUDLY SERVING THE PURE.

Purity, a zealous off-shoot of modern religion preaching wholesale eradication of magical beings, had been gaining favor since the summer murders. The killer was gone, thanks to me and my friends, but the fear remained. I wished I could shake every last one of the Purists and scream in their faces that it had been a man like them, a human bent on a violent end to magic, that had committed the crimes. A human willing to sacrifice the world for his ideals.

If men like me won't stand up to stop them, who will? I steadied myself on the wall of the shop as my father's voice cut through my thoughts. I'd almost forgotten what it sounded like, but the memory was bright and clear. His words echoed in my head as they'd drifted up the stairs the first time I overheard that argument.

What harm would it do to let them stay when they've already been here for years? Mom, the voice of reason and tolerance in our household.

They don't belong. A door slammed, and Dad's voice drifted back into the recesses of my mind.

I took a shuddering breath, and reminded myself I wasn't a child hiding on the stairs anymore. I frowned at the sign in the window. I wasn't, strictly speaking, human anymore either.

A cold wind tore up the street, setting the beads to jingling. I tugged my coat tighter with a shiver, pulled the last three dollars from my wallet, and dropped them in the musician's open guitar case. Then I continued up the street, scanning windows for similar stickers.

Three more shops boasted the Purity stamp. I had no doubt that number would increase once Anderson officially took office as Governor of Colorado and gave Purity a legitimate foothold in local politics. Despite everything I'd done to stop it, we might be headed for another war after all—a second Faerie War that wouldn't end until one side was wiped out.

I continued to walk between shops that glittered with holiday lights and mile upon mile of tinsel. Banners hung over entrances and shouted out from windows, "Happy Holidays," avoiding the now taboo C-word for fear of pissing off any and every side of the religious community. In the middle of the walkway, ornaments pulled down the branches of a tall tree whose life had been cut short for a single month of splendor. I took a deep breath, steadying my nerves, and let my eyes scroll over the green needles decked out in their holiday finest, all the way down to the colorfully wrapped boxes peeking beneath the branches; piles of beautiful, empty promises.

Pearl Street had always been one of my favorite places to wander and think—I'd spent hours people watching, sketching all the different characters who walked by—but tonight it was just a reminder of everything that was wrong in my life. Every laughing face, every glittering ornament, was a knife in my heart. Couples walked arm in arm, while the guy I thought I could love wouldn't even return my calls. Parents swarmed the toy stores, granting their children's wishes, while my parents were dead and gone. And now there were signs in the shop windows telling me I wasn't welcome. Sure, I could pass through the beads. I could lie. But I wouldn't belong any more than those glamoured fae hiding in the crowd.

The night grew colder as the last of the lingering heat bled out of the world. I pushed my fists into the pockets of my jacket. My knuckles brushed something hard. Wrapping my fingers around the smooth surface, I pulled the little vial Kayla had given me out of my pocket. The pixie dust glinted under the holiday lights.

Just dip your pinky and lick. Pure happiness, easy as that.

Shoppers streamed around me, bundled in colorful scarves and hats with floppy pompoms, a tide of humanity. Their smiles mocked my melancholy mood.

Setting my jaw, I popped the cork out of the tiny bottle, wiped the tip of my pinky around the rim, and stuck the clinging glitter in my mouth before I could think too much about where it came from, or where it might lead.

I licked my lips and waited. The chill receded a little, and the ropes around my stomach stopped twisting, but the world didn't turn to roses. Guess my stress was more than a little pixie dust could handle. Then again, Kayla said fae took more than mortals. Perhaps I just needed a stronger dose. But how much? And how long did it usually take to kick in?

Tipping my head back, I looked up at the black expanse of the night sky and waited for some reaction. Light pollution hid the stars. The moon was nowhere to be seen.

I took a second dip of dust, then tucked the vial back in my pocket and started walking again. I turned away from the crowds and left the bright lights of the main thoroughfare. Since I couldn't seem to relax among the humans, perhaps I should try my luck among the fae.

Chapter 7

MY FEET CONTINUED eating the sidewalk, away from the holiday shoppers and light watchers. After a few blocks, only the lonely lamps of the neighborhood and an occasional traffic light broke the night. I kept walking, trying to remember the way to the fae bar I'd visited only once before. After a few minutes, I took another dose of pixie dust, trying to dull the sharp edges of my thoughts.

By the time I stopped in front of a dingy wooden door halfway down a dark alley at the edge of town, a fuzzy warmth had settled over me. The glittery powder hadn't made me happy, but it made me care a little less that I wasn't. My knotted muscles had loosened, and I was breathing easy for the first time in days.

The door to Crossroads had no sign, there was no line to get in. It wasn't the kind of place most people would look at twice. Not most mortals anyway.

The fae-exclusive bar didn't exactly welcome halfers, but we weren't banned either. More like tolerated, as long as we didn't cause trouble or get in the way.

Straightening my shoulders, I walked up to the door only fae could pass through and knocked on the splintered gray wood. The door swung open before the echo died, and the living mountain I remembered from my previous visit stepped out. I lifted my chin until I was looking nearly straight up, and smiled at the sharp crags that made up the troll's face.

"Hi." I gave a little finger wave, and the jagged edges of his mouth might have lifted a little. "Mind if I come in?"

He leaned forward with a groan of glaciers moving, and peered through two tiny fissures below the ridge of his brow. For one heart-pounding moment I thought he might squish me, and there wasn't a damn thing I could do about it. Then he moved aside.

I choked back an instinctive thank you, overriding a lifetime of human conditioning. Those words meant more to the fae, and I had no desire to indebt myself to the troll just for opening a door. Instead, I gave the small nod Kai said I should use when addressing servants.

Slipping past the doorman, I wound my way along a dark corridor that seemed longer than the exterior dimensions of the building should have allowed. When I rounded the last corner, I stepped into a scene of chaos.

The last time Kai brought me to Crossroads, it had been mid-morning and only the most stalwart drinkers had lingered about the place. Now, the three short steps that led into the room dead-ended in a wall of bodies. A raised stage at the far end held a band whose members ranged from a pale gray man with black wings who hovered above the stage with an instrument that looked like a guitar but sounded like a xylophone, to a three-foot creature covered in orange fur who was beating a set of drums as though they'd offended him. The singer was covered in shimmery purple scales and wore a dress that seemed to be made of seaweed.

Between the band and me was a writhing sea of bodies, too many to identify. I smiled. This was just the sort of distraction I needed.

My pocket vibrated, making me jump.

I dug out my phone and frowned. James had finally decided to call. The phone vibrated in my hand, the sound drowned out by the noise of the bar. I wouldn't be able to hear him in here, and I wasn't about to leave after just arriving. He'd ignored me until the timing was convenient for him. Well, it wasn't convenient for me. Let him feel unimportant for a change.

I swiped my thumb over the dismiss symbol and dropped the phone back into my pocket. Then I let the beat of the music and the motion of the crowd wash over me and pull me onto the dance floor.

Some dancers towered over the crowd or flew above it. Others darted between legs in a mad scurry. Colors flashed as fae in every hue of the rainbow flitted past, and I spun and smiled and lost myself to the manic pulse of the dance. I couldn't make out the lyrics, if there were any, but a voice seemed to spiral through my mind, telling me to relax, to let go.

It was a Halloween rave on acid. Better than the time Maggie and I snuck into a dance club on fake IDs for my nineteenth birthday. Better than getting wasted in Cancun with David and Aiden. After all the drama with James, and the pressure coming from Kai and the fae court, it was good to feel reckless and young again, if only for a night.

At some point a girl offered to take my coat and I gave it to her. After half an hour, I was drenched in sweat and breathing hard. Kai was right, I needed to work on my stamina.

Weaving through the gyrating crowd, I stumbled up to the bar in the center of the room and waved at the bartender.

"You'll never get a drink that way."

I turned to the voice and rubbed noses with a high-cheeked girl with amber eyes and skin the color of an overcast sky.

"Allow me." She stuck two fingers in her mouth and blew out a whistle that cut through the music and brought around the bartender's attention. "Two shots in the dark and four ambros."

"Come on." Grabbing my elbow, she dragged me away from the bar.

"What about my drink?"

"They'll bring it." She tossed a grin of blinding white over her shoulder and kept pulling. The hem of a calf-length coat the color of soot billowed around her, but her grip was cool and dry. Six stiff pigtails arced from her head like the hairy black legs of a giant spider, and I couldn't shake the feeling I was already caught in her web.

She pushed me onto the vinyl cushion at one end of a U-shaped booth and slid in across from me. "Never seen you in here before." She flashed another brilliant smile, her teeth ever-so-slightly too sharp to be human.

"You come here a lot?" I raised my voice to be heard over the music.

She gave a half shrug and started playing with a thin silver chain around the high-necked collar of her blouse. A Gothic-style cross dangled between her fingers, a dark, faceted stone in the center glinting red in the lights of the single lamp that illuminated our little alcove.

Six drinks appeared at the end of the table, blinking into existence like a granted wish. My impromptu companion pushed a tiny shot glass toward me, the liquid so dark it seemed to absorb the light. She lifted its twin in salute. "To new friends."

I waited until she tipped the glass to her lips, then held my breath and threw the inky drink into my mouth. My throat burned then went numb in quick succession, and a pleasant warmth settled in the pit of my stomach. The hard edges of the world softened slightly, and the remaining knots in my neck and shoulders melted away.

"So what brings you in tonight?" She slid one of the remaining drinks in my direction. It was bright pink, and little bubbles danced on its surface like microscopic fish leaping for bugs.

I shrugged. "Just needed a change of scenery." The drink tasted of blackberries and had the consistency of champagne. "Mmmm, this is amazing. What's in it?"

"Does it matter?" Her lips were the same soot color as her coat, like she'd just stepped out of a chimney.

I took another, longer sip, and the warmth spread to my limbs. I pushed the sleeves up on my sweater and drained the glass.

"So what should I call you?" she asked.

I opened my mouth, closed it. She hadn't asked for my name. That was taboo for fae. I considered making something up, a new name to go with the night's personality, but I'd have a hard time keeping up the lie with the cotton that was filling my head.

"Call me Alex."

"And I'm Morgan." She held out her hand and I reached across the table to clasp it.

Her eyes dipped, and I followed those amber pools to the tattoo running up my arm.

Yanking my hand out of hers, I pushed down my sleeve. *Stupid, stupid, stupid!*

Two pale umber hands slammed down on the table at the entrance to our booth. "What in the realms are you doing?"

I jumped and stammered at the stranger looming over me, but I could have been a fly on the wall. His focus was all for Morgan.

"You're supposed to be looking for Galen." The man's growl rattled the chains on the dog collar around his neck.

"Relax, Enzo." Morgan patted the tattoo-covered arm of the newcomer as though he really were a pet. "Gale will be fine."

Enzo's already narrow eyes shrank to slits. "Dimitri doesn't think so."

I squinted at the hazy shimmer around Enzo, but couldn't find anything beyond the black on black ensemble, tattooed skin, and fashion magazine hair that probably took three hours with a blow dryer to get that perfect "just rolled out of bed" look.

As if sensing my scrutiny, Enzo's gaze swung in my direction. For a split second, lightning flashed in those eyes, then it was swallowed by the dull brown of his glamour.

"I wass jus leaving." I snapped my mouth closed on the slurred words.

My empty glass came into focus, the tiny shot glass crouched beside it. Since when was I such a lightweight? Then I remembered the pixie dust. What if it took a while to kick in? What if it reacted with alcohol in some weird way?

"I'll jusss—"

"Out." The tattooed bulldog stepped back and crossed his arms over his chest.

"She could be useful." Morgan inspected the nails of one hand, her arm making after-images across my vision when it moved.

Enzo cut his eyes to the side. "How?"

"Haven't you heard about Enchantment's new toy? Word is she can see things. Like maybe where my wayward brother's got off to."

Enzo leaned over the table.

Static crackled over my skin and a blue arc skipped across the table like a stone over water.

"Really?" He purred the word, and a shiver ran down my spine.

"No idea what you're talkin' 'bout." I lurched out of my seat, stumbling against the man blocking my path. He wasn't as tall as I'd first thought, an inch or two shorter than I was, but his thin fingers were strong around my upper arm.

"Le'go." Again, the words were a jumble I couldn't be sure anyone understood, so I pushed him with my free hand.

His grip tightened.

My right arm started to tingle. Then it started to burn.

I opened my mouth to demand he stop whatever he was doing, but before I could get the words out he dropped my arm and stepped back, cradling his hand.

Morgan *tsked* and set her fingers lightly on Enzo's elbow. "I apologize for Enzo. He gets a little thick where my brother's concerned."

"Stay 'way from me," I slurred, taking an unsteady step away from the table.

She nodded, amber eyes glittering. "Perhaps another time. It was lovely to meet you, Alex."

The soot black clothes faded first, then the ashy skin. Finally, the two glowing orbs of her amber eyes winked out.

Enzo shot me a glare, then popped out of existence in a flash of light that folded in on itself like a collapsing star.

I blinked, rubbed my eyes, and stared at the empty booth for a moment. The warmth I'd been enjoying became a distant memory as tremors shook my limbs and my damp skin turned cold.

Turning, I stumbled a weaving line onto the dance floor that separated me from the exit.

The dancers that had seemed fun and lively when I arrived now struck me as dangerous and terrifying. Where before I'd seen only feathers and gauze, now I noticed claws and fangs. All around me were smiling faces, but the smiles were too sharp, too wide, too hungry. As I backed away from each new threat, I bumped into others, bouncing from body to body as I jostled through the crowd.

I tripped over a leathery tail, and would have fallen except a hand reached out of the darkness to pull me up. Talons as long as my index finger circled my forearm, glinting in the chaotic light of the dance floor.

I screamed.

The hand fell away and the nearest dancers glanced in my direction, but my scream dissipated into the overwhelming din of the club, just another beat in the music. I looked for the exit, but couldn't see past the wall of bodies. My breath was coming too fast and sparks that had nothing to do with the flitting pixies danced in my vision.

Two solid hands settled on the tops of my shoulders, and I found myself at the center of a suddenly clear patch of dance floor.

Swiveling my neck, I looked back at who, or what, was standing behind me.

The man was six and a half feet tall and half that wide. He looked almost human, but for the dull red glow of his eyes and the slight point of his ears peeking through a tuft of orange hair. His hands, thick and weathered, steered me through the crowd with an irresistible force.

Where we walked, a path opened—faerie Moses parting a sea of thrashing bodies. When we reached the edge of the room, dancers flooded back into the vacuum left by our passage.

"I don't appreciate people causing a ruckus in my bar." The man's voice was an avalanche in the high country, deep, cold, and indisputable.

"Sorry." The slur was still there, but the fog in my brain was starting to lift. "I didn't think I'd get so . . ." I waved one unsteady hand. "On such a little drink."

"Depends on the drink." He let go of my shoulders and sighed. "A halfer with as little sense as you has no business here. Go home and don't come back until you've grown up."

He pointed over my shoulder, and I followed his finger with my eyes.

There was the exit. Standing beside it was a girl with burgundy pigtails, my coat draped over one arm.

My heart was a puddle in the soles of my feet, but somehow still managed to pump enough blood to heat my cheeks. Nearly thirty years old and I was a teenager caught with a fake ID. At least they couldn't call my parents.

I reached for my coat and sighed.

"Don't worry," the girl whispered. "I'm sure he'll let you back in once a little time has passed."

There was a snort behind me.

"It's not that." Well, not only that.

She tilted her head to one side, pigtail brushing the shoulder of her button-up blouse.

"My car is across town."

"Of all the—" I could almost hear the bartender counting in his head as he tried not to strangle the idiot who'd stumbled into his bar. "Can you call someone?"

I scrunched my nose at the thought. No way was I going to face James in this condition. Kai would have left for work by now, and Chase couldn't drive. I could wake David, but the ride would come with a lecture I wasn't in the mood for. Maggie would come, she might not even lecture me. I'd certainly held her hair after enough misadventures to earn a little leeway. But this was Thanksgiving. She'd be happily sated, enjoying a nice, normal, human evening with her husband. I wasn't feeling particularly normal or nice at the moment, let alone human. I wouldn't ruin her night just because I'd ruined mine.

I shook my head. "I'll be fine."

One big hand slid over the man's expression. "No sense at all."

"I'll take her, Uncle Targe." The pigtailed girl bobbed on the balls of her feet.

He glared at her. "Fine. But just to her car. She's on her own from there."

Shooting me one last look, he grumbled, "Those guardians should keep you on a shorter leash." Then he tromped back through the sea of bodies, dancers shying away as though repulsed by a magnet.

"Guardians?" I muttered.

"Come on." The girl grabbed my wrist and turned down the dark hall toward the exit. "I'm Ava, by the way."

Ava reminded me of a two-year-old, all excited energy but no sense of urgency. Following the swish of her pigtails, I realized she was the same girl who'd greeted us when I first came to Crossroads with Kai.

"Did you say *Uncle* Targe?"

"Yep." She spun to face me so fast I almost collided with her. "This is my uncle's bar." She beamed brightly, then started out again, yanking me after. "Don't worry about getting scolded. He thinks of just about everyone as a child. I think he actually likes you."

"Not the impression I got," I grumbled.

"He was just annoyed no one was watching out for you. Halfers really shouldn't drink ambrosia unless they know what they're doing. It hits you hard and fast. But don't worry, the effects don't last long."

My head was already clearer, the hazy edges of the world coming into sharper focus, but my tongue still felt swollen and sluggish, and the hallway seemed to sway as I walked. When we paused, it spun like a lethargic merry-go-round.

A wall with arms and legs appeared out of the darkness and I yelped, pulling away from Ava and crashing to the floor.

Ava laughed. "Don't worry, it's only Arthur."

I peered up at the living mountain who'd let me in, and my cheeks grew warm again.

Ava patted the creature's stony arm with one tiny hand. "Trolls can be intimidating, which makes them great bouncers, but Arthur's a sweetie."

"Sorry." I got to my feet and brushed invisible dust off my pants.

Arthur the troll nodded his enormous head at the speed of molasses and stepped aside, fading into the darkness even as light from the alley flickered across the hall from the now open door.

"How can he move so quietly?"

Ava giggled. "Magic of course." Taking my hand once more, she pulled me into the night.

The alley outside Crossroads was deserted.

Ava took me three steps away from the club door and dropped my hand. "Where's your car?"

"Just north of Pearl Street, near Sushi Zanmai." I looked around the empty alley. "Where's yours?"

She smiled and lifted one arm. A shimmer appeared in the air. I could still see newspapers blowing around the far side of the alley, but there was a slight distortion, like looking through the surface of very clear water or heat waves over asphalt on a summer day.

I leaned forward, squinting, trying to find the edges.

Then Ava pushed me.

Chapter 8

FOR THE SPLIT second I was in that shimmering space, I felt turned inside out. Then I fell to my knees on the sidewalk of Pearl Street and heaved the contents of my stomach into the gutter. A few pedestrians looked my way, but quickly went back to their business. Had they seen me materialize out of thin air? Or was I just a drunk who couldn't hold her liquor?

Ava appeared on the sidewalk beside me. "It's always rough the first time."

She tucked a hand under my arm, and together we stumbled the two blocks to my car.

"You gonna be okay from here?" She tipped her head to one side again and a tiny crease appeared between her eyebrows.

I cleared my throat, grimacing at the flavor. My thoughts weren't so hazy anymore, and the world no longer swayed or spun around me. "Not that I enjoyed it, but I think throwing up actually helped."

She nodded. "Drive safe." Then she stepped into a solid wall.

I stared at the dull brown bricks. I was definitely going to have to ask Kai about that one.

Settling behind the Jeep's steering wheel, I sat for another few minutes, testing my senses. When I was fairly confident I could make it home safely, I put the car in gear and started up the canyon. There wasn't much traffic heading up to Nederland in the middle of the night, so other drivers weren't a problem. Slow and steady, I made it to my turnoff, up the long, winding dirt road that passed for my driveway, and into the clearing in front of my house.

Unclenching my hands from the steering wheel, I pulled the parking break and heaved a sigh of thanks to the universe for protecting my stupid ass from getting into an accident or receiving a DUI.

An inch or so of fresh snow had blanketed the clearing while I was gone. Moonlight peeked between patchy clouds, bathing the world in silvery-blue. I opened my car door, and in the frozen silence of the night, my feet crunched through the snow and sank to the earth hidden beneath. I breathed out a warm cloud that hovered a moment in the still night, then sucked in a lungful of arctic air that snapped at the cobwebs clinging to my mind from drink, fatigue, and pixie dust.

There was a soft crunch behind me, loud in the quiet of the night. Probably a rabbit or deer, but my thoughts jumped to Enzo, and Morgan's parting comment. *Perhaps another time.*

Fingers curling, I turned, and an incoming fist connected with the side of my face.

I hit the ground on hands and knees, ice stinging my exposed skin. Bracing against the frozen ground, I kicked blindly behind me and was rewarded by a deep grunt as my foot connected with something soft.

Without looking at the damage, I lunged to my feet and ran for the house, but strong arms wrapped around my ankles and I toppled once more into the snow.

This time, I twisted to get a better look at the situation.

Besides the man crawling up my legs, there were four others in the clearing. One was leaning against my Jeep clutching his gut.

If only I'd hit a few inches lower.

The other three were harder to make out in the darkness. They'd just cleared the tree line and were loping across the snow. No way I could take all five, even with Kai's training and the extra Aikido classes I'd been going to, but I was damn well gonna try.

I grabbed a handful of slushy gravel and threw it into the face of the man clinging to my knees, hoping for an opening when he wiped the debris away, but he just heaved forward onto my thighs. Grit stuck to his face, caught in his teeth and feverish eyes.

I smashed my palm into his nose, but he held on. Blood coursed over his chin to make a crimson goatee.

He reached my waist, his body trapping my legs. I thrashed in the snow, trying to get away from the dirt-and blood-encrusted visage creeping closer.

The first of his backup skidded to a stop near my shoulder and pulled my arm to the side, collapsing my support. I flopped to my back. The man on my waist scooted up again. Thick, dark drops of blood soaked into my sweater where my coat gaped at the collar. My diaphragm struggled under the weight that wouldn't let my lungs fill.

I swung out with my free hand, but couldn't get enough force behind it to do any good. My knuckles connected with his chin in a splatter of blood, but it was just a glancing blow. Grunting, I clawed at his face, driving my thumb into one unblinking eye. It sank in with a wet squelch, sliding along the side of the bulging orb, and bile rose to the back of my throat.

The man's remaining eye stayed fixed on my face, unblinking. It held no anger or pain, or any emotion I could recognize. It was the glazed eye of a dead man.

My shallow breaths came faster, straining at the weight crushing my chest. Ink swirled at the edges of my vision. Someone grabbed my remaining arm, jerking my hand away from his eye with a sickening slurp. My thumb was warm and wet with something viscous.

Screaming, I bucked and thrashed, and closed my eyes against the ruined face above me.

A damp splash hit my face, hot against my cheek.

I opened my eyes.

There was a ragged, gaping hole where my attacker's neck used to be.

Strong hands gripped my shoulders and pulled me out from under my attacker. Blackish blood smeared down my torso and over my legs. The ground was a cheese grater against my back. Then my shoulders hit the porch steps, and the hands let go.

I tipped my head back and found Chase crouched above me, teeth bared. He was staring at the clearing.

I followed his gaze.

Time had become a series of fragmented images, a flip book with half the pages missing.

A living shadow flitted through the darkness, and where it passed, men fell. Some were dead before they hit the ground. Others tried to get back up and carry on. One man's arm was dislocated from its socket, and it dragged uselessly at his side as he clawed forward with his remaining appendage, dead eyes focused on me. Then the shadow was on him. A swift snap and the man's head fell limp to the ground.

I was staring right at him when he died, and I still couldn't say what killed him. I might have seen hands for the briefest instant. Then they were gone and I couldn't be sure they'd been there at all.

I pushed up to my elbows, but Chase placed a hand on my shoulder to stop me rising any higher.

"It's almost over," he said quietly.

As the last man fell, the shadow finally stopped, coalescing into a body born from darkness.

There, in the gruesome aftermath of the red-stained snow, stood James.

For a long time we just looked at each other.

Chase's hand left my shoulder, tucked under my armpit, and lifted me to my unsteady feet.

"James." My voice was a hollow rasp. Was I in shock from the attack, or. . . . "What are you doing here?"

"I came to talk. Since you didn't answer your phone, I've been waiting with your . . . roommate . . . for you to come home."

Chase grumbled, "Pain in the ass wouldn't take piss off for an answer."

James took a step toward the porch. "Where have you been?"

Like I was going to admit to him about my drunken escapade at the faerie bar. "None of your business." I pointed at the crimson snow. "What about this?"

He glanced at the bodies and body parts strewn about the field as though seeing them for the first time. "Merak's servants."

I crossed my arms. "Like Bryce?"

He nodded.

I ground my teeth and tried to keep my voice from rising to a shout. "You told me the negotiations were going well."

"Perhaps not well, but I hadn't realized they'd deteriorated to this level. I fear I am a step behind in this game."

"Game?" I gestured to the bodies. "You call this a game?" A shrill note crept into the last word. I was *so* done with this night.

James at least had the decency to bow his head. "That's not what I meant."

"What the hell happened here anyway? Did you really just—"

"Yes."

A chill ran down my spine and I hugged myself tight to keep from shivering. "Humans can't move like that."

"No," he agreed. "They can't."

"You said you weren't a fae."

"Might as well spill," said Chase. His smile was colder than the night.

James looked away.

Chase snorted and gave me a pat on the back that felt more like a shove. "Your boy James is what you'd call a vampire."

I waited for James to laugh, to say such things didn't exist, but he just stood there, blood dripping from his hands.

From the corner of my eye, I saw a gray tabby disappear around the side of the house. I cursed Chase for abandoning me after dropping that bombshell, but I couldn't take my eyes off the man who wore James's face but felt like a stranger.

"James?"

James's pale eyes were as dull and empty as the men who'd attacked me. "I didn't want you to find out this way. To see me—" He shook his head.

My body started to shake. I clamped my arms tighter to stop it, but the vibrations continued, threatening to pull me apart at the seams. The moon dipped behind its mottled cover and stole the color from the world. The clearing became a contrast of black and white.

There were stories about vampires—there were stories about aliens and ghosts too—there had never been any proof that they existed. But then, people hadn't believed the stories about faeries until the fae came out. I never put much stock in stories of werewolves till I was staring down the snarling muzzle of one. I knew better than to discount stories, proof or no, and I was staring at a whole field of proof that James wasn't human.

Suddenly, the enigmatic personality and quirky idiosyncrasies I'd passed off as harmless took on a different light. Then there was his past with Kai, and the way Marc and Sarah both hinted that he was hiding something from me.

But for every piece added to the puzzle, there were others that just didn't fit.

I'd seen James during the day. Not often, granted, but we'd gone for walks and eaten lunch on sunny days. Weren't vampires supposed to explode or something if sunlight hit them? And then there was food. In all the stories I'd ever heard of vampires they fed off human blood, but James ate with me on a regular basis.

I rubbed my temples, trying to make sense of . . . anything.

"You should go inside, Alex. Get some rest."

"What?" I let my hands fall and blinked.

"Leave the bodies where they are," he continued. "I'll take care of them."

"You'll *take care* of them? What does that mean?"

"It means you don't need to notify anyone of what happened here tonight."

My jaw dropped. "These people are *dead*, James."

"No one will miss these men. No one will come looking for them."

"How can you possibly know that?" I balled my hands into fists. "Besides, they attacked me. God only knows what would have happened if you weren't here. I need to report this." But even as the words left my mouth, my mind raced ahead to interrogations and interviews, and Uncle Sol's disapproving voice in my head. *You've been drawing a lot of attention from the wrong kinds of people lately.*

Calling the authorities was what any law-abiding human would do, but I'd left that path a month ago. The last thing I needed was to explain how a bunch of men ended up ripped to pieces in my front yard. Not when PTF Agent O'Connell was looking for an excuse to tear my secrets open.

"Please," James said. "Give me time to get to the bottom of this."

The plea in his voice stopped me cold. In the two years since he showed up at my door, I'd never heard James beg.

"What if the police pay me another visit in the meantime? Not unlikely considering—" I gestured to him.

"Unless you tell them otherwise, the police will never know these men were here."

I gritted my teeth and looked around the gore-splattered field. "So what do we do about—" I wrinkled my nose, unsure what to call the dead meat on my lawn.

"Your yard will look as it should in the morning. In the meantime, please erase tonight's footage from your surveillance system." He gestured to the cameras pointed at him.

"You must have one hell of a clean-up crew."

He turned away, stepping lightly across the snow toward the Lexus I hadn't noticed parked under the trees.

"Hey, we're not done yet. We need to talk about the whole you being a vampire thing."

James kept walking. "Talk to Kai. If you still wish to speak with me after he explains, come see me."

"Explain it yourself."

He strode purposefully toward his escape.

I scooped up a slushy snowball and threw it as hard as I could at his back as he opened the door to his car.

The snowball fell two feet short, but his shoulders jerked when it impacted as though I'd hit my mark.

"Chickenshit!" I shouted.

He climbed inside and drove away.

I SLAMMED THE door to the bathroom, just like I'd slammed the door to my bedroom and the door to the front of my house. Doors were a poor substitute for what I really wanted to slam, but they'd have to do for now.

Yanking off my ruined winter coat, I threw it in a trash bag. Then I glared at my reflection in the mirror. The skin around my left eye was red and starting to swell. The thick sweater I'd been wearing was streaked and splattered with reddish-brown splotches. It would also need to be thrown out, or burned. I tugged the heavy fabric over my head and dropped it on top of my coat. Then I stared at my hiking boots. It had taken years to break them in. I loved those boots.

I pursed my lips. Good boots were hard to find, but the chunks of dead guy goo clinging to them weren't likely to come off. Sighing, I dropped them in the bag as well. The jeans were next, sticking to my skin where dark stains had soaked through. Red smears streaked my arm when I pulled it out of the bag.

The sack hit the floor with a squelch and a puff of rank air. I kicked it into a corner and used my "relatively" clean hand to turn on the shower. The faucet knob was red when I released it. I'd need to pick up some bleach next time I went to town.

Standing under the beating heat of the shower, I tipped my head against the wall and let my eyes slide closed.

Let it be a dream, some horrible nightmare I was about to wake up from. James was a human gallery owner who didn't deal drugs, or sleep with prostitutes, or rip the limbs off zombie attackers in the middle of the night. He was my friend, and I'd hoped more. He was supposed to be someone I could trust. . . . Except he wasn't.

I slid down the wall until my butt hit the cold porcelain of the tub. My gaze was pulled to the reddish-brown sludge spiraling the drain. I started to shake.

I didn't try to stop it this time. I let the waves of adrenaline and anger and fear wash over me and trickle away. By the time the water ran clear, I was limp beneath the cooling stream.

Shutting the water off, I heaved myself over the edge of the tub and did a quick once-over with a towel. Then I grabbed a nightshirt off the floor and stumbled toward the bed.

My body weighed a thousand pounds and my feet dragged along the carpet, static arcs leaping like fish in my wake. No furry body purred in my bed. Another coward, probably hiding in case I blamed him for keeping James's secret.

I sank into the mattress, pulled the covers up to my chin, and melted away to nothing.

MY HAND IS SO small compared to his, it disappears completely in his grip. I look up, past our linked hands and the length of his arm. My father smiles down at me. As long as he holds my hand, everything will be all right.

"What do you think of Venice, sweetie?"

We are standing in San Marco Square, at the foot of a great cathedral. Its domes and spires rise into the sky, and more pigeons than I can count swarm around it in perfect aerial choreography. Behind us, ships both large and small drift along the waterway. The sun rests low on the horizon, spreading fingers of pink and gold to tickle the clouds, and the surface of the water shimmers in the light.

"It's beautiful, Papa."

The last curve of the sun falls out of sight.

Night descends, and with it come the dancers. Men and women in colorful masks and fancy costumes. I laugh, delighted by the Carnival characters that pour into the streets around us. There are masks made to resemble the sun and moon and masks of fairytale monsters. Some have long noses that resemble beaks. Some are purest white with intricate patterns painted around the eyes. No two masks are the same.

"Venice is a city of demons, Alyssandra. Beware its beauty."

I look at my father, not understanding, but as I turn, my fingers slip from his hand. In the space where he'd been just a moment before, dancers crowd in around me. I scramble through them, calling for my father, searching for some sign of his passing. All around, the masks watch me, beautiful and silent.

I stop running. Tears slide down my cheeks and snot runs from my nose. I am only a child, lost and alone.

"Why do you cry, pretty one?"

The masked figures surround me. They are pressed so closely there is no way out. As if on some prearranged cue, the dancers reach up to pull their masks away, and the illusion is destroyed. Gone are the porcelain smiles and glittery paint. In their place I find empty eyes and grins of fangs dripping with blood. I recognize one man, but he is not my father. He has black hair bound by a ribbon, and eyes as cold as ice.

He whispers something, and the circle constricts. Clawed hands reach for me, tearing my skin, pulling my bones apart, and I scream.

"Alex, wake up!"

My forehead slammed into something solid and I fell back against my pillow, clamping my hands over the pain.

Kai sat back, rubbing his own head gingerly with one hand. "You were having a nightmare."

"No kidding," I moaned with the gravelly voice of a pack-a-day smoker.

I rolled my head to make out the fuzzy red numbers on my clock. It was nearly dawn. Kai was still wearing his smock from the convenience store.

"Did you just get home?"

He nodded, hands falling to his lap. "Chase told me what happened."

The bar, the fae, the dead men in my driveway. It all came back. I slumped against my pillow. "You knew what James was. That's why you disapproved of me dating him."

He raised an eyebrow. "Can you blame me?"

"Why not just tell me?"

He sighed. "It wasn't my truth to tell."

We'd had this conversation several times since he'd come to live with me. Paranaturals were fiercely protective of their secrets, and by extension, the secrets of others. It was an unspoken agreement that you didn't go blabbing other people's secrets, because once lips started flapping in the paranatural community there would be no end to it.

"No exceptions, huh?" I tried to smile, but my face was too tight. Pain lanced through my cheek, and I raised a hand to the puffy skin around my eye, flinching at the pressure.

Kai and I stared into the middle distance for a while, the silence broken only by the soft hum of my clock and the occasional creak old houses were prone to.

"So . . ." I said at last. "Vampires."

He patted my blanket-clad knee. "I'm afraid so."

"Do they really drink blood?"

Kai tipped his head in thoughtful silence. "Yes and no. They do drink blood, but that's just the delivery system. They drink life."

I shivered. "What about the sun? Shouldn't vampires burst into flames in sunlight?"

"Vampires are allergic to sunlight the way most fae are allergic to metal."

"Then why can James walk around in the day?" My fingers dug into the comforter. "Does it hurt him?"

"He's a special case." Kai's smile was strained. "Sort of like you."

"Are they immortal?"

"Yes, but not indestructible."

"So putting a stake through his heart and cutting off his head would kill him?"

Kai snorted. "I can't think of many things decapitation *wouldn't* kill."

"Good to know." I drummed my fingers against my thigh, staring at the wave made by my knuckles.

Kai rubbed his hands over his face. "James isn't bad for what he is, but he's still a vampire. Now that you know, will you stay away from him?"

Would I? I'd taken a chance opening up to James, letting him into my life, and he'd repaid me with lies. But I knew a little about hiding who you were from the people you cared about.

"I don't know. It's a lot to take in." I chewed the inside of my cheek. "What have you got against vampires? Aren't they just another breed of paranatural, like Marc and the wolves?"

"No," he said. "They're not."

The springs squeaked when he stood up, and he was out the door before I could say another word.

I sat up, mouth open. Was he running too?

I flipped the covers back to follow, but Kai stepped through the door before my feet hit the floor.

"I had a feeling you might need this." He held out a slim, black, leather-bound book.

I frowned. "More homework?"

"A story," he corrected. "Of how the vampires came to be."

Chapter 9

THE WORDS WERE written in a tight script, and I squinted to make out the fading ink. I hunched around the pages, the book propped up on my blanket-covered knees.

Kai lay at the foot of my bed, arms tucked behind his head, feet dangling over the edge. His eyes were closed, but the lines around his eyes and mouth were too tight for sleep.

I tapped the passage I'd just read. "In this bit about the practitioner, it says he shone like a beacon across the realms. What does that mean?"

Kai opened his eyes but kept them focused on the crack in my ceiling. "Demons exist in the space between realms, the Rift, as we call it. They can only enter a physical plane through a conduit. When a practitioner of sufficient strength draws magic, he becomes such a conduit. The concentrated magic illuminates the Rift like someone turning on a light, and demons are drawn to that light without fail. The more magic a practitioner draws, the stronger the light."

I chewed a piece of dry skin off my lip. "That explains why practitioners are more susceptible to demon possession. Do the demons cause practitioner burnouts?"

He shifted to look at me. "That's good old-fashioned human greed, though a practitioner is more likely to suffer a backlash if he's busy fending off a demon trying to consume his soul."

Turning the page, I found an image of a willowy-looking elf. I skimmed through the caption below. The man had a fae lover.

I turned the book toward Kai, showing him the picture. "If fae are immune to demons, couldn't his girlfriend have protected him the way paladins do for the Church's sorcerers?"

Every practitioner was assigned a paladin when they began their training to join the Sorcerer Troop—humanity's weapon in the war against the fae, the only practitioners allowed to study the powerful magic texts guarded by the Church. I didn't know much about paladins except that they were holy men and women who trained for years to guard the souls of their sorcerer charges.

Kai pursed his lips and went back to studying the ceiling. "The illusionist in that story was young and not very powerful. The rifter—that's what we call a practitioner possessed by a demon—brutally raped her and left her on the brink of death."

I swallowed.

"She managed to survive, though there are many among the fae who consider that the greatest tragedy of this story."

"They'd rather she died?"

He shrugged.

"That's terrible."

"The rape left her pregnant, and the baby . . ."

"What?"

"It was killing her. Draining her life. Her family wanted to destroy it, but she refused. She fled to the mortal realm to keep it safe."

"So the first vampire was a child born from a rifter father and a fae mother?"

He nodded. "Though that first child wasn't really a vampire as we now define them. It was unique, a demon with a body of its own."

"How is that even possible?"

"We don't know. Since fae and demon magic are antithetical, common wisdom says the opposing forces should have ripped the child apart as soon as it was born." He shrugged. "But here we are."

"So the fae hate vampires because they're part demon?"

"That . . . creature was an abomination. A plague upon the world, with the psyche of a demon, the longevity of a fae, and the ambition of a human. To protect all the realms, the fae hunted it down."

I flipped the page and traced my finger over an illustration of writhing black bodies. "But he wasn't alone."

Kai shook his head. "At some point, the creature learned it could drain a person to the edge of death, then break off a piece of its own demon soul and merge it with that of the dying human to bring them back. By the time the fae found it, there was an army."

I skimmed an account of the battle that followed. "You thought killing the original would kill the rest."

"Didn't work out that way."

"Why didn't the fae go after the offspring?"

He settled back on his elbows, once more looking toward the ceiling. "We'd taken heavy losses in the battle, and the surviving vampires scattered. I think the deciding factor was that a fae scholar developed a way to ward the portals between realms. With the vampires contained in the mortal world, there was no reason to waste further resources."

I rolled my eyes and closed the book in my lap. The leather cover had grown warm in my hands. "Do you think James is evil?"

Kai frowned. "In so far as it's possible, I believe James is a decent man."

I set the book on the nightstand. "That's quite the caveat."

"Vampires drain the life from other sentient beings. I'd think you'd find that abhorrent."

"I do, but there are fae who feed off humans too, and you don't want me condemning them." Was I really defending murder? I shook my head. My recent exploits had clearly damaged my moral compass. Then again, was it right to condemn someone for trying to survive just because his food source could beg for its life?

A solid weight settled in the pit of my stomach. How many lives had James taken to survive?

"Vampires live a long time, right?"

Kai nodded. "So long as they continue to feed, it's conceivable a vampire might live forever."

"Do you know how old James is?" I held my breath.

"No."

I exhaled, and rubbed my eyes.

If James was conceivably immortal, a human life would be little more than a blip on his timeline. Even if I wanted to try again with James. . . . What would be the point?

"May I make a suggestion?" Kai's voice was soft.

"Go ahead."

"Knowing his true nature, do you hate James now?"

I tried to catalog my tumultuous feelings. Anger, confusion, frustration, disappointment, concern, doubt. . . . "No."

"Do you fear him?"

I thought of the mutilated corpses in my driveway, and crazy as it was, shook my head.

"Then talk to him."

I frowned. "You didn't want me dating him in the first place, why encourage me to go back to him?"

"I said *talk*, not date. I still think you should distance yourself from him. I just don't want you to have any regrets." He rolled smoothly off the bed. "Human lives are too short for regrets."

He was halfway to the door when another thought popped into my head. "Hey, Kai? Can I borrow that encyclopedia of fae we were looking at the other day?"

He turned, eyes narrowed. "Why?"

"Can't a girl show a little initiative in her studies?"

"Not if you're the girl."

I sighed. I didn't have the energy for a lecture, and that's what I'd get if I told him I'd gone to Crossroads on my own. Especially considering how it turned out. "I saw a fae earlier and didn't recognize the species. Thought it might be a good project to look him up."

He snorted, but gave a sharp nod. With luck, I'd be able to figure out who, or at least what, Morgan and Enzo were before they caught up with me again.

JAMES WAS TRUE to his word. When I stepped onto my front porch, cradling a steaming mug of coffee, I couldn't tell there'd been a fight. A fresh layer of frost covered the gravel, blissfully free of stains. The bodies, and the contaminated snow, were gone. It was so perfectly normal-looking I could almost believe the whole attack had been a terrible dream brought on by stress and a bad reaction to pixie dust. But then, there'd still been the trash bag in my bathroom.

While I was glad not to be greeted by a pile of corpses first thing in the morning, it was more than a little disturbing to know James could make all that evidence disappear overnight. This was definitely not the first mess he'd had to clean up, and that more than anything convinced me he had nothing to do with the dead hooker in his apartment. David was right, James wouldn't have been so sloppy.

A gust of wind twisted my hair, and the exposed skin on my face and hands started to ache from the cold.

What I remembered of last night's fight was a blur, literally, and I didn't think it was due to my semi-inebriated condition or the darkness that I hadn't been able to track what was happening. I glanced at one of the security cameras mounted to the side of my house.

Retreating to the warmth inside, I shut the door on the picturesque forest with a shudder, and settled in front of my computer. I took a pull from my mug, but the coffee had lost its heat. Setting it aside, I brought up the footage from last night.

The cameras covered a number of angles around my house, but only one had caught the fight. I watched myself step out of the Jeep. Then the first man came up behind me on the screen. There was no sound in this version, but the noise that had alerted me to his presence echoed in my head as my past self turned to take the punch.

I reached up and touched the swollen bruise under my eye with a grimace as my attacker went down.

I caught the first guy just above the groin with my kick, then ran for the house. A second man tackled me from behind, and the two tiny figures struggled. My mouth went dry when the me from last night gouged the man's eye, and I scrubbed my hand over my jeans as though I could wipe off the memory.

My struggle had seemed to go on forever last night. On the screen, it only lasted a few seconds.

I leaned forward, willing myself not to blink even as my eyes began to itch.

A black shadow passed above the struggling figures like a billow of smoke. In that shadow was the barest glimmer of a face, perhaps the glint of a ribbon streaming behind. Then Chase was there, pulling me from beneath the falling weight of the dead man.

I ignored the two figures retreating to the safety of the porch, I already knew that story. I followed the shadow.

Even watching as closely as I could, that shadowy figure flitted across the screen almost too fast to track. It was only when he actually landed a blow that he slowed enough to be seen.

The last man standing tumbled to his knees, clutching his abdomen in a vain effort to keep his insides from spilling to the ground. He toppled forward. After that, nothing moved on the screen. James stood statue still. He never so much as glanced at the carnage around him.

I fast-forwarded to see how he'd managed to clean up that god-awful mess in the few short hours I'd been asleep.

An hour after James fled the scene, a van lumbered up my driveway, and out climbed Joe with a pressed suit and slicked back hair. Guess he helped with more than just gallery operations.

I shook my head. How well must he know James to clean a field of dead bodies without batting an eye?

Better than me, that was for damn sure.

Bracing my elbows on the desk, I propped my chin and studied the tiny figure on the screen, the person James trusted with his secrets. A twinge of jealousy stabbed through me.

Joe bent over on the screen, crouching just above the blood-streaked snow. His mouth was moving, but there was no way to make out what he said. Then a slightly lighter shadow detached itself from the darkness, and a gray tabby trotted across the snow. Joe spoke again, and the tabby stepped briskly to the house, careful to avoid the contaminated snow.

A moment later, the screen went blank. The system had been shut off.

I glared over my shoulder at the furry gray ball sleeping on the back of the couch. "Why did you turn off the cameras?"

Lifting his head, he yawned far enough to expose the back of his throat. Two luminous green eyes blinked at me.

"Well?"

He closed his eyes and returned to his nap.

"No one needs to see what happened last night." Kai stepped out of the hall, hair damp from the shower. His baggy pajama pants swished as he walked toward the kitchen.

"I thought you were headed to bed."

"Food first."

Pressing the button to delete all the stored footage, I followed him. "I was going to delete the recording anyway."

Kai shrugged. "Better not to record it in the first place."

"But I want to know how they cleaned it up."

He pinned me with a level stare. "No, you don't. Trust me."

I crossed my arms and flopped into a seat at the kitchen table while he poured himself a bowl of frosted flakes.

He glanced at the computer. "I take it you watched the fight?"

I nodded and sank a little lower in my seat.

"Change your mind about James?"

"What he did was terrifying, but I'm not afraid he'll hurt me. Not physically at least." I crossed my arms with a sigh. "The lies are a bigger deal. I can understand his reasoning, but—"

Kai cocked his head to one side, crunching away at his sugar- encrusted breakfast.

"He didn't trust me. Even knowing I'm a halfer with my own secrets, he didn't trust me."

Kai swallowed. "Trust can be hard when you've been alone a long time."

I snorted. "Maggie said something similar to me back in college." That had been three years after mom died. Even before that. . . . "My mom was a single parent working three jobs to keep food on the table, and we moved around a lot. I got pretty used to being on my own."

Kai pointed his spoon at me. "Now multiply that by a few centuries."

"I thought you didn't know how old James was?"

"I don't." He shrugged. "But I can guess." He took another bite, swallowed, and sighed. "James is not human and never will be. He'll always have secrets. He'll bring danger into your life as long as you stay near him, and the closer you are, the more danger you'll be in."

"Says the faerie who turned my life upside down and got me stabbed." I crossed my arms.

He shrugged again. "I never claimed to be safe company. But you can't run from who you are. You *can* distance yourself from James."

I chewed my lower lip. Was it fair to judge James by *what* he was rather than *who* he was? I'd told Loni I had no problem with Emma being a practitioner, so why did James not being human change how I saw him? Then again, practitioners didn't go around decapitating people. By PTF decree, they were only allowed to study passive and healing magics, good for things like stabilizing ecosystems or knitting broken bones. Anything stronger and they became sorcerers, controlled by the Church and kept in line by their paladins.

But James had killed the men on my lawn to protect me, and he hadn't asked to be a vampire any more than I'd asked to be part fae. It didn't change who we were.

My memories kicked up like an old projector, showing me Johnson, the PTF agent I'd stabbed with his own knife, and Neil, the fae whose skull I'd crushed with an iron bar. I never would have thought myself capable of killing a man, but in the past month, I'd killed two. Did I have any right to point fingers at James?

I gripped the sides of my head, grabbing clumps of hair as my thoughts ran in circles.

"Is your friend still coming over this morning?" Kai dropped his empty bowl in the sink.

I glanced up, frowning. Then I remembered. David. Guns. I looked at the clock. He'd already be on his way.

I sighed and tried to push my confusion about James and the definition of monsters aside. I needed to pull myself together before David showed up.

Chapter 10

"WHAT THE HELL happened to your face?" David said when I opened the front door.

"Nice to see you too." I walked back to the couch and my third cup of coffee. I'd had barely four hours of sleep, and I was starting to feel it. The cobwebs in my brain snagged passing thoughts, tangling them up, dulling my senses. A nap would have been ideal, but David had no sympathy for late nights. A black eye on the other hand . . .

"Seriously, Alex." He closed the door and followed me. "What happened?"

"I went to a bar last night and got a little tipsy. I fell walking back to my car."

"Your car? You drove home when you were too smashed to walk?" David scowled, his dark brown eyes seeming almost black.

I glared back. "I wasn't smashed. I just lost my balance."

"Yeah, right. Why didn't you call me? I would have given you a ride."

"It was the middle of the night." I took a sip of coffee, willing the caffeine to clear my head. "What would Steven have thought if you jumped out of bed to run to my rescue?"

"That you'd done something stupid," he deadpanned. "Again."

I stuck out my tongue.

"Besides, he wasn't there last night."

I quirked an eyebrow. "Trouble in paradise?"

"Says the girl whose boyfriend is wanted for drug-trafficking."

The smile melted from my face.

David heaved a sigh and pulled both hands back along the sides of his dark, close-cropped hair. He sat down beside me and the cushions sank in his direction so my shoulder bumped into his.

"Sorry. That was over the line."

I shook my head. "It's not you." David's teasing was natural, familiar, like an annoying brother.

His eyes widened, and he lifted a hand, pointing. "Is that a Christmas tree?"

I followed the direction of his finger. Kai's saggy little tree was propped near the wall. Bright blue and silver balls dangled from its branches, and glittery white tinsel hung like icicles among its needles. It was a testament to my distraction that I hadn't even noticed it that morning.

"I thought you didn't do trees?" David continued.

I shrugged. "It was Kai's idea."

"And you're okay with it?" He shifted his gaze to me, narrowing his eyes. David knew why I hated Christmas trees. I'd broken down during a Christmas party my first year of college and blabbed the whole story.

I studied the little tree. "You know, I think I am."

He bumped my shoulder. "Wanna talk about it?"

I grimaced.

He slapped me on the knee. "Then let's go shoot some guns."

Living in the mountains had its advantages. No one complained about the noise when I left the studio door open in the summer, or called the cops when my boyfriend decimated a gang of thugs in the front yard. It also meant I could use my property as a practice range without anyone reporting gunshots.

"This is for you." David handed me a small handgun in a leather holster. "It's a Ruger LC9. Don't carry it around unless you get a permit, but you can keep it in your house or car in case of emergencies." He held up a finger to draw my attention away from the gun. "Unless you're shooting, it should *always* be in the holster."

I lifted the gun gingerly, keeping my fingers far from the trigger as I slid it free of its holster. "I'm still not sure this is a good idea."

"Even after what happened with Johnson?"

The name of the PTF agent I'd killed sent a shiver through me. Getting strangled, mauled, zapped with a Taser, and stabbed had certainly brought to light some shortcomings in my ability to protect myself, hence the sword and extra Aikido lessons. Being able to land a hit before the bad guys were close enough to hit back would be a nice advantage. David was right. Learning to use a gun was a good idea.

He stepped up beside me, a slightly larger gun in his own hand, and held out a pair of bright orange ear plugs and clear plastic glasses.

I slipped on the glasses and stuffed the plugs in my ears.

"Set your feet shoulder width apart and use your left hand to steady your right." He demonstrated as he spoke. "Sight down the barrel, exhale, hold, and squeeze the trigger."

Even with the ear protection it was loud.

"Now you try."

"One demonstration? That's all I get?"

He shrugged. "Best way to learn is by doing."

Wiping my palms on my jeans, I set my feet apart and squared off against the hillside. I exhaled. Even before I tightened my finger on the trigger I began to cringe, anticipating the kick and bang that would follow.

The shot rang out.

I turned to David.

"Not bad," he said. "You managed to hit a mountain. Let's see if we can tighten that up a bit."

David had me fire until my gun was empty, then showed me how to reload it. For the second round he placed various-sized plastic containers around the landscape.

I reloaded the gun three more times before I managed to hit the gallon milk jug.

"I got it," I crowed.

"Don't get too excited. That's one out of how many shots?" David stepped up beside me, and in the blink of an eye five tiny water bottles flew off their perches. The fifth shot was still ringing in my ears when the gun went back in its holster.

I whistled. "When did you become such a bad ass?"

"About the time I stopped hanging out with you so much."

I slapped his arm, but kept staring at the decimated remains of the bottles. If I wanted to get that good, I was going to need more bullets.

SWIPING MY FINGER around the mixing bowl, I popped a wad of brownie dough into my mouth and moaned with pleasure. The rest of the batter was already in the oven, and soon the house would fill with the scent of baking chocolaty goodness—my reward for finally hitting a target with every bullet fired from my gun.

After two hours, once I could be trusted to land most of my shots, David told me to keep practicing and took off. I'd blown through half the ammo he left me before calling it quits, and my arm, shoulder, and neck muscles felt fused in place, but I had another weapon for my arsenal.

I rinsed the remaining chocolate out of the bowl and dropped it in the dishwasher. Then I grabbed my sketchbook and moved into the living room to wait.

Flipping to a blank page, I pictured Morgan. Then I started sketching.

According to the book Kai had lent me, she was most likely a shadow-walker—a fae who could travel through patches of darkness by opening something called a shadow road.

I created a basic outline for her face, round and full. Then I started filling in details. The slant of her eyes. The little bow shape of her lips. I imagined I was creating a suspect sketch for an APB.

I'd just started on the creepy spider-leg tendrils of her hair when there was a knock at the door.

I jumped, my pencil marking the page unintentionally. I'd been so focused I hadn't even heard an engine approach. Then again, not all my visitors these days drove cars.

I glanced toward the back of the house, but Kai had left twenty minutes into gun practice, complaining about the noise. Chase was questionable backup at best, but he'd probably de-fur if someone tried to kill me . . . eventually. I set my sketch pad aside.

"Police," came a muffled call through the door.

I froze in the process of getting up.

James had promised no one would miss the men, no one would know. But here were the police, knocking on my door. I swallowed the boulder lodged in my throat.

"Just a minute," I called, trying to gather my thoughts.

The trash bag with my stained clothes and ruined boots was still slumped in a corner under the sink like a melted candle. I should have burned it all first thing that morning. I'd do it as soon as they left.

Please let them not have a warrant.

Plastering on my best customer service smile, I took a deep breath and pulled the door open enough for them to see me, but not enough to be mistaken as an invitation. "Yes?"

Detective Herrera was in front. Sarah loomed behind him, arms crossed, scowling like she wanted to drill a hole through my head with her glare. "What happened to your eye?"

"I fell." It was the bullshit answer of a battered housewife in an emergency room, and we all knew it. It as much as screamed, "I don't want to tell you," but anything else would just lead to more questions. Questions I couldn't safely answer.

"You seem nervous, Ms. Blackwood. Is everything all right?" Sarah was still glaring daggers over Herrera's shoulder. I wasn't sure what bug had crawled up her butt to put her in such a mood, but I could guess. No matter how good James's cleanup crew was, there was no way they could mask the smell of that much spilled blood from a werewolf's nose.

"Right as rain," I said.

"We have some questions to ask you," Herrera said. "May we come in?"

I hesitated, thinking of the bag of bloody evidence slumped in my bathroom.

"Something wrong, Ms. Blackwood?" Sarah's smile was all teeth.

Clenching my jaw, I stepped away from the door.

Herrera walked past me, eyes straight forward. Sarah's gaze continued to bore into me like she was drilling for oil. When she passed, she leaned in close and rumbled in a barely audible voice, "I'm going to find out what happened here."

I swallowed hard and closed the door behind her.

"Make yourselves comfortable." I gestured to the dining table, arguably the least comfortable seats in existence.

The cops sat side by side, and I pulled out a chair at the end, forcing them to turn.

Herrera whipped out a little notebook and flipped it open. "What do you know about Elsa McNamara?"

All the tension rushed out of me, leaving me lightheaded. They weren't here about last night's massacre, just more questions about James.

Sarah's whispered promise still rang in my mind, but I pushed it aside.

"She's James's housekeeper. Short, polite. She has grayish-brown hair and wears too much lipstick." I shrugged. "I don't know her very well."

"When was the last time you saw Ms. McNamara?"

I looked up at the ceiling. "Last Thursday, I guess." I'd stopped by James's house, and she answered the door with an honest-to-gods feather duster in her liver-spotted hand. Did real people actually use those things? I shook my head at the memory and glanced at the dusty knickknacks on my mantel.

Sarah leaned forward. "She's missing."

I stared at them, processing the words.

"We tried to interview her regarding the incident at the gallery, but no one's seen her since Tuesday afternoon. It seems Mr. Abernathy was the last person to have contact with her," she added.

"Do you think it has something to do with the dead girl?"

Sarah arched an eyebrow. "Do you?"

"What? No. I mean, I don't know." I shook my head.

First a dead escort, then the attack last night, now a missing housekeeper. I had no idea what to think. The only connection . . . was James.

Sarah and Herrera asked more questions about James's routines, who he knew, where he went. It was sad how few of them I could answer, and each blank widened the hole in the fiction I'd been weaving about having a man in my life.

"Let us know if you think of anything." Herrera handed me another card and I took it numbly, reacting on autopilot.

Sarah gave me one last glare in lieu of a parting remark and pulled the door closed behind her.

I waited until their engine turned over and the crunch of gravel faded away, then I tossed the card beside its twin on the end table. The smell of chocolate was starting to waft from the oven, but even the thought of brownies didn't make me as happy as it had twenty minutes ago. Dropping onto the couch, I rubbed at the pressure building in my skull. Every thought that flitted through my mind seemed to lead to more questions.

I sighed. If I wanted answers, there was only one place to get them. Sooner or later, I'd have to face James.

Chapter 11

MY FINGER STOPPED an inch from the doorbell.

Behind me, snow fluttered through cones of light cast by street lamps over the empty road. I licked my lips and tried to blink away the image of James silhouetted on a field of snow stained red, blood dripping from his hands. Goosebumps pimpled my skin, and I hunched my shoulders against a cold that was as much inside as out.

I wasn't afraid of James, but wasn't sure which version of him I'd find when he answered the door. *If* he answered the door. Gritting my teeth, I pressed the button.

The door swung open before the chime died.

"I didn't think you'd come." James's voice was low and even. His clear blue gaze traced my features as though searching for verification that I was truly there.

"I wasn't sure you'd answer."

A small smile played around the edge of his mouth. He stepped back from the door.

I took a deep breath, straightened my shoulders, and followed James into a large living room near the back of his house. Flames crackled in the fireplace that dominated one wall, chasing back the chill winter air and throwing shadows that danced in the wavering light like the masked creatures from my dream.

James braced one hand against the mantel and looked into the fire. "Coming alone to the lair of a vampire was brave . . . and foolish."

I forced my hands to relax. "I'm not afraid of you."

"Liar."

"It's not a—"

"Your heart is racing like a rabbit bolting from a fox." He tipped his face up. Hunger glinted in his eyes.

I cleared my throat. "You won't hurt me."

I was pinned to the wall before I could blink, feet dangling above the ground. I clutched at the fingers circling my throat, but they were bands of steel. My mind flashed to another hand around my neck, and for a moment the warm room was replaced by a clear autumn night that filled me with panic.

James leaned in so his breath warmed my face. "Do you understand what I am?"

His complexion had washed out to the pallor of a drown victim, translucent flesh stretched thin over bluish veins. His lips pulled back to reveal vicious fangs that glinted in the firelight, and silver eyes looked out from dark sockets, pools of mercury at the bottom of twin wells. Those eyes held hunger, and pain, and sadness . . . but behind it all was James.

It took every ounce of my self-control to relax my arms at my sides. My heart was still racing, but at least I was back in the here and now. This wasn't Bryce delivering a message. This was James. He was trying to scare me, to make a point, but I could see the fear behind his eyes. What was he afraid I'd see? The monster? Or the man?

Searching my memory, I pulled up the lecture James had given me when I found out I wasn't human, when I wasn't sure *what* I was anymore. My voice was a thready whisper squeezing past the vise of his grip. "You are who you always were. Your abilities don't matter. What matters is what you feel, and think, and how you live your life. Those are the things that define you as a person."

The shadow moved, and I crumpled to the floor like a broken doll.

"Dammit, Alex." James was standing across the room, his back to me.

I stood up and brushed the knees of my pants with shaky hands. "You seem disappointed."

He looked over his shoulder and the mask I'd known for years was back in place. "You have never disappointed me."

"Then why the letdown?"

He stiffened his jaw, frowning. "I never should have let you believe we could have a future together. I'm a monster."

"If my misadventures since October have taught me anything, it's that fangs and magic do not a monster make."

"And murder? Don't fool yourself into thinking me innocent."

I crossed my arms. "My hands aren't exactly clean either."

I hadn't told James about the fae I killed in a dark field outside Boulder, and I had no idea how many lives he'd taken in however long he'd been walking the earth, but the tension between us splintered and fled, chased away by our mutual culpability.

I stepped to one of the overstuffed chairs that framed the fireplace and lowered myself into the creaking leather.

James ambled to the liquor cabinet at the speed of a mere human. "Care for a drink?"

"Are you ready to have a real conversation?"

He nodded and I mirrored the gesture.

James pulled down a bottle of dark liquid and two crystal glasses. Pouring a generous portion into each, he handed one over and settled in the seat across from me.

The thick drink glinted red in the firelight and made my heart beat faster.

I sniffed, and relaxed slightly at the aroma of fruit and alcohol.

"I'm hardly going to keep blood in a decanter on my shelf."

Blushing, I tipped the glass to my lips. The wine was rich and tart, and flooded my stomach with warmth. I took a second, longer drink, letting the alcohol smooth out the rough edges of my thoughts.

I lifted the half-empty glass in salute. "So vampires drink more than blood."

"Wine helps dull the hunger, though it can never truly satisfy."

I cradled the glass in my lap and stared into its wavering surface. "Why didn't you tell me?"

He took a long pull from his glass, then rested it on his knee. "Perhaps I was too enamored with the lie."

"Joe knows."

He nodded. "And Elsa."

I stiffened. That cast the woman's disappearance in a new light.

"But not me." The hollow pit in my stomach swallowed the meager warmth of the wine and spread through me, emptying me out.

Ducking his chin, he closed his eyes and sighed.

"When were you going to tell me?" The ache in my chest twisted. "*Were* you going to tell me?"

"I don't know." His voice was cracked glass, and it flayed my heart.

"And what about now? Do you trust me now?"

"It was never about trust, Alex."

"Bullshit."

"I didn't want to lose you."

I opened my mouth, closed it, then downed the last of my wine and leaned back enough to make the leather groan.

Rising in one fluid motion, James prowled back to the liquor cabinet like a tiger in a cage, each shift of muscle clear beneath the lines of his perfectly fitted shirt. "You should go."

Scowling, I crossed my arms. "You didn't want to lose me, but now you're kicking me out?"

"I've been down this road before." His head swung slowly from side to side. "I was foolish to think I could have a normal relationship, however briefly."

"I'm not going anywhere."

The decanter slammed down, ruby liquid sloshing up the sides.

"You and me—" I shook my head, setting my empty glass on the floor. "I don't know. But you're still my friend. I won't just cut and run."

The corners of his mouth curved up. "You really are remarkable."

"So what's really going on?"

He downed his drink and refilled the glass, then stalked back to the fireplace. The light cast his profile in sharp contrast. "Merak, the man I've been negotiating with, the one who sent those thralls after you—"

"Thralls?"

His eyes shifted in my direction. "Humans whose wills have been overridden by a vampire."

"So Merak is a vampire too."

"Not just any. He's the master of this territory, a depraved creature." He rubbed a hand over his forehead. "And a serious pain in my ass."

I raised my eyebrows. James didn't often swear. "Why does he hate you so much?"

James shrugged. "It's in the nature of all things to fear that which they don't understand."

"But you're both vampires."

"He is young, driven by power and ambition. He cannot comprehend that I have no such desires."

"Master of a territory sounds important. How come he doesn't just kill you, or exile you, or something?"

"He hasn't the strength. He can, however, undermine the life I've built here."

"So he planted the escort, paid for the witness?"

James shifted, and something dark flitted through his expression.

"James?"

"The woman was there to service me." He downed the last of his drink.

I braced my hands on the armrests, squeezing the warm leather. "She was your meal."

He nodded. "But I didn't kill her. We had an . . . arrangement."

I rubbed my temples. "And Elsa? Did you have an arrangement with her as well?"

He nodded again.

"Merak is cutting off your food supply."

"So it would seem."

"Does Joe . . ." I waved a hand.

"Rarely. Though Merak wouldn't know that." He gestured to me. "I've never fed from you, yet you were no less a target."

"Where do the drugs fit in?"

He spread his hands wide. "I have no need of heroin, and no idea how it got into her system."

I pursed my lips, tapping one finger against the leather armrest. "Maybe I can help with that."

THE GALLERY WAS closed, and the parking garage was empty. I idled around the corner until James cut the security. Neither of us wanted to explain to the cops what I was doing at the crime scene. When the coast was clear, we rode the elevator in silence to the third floor.

His breath stirred the hairs on my neck, and a warm flutter spread through my abdomen. My head was still struggling with the complexities of a possible cross-species relationship, my heart was screaming that he couldn't be trusted, but my body. . . . My body didn't care about vampires or lies. Taking a deep breath, I clamped a hand over the treacherous feeling and stepped away from him as soon as the doors opened.

City lights flickered like stars beyond the floor-to-ceiling windows that wrapped two sides of the dark living room. James flipped a switch, and the overhead lights flared to life. I blinked, and the world beyond the windows was gone. My eyes focused on the dark figure looming over my reflection's shoulder, and another old myth drifted to mind.

"You have a reflection."

He snorted. "One of many inaccuracies fabricated over the years."

My gaze dropped to furniture straight out of a decorator's catalog, tasteful but subdued. The same could be said of the pictures on the wall, the polished floors, and the plush, stain-free rugs. This wasn't a place someone lived.

"Do you know where she died?"

"The bedroom." He pointed to a room at the back of the apartment. "They found her on the bed."

I wrinkled my nose. I'd napped in that bed.

Stepping into the bedroom, I ran my hands over my upper arms with a shudder and glanced around the room. Other than the crumpled bedspread, nothing was out of order. Skewed covers were the only evidence the room had been used at all.

"If someone tried to jab a needle in her veins, why didn't she put up a fight?"

James's eyes grew distant. "She was in no condition."

"Blood loss?"

He shifted his feet. "Not exactly."

I crossed my arms and marked each second that passed in silence with a toe-tap against polished wood.

"It's possible to change the . . . flavor of a person by changing their emotional state."

I blinked, trying to wrap my mind around the words.

He shrugged. "I prefer the taste of bliss. Abigail," he gestured to the bed, "the woman who died here, was euphoric when I left."

A cold shiver dripped down my spine at the word euphoric, and the tip of my smallest finger itched. "So she was getting high while you were . . ."

He nodded. "And in no condition to fend off an attack. I doubt she was even aware it was happening."

Shuddering, I took a deep breath, knelt in front of the bed, and placed both hands palm-down on the sheets.

I'd always been more comfortable keeping my emotions at a distance, preferably sealed in a metal box and dropped into the deepest trench in the ocean. But as fate would have it, one of my fae abilities was to access imbued memories, and the only way to do that was to open myself up to the emotions around me, including my own.

With James standing three feet away, my emotions were a storm threatening to tear me apart if I got too close. Anger twisted with lust, friendship with betrayal, hope with fear.

The only people we can depend on in this world are you and me. Mom's words rang like a chant in my head. How many times had she said that after my father left?

Then she left me too.

But James hadn't left. Not yet. Did he want to? Did I want him to?

I shook my head and dug my fingers deeper into the sheets, moving my hands, searching for an emotion that wasn't my own, but the doubt pounding my mind drove out all else. I couldn't break through the cloud of my own confusion. If there was a memory imbued on the bed, I was blind to it.

I stretched as far as I could, reaching to the middle of the bed and sliding my hands to the edges. When I'd touched every inch of the bed, I straightened, hands on hips, and shook my head. "It's not working."

James frowned. "What exactly were you looking for?"

"The other side of imbuing is sort of like reading." I shrugged. "Strong emotions leave an imprint. Getting killed usually involves a pretty strong emotion, but—"

"Not in this case. She was too high to be scared."

I chewed my lip. Imbued emotions didn't have to be negative, and euphoria seemed pretty strong. I couldn't shake the thought that it was my confused feelings that let us down, just like the mess they'd made of my metalwork. Chances were my magic wouldn't work properly until I'd sorted myself out. "I'm sorry."

"Thank you for trying." Stepping forward, James took my hands. "The fact that you're even here is—"

I pulled away, wrapping my arms around myself. I gave him a tight smile. "We'll get to the bottom this."

His features could have been carved from ice.

Chapter 12

RYAN-SENSEI HELD out his hand. "Your ukemi has really improved."

"Thanks." I grabbed his forearm and used his pull to spring to my feet.

I might not have been up to Kai's standards yet, but I was killing it at Aikido. Not only was I understanding the techniques better lately, but we were more than halfway through class and I wasn't counting the seconds till I could collapse.

I tugged the rough fabric of my gi to close the gap over my sweat-soaked sports bra and wiped my forehead. Saturday morning shoppers, loaded down with bags from the strip mall that housed our dojo, peeked through the large windows that heated the room like a greenhouse and softened the mats with squares of mid-morning light.

Ryan-sensei gestured to my partner, Kate. "Again."

I bowed to the teacher and turned to face Kate. I was the uke—the attacker—in this scenario, so I reached out to grab Kate's wrist. Swinging her arm wide, she twisted our bodies together and positioned herself behind me, bringing her free hand up under my chin.

"Freeze," came Ryan-sensei's command. We stood perfectly still, awkward though it was, as he walked a full circle around us. He repositioned Kate's stance. "Your feet are too close together. Feel this?" He pressed against her shoulder with a single finger and we swayed to one side, fighting for balance. "Keep your center over your hips or you're just twisting with your arms. Your whole body needs to move together."

"Yes, Sensei."

"Continue."

Kate shifted her weight, leading me in a circle around her body. The technique we were practicing, irimi-nage, involved a drop followed by a lift that would take me off my feet—to the untrained eye it looked a lot like getting clothes-lined. Around and around we went. I felt Kate's weight shift several times, preparing to drop, but she hesitated and the momentum of our circle carried her on. Finally Ryan-sensei stepped in to save us from our dizziness.

He demonstrated how to create the necessary opening. "Remember, you are making a space for the uke to fall into. To redirect energy you have to stay ahead of it, not tag along behind."

Kate bowed. "Yes, Sensei."

Ryan-sensei gestured to me. "Now you, Alex."

Kate and I returned to our starting positions, and I centered myself, waiting for the attack. In almost comical slow motion, Kate moved forward, intent on my right wrist. Irimi-nage had never been my strongest technique, but did she really think I was that bad?

I waited until I felt the brush of her grip, but didn't give her a chance to clamp down. Pivoting, I used the lure of that last inch to draw her in farther. My second hand came up to guide, resting lightly against her neck. A half turn later I settled my weight, sinking slightly onto my right knee. As soon as Kate shifted to follow I scooped my arm back up like a cresting wave, dropping her into the vacuum that wave created.

Kate's feet left the ground. She plummeted straight down, slapping the mat in a hard fall rather than rolling out.

I offered her a hand up, but she stared at me as though I'd grown a second head.

"Excellent." There was an edge in Ryan-sensei's voice that twisted my gut and wiped the smile off my face. When I looked over, he was already walking away.

Kate climbed to her feet without help and planted her fists on her hips. "Where did that come from?"

Kate had been with the dojo a year before I joined. She was one rank higher than me, and the closest to my skill level. At least, she had been. My thrill at doing well was tempered by a sinking feeling that my improvement was somehow wrong. The hairs on the back of my neck started to itch, and out of the corner of my eye I caught glimpses of other students watching me.

I shrugged self-consciously. "Guess I'm in the zone tonight."

"Hmph." She flipped her long brown ponytail over her shoulder and brushed a few sweat-soaked strands from her forehead. "Wish I could find a zone like that."

"Do you want to go again?"

Her answer was cut off by a loud clap.

"Let's finish up with koku-dosa," said Ryan-sensei.

Kate grabbed Amber, the only other woman in the class. I glanced around, looking for eye contact. As students paired off, Sensei waved me over. "Alex, come be my partner."

Kneeling, we bowed to each other and took up the starting position. With our knees almost touching, I grabbed his raised forearms, creating a circle of empty space between us. I centered myself and tried to create a solid wall of pressure for my partner, picturing myself as an immovable object. Ryan-sensei shifted his arms, subtly testing my balance. When he found a weak point, he twisted slightly, and I rolled to the side.

Facing off again, Ryan-sensei took hold of my forearms. His grip wasn't tight, but beneath that soft hold was a steel framework. My job was to find the weakness in that framework, like toppling a building with one well-placed charge. I rotated my arms, moved them side to side, forward, backward, testing his defenses. Finally, I saw an opening.

Ryan-sensei rolled to the side.

Back and forth, back and forth. Each time we traded off I was able to find the weakness sooner, adjust faster, keep my center longer. Kneel, roll, kneel, roll until Sensei held up his hands.

Clap. Class was over.

We hustled into a line facing the front wall, where photos of past teachers hung between decorative scrolls. We sat according to rank, with Tony, the teacher's assistant, at one end and our newest member at the other. Ryan-sensei sat to one side. On cue, we bowed to the shrine. Then the teacher turned to face his students and we all bowed again.

"*Domo arigato gozaimashita,*" we recited together.

"Good class, everyone," Ryan-sensei said. "Remember, next week we'll discuss the New Year's seminar." The teacher bowed once more, and we were dismissed. Students began to wander away, chatting amiably as they strolled to the locker rooms. Those on cleaning duty grabbed rags to wipe down the mats.

"Alex," Ryan-sensei called. "Do you have a minute?"

"Of course, Sensei." I followed him to the edge of the mat.

He clasped his hands in front of him. "Have you been training outside the dojo?"

My mind flashed to morning practices with Kai. "A friend's been giving me private lessons. Is that a problem?"

He shook his head. "I was just curious. You've advanced more than I would have thought possible in such a short time. Less than a month ago you were struggling with irimi-nage, and today you performed it beautifully."

"Thank you," I said.

"It's wonderful that you've improved so much, but it seems your

87

skill level has outstripped your training. During koku-dosa your center was more grounded than the last time I worked with you, and your energy control was phenomenal. You were able to react to minute changes before I'd fully executed them, anticipating my moves. That's something most students spend a lifetime learning, and you seem to have picked it up almost overnight."

It wasn't exactly an accusation, but Sensei was clearly looking for an explanation. I pressed my lips together. The writhing worm in my abdomen twisted tighter.

"What kind of training is your friend providing?" he asked.

I shrugged. "General combat and some sword work."

"I'd be interested to meet this friend of yours. Perhaps you could bring him to class once the seminar is over." Ryan-sensei smiled and headed for the men's locker room.

My shoulders sagged as I breathed out. I pushed through the door to the women's changing room.

"... believe how fast she was moving?" Kate's voice carried around the corner of the lockers.

I froze, just out of sight, and eased the door closed behind me.

"Maybe she's on drugs." Amber pitched her voice low, and I leaned closer to the edge of my cover, straining to hear. "Something's been off about her lately, and artists are always getting into trouble with stuff like that, right?"

"True," Kate agreed, "but I'd never thought of Alex as the brooding, substance-abusing, cut-their-own-ear-off kind of artist."

"I heard there's this new drug on the streets," Amber offered. "It's supposed to make you really fast, like everything around you is moving in slow motion."

"That sounds about right," Kate's voice became muffled by fabric. They'd be done changing soon. "Still, I wouldn't have pegged her for a user."

"Well, no *normal* person can suddenly move like that. If it's not drugs, what is it?"

A shiver raced down my spine. Would they think to report my behavior to the PTF? O'Connell would love that, another reason to pry into my life.

No normal person . . .

DROPPING MY GYM bag just inside the front door, I marched to Kai's room and knocked.

"Come in," he called.

I pushed the door open, crossed my arms, and leaned against the door frame. Kai had the personal hygiene of a teenage boy, and my spare bedroom had become a sea of corruption with him lounging on his island bed, a book propped open on his stomach.

"Got a minute?" I asked.

"I wouldn't have invited you in otherwise."

I quirked my lips in a stillborn smile. "Something strange happened at Aikido today."

"Oh?" He raised an eyebrow.

"While I was working with the other students, they all seemed sort of . . . slow. Even people who are more advanced than me. It was like they were having trouble keeping up. Then, after class, my teacher asked if I was getting outside instruction. He said my skills had advanced past my level of training."

Kai closed the book and set it aside. "What did you tell him?"

"That I'd been taking lessons from a friend."

Kai smiled and sat up. "I'm flattered."

"When I walked into the locker room, I overheard someone say I was moving faster than a human should. They thought I'd taken some sort of drug . . ." I shook my head.

Kai pointed his steepled fingers at my tattooed arm. "I told you at the beginning, didn't I? That charm strengthens your fae blood."

I nodded. "So I can read imbued objects."

"It's not as though it can pick and choose which aspects of your heritage to awaken. It's strengthening your magic. All of it. You'll eventually gain all the attributes of your fae lineage."

"Wait." I held up a hand as a cold knot coiled through my torso and squeezed my lungs. "I'm becoming less human?"

"You're becoming faster, stronger, and altogether more powerful than a regular human being."

I sagged more heavily against the door frame.

Kai leaned forward, gesturing. "Humans, by and large, stumble through the world like children in the dark. The fae are made of magic, and therefore are more connected to the magic that flows through every living thing. This gift is simply bringing out your potential, letting you see the world more clearly."

I licked my lips, bracing shaky hands against the wall. "Will I become fully fae?"

He shook his head. "You'll always be part human. While you may be faster than your mortal counterparts, compared to most fae, werewolves, and vampires you might as well be standing still."

Too fae for the humans and too human for the fae. The story of my life.

"You should have warned me. What if someone decides my sudden jump in abilities is worth reporting to the PTF?" I ran a hand over my face. "That O'Connell guy is just itching to—"

"Even if the PTF tested you, and no doubt Agent O'Connell would love the opportunity, they have nothing you couldn't pass. Besides, you've always got that *uncle* of yours."

I narrowed my eyes at his sarcastic tone. "Sol has better things to do than bail me out of trouble."

Kai sighed. "If you're worried about standing out, maybe you should stop going. Mortal partners will soon lose their effectiveness anyway."

I pushed off the wall and crossed my arms. "I've given up enough."

"Then you'll have to learn to live with it."

Grinding my teeth until my jaw ached, I stormed back through the living room and out to the studio. It wasn't a great idea to work while upset, but keeping my hands busy helped me blow off steam, and the studio was the one place that felt safe from all things fae thanks to the steel and iron decorating its walls.

Too bad I couldn't block out the magic inside me as easily.

Closing the door on the rest of the world, I draped my second-warmest jacket over the back of a chair. It was a poor substitute for the one I'd burned and buried, but better than nothing.

Twenty-seven metal soldiers sat on my desk, waiting for their missing comrades and the board that would be their battlefield. Half were polished to a bright bronze shine, the others dipped in darkness to create an oil-slick patina. I lifted a pawn from each faction, rolling them in my palms. They were equally heavy, cast from the same metal. Both cleaned and polished with the same tools. Both capped with the same black felt on the bottom to prevent scratching. Only the shapes they'd been forced into and a thin coat of color distinguished them. In a week, they'd all be in a box on their way to Sol, ready to wage war.

Setting the soldiers down, I pulled out a block of modeling clay. I rolled it into a ball, stretched it into a rope, twisted it together, and pressed it back into a ball. As I reshaped the clay, I thought about how much my life had changed. Yet, it was still recognizable as my life. The clay was the clay no matter what form I gave it.

Taking a deep breath, I cleared my mind. When I started working the clay again I thought of my magic, a gift that had slept through generations. Had my mother had any inkling, or her parents, or theirs? How long ago had the fae blood that ran in my veins seeped into the line? I'd had a great-uncle when I was little who made his living as a circus magician. Mom called them parlor tricks, but could he have been doing real magic?

Then there was my father. My stomach twisted. Probably best he died before finding out what I was. As much as he hated the fae, being his daughter might not have saved me.

I stretched the clay between my hands and watched it drip with the strain of its own weight, pulled thin between its anchors.

James, Chase, Marc, Kai, and all the people who weren't quite human, balanced against Maggie, David, Loni, Sol, and everyone who was. Would I have to choose a side? Could I?

The clay tore through the middle.

I stared at the swinging ends until the blare of my ringtone cut through my thoughts.

Slamming my hands together, I rolled the clay back into a single ball and set it on the counter. Then I wiped my palms and reached into my jacket pocket.

It was a number I didn't recognize.

"Hello?"

"Alex? It's Sophie."

Chapter 13

"ALEX? ARE YOU there?"

I struggled to make an articulate sound. "Soph? Is that really you?"

"Yeah, Alex. It's me." There was an edge to her voice that made her sound like a stranger. Even when we really were strangers, she'd been open and friendly. Of course, that was before—

I shuddered at a memory of teeth, and claws, and shreds of Sophie's designer jacket waving like flags in the dry autumn grass.

"What . . . How . . ." I tripped over the questions pressing to get out, finally settling for, "It's so great to hear from you."

"I miss you too. In fact, that's why I'm calling. Will you go out with me tonight? Just us."

My brain refused to focus.

Marc had said it could be months before Sophie had enough control to rejoin society, but he'd also said Sophie recently had a couple expeditions out of solitude, so she had to be doing better. And the moon was about as far from full as it could get.

"Is it okay with Marc?"

"It's fine." Her voice was tight, and there was a deep exhale on her end of the line. "Besides, you don't really believe I could hurt you, right?"

Remembered pain lanced through my left arm and I rubbed at the thin, pale scars. "I know you wouldn't hurt me on purpose."

"Look, I just need a night to act normal, be myself. I thought you could understand needing a break from all this freaky stuff, but if you don't want to go I can find someone else."

"It's not that I don't want to, I just want to make sure it's safe. Marc told me it'd be a while before I got to see you."

"Yeah, Marc's a worrier, but I already cleared it with him. He said as long as I didn't stay out too long it would be fine. He said it might even do me some good to see an old friend."

I looked at the ceiling, weighing my options. "What did you have in mind?"

"There's a club in Denver I've been dying to check out."

"A club? Really? Wouldn't you rather go somewhere . . ." I thought of all those unsuspecting mortals. ". . . quieter?"

"I've spent the last few weeks in the middle of nowhere. I'm sick of quiet. What I need is a night to forget about all the awful shit that's happened. So are you in?"

"Okay, Soph. If that's what you want, I'm in."

"Good. The club's called Abandon. I'll meet you out front at ten. Don't be late."

I disconnected and leaned back with a sigh.

Sophie. I hadn't dared hope to see her so soon. The thought rode a wave of joy through my mind, followed by a wash of dread.

I might not have been the one to snatch her life away, but it had been my idea to go for a hike that night. I'd chosen the place. I'd wandered far enough away from her that I couldn't help when the beast burst into the clearing.

My last clear image of Sophie was of a mangled, blood-soaked rag doll lying motionless in a moonlit meadow, and nothing I could do would ever make that right.

CHILL, WINTER AIR caressed my legs below the gray-blue dress that swished just above my knees as I stumbled over pavement cracked by weeds and neglect. Rounding the corner of the side street where I'd been forced to park, I came into view of the renovated church Abandon had taken over. Sophie was pacing under one of the few unbroken street lamps in front of the club, stalking from edge to edge of the pool of light, biting her nails. Long blond hair trailed down her back and over a bright red dress. Protruding bumps of hips and ribs broke the smooth curve of the clinging fabric. Tall black boots crested her knees, leaving a scant few inches of skin exposed beneath the red hem.

I released a breath, along with some of the tension I'd been holding. Sophie looked like Sophie. Thinner, sharper, but still Sophie. Everything was going to be fine.

"Soph!" I raised an arm.

Sophie whipped around. When she caught sight of me, her eyes went wide.

I stopped at the edge of her pool of light. "Sorry I'm late. I had a hell of a time finding a place to park."

Sophie was still staring. "I didn't believe Marc at first, when he told me you'd survived unchanged; figured he was lying to keep me calm." She shook her head. "Part of me was convinced you were dead, right up until you answered your phone."

I spread my arms to the sides. "Still here."

She looked me up and down. "You really are just the same."

The same, huh? I pulled my jacket tight and tipped my head toward the line of party-goers waiting under the neon sign that proclaimed the club's name. "There are a lot of people here. You sure you're up for this?"

Her eyes narrowed, and a hard edge crept into her voice. "Of course."

"I'm just saying, we could—"

"I need this." She rolled her neck and shook out her arms, a boxer limbering up before a fight. "Let's go."

I bit my lower lip. If Sophie lost control near all these people. . . . But Marc wouldn't have let her come if he wasn't sure.

I turned toward the line that wrapped the length of the brick building and disappeared around the corner, but Sophie headed straight for the entrance.

"What are you doing?" I asked, trotting after her.

"You don't want to stand outside all night, do you?"

"But," I gestured to the people shuffling their feet in front of the brick façade, "the line?"

She swatted my concern away. "These places always admit pretty girls without escorts. It's good for business. Watch and learn, Alex."

Sophie had a lot more experience with clubs than I did. She also had more experience using her feminine wiles to get what she wanted, so I quietly trailed a pace behind her.

"Hey there," she said as we approached the gatekeeper. Sophie's long lashes, padded by mascara, blinked slowly, and a coy smile played on her lips.

I rolled my eyes.

Sophie pressed a little closer to the man at the door and whispered something to him. He was a big guy, tall enough that Sophie had to stand on tip-toe to reach his ear. His black leather coat and dark jeans were calculated to up the intimidation factor, and his expression stated clearly that he was prepared to break a few bones if anyone started shit with him.

His eyes shifted to me, then back to Sophie. He gave a little nod and motioned her in.

"Come on." Sophie grabbed my wrist and pulled me past the watchful eyes of the bouncer.

"That actually worked?"

She tugged me through a small, dark anteroom with a coat-check counter and into the vaulted expanse of Abandon.

The club overlaid the old church like a second skin, the congregation writhing on the dance floor while a DJ played for his worshipers from the pulpit above. Arches lined the walls, giving access to a black-light hallway that ran around three-quarters of the perimeter. Couples popped in and out of confessionals, clothes in disarray. Below the central arch of the back wall nestled a full-service bar pressed with hot sweaty bodies. Above the bar, a sign in glowing LED script proclaimed, "Abandon all hope, ye who enter here."

"Charming," I murmured.

Sophie led me onto the dance floor, and I was hit by the sudden heat of the gyrating crowd. Bodies flashed in and out of view, a series of still-frames burned into my retinas as colored lights strobed to a pulsing techno beat. It was impossible to tell how many people were present in the enormous room. Sweat trickled down my back and soaked my bra, but I resisted the urge to push up the sleeves on the loose knit sweater I'd pulled on over my spaghetti strap dress to cover the tattoo. I wouldn't make that mistake again.

We danced to the hypnotic rhythm of the music, the room shaking with bass, vibrating my bones. Tipping my head back, I squinted into the vault above but couldn't find the ceiling, which was painted black and obscured by flashing lights. Dizzy, I swayed on the high heels of my strappy sandals.

A woman bumped into me and spun away. A stray hand slapped my shoulder and disappeared into the crowd. Fingers began to look like claws, teeth like fangs.

I shook my head to clear the image.

This was a human club. No faeries here. Just a halfer and a werewolf out on the town.

Sophie was swaying and spinning, but her expression was pinched. Her eyes were rolling a little too wild for my liking, and there was too much white showing around the edges.

I closed the distance between us.

"Are you okay?" I had to shout to be heard over the beat of the music and the roar of the crowd.

She didn't seem to register my words, just kept dancing, eyes wide but unseeing, as if she was in a trance.

I touched her shoulder, and she jumped, spinning into a crouch.

She stared at me for a moment, as though I was a stranger. Then she straightened and pointed toward the bar. "I need a drink."

Sophie and I wedged our way up to the bar, pressing through the crowd of thirsty dancers.

She flagged down the bartender and called, "Two Blue Lagoons."

A woman in a white sequined top abandoned her barstool, and Sophie pounced on it. I pressed in between her and the man on the next stool who had a petite blond perched on his lap. I fanned myself with the little black purse that held my phone, cards, and cash. I'd underestimated the heat so many moving bodies could produce.

Sophie propped her elbows on the counter with a sigh and mumbled something.

"What was that?" I leaned closer.

"Just one night," she said. "That's all I wanted. One night to feel normal, to feel . . ."

Human, I thought. I knew all too well what it felt like to lose who you were. At least I could still pretend sometimes. But Sophie . . .

Sophie was hunched over the bar. Her back rose and fell in heaving breaths, too fast for comfort.

The bartender set two frosted glasses of turquoise liquid on the bar in front of Sophie and gave her an assessing look.

I offered him a smile and dropped some money on the counter to pay for the drinks.

He swept it up and moved down the line to fill the next order.

Sophie groaned. Her fingers curled, digging furrows into the polished wood.

Dread pounded in my veins to the rhythm of the music. Sophie was losing control. "I think we should go."

"Is that so?" She turned on me with a snarl, and it was all I could do not to jump away from the anger in her eyes. She raised her arms, a carnival barker calling to the crowd. "Alex Blackwood, decider of fates."

The bartender glanced in our direction, then went to the end of the bar and waved over a man in a black t-shirt and black cargo pants. Probably security for when dancers had too much to drink and got out of hand. The bartender whispered something in the man's ear and gestured at Sophie and me.

"Seriously, Soph." I set my hand on her arm. "It's time to go."

She shoved me away. "Don't patronize me. I could kill you. I *should* kill you. Why should you get to go on with your life like nothing happened when I'm," she indicated her own body, "this . . . thing?"

Her voice was taking on a hysterical pitch, and people were starting to notice, even above the thrum of the music.

I made a calming gesture. "My life is *not* fine, Sophie."

"Why didn't you change?"

That stopped me dead. Marc hadn't told her? But then, why would he? It wasn't his secret to tell, and Sophie had enough on her plate, why add one more impossible truth to the pile? I exhaled a shaky breath. If Sophie thought I'd both survived the attack *and* remained human . . . No wonder she was angry. But I couldn't tell her the truth here, shouting to be heard and surrounded by gawkers.

The black-clad man was moving in our direction, one hand pressed to his ear. Definitely security. What would an angry werewolf do if a strange man grabbed her? I swallowed the lump in my throat. I *really* didn't want to find out.

"Sophie, we have to leave. Now."

"Stop telling me what to do!" She jumped off her stool and rounded on me. Her pupils were dilated, turning her eyes black. Her teeth had grown longer, sharper. Her arms were shaking at her sides, fists balled, and tufts of fur had sprouted on the backs of her hands.

She grunted, and doubled over. Her whole body was shaking now. A sign of the change? Or the effort of holding it back? Then she cried out and dove into the crowd, racing toward the exit.

"Sophie!" I took a step to follow her, but was brought up short by a steely grip. The security guard's fingers caged my upper arm.

"You need to come with me."

I tried to shake him off. "We're already leaving." I lost sight of Sophie as she darted through the gyrating bodies. *Please let her get out without changing.* "I need to catch up with my friend."

"You're not going anywhere, and neither is she." He pressed a hand to his ear and said, "Blond woman in a red dress heading for the door. Stop her."

"You don't understand. She's . . . dangerous."

"I know." He leaned in close and whispered, "My master is dying to meet you, Alex Blackwood."

I froze. Humans didn't have *masters.* I'd only heard that term in reference to one man . . . one vampire. Sophie had said my name, screamed it so the whole club could hear, and the bartender had recognized it. Recognized it, and reported to his master.

I licked my lips. "People could die."

"So?"

I stared into his unblinking eyes and knew he'd relish the carnage of a werewolf let loose on a room full of mortals. "Fine. I'll come. Just let her leave."

He led me beneath an arch and into one of the corridors that lined the room. The bright lights of the dance floor were blocked here, replaced by the intermittent glow of black lights, the shadows between them long and deep. Couples were tucked into corners, skin and clothes glowing in the purplish glare.

At the end of the hall stood an open door, and waiting at the edge of a darkness even deeper than the twilight of the club was a giant of a man with familiar waxy chocolate skin and eyes like an abyss. His tongue slid between his lips, arcing from one side to the other. The muscles in my legs melted. *Bryce.*

I tried to stop, to pull away, all thoughts of Sophie and the dozens of two-legged snacks trapped in the club forgotten. But the man on my arm propelled me forward like an ocean tide, right into Bryce's waiting embrace.

"So nice to see you again, Alex." His breath was warm against my neck.

Cold sweat broke out across my skin, but I willed my voice to hold steady. "You don't want a massacre in your club. Lots of unwanted attention. Do the smart thing. Let my friend go."

Bryce's eyes flicked to the man who'd escorted me. Then he smiled, and his chest vibrated with laughter. "You think I'm dumb enough to hold a wolf in my club?" He shook his head. "Bad for business."

His words poured over me like a bucket of ice. They'd tricked me. I'd given up my freedom . . . for nothing.

Twisting from Bryce's grasp, I dove toward the door. "Hel—"

I was jerked back with such force my mouth snapped shut, cutting off my plea. My back slammed into bricks, and Bryce's hand compressed my chest with the weight of an anvil. The dim rectangle of light in the doorway narrowed and closed, sealing me in darkness.

"Behave, or I'll knock you out."

My heart was pounding with adrenaline, and every muscle in my body screamed at me to fight. But Bryce was stronger than me. He was faster than me. And apparently, he could see in the pitch black surrounding us.

I forced my hands to my sides. So long as I was conscious, there was hope.

"Good girl."

Bryce didn't keep up the pretense of having me walk, he hefted me over one shoulder as though carrying a bag of dirt. Blood rushed to my head, and Bryce's broad shoulder dug into my gut, making it hard to breathe.

He walked, twisting and turning down invisible tunnels. Sometimes there were stairs, sometimes inclines. I blinked and squinted, willing my eyes to adjust, but the darkness was absolute.

The air grew cooler, filled with a dampness that tickled my nose and made me shiver. Bryce's footsteps echoed back from the darkness, sometimes close, sometimes far away, sometimes joined by other sounds— the quiet drip of water against rock, the sigh of wind with nowhere to go.

My muscles could only stay taut so long. My frayed nerves burned out. The adrenaline in my system crashed, leaving me at the mercy of my spiraling thoughts. My teeth chattered from cold, and frustration, and fear.

Then Bryce shrugged, and I fell to the cold, hard ground, gravel biting my skin.

There was a screech and scraping sound behind me. I twisted toward it, but my eyes might as well have been closed. The noise stopped, and there was a moment of silence filled only by the pounding of my heart. Then a hand twisted into the front of my sweater.

My head snapped back as I was jerked up and tossed into an abyss, arms pinwheeling as I fell through space. With no point of reference, it felt as though I could fall forever. Perhaps the impact of my eventual landing would shatter me.

But it was with a splash that I came down.

Sputtering out the viscous fluid that filled my open mouth, I struggled into a sitting position. Cold liquid sloshed around my waist. My clothes hung like a prison, tight against my skin. The air was sharp with mold and fear.

As I coughed and gagged, something brushed against my hand. I jerked away from the feeling of scales against my skin. Something glided past my ankle, my back. I twisted and splashed, but the more I thrashed the more creatures there seemed to be.

I couldn't control my body properly, my limbs were heavy and thoughts were elusive. Logic and reason fled in the face of terror as my remaining senses struggled to make up for my lost sight. I tried to scream, but pulled in a lungful of bitter sludge as I slipped beneath the surface again.

"Easy there, sweetheart." Bryce's deep voice drifted out of the darkness. "Wouldn't want you dying early."

Rough hands pulled me to my feet, but my balance was shot. I could barely tell which way was up in this inky world. I coughed out something that tasted like bile and grabbed blindly for the hands that held me upright, not caring that he was the one who'd thrown me down there. He was solid, something I could hold on to.

My back slammed against an unyielding wall and the air fled my lungs in a burning *whoosh*. Then Bryce snapped something cold and heavy around my wrists. My dubious support disappeared and I toppled to my knees, gasping, unable to lift the weights my hands had become.

My fingers scraped against dirt, the air was dry. What happened to the water?

"You seem to have trouble keeping your feet," taunted the voice in the darkness. "Here, let me help."

Hard edges bit into my wrists as my arms were jerked up by heavy metal rings. My body followed. When I could scarcely scrape the floor with my feet, the ratcheting noise of chain feeding through a loop stopped, leaving me stretched from my fingertips to my toes.

"That's better."

My sweater tugged forward, and the darkness was filled with the sound of tearing. Cold air hit my torso. Then my sleeves ripped free, exposing my arms.

"Won't be needing these," Bryce said as he snapped the straps that held my sandals on.

Goosebumps prickled across my body, but my right arm was burning. Not painfully, but the itchy tingle I'd felt at Crossroads when Enzo grabbed me.

"You're trying to get to James through me," I said. "But it won't work."

"Wanna bet?"

"We split up. I dumped him and broke his heart when I found out what he was."

Bryce's laughter filled the room. "You think he has a heart?"

I swallowed, forcing my voice to stay steady. "What are you going to do to me?"

"I'll leave that for my master to explain. He's busy entertaining other guests at the moment, but he told me to keep you company while you wait." A puff of air blew across the back of my neck, making the hair there twist and tickle. "I missed this neck." His lips brushed my ear. "I've dreamed about it."

Something slid along my skin, leaving a damp trail from my jaw to my shoulder. The same path his tongue took the night we met.

I bit down on my lip until I tasted blood, straining against the iron rings holding me in place.

"Merak promised I could have you once he's done with James." Hands traced my curves, tugging the thin cotton that protected me. "But who knows what will be left of you by then. I wonder if he'd mind me sneaking a little preview?"

The hands slid down my waist, over my hips, and paused.

Inch by inch the hem of my dress rose as he wound it up with his fingertips. *Snap!* The band of my panties tore loose and the fabric slid between my thighs. "Won't be needing these either."

The creak of hinges split the air.

"Bryce," said a new voice. "He's ready for her."

Bryce's hands fell away, but his breath still shivered over my skin. "Another time."

Chapter 14

PALE BLUE LIGHTS illuminated the path Bryce pushed me along, piercing the darkness. I winced and stumbled as my bare feet found jagged bits of debris half-hidden in the watery light.

Crunch. Crunch.

Something sharp cut into the soft underside of my foot, and I yelped. Part of a skeletal jaw grinned up at me, teeth slick with my blood.

Another shove propelled me forward.

The small blue torches flared to life one step ahead of me as we moved, but never gave me enough time see what was coming until I was in the middle of it.

Femurs, ribs, and skulls littered the ground. Cold air crept under my dress, and when an ache in my chest reminded me to breathe, I gagged on the scent of putrefaction.

I struggled to keep my footing on the uneven ground, slipping in a thick, black ooze that coated everything. My feet squelched with each step, putrid sludge splattering my calves. When I stumbled, my hands came up black.

My stomach heaved, and the contents of my stomach joined the sludge on the floor.

Bryce gave me little more than a moment to spit the burning bile from my mouth, then jabbed his knuckles into my side to keep me moving. The bodies grew fresher, pieces of skin and muscle hanging from their frames. Exposed organs intensified the smell of rot and I heaved again, but my stomach was empty.

I wiped the back of my wrist across my mouth and stumbled on, trying to steady my racing heart. I had to get my shit together. As terrifying as Bryce was, he was only the opening act.

A wet slap caught my attention, and a fresh corpse rolled limply down the pile in front of me. It settled with a sickening squelch at my feet, blood bubbling from a ragged gash on his neck. The man's hair was blond speckled with crimson, and I watched the light fade from eyes the color of fresh-cut grass.

"Welcome." The voice was a harsh rasp, like rodents crawling through walls or branches scraping against a window pane. It echoed eerily around me from everywhere and nowhere.

Blue flame raced around the room to either side, lighting the remaining torches.

Merak smiled from atop a throne of bones, a thin trail of crimson trickling from the corner of his mouth to drip from his chin.

His waxy pallor reflected the wavering blue light, making him look like a drowned corpse. An image strengthened by lank tendrils of long, black hair that dangled like seaweed over his face. The dark recesses of his eyes were impenetrable, black holes that wanted to pull me in and never let go.

I stumbled back, ankle twisting in loose flesh and rolling bones, and crashed to my back. This was the monster James and Kai had warned me a vampire was, what I hadn't wanted to believe James could be.

Dark robes billowed as Merak flowed toward me, not with the measured gait of legs but as though riding the crest of a tidal surge. From beneath his robes skittered cockroaches, spiders, and all the tiny creatures that scurry through the dark corners of the world. They cascaded over my skin, slid under my dress, burrowed in my hair, and I screamed until I gagged on the questing legs that found their way into my mouth.

Then Merak's weight was on me, pressing me deeper into the rancid muck of decaying bodies. A million tiny lights of pain flared across my skin as the insects began to bite. My right arm burned as though my skin had ignited. I squirmed and flailed, sinking farther into the remains of those who'd come before. Then a pain brighter than the others flashed through me.

I looked down past the crumpled folds of fabric bunched around my waist.

Merak's chin was red, fangs buried deep in the soft flesh of my inner thigh.

I screamed again, thrashing, rolling to dislodge the creatures that were devouring me, but my limbs became heavy, my movements sluggish.

Where was the euphoria James had mentioned? Had he lied? Was this . . . nightmare . . . what the dead escort in his apartment actually experienced?

When I teetered on the edge of oblivion, Merak rose from his feast to grin over the length of my body. Those bloody teeth inched closer, creeping over my abdomen, hovering above my breasts, until drops of my own blood fell against my cheek and ran into my hair like crimson tears.

The bloody lips moved above me. Words came a moment later, a movie with the audio out of sync. "James always did have impeccable taste."

Merak vanished from my field of vision. Then rough hands slid under my armpits. I was lifted up only to be tossed forward, knees and palms scraping against hard stone.

I blinked at the gray slate in confusion.

Where were the bodies? The muck? The hundreds of biting insects?

The only part of my nightmare that remained was a cooling stream of blood that trickled down my thigh.

I raised my eyes to Merak's throne, but his seat, now thick leather and stained wood, rested atop a simple concrete dais rather than a mountain of rotting corpses. Blue torches still lined the walls, but their light traveled farther, filling in the shadows to reveal a large stone chamber that mirrored the club above. The ceiling was high, and the walls were lined with archways. Men and women stood in the halls behind those arches, watching me with hungry eyes.

"Not what you were expecting?"

I jerked at the voice.

Merak was standing beside his throne, idly stroking the wine-colored leather. The skin that framed his sunken eyes was still pallid, but I could see those eyes now, peering out from the shadows. The midnight robes had become simple fabric draped over a dark blue suit.

He raised one thin, long-fingered hand with vellum skin and thick yellow nails, and wiped the blood from his chin with a thumb. Then he slid it into his mouth with a smile. "No point wasting more magic. Much as I loved the fear in your veins, I've got other plans for you."

I shook my head and immediately became dizzy. "It . . . wasn't real."

He waved a hand. "Real is such a tired term."

"Why?" I croaked. My throat was raw. My screams at least had been real.

"Because it's fun." He smiled. "And because people taste so much better when they're afraid."

His voice no longer echoed through the darkness, but it sent shivers across my sweat-soaked skin. He was a psychopath. He enjoyed hurting people. Even without magic augmenting my fear, no sane person could have looked at Merak and not been afraid.

"What do you want?"

Merak stepped to the front of his throne and sat down with a flourish. "An interesting question, the answer to which I doubt your feeble mind could understand."

I licked my lips, grasping at scattered thoughts. "James."

Merak gave a slow, resounding clap that echoed off the walls and bounced back in mock applause. "He's been a thorn in my side far too long."

I shook my head. "He just wants to be left alone."

"Oh? You think you know him so well?"

I pushed away the cold knot his words twisted around my heart.

Merak's mouth twisted into a sneer. "He's no different than me."

I clenched my fingers into fists and ground my knuckles into the floor. "You may be the same species, but you're nothing alike."

"He let you in on our little secret, did he? How nice for you." His smile was all teeth. "Then you'll know all about his time in Los Angeles, when he was considered the most ruthless master in the New World. And of course he told you about his escapades in Prague. Oh, and London, who could forget London? Pure genius. His body count that night was. . . ." He brought his fingers to his lips and kissed them. "It's enough to give even monsters nightmares."

I gritted my teeth. "I know what you're trying to do."

"I very much doubt that." The sardonic smile melted from his lips. "Let's get down to business."

I straightened up as much as I could on my knees and raised my chin.

"Do you know why James can live as he does?" He pressed his fingertips together. "He cheats. He has a little trinket that lets him enjoy the sunlight denied the rest of our kind."

I resisted the urge to frown. Kai had said James was a special case. He hadn't mentioned any trinket.

"But that's all about to change. James has hoarded his faerie amulet long enough."

My pulse stuttered, and I swayed on my knees. The necklace with the strange glowing stone, the one he never took off. James once told me my grandfather made him an imbued object as payment for services rendered. That had to be it.

I shifted my tattooed arm behind me. Did Merak know I was related to the fae who made James's necklace? If he was keeping me alive because he wanted a sun-proof pendant of his own, that could buy me some time. Not that I'd make him one. Not that I even could.

"Are you listening?" The furrow on Merak's brow was an almost human expression. "Perhaps I took too much."

Merak straightened from his throne and strolled down the steps of the dais until he stood directly in front of me. He gripped my chin between his finger and thumb so tightly tears welled in my eyes, and tilted my head until I was looking into his cold anger. "Do I have your attention now?"

Unable to form words, or even nod, I gave an affirmative grunt.

"Good." He dropped his hand so quickly I fell forward.

Merak blurred to a flash of shadows—an image forever tied in my mind to blood-spattered snow—then my head jerked back, pulled by fingers in my hair. One deceptively soft fingertip traced my skin, pausing when my swallow rippled under it.

Merak's cheek was warm against mine, heated by the blood he'd stolen. "Pretty boy James has a soft spot for hopeless causes, and you're about as hopeless as they come."

He pressed his nose into my skin and breathed deep, then exhaled with a sigh.

I started to shake. My mind was coated in a thick haze, my limbs were dead weight, and I was getting colder by the second.

"He'll come to trade, and then he'll die, and you'll spend the rest of your tormented life as my midnight snack." He licked his lips, and we were close enough that his tongue skimmed my skin.

"James isn't stupid."

"He doesn't have a choice."

I swallowed again, straining against the hand in my hair. "Why are you telling me this?"

"Because," he tipped my head until my whole torso arced like a dancer caught mid-dip, "despair tastes almost as good as fear."

His fangs sank into the flesh between my neck and shoulder and stole what little warmth remained.

A SCRAPE ECHOED through the room, and it was an avalanche in my ears. My eyes fluttered open. A handful of torches cast dim blue light around the chamber, dancing in a stale wind. I shifted, and my knees screamed. How long had I been kneeling?

Time had lost all meaning. Seconds became hours, days, years. I traced the thin silver chain that dangled from my collar to where it wound between the fingers of my master.

My traitorous heart swelled at the sight of him, beautiful and terrible, while my mind shrieked and rattled the bars of its immaterial cage. My eyes had become a window to watch a world I couldn't control.

Merak ran a hand absently over my cheek, and his touch was a jolt of electricity through every cell. My body leaned into the caress even as I recoiled into the farthest corner of my mind.

He leaned down so our heads were side-by-side. "Look, Alex. Your lover has come to join us. Aren't you happy?"

James stepped out of the shadows between the farthest torches, his pale skin almost the same blue as his eyes under the flickering lights. Bryce stood at one shoulder while another, equally large man stood at the other. Neither touched him.

I sat up a little straighter. My master's enemy had come. This was a good thing.

No, no, no! My fingers curved to claws, nails scraping my thighs. I pounded against the one-way mirror of my vision, willing James to see me. *You shouldn't be here! Run!*

When my master had his prize there would be less pain. Yes, it was good to give the master what he wanted.

I screamed in silence.

"Merak." James's voice was deep and steady as the stone that bounced it back to me.

"James." Merak spread his hands wide to mirror his smile. "So glad you could join us."

"Let her go."

"And why should I do that?" Merak slid the end of my leash through his fingers. "She really does have a most unique flavor. But then, I'm sure you knew that."

James's fists closed, then his fingers stretched wide and relaxed at his sides.

Taking a step forward, he reached up and tugged at the chain around his neck, snapping it free. "This is what you want."

The yellow gem was a beacon in the pale blue cavern, and it pulled my eyes like a magnet. Faces drifted out from alcoves, half-shadowed creatures with sunken skin and hollow eyes. Merak leaned forward in his chair, hands gripping the armrests. Then, as though regretting his movement, he settled back in his seat and folded his hands in his lap.

"And now I have it." He smiled. "I have it, and you," his eyes cut to me, "and her."

He ran a thumb along the side of my face and under my chin. "Time for a snack, darling."

No, no, no. I pulled and thrashed in the confines of my mind, but my body rose, knees popping as they straightened. I swung around to straddle Merak's lap, the tatters of my dress parting to expose my thighs and hips.

My right arm was on fire, and I focused on the pain. It burned non-stop these days, and the more I struggled the more it burned.

"Stop this." James's voice seemed distant, muffled.

Merak pulled at the one remaining strap on my dress and it released with a snap, the fabric sliding down to expose my breasts. I shivered.

In my mind, I was fighting as hard as I could, knowing it just made me taste better. That was why I could still see, still feel. He'd made a prison of my flesh.

One hand pressed into my lower back while the other pulled my hair. I arched until James was framed in my vision again, upside down. Bryce and his companion were holding him now, one arm each. His face was twisted, his teeth too sharp, and his eyes were no longer blue. Twin pools of mercury bore into me.

Then came the pain. A tearing sensation just above my left breast. My heart beat faster, pumping the blood out as fast as it could. My body grew light and distant. My arm became an iron straight from the fire and I wondered that it wasn't glowing. I tried to close my eyes, to block the image of James struggling and screaming the way I wished I could, but my eyes were not my own and they did not obey.

When my heart slowed, Merak released me. I slid to the side and crumpled against the dais in a boneless heap. My breaths were shallow, each one taking all my strength. The steps of the dais dug into my arm, my side, but I was numb and the pressure was dulled by that numbness.

James's guards were on the ground. Bryce was rolling to his feet, but the man who'd been holding James's left arm stared with empty eyes, his head twisted so shoulder blades protruded where his collar bone should have been. Three other forms detached from the shadows, surging forward, but James had crossed half the distance to the throne.

"You should be happy, James. I finally took your advice." A hand swept over me. "Feeding without killing."

James threw off one of the smaller vampires and raised his pendant once more. The remaining vampires shied away. "Guarantee her safety or I break this now. We'll all burn together."

Merak sneered. "You're not the suicide type."

"You think I won't?" Those quicksilver eyes shifted to me. "For her?"

Merak's lips pressed to a thin line, then pursed. He flicked a finger, and Bryce and the rest of the vampires fell back. "Fine."

James's fist tightened on the chain. "Your word."

"Neither I nor mine shall harm your precious halfer. You have my word."

With a nod, James held his pendant out to Bryce, who took it by the chain like a snake by the tail.

"Release her," James demanded.

A wicked smile revealed Merak's teeth.

The burning in my arm quenched, a red hot iron plunged into an ice bath, and I wondered that my skin didn't split apart at the change.

I lifted my gaze to meet James's.

"Run." My voice was a hoarse whisper that didn't travel past the dais, but it was there and it was mine. It gave me hope.

Merak settled back in his throne. "You really are a fool."

"You gave your word." James took a step forward.

I shook my head. Did James really believe Merak would let me go? He'd never let me go. Never let either of us go.

I couldn't let it end like this.

Tearing the dangling strap off my dress, I curled around it, cradling it with my body, and imagined the sun on my skin in all its blistering glory.

"I'll keep my word. She will not be harmed. In fact, I'm going to ensure that she lives a very long time." He raised his hands to indicate the chamber around us. "Right here."

I started knotting, looping the strap over and over, threading sunlight into each strand.

"You bastard." James lunged, but dozens of black-clad vampires and thralls poured from the arches. Several fell, but they were quickly replaced. The floor in front of the dais filled with writhing bodies, and James was pulled to his knees.

Almost!

Bryce waded into the fight, and the tip of a shining blade erupted from James's stomach.

He grunted, but continued to struggle.

"Put him in the lower dungeon." Merak flicked a wrist toward the exit. "He'll make a good meal if I ever need a power boost."

James screamed, thrashing as the mass of vampires carried him through one of the arches, the black-slicked blade still protruding from his abdomen.

My body was a wet dishrag, but I pushed to my knees, panting. My vision swam.

One shot. That's all I was going to get.

Coiling on the steps, I lunged at the throne and forced my hand right into Merak's toothy grin.

Light exploded around us. Blinding, burning light. I screamed, he screamed, the vampires in the hall screamed. The stones shook with our voices. Blisters formed and burst on my palm, and the world washed out in a sea of white.

Chapter 15

A FIST CAME OUT of nowhere to backhand me across the face. Dark sparks popped like fireworks across my white-washed vision. Hard edges dug into my ribs as I rolled. Thin loops of metal tangled my legs.

I blinked, and the light was replaced by a black so deep I might have been blind.

My skin ached. Something damp oozed from flaking cracks on my right hand. The smell of charred flesh choked me, and I gagged.

Wails filled the chamber, echoing back in a hundred different voices. *No time.*

Clenching my teeth, I unwound the chain from my ankles and pulled at the slack. The line went taut.

I blinked a few more times, and blue highlights emerged from the deepest shadows. The world was a high-contrast monochrome of writhing bodies, each clutching their heads in mimic of Merak on his throne, long pale fingers splayed over a backdrop of blackened flesh.

I pulled at the thin chain glinting between us, gasping when it dug into my palms and bit across my fingers. Tears leaked down my cheeks. I braced my feet against the lowest step and strained, but it only sank the chain deeper into my flesh.

Blue light flashed along a silver edge, and sparks flew off the dais.

I tumbled back, a ship cut adrift.

"Can you run?" Kai's mouth was pressed to my ear, but his yell was a whispered counter-note to the sustained cries still filling the cavern.

I threw my arms around him and shook my head into his shoulder with a sob.

Unlatching my hands, he stood and slid the long blade of his sword back into its sheath. Then he pulled me to my feet.

I teetered for a second, then grunted as he pressed his shoulder to my stomach and straightened. What little blood I had rushed into my head and the world swam.

The echo of pain died to a rolling whimper, and shadows started to move around us.

I dug my fingers into Kai's side. "What about James?"

Kai set off running, and I tipped my chin to see Merak's abyss-eyes staring after me from a face that now resembled a lava flow. His hatred was framed for a moment in a blue-lit arch, then Kai carried me into the darkness.

"MMM." I SHIFTED, and springs creaked beneath me.

"Don't move."

My eyes snapped open. Kai was sitting at the edge of my bed, a damp washcloth in one hand.

I searched my fractured memories, struggling to fit together a jigsaw puzzle with half the pieces missing.

Darkness like the depths of the ocean. Teeth. Bones. James.

"You left him," I whispered.

"I couldn't save you both."

"You could have tried."

He straightened. "James knew what he was getting into."

Chase, gray and furry, stretched at the end of my bed with a yawn that showed entirely too many teeth for my liking.

Kai wiped dry blood from the raw flesh of my right hand.

"It'll heal fast now that your fae blood is stronger, but you'll need to take it easy."

"We have to go back."

He silently wrapped a bandage around the angry red skin.

I ground my teeth. "*I* have to go back."

He clipped the end of the bandage in place and lifted a bowl of pink water and stained rags from the nightstand. "You need to heal. Get some rest."

"I'm going back."

Kai sighed, opened his mouth—

A bang sounded from the front of the house.

Kai sighed again and stepped to the side as a blur of brown leather and coppery curls streaked into the room. Chase sprang from the bed with a hiss, tail puffed up like a feather duster.

Tanned hands stopped just short of grabbing my shoulders, hovering close enough to feel their heat against my bare skin.

Marc's star-burst eyes traveled the length of me then came back to my face. "Alex, I—"

"Where's Sophie?" Holding the covers to my chest, I sat up and scooted back against my headboard. The movement hurt, but at least I didn't have to keep looking up at everyone. "Did she make it out before she . . ."

Marc straightened with a deep breath and ran a hand through his hair, making the curls pull and bounce. "I found her mid-change, about a block from the club."

Bandages strained against my knuckles as I bunched my fists in the comforter. "Did she hurt anyone?"

He shook his head.

"Did anyone see her?"

His expression tightened. "I don't think so. No one's reported her anyway."

"How the hell could you let her out when she was—"

"I didn't let her out," he snapped.

Kai stood in the doorway to my bathroom, the now empty bowl dangling from one hand. "He's the one who told us what had happened."

"The pup I had watching her was . . . " Marc shook his head. "He won't be watching her anymore." His voice grew quiet. "I'm sorry, Alex. I knew she was impatient. I didn't realize she'd be so stupid."

Impatient, angry, frustrated. Yeah, I could relate. Maybe she had just wanted a night out with an old friend. Maybe she'd just wanted to feel human again. But her selfishness had landed me in hell. And now James. . . . Accident or not, I wasn't sure I could forgive her.

Marc shifted his feet and glanced around my bedroom like he wanted to pace, or run, but the walls were too close. "When I heard she'd gone out, I tracked her to the club. Unfortunately, by the time I found her and got the whole story, you were already beyond my reach."

"That's where James and I came in," Kai finished.

I frowned at Marc. My memories of the escape were still hazy. "You weren't there. Or did I just not see you?"

He shook his head. "I wasn't there."

"It would have been impossible to sneak a pack of wolves into the nest," Kai said. "A small infiltration was our best bet to get close to you."

"So James made himself a target while you snuck in." The memory of James being carried away made my heart pound, each pulse throbbing in my aching skull. I fixed my gaze on Marc. "Will you help me get him back?"

Marc cut his eyes across to Kai. "You're going after James?"

Kai gave half a shrug and looked away.

My chest tightened. Kai and Marc were willing to leave James to his fate.

I'd learned a long time ago that people couldn't be counted on. People left when things got tough, and most never came back. But James had come. Suddenly, all the missed dates didn't seem so important. He'd been a terrible boyfriend, true, but he was there for me when I needed him most. Even though our relationship had fallen apart before it really got started. Even though our friendship was fraying under the strain of lies and secrets. He'd come for me.

How could I do any less? "Of course I am, and I need your help."

Marc shook his head.

I slammed my fist into the bed, gritting my teeth at the pain of friction on my raw skin. "If you'd kept Sophie under proper control in the first—"

He leaned down so our noses were inches apart. His teeth were bared. His breath smelled of garlic and rosemary. "I might have felt responsible for you, but James's actions were his own."

"He only—"

"I'll not risk my pack in a war with the vampires." He straightened, crossing his arms. "I'm glad you're all right, Alex. And I'm sorry about James, I really am, but going after him would be suicide. Don't make his sacrifice in vain."

I clamped my jaw tight. I couldn't believe he wanted me to give up. To abandon James to his fate, be that death or eternal torment. "Who knew werewolves were such cowards?"

Sighing, Marc swung his head and let his arms fall to his sides. "I can't stop you, Alex. But I can't help you either." He shared a look with Kai, then paused at the door with his back to me. "I hope you change your mind."

His footsteps grew distant, and the whine of a motorcycle shrieked his retreat.

I crossed my arms and leveled my gaze at Kai. "I'm going back."

He shook his head, a sad smile on his lips. "*We're* going back."

I STARED UP AT the crack in my ceiling. It was getting longer, a dark vein creeping across the white when no one was looking. Sunlight splashed across it, but the light was cold and couldn't reach its depths.

Throwing back my covers, I glanced down at the bruised semi-circles that pocked my skin like a festering disease, and quickly looked away. Kai promised the wounds would heal soon enough. Apparently, the tattoo on my arm had picked up the pace of waking my abilities, increasing the magic in my blood in response to a life-threatening circumstance. I'd moved closer to fae, and further from human.

My feet sank into the carpet, and I just sat at the edge of the bed for a moment, scrunching my toes into the threads. I wobbled a little when I pushed upright. My vision flared and faded, and my heart pounded harder for a moment to compensate. When I could see, I shuffled to the bathroom and turned on the shower.

The bandages stuck when I unwound my hand, but flesh as pink and smooth as a newborn babe's coated my palm. I opened and closed my hand a few times, watching the new skin stretch and wrinkle. Tight but usable.

I stepped into the shower and gasped. The water burned like acid against the puckered bite wounds dotting my body. The marks were scabbed over and itchy, but still visible. The punctures had been deep, and the vampires hadn't taken care to leave clean wounds. Even fae healing couldn't erase them overnight.

When the initial shock dulled, I grabbed a loofah and started scrubbing, taking inventory while I worked. Most of the bites were clustered on my thighs and torso. A few marked my back, and those were harder to reach. The insides of my wrists and elbows each bore a perfect imprint of teeth. Just how long had I been down there? How often had he fed? How many mouths had pierced me?

I shivered in the steam and scrubbed harder, stripping the defiled skin like a woodworker with a rasp.

A trickle of sound too steady and short for the shower caught my attention, and I turned to find a shadow cast across the shower curtain. The toilet flushed.

Grabbing my shampoo bottle by the neck, I raised it like a club and peeked around the edge of the curtain. A young woman with snowy-white hair that stood in short spikes above pointed ears turned on me with eyes the endless blue of an August sky.

My mouth fell open. Then all the blood rushed to my face. "Who the hell are you?"

"Jynx." She cocked her head sideways and smiled. "Kai was in the other bathroom, and I really had to pee."

"How—Why—"

The bathroom door banged against the wall and a wide-eyed Kai stood fuming in the doorway. He grabbed the girl by the arm and propelled her out of the room.

"What—" I was still brandishing the shampoo, staring after the girl.

"She showed up just after you went missing."

"Who is she?" My voice was an octave too high.

"Chase's sister." Kai shook his head. "We can talk after your shower."

I looked down at the plastic curtain protecting my illusion of modesty, and the door clicked shut.

Sealing the shower, I pressed my back to the slick tiles and sank into the tub. Water pooled and swirled around my legs and hips, collecting and cooling where my skin creased. A tiny whirlpool circled the drain with the hypnotic pull of a spinning top and I stared into it until the water ran cold.

Sighing, I turned off the faucet and climbed out of the tub. The mirror was steamed over, for which I was grateful. I wrapped a towel around my torso and squeezed the water from my hair like I was wringing someone's neck.

A distant knock sounded at the front of the house. Then a closer knock echoed on the bathroom door.

"Alex," Kai said through the wood. "The police are here."

My hands froze, still tangled in my damp hair. "Can't you just magic them away?"

"They want you to accompany them to the police station."

My breath caught. "They're arresting me? For what?"

"Not arresting. They probably just want to know why James is missing."

Pinning my towel in place, I opened the door so I could glare at him. "So tell them."

"You know we can't."

"Then what am I supposed to say? *I* don't even know exactly what happened. Hell, I don't even know how long I was down there."

"Keep your voice down. I don't need to tell you how good Detective Nazari's hearing is."

I snapped my mouth closed. If Sarah was waiting in the living room, she'd probably heard the whole exchange. Then again, Sarah might have gotten the story from Marc already. Or Sophie for that matter. Hard to know who was keeping which secrets these days.

"Short story, you've been incommunicado for three days." Kai raised his hand to forestall my outburst. "I called in sick for you at the bookstore. James has only been missing since yesterday, but I'm sure the cops are keeping pretty close tabs. Joe is also missing in their eyes, but he isn't really."

"Where—"

Again he held up his hand. "Better you don't have to lie."

THE BOULDER POLICE station was a gray and white building on Thirty-third. Just passing through those doors made me feel guilty, and it didn't help that I was led to a room without windows. Just a mirrored wall and a single metal table with three chairs.

I was alone on my side. Sarah and Herrera sat across from me. The red eye of a camera watched from one corner, recording my every twitch for later review.

I shifted on my hard metal seat. "Why couldn't we do this at my house?"

"Why haven't you been answering your phone?" Herrera countered.

"I lost it."

He flipped open a yellow folder. "Says here you missed work yesterday."

I nodded. "I was sick."

Both cops looked me over, and I waited while they took in my anemic complexion, the dark circles under my eyes.

Sarah's gaze caught mine. "Nothing serious, I hope."

I clenched my jaw. As a member of Marc's pack, she must have known about Sophie's impromptu outing and where it had landed me . . . and James. "I'll live."

"The thing is, Ms. Blackwood," Herrera continued. "You aren't the only one who fell off our radar this weekend."

He gave me a level stare, which I returned in kind. After Merak, the idea of someone like Herrera trying to intimidate me was just laughable. Sure, he could throw me in jail, but he couldn't trap me in a living prison and suck out my soul one sip at a time. He couldn't make me betray my own nature. He was only human.

"We haven't been able to locate James Abernathy or Joseph Carmichael since Sunday morning. Along with the housekeeper and. . . . Well, it's a lot of people to go missing."

Herrera's "and" hung between us, a bomb waiting to drop. Who else was missing?

"I'm not sure what you want me to say." I raised my palms. "I don't know where James, Joe, or Elsa are."

Sarah scratched a finger along her jaw. "When was the last time you saw Mr. Abernathy?"

"I stopped by his house Friday night." I crossed my fingers that we'd been careful enough to hide our subsequent trip to the apartment. The last thing I needed was to be caught "returning to the scene of the crime" and then lying about it.

"How did he seem?"

"What do you mean?"

Herrera gestured with one hand. "Was he . . . agitated?"

I pressed my palms flat on the table and narrowed my eyes. "He was accused of selling drugs. A woman died in his apartment. Of course he was agitated."

Someone tapped on the other side of the mirror, and Herrera pressed a hand to his ear.

Sarah caught my eye and glanced down, lips a thin white line.

Following her gaze, I adjusted the cuff of my sweater a little lower to cover the purplish skin peeking out at my wrist and folded my hands in my lap.

"Were you at a club called Abandon on Saturday night?" Herrera asked.

"What's that got to do with anything?"

"Just answer the question."

"Yeah. I went dancing. Is that a crime now?"

"Were you alone?"

I did my best not to look at Sarah. Did she know where this line of questioning was going? Surely she wouldn't want police attention on Sophie. Attention that might lead to exposure. "There were about a hundred other people there."

"Was one of them Ms. Sophie Devereaux?"

My fingers cramped in my lap and I sucked a breath through flared nostrils. My heart was a staccato in my ears. Had someone seen her change after all?

Herrera leaned forward. "It seems an awful lot of your associates have been disappearing lately."

I exhaled. He didn't know.

"Sophie didn't disappear." I tried to recall the cover story Marc had made for her. "Was she the 'and' you mentioned earlier?"

"Actually," Sarah cut in, "some homeless people have gone missing."

I frowned. "You keep tabs on homeless people?"

"We do when they're witnesses."

"Funny thing." Herrera leaned back in his chair and flipped to a new page in his file. "Three people confessed to buying drugs off your boyfriend. Two of them disappeared about the same time he did." Herrera tossed a photo on the table between us. "Here's the only one we found."

In the picture, a man of about sixty sprawled amid black plastic trash bags in a brick alley. His eyes were cataract-white. A dark stain covered his chest, soaked into layers of patched clothes and a thick flannel-lined coat.

"That alley is across the street from your boyfriend's gallery. And that," he pressed a finger to the picture, "is the man who reported Mr. Abernathy leaving the scene of a murder."

Chapter 16

I DRUMMED MY fingers on the table and looked around for a clock. All I found was my own reflection and the unwavering red eye of the camera. Guess they didn't want people to know how long they'd been stuck there.

I chewed my lip and tried not to look at the mirror across from me. Behind that glass, my fate was being decided. Did they have enough to hold me? Herrera had made a big fuss about obstruction of justice and accessory charges before they left me to stew. That had been what felt like hours ago. Bad enough they'd taken up most of my afternoon with pointless questions, if they locked me up . . . . Every second I wasted here was a second James was at Merak's mercy. Assuming he wasn't dead already.

No. I shook my head. I couldn't believe that, couldn't even think it.

The door swung open, and Sarah stuck her head into the room. "Okay, Ms. Blackwood, you're free to go."

I pushed my palms to the table and levered out of my seat. My right leg tingled with the pins and needles of staying still too long.

Stepping past Sarah, I turned in the direction she indicated. Two steps down the hall, the door to the observation room opened and Herrera came out. I nodded to him, then shifted my eyes to the man at his back.

PTF agent Ben O'Connell stepped into the hall. Eyes the color of molasses glared from sun-stained skin. Deep lines bore into his forehead and around his tight frown. He slipped a PTF ball cap over short, dark hair. "Ms. Blackwood."

My stomach became a writhing snake, strangling the other organs.

I'm gonna prove you murdered him. O'Connell had delivered that threat after I killed his friend and fellow PTF agent in self-defense. Johnson had tortured and killed people, including one of my best friends, then come after me. I wasn't losing any sleep over his death, but O'Connell's threat filled me with a paranoid dread. I'd tried to steer clear of the PTF, and O'Connell in particular, since that encounter. Yet here he was.

I swallowed the dry lump in my throat. "What are you doing here?"

O'Connell tipped a hand toward Herrera. "I offered to help with the investigation."

With Sarah at my back and Herrera and O'Connell in front of me, the hallway was starting to feel claustrophobic. "I hadn't heard there was anything paranatural about the case."

The corner of O'Connell's mouth pulled up, more sneer than smile. "Your involvement with the fae is documented. It seemed prudent to take precautions with your interrogation."

I threw a glance over my shoulder, but Sarah was studying her shoes. "Letting a fae live with me doesn't give me special powers."

He shrugged. "Better safe than sorry."

Herrera leaned away from O'Connell, moving out of the crossfire of glares flying between us. "You're free to go, Ms. Blackwood, but call us the second you hear from Mr. Abernathy or if you learn of his whereabouts."

I nodded and squeezed past O'Connell.

"Be seeing you," he said.

The air as I trotted down the stone steps of the Public Safety building was cold, heavy with moisture the clouds refused to release as they scraped their bellies over the Flatirons. The sun was a dull orb, diffused so the whole sky seemed to shine with pale light. I paused on the sidewalk and breathed deep.

O'Connell had no reason to stick his nose into James's investigation. He was there for one reason. Me. If he could nail me on something, anything, he would.

Turning away from the parking lot, I walked south toward the river.

I didn't have time to tiptoe around O'Connell, not when James was still a prisoner, but if I rushed off half-cocked, O'Connell would be waiting for me with a pair of handcuffs when I came back. Worse, he might learn the truth about James, and that would open a whole other can of worms. I'd promised Uncle Sol to stay off the PTF's radar, but O'Connell wasn't going to make that easy.

I cut through a shopping center and passed near one edge of a shanty town that filled what used to be a park backing up to the river. Areas like that had sprung up in every major city during the Faerie War, flooding with refugees displaced by fighting in the countryside and the unlivable wastes those conflicts created. Since both the fae and human armies preferred to fight on open land, the cities were left mostly un-touched, so that's where everyone fled. The number of homeless now was nothing compared to the first few years following the war, but some people never got back on their feet.

I scrambled down a hill to the greenbelt path that traced the edge of the river. A single jogger wearing day-glow green shoes and a construction orange windbreaker flashed past. Farther up the river, just before the next bend, three women were scrubbing laundry in the icy stream.

Stepping off the path, I skipped a stone into water that would be clogged with tubes and kayaks in the summer, but now rolled with sluggish ebbs of slush. Crouching over a bed of matted leaves, brown and rotting from the constant spray of the river, I tried to collect my thoughts.

I'd never made anything like the light bomb I created from my dress strap before. I'd been working on instinct and adrenaline, trying to make a distraction so James could get away. That last part had been a failure, but the bomb. . . . The bomb had worked.

I stared at the new flesh on my palm, then flipped my hand to inspect the back. If I squinted, paper-thin white lines marred my skin.

I'd done almost as much damage to myself as I had to Merak, and probably he was already healed, but I'd *hurt* him. If I could hurt the master vampire of Denver, there had to be a chance I could save James.

Bubbles formed and popped on the surface of the water.

Even if I managed to get James back from Merak, what good would it do if he was immediately arrested for murder? And with O'Connell involved—

I rubbed my upper arms, hugging myself. Could a vampire pass PTF testing?

The hairs on the back of my neck prickled, drawing me back to the present. Branches swayed and scraped in the wind, water burbled near my feet. A scuff sounded on the sidewalk behind me.

I adjusted my feet, shifted my balance, and turned.

Sarah was standing beside a thick oak tree, arms crossed, lips a tight, unhappy line. I scanned the area behind her and to either side. We were alone on the path.

I straightened, forcing my hands to my sides. The gray sidewalk was a second river between us, and we stood on opposite banks.

"I take it you know what happened?" I shifted my gaze to the mark on my wrist she'd reminded me to cover during the interview.

She nodded.

"And you know about James."

Another nod. Her frown grew even tighter.

"Then you know he's being set up."

"Chances are he won't be back to face the charges anyway."

I ground my teeth and bunched my hands into fists until they shook.

"I heard you and your roommate are planning to commit suicide. My advice? Don't. Keep your head down and get on with your life."

"Not an option."

"You're in way over your head."

"Then help me."

"I can't."

"Then what are you doing here? Why follow me?"

She tipped her chin up and squinted into the overcast sky. "Marc asked me to keep an eye on you, just in case. Figured I should see why you didn't head straight home."

The wind caught my loose hair, and I pulled it away from my face. "I don't need a babysitter. I need allies. If you won't help me save him, at least do your job. Prove he's innocent."

Her shoulders stiffened. "I can only follow the facts."

"And only so far." I softened my voice. "I know you've got your own secrets to look out for, and James wouldn't thank you for sharing his, but there must be *something* you can do. You wouldn't be a cop if you didn't care about justice."

She pinned me with eyes too old for her face. "If you make it back, I'll try to see that James has more than a six by eight cell to look forward to."

I nodded and watched her stroll out of sight, hands in her pockets. The wind grabbed my hair again, and I shivered.

DROPPING THE LITTLE suede purse I'd carried to the precinct despite no longer having any phone or wallet to put in it, I flopped onto the couch. "We have a problem."

"Just one?" Kai stepped out of the kitchen, a half-empty bowl of Fruit Loops in one hand, plastic spoon in the other.

"Don't you ever get sick of that crap?"

He shrugged, crunching a bite of sugar-encrusted cereal. "What's the problem?"

"Remember O'Connell?"

The spoon paused partway to his mouth. "The unpleasant PTF agent who interrogated me after we saved the world from his friend?"

"That's the one. He was at the precinct today when they questioned me. He's poking around James's case."

He chewed, swallowed. "We'll just have to be extra careful."

I tipped over and stretched out, resting my feet on one armrest, my head on the other. I'd only been up for half a day, but I was already exhausted, mentally and physically. "So what happened to Joe? Where is he?"

Kai slurped up the last of his milk and wiped a wrist across his mouth. "The necklace James took to Merak was a fake. He sent Joe to the reservation with the real one to keep it safe."

"The reservation? But Joe's human."

He shrugged. "There's no law prohibiting humans from entering the reservation, there just isn't anything to protect them if they do. I gave Joe the necessary protection." He settled on a chair across from me. "You could be safe there too."

"Sure, except for all the fae you say want me dead and the fact that I've had almost no time to prepare for them." I shook my head. If my time with Merak taught me anything, it was that I was way out of my league in the paranatural world. "Besides, I won't abandon James."

I ran a hand through my hair, snagging tangles. "At least, with the necklace out of reach, that's one less thing to worry about. Though Joe's disappearance isn't helping James's case."

Kai spread his hands. "Not much that would at this point."

A black-spotted, grayish-white ball of fur hurdled the back of the couch and landed on my lap with the weight of a bowling ball, folding me nearly in half.

"Jynx!" Kai snapped.

Eyes of unblinking blue stared down at me as I tried to catch my breath. Then a wet tongue flicked out to dampen the tip of my nose.

Chase rounded the end of the couch, bare-chested, in a pair of faded jeans.

I looked back at the giant kitten. "*This* is your—"

She launched off my chest, and I lost the air to speak.

The cat melted in midair, and a slim, teenage girl crouched where it should have landed. She smiled over her shoulder.

"His sister," she said with a wink.

Sitting up, I grabbed the afghan off the back of the couch and threw it at the naked girl.

"You look younger." I shifted my eyes between the siblings. "Why are you so much bigger as a cat?"

Chase sniffed and looked away.

Jynx laughed. "I'm not a cat."

"Believe it or not, she's going to get bigger still," Chase added. "Jynx is a snow leopard."

I pinched the bridge of my nose. "Right. So what are you doing here?"

The laughter died out of her eyes and she glanced at Chase. "I wanted to visit my brother."

"You wanted to visit the mortal world," Chase chided. "Again."

She shrugged. "Is that so bad?"

Chase frowned and cocked his head toward me.

Taking a deep breath, Jynx knelt next to the couch and took my hand with one of her own. The other kept her paltry cover from slipping. "Can I stay here?"

I looked from her to Chase to Kai and back again, then shook my head. "That's not a good idea."

Her grip tightened, grinding my fingers together. "Please, I'll do anything. I . . ." Her voice dropped to a whisper. "I can't go back."

"Back where?"

"To our parents," Chase said. He crossed his arms. "Jynx has run away from home."

"You're one to talk," she snapped.

"I'm an adult."

I used my free hand to pry Jynx's fingers loose. "How old are you?"

She shrugged. "Old enough."

Chase snorted. "She's forty-seven, roughly fourteen by human standards."

I shook my head, trying to wrap my brain around that fact. "Why did you run away?"

She settled back on her heels. "My parents don't understand."

"Parents are like that. It doesn't answer the question."

"She thinks she's in love." Jynx and I both glared at Chase, but he just shrugged.

"Your parents don't approve?"

She shook her head.

I sighed. "I'm sorry. I really wish I could help, but right now is just—"

"I know all about it." She jumped to her feet. "I was here when Chase and Kai were talking about what happened to you, and I heard you last night. You're going to rescue your boyfriend."

"It's not that simple, but—"

"I can help," she said.

"No. No way. You're just a—"

"You need a scout. Otherwise you'll never make it through a vampire nest."

"Kai already—"

"He only had to get to the main chamber. James will be much deeper. They probably have miles of tunnels down there."

Chase stepped forward, reaching for her. "You're being—"

She shrugged off his hand. "I can do this."

"Would you let someone finish a sentence?" I snapped.

All three fae turned to me.

"You need me," Jynx said. "And I can prove it."

Darting around her brother, she wrenched open the front door. The afghan hit the floor as a half-sized snow leopard streaked outside.

Chase cursed, and a gray tabby raced after the leopard, leaving behind a pair of empty jeans.

A cold breeze blew into the house. Standing, I lifted the discarded afghan, twisting it in my hands, and stared out the open door. I itched to follow them. To charge straight into Merak's dungeon and free James.

"Should we—"

"No." Kai pushed the door shut. "We need a plan before we move against Merak. James can hold out a little longer."

"But . . ." I gestured toward the closed door. "Jynx."

"Chase can look after his sister. And if they intend to scout the nest, all the more reason to wait. Or would you rather stumble around in the dark?"

I recalled the seemingly endless tunnels beneath the club, and shivered. Having a map *would* be helpful. Still . . . "I can't just sit here."

Kai smiled. "Who said anything about sitting?"

Chapter 17

METAL CLANGED against wood, wood slammed into meat, and I got another bruise on my battered torso.

"Again."

"This is impossible."

"If you want any chance of surviving a raid on a vampire nest, you need to do better." Kai lifted his sword. "Again."

"You're too fast." I cringed at the pinch in my lungs when I tried to straighten.

"Not nearly as fast as a vampire. Again."

"You've made your point."

"Are you going after James?"

I pressed my lips together.

"Then I haven't made my point."

"Fine." I lifted my sword and settled my stance.

We'd been sparring since Chase and Jynx bolted. The sun hung, heavy and swollen, just over the tree line, casting a warm, red light that contrasted sharply with the bite in the air and the bruised shadows around us. Neither feline had returned, so we had to assume they'd followed Jynx's plan to scout the nest.

Kai came in with a flurry of strikes that caught in my vision like the wings of a flip-book butterfly. Somewhere in the missing frames I received another bruise on my arm, one on my leg, and a slap across my back.

I stopped an overhead slash an inch from my head, arms vibrating from the impact. If that had hit . . .

Thick boot treads drove into my stomach, and my feet left the ground.

I crashed to the frozen earth in a rushed exhale, numb and gasping.

Kai set the point of his wooden blade against my neck and shook his head. "You focus too much on the blade."

I sucked cold air into my burning lungs. "You said body strikes were illegal."

"In duels. In a real fight, your opponent will use every weapon they can."

A *tsking* noise brought both our heads around.

"It seems academics aren't the only area in which you fall short." Hortense stepped out of the long purple shadow of a Douglas fir. "You are apparently an equally poor student in all your endeavors."

Kai pulled the blade away from my throat and turned to bow to the tutor.

I raised to one elbow and glared. "Like you could do better."

Kai cringed.

Hortense raised one snowy eyebrow, and the wrinkles around her mouth rearranged into a smile. "A gremlin could do better than you."

Recalling the tiny dark shapes that spilled out of my enemies' van the night I first killed a man, I shuddered. "Cannon fodder," Kai had called them. Mindless, expendable.

I pushed to my feet, only wobbling a little. "Prove it."

The other eyebrow rose to match the first in twin arches.

Kai stepped between us. "Please forgive—"

"Accepted." Hortense held one hand, palm up, toward Kai.

His shoulders slumped. He glanced back at me, but I couldn't read his expression. Then he set the hilt of his sword in the ancient scholar's hand.

Hortense tossed the edge of her heavy, midnight cloak over her shoulder to reveal an impractical brocade dress. She slid one soft leather boot forward to peek out beneath the luxuriant fabric, and relaxed into her stance with a slow, even breath that made my gut cramp. Hortense knew what she was doing.

I mirrored her stance. "Will you be able to fight in that getup?"

She moved so fast I almost missed it. A blur of wood and fabric, a streak of silver-white.

Then the swords clashed. My hands went numb from the impact. The connection lasted less than a second, a lightning strike against my defenses, then Hortense was spinning away.

Was that how I'd looked to Kate at Aikido? My chest tightened. Kai was right. I'd have to give up training with mortals if I wanted to keep my secret.

I pushed the thought away. One fight at a time.

My arms shook as I raised my blade. I tightened my grip until the wrapped fabric scraped like sandpaper across my healing palm.

Hortense moved with the fluid grace of a dancer. When she paused, the world seemed to pull in around the edges, gathering toward her. Then she burst into motion and it was all I could do to keep my eyes on her.

My body reacted from some deep instinct for self-preservation, blocking and dodging before I even saw the attacks. But I was losing ground, barely slowing the strikes to minimize bruising. My lungs pumped like leaky bellows, fighting to fill. My blood raced, delivering half-spent oxygen to over-used muscles.

Our blades came together again, and I stared into her impassive face from inches away. There was no emotion in her eyes, no strain in her expression. She might have been sleeping for all the tension I could find there.

My own heaving breath stirred silver tendrils of hair on her forehead, too short to be contained by her coiled braid, and I felt the giddy urge to head-butt her or spit. Anything to break that calm façade.

She spun away on soundless feet.

At the edge of the trampled clearing, Kai paced like a beast in a cage, one hand raised to his mouth while the other hugged his ribs.

What was he so worried about? It was only practice.

Hortense coiled again, and I felt my balance shift as though gravity itself had found a new center. Clear, cold eyes settled on me with the weight of time.

I'd met plenty of old people, dealt with them as customers. Humans degraded with age, sad but true. Minds lost their edge, bodies lost their resilience. Age was the unfair punishment of a long life.

Hortense wasn't old, she was ancient, but the time that wore mere mortals down had sharpened her. The woman before me hadn't been hindered by a long life, she'd been honed by it.

Cold sweat trickled between my shoulder blades.

With a step to the side, Hortense swung her blade in a wide arc toward my chest. It seemed almost sloppy compared to her other strikes, and I brought my own blade up in plenty of time to block. But instead of colliding with my blade, she twisted her wrist so the wood slid along the length of my defense and up over my head. Her stance sank lower, and the arc of her blade swung a full circle to impact the back of my knee.

My weight collapsed on the screaming ligaments, and my leg folded beneath me. The moment my back hit the ground, a second impact landed on my chest to press me into the cold dirt.

Hortense knelt above me, one knee drilling into my sternum. She lifted her blade in both hands, and buried it into the earth beside my head. Smooth wood brushed my cheek.

I tightened my grip on the sword still in my hand, then let it fall from numb fingers and closed my eyes with a sigh.

"Against my recommendations, the Lord of Enchantment has conceded that Malakai will remain your primary tutor," she said.

My eyes snapped open.

The weight shifted off my chest, and Hortense brushed a smudge of dirt off her skirt. "I shall do what I can to supplement your education, but considering your abysmal retention of knowledge, you should improve your dueling. Chances are you'll need it."

Tucking a stray wisp of silver behind her ear, she stepped primly toward the house.

Kai knelt beside me, and I smiled up at him.

"You get to stay." I gestured after Hortense. "And I get professional tutoring. Best of both worlds."

"So it would seem." He pitched his voice low. "But best not to mention our rescue plans."

I nodded.

He patted my shoulder, then tugged the practice blade free with a grunt. "Run through your kata a few more times before heading in. I'll see that our guest gets settled."

He followed Hortense into the house.

I thumped my head back against the frozen ground and stared at orange-tinged clouds streaked across an indigo sky.

I LIFTED MY HAND in the dark of my bedroom and spread my fingers wide, imagining shiny pink skin stretched tight across my palm. My mind was filled with the howl of a dozen vampires, and a vision of Merak's melted face.

I let the hand drop to my side, where it bounced on the bedsprings.

My impromptu sunlight bomb had burned itself out nearly as soon as it was complete, but it had worked. There had to be a way to delay it, to build in some sort of fuse. I drummed my fingers against the covers.

I rolled over, tugging the tangled blankets.

Chase hadn't come back, neither had Jynx, and the bed felt oddly empty without a warm ball of fur to bump against.

I rolled onto my back once more, swore, and sat up. Between my nightmares, memories, and racing thoughts, sleep was clearly out of the question. I might as well use the time to run my idea by Kai.

My slippers scuffed down the hall, past the closed door to Kai's room where Hortense was spending the night. Thick flannel pants kept the chill off my legs, and I'd pulled a heavy cable sweater over the loose t-shirt that was my standard nightgown.

Starlight dripped through the windows to dapple the living room floor.

Holding my breath, I peeked over the back of the couch.

"Couldn't sleep?" Kai closed the book he'd been reading.

I stepped around the couch and took a seat in one of the chairs. "How can you read in the dark?"

Kai looked around and shrugged. "Does this seem dark to you?"

I opened my mouth, then shut it and looked around again. I could make out the computer in the corner, the appliances on the counter, the pattern of the rug.

Kai sat up. "Another gift of fae genetics. So what has you out of bed so late?"

I snorted. "Ten o'clock isn't late."

"You're the one who went to bed at nine."

"Only because I couldn't stand—" I snapped my mouth closed. An echo of my voice hung in the still night.

Kai's smile was tight. "Probably best not to wake her then."

I ran both hands over my head, pulling back my hair. "When you first offered to teach me magic, you said learning enchantment would help direct my imbuing, make it less . . ." I waffled a hand in the air. "Random."

He nodded. "It will allow you to focus your power, to imbue with specific intent. You'll also be able to imbue things with more than simple emotions or attributes."

"How long would it take?"

"To learn to imbue a relic?"

"To actually do it."

He arched an eyebrow. "I suppose that depends on what you're trying to create."

"When you saved me from—" I glanced at the dark hallway. "When you saved me, I made a kind of . . ." I held my hands so the fingers formed a ball. "Light bomb."

He nodded. "I noticed."

"Could I do that again, but be able to carry it around and use it at will?"

Kai stroked his chin. "Possibly, but. . . . An item like that would be difficult. Your best bet is probably to imbue a single object with a constant output, like a blade. The effect would be smaller, more localized, but it would be easier than designing the parameters of a bomb so it didn't explode unexpectedly. That would require more refinement than either of us can manage right now."

I slumped, frowned, then gave a sharp nod. "A knife then, imbued with sunlight. Can it be done?"

He nodded. "In time?" He raised his palms to the ceiling. "I guess that depends on how good a student you are."

"ALEX?"

I blinked and looked around.

Maggie's lips were a thin frown, her emerald eyes narrowed.

I wiped a hand over my face. "Sorry, Mags. Long night."

Kai and I had stayed up, designing the knife we'd make, until well after midnight. I'd wanted to start on the actual forging right away, but Kai had insisted on getting a second opinion on the incantation he'd written. He left before sunrise to visit the fae contact he intended to ask. I would have gone with him, but apparently the guy had a pretty strong hatred of humans. Even halfers weren't welcome in his presence.

That left me with either eight hours of lessons with Hortense, during which I'd have to avoid giving away my intention to infiltrate a vampire nest, or actually showing up for my job at the bookstore for a change.

Maggie sighed and lowered her hands from her hips. "I know you've got a lot going on, what with James and all, but I need you to be *here* when you're here."

"I know, Mags. I'm sorry." I smiled and patted her shoulder. "I'll try."

I glanced over to the café, where Emma's co-barista, Akshata, was serving a growing line of customers. "Speaking of here, where's Emma?"

Maggie's frown deepened. "Took some time."

"Akshata can't fill all the hours herself."

"Tell *her* that."

Maggie headed for the back room. "I've got some orders to fill. Hold down the fort up here."

I saluted until she was out of sight, then rested my elbows on the counter to prop up my chin. I probably should have been working on displays, or shelving inventory, or at least straightening, but . . .

I yawned and let my eyes slide shut.

Assuming Kai got what he wanted from the hermit who hated halfers, we could start making the knife as soon as I got home, though we'd have to find a way to distract Hortense.

Then all we needed was the map Chase and Jynx would provide upon their safe return.

I pushed aside the little voice telling me they'd been gone too long. Of course it would take a while to scout out the whole nest without being seen. And James was likely well hidden and guarded. If I wanted this rescue to succeed, I couldn't go off half-cocked. I needed to be patient.

I frowned. I still wasn't sure what I'd do about James once we were both safe. Assuming he could find some way out of the drug and murder charges, there was still the issue of—

"Glad to see you're back at work."

My eyes snapped open to find Marc's gold and green star-bursts staring at me.

"I hope this means you've given up on—"

"Not a chance."

He frowned and rubbed a hand over the back of his neck, jostling reddish-brown curls. "Look, I—" He blew out a breath. "I just wanted to apologize. Again. For what happened."

I leaned forward. "Then help me."

He shook his head. "I wish I could, Alex. I really do. But—"

"You've got your own ass to cover."

"More than mine."

I nodded.

"If it was just me . . ."

"But you're the alpha."

We both stared at the counter between us.

"Will it always be like this?" I asked.

"My people come first."

"Your secret you mean." I crossed my arms, hugging myself. "You, me, James, all of us. It makes me sick."

He shook his head again. "Exposure didn't work out so well for the fae. And with Anderson taking office . . ."

The election had been a landslide. Come January, Purity would have a seat in the government. Marc was right, our secrets came first. They had to.

He leaned across the counter and pitched his voice low. "Sarah will keep an eye out. That's the best we can do."

I offered a tight smile.

Marc set his hand on my shoulder, squeezed, then headed toward the café for his daily dose of caffeine.

Leaning back against the shelves behind the register, I tipped my chin to the ceiling and closed my eyes again. The sweet potpourri of cinnamon and evergreen hung heavy in the air, making my nose itch with the smells of Christmas. Steam hissed and dishes clattered, feet scuffed around the store, all blending to a soothing backdrop as my mind churned with the dreams I'd failed to have last night.

I sighed. Lies and secrets, secrets and lies. That seemed to be all my life was anymore.

"Really Alex?" Maggie's hands were back on her hips, the frown deeper than ever.

I straightened up, heat rushing to my cheeks. "I was just—"

"Daydreaming," she snapped.

Pushing me out of the way, she held her hand out to the customer waiting on the other side of the counter and rang up their book. How long had they been standing there?

Maggie slammed the register drawer. When she turned to me, her eyes had a wet sheen. "Can't you at least talk to me about what's going on?"

I opened my mouth, closed it, and shook my head.

"Fine." She wiped one cheek, then the other. "You've never been one to share. But Alex, you should talk to *somebody*. First Aiden's murder, then that PTF psycho who came after you, now James and his—" She braced her hands on my shoulders. "It's no wonder you're gutted, but you need to pull yourself together."

She took a deep breath and gestured to the door. "Take the rest of the day off."

"But—"

"I'll get Jake to come in. He's always looking for extra hours."

I bit my lip. "Are you sure?"

She shook her head. "Sort this out and come back to us."

I wrapped my arms around Maggie, wishing I could tell her everything, knowing I couldn't, and pulled away with a sinking feeling. Secrets and lies. That was my life now, and it was only going to get harder.

Chapter 18

I TOSSED MY purse in a corner and padded through my empty living room. Kai's car had been out front when I pulled up, but there was no sign of him inside. The kitchen was empty of all but a collection of dishes drying by the sink. Kai's door was closed, and I passed it on tiptoe, not wanting to alert Hortense of my return just yet. I gritted my teeth at being reduced to sneaking in my own home.

My room was just the way I'd left it, blankets pulled semi-straight over the bed, clothes in piles ranging from freshly laundered to stained rags. Still no sign of Chase or Jynx. No sign of Kai, either. Everyone was out making progress toward James's rescue. I bunched my fists. Everyone except me.

"You're home early."

I jumped and turned, placing a hand over my speeding heart.

Kai slouched against my door frame, hands stuffed in his pockets.

Pushing past him, I marched back to the living room. The door to his room stood open. "Where's Hortense?"

He lifted one shoulder. "I told her you'd be working till four. She chose to spend the time elsewhere. Speaking of which," he crossed his arms, "what are you doing here?"

Grimacing, I flopped onto the couch. "I got sent home early."

"You were fired?"

"No," I snapped, glaring over the back of the couch. "I just—" I fell back against the cushions, deflated. "I couldn't concentrate."

"Because of James?"

"James, and Hortense, and Chase, and Jynx, and Elsa, and O'Connell, and Maggie, and the homeless junkie in the alley, and the dead girl in the apartment." I dragged my fingers over my face with a groan. "All of it."

He pushed my legs out of the way and settled at the end of the couch.

"Just when I think I've found some kind of balance in my life, everything falls apart."

He smiled. "That's because you're thinking of "balance" as "stable.""

Balance is something that is constantly changing."

I shifted to look into the twin galaxies of his eyes. "Did you get what you needed from your friend?"

He snorted. "He's hardly a friend, but the old hermit was helpful. We made a couple adjustments. The incantation is ready to go."

"Then let's get to work." I pushed off the couch, itching to have something productive to bend my frustrated energy toward.

I padded down the hall to the extra bedroom I used for storage, and flicked on the light. Boxes lined one wall, shelves the other. In the back corner was a nest of blankets and pillows that shouldn't have been there.

I crouched beside what looked like a child's fort and trailed my fingers along the fabric. A tuft of white fur lifted free.

My mouth tightened. So this was where Jynx had been sleeping. I hadn't even had time to ask.

My stomach rolled at the thought of the still-missing teenager. Surely Chase would keep her safe. Assuming he caught up to her. Assuming they weren't both caught and sitting next to James in Merak's dungeon. Assuming they weren't dead.

I shook my head and took a shuddering breath.

They were fine. They'd all be fine. And if the cats didn't come home tonight, I'd storm the nest tomorrow, map or no, consequences be damned.

Straightening, I grabbed two bars of steel and headed for the studio.

THE END OF THE steel glowed like a field of wheat caught in the midday sun. Nothing magical about that, not yet.

I clamped a gloved hand over the metal protruding from the blackened brick forge that crouched in one corner of my studio. Coals crackled and flared when I pulled the rod free, sending sparks that made Kai cringe.

He pressed against the cabinet on one wall, as far from the anvil as he could get and still see what was happening. Sweat coated his forehead and dripped from his chin. The furnace was hot, and sweat ran down my back as well, but the white showing all around his eyes and the way he kept licking his lips made me think his discomfort had more to do with my tools than the heat.

Setting the glowing steel against the anvil, I picked up a three-pound sledge. "You don't have to be in the studio for this. You could stand by the door."

He shook his head. "I need to see what's happening. I won't be able to direct from that far away, or channel the necessary energy."

I nodded and lifted the hammer. "You sure?"

He pressed his lips together until they disappeared, but lifted his chin.

The hammer came down with a clang that echoed through my hand and up my arm.

Kai clamped his hands over his ears despite the plugs I'd given him, and started reciting.

His voice wavered with each cringe-inducing strike, but he kept chanting, pouring his magic into and through me as I forged, providing power and direction for the spell. My own voice flowed alongside his with the even rhythm of my hammer, reciting the words I'd spent the last hour memorizing as the forge heated. My shoulder strained, my fingers tingled with each impact even through the thick leather of my gloves. Kai's voice carried me along, and the words etched in my memory poured out to join his, even as his magic mingled with my own and was bound to the metal.

When the steel was thinned out to the rough shape of a six-inch blade with a dramatic recurve, I set my hammer aside and slid the metal back into the coals. A sheen of sweat kept the desert of my skin from cracking under the heat of the forge.

Once the metal was situated, I turned to Kai. "You okay?"

He licked one quivering lip. His skin was waxy and pale. The galaxy of his eyes was dull, as though half the stars had burnt out.

He nodded.

I stretched my shoulders and back, rolled my neck. Then I leaned my hip against a workbench, jostling Sol's bronze soldiers. "If this works," I gestured to the heating metal, "will it be enough to kill a vampire?"

"Doubtful." His voice was tight and cracked. "But the light should keep any inflicted wounds from closing at the incredible rate of vampire healing."

"If it works."

"If it works."

I sighed and crossed my arms, glancing at the color of the steel. "Do vampires heal as fast as werewolves?"

"Faster."

I tapped my fingers against the workbench. "Since halfers have fae blood, do they live longer than normal humans?"

He raised an eyebrow. "Is this about James?"

I lifted one shoulder. "I don't know where things stand with him, but—" I squeezed my arms a little tighter.

"But you want to know if there's a chance." He ran a hand through his hair, then seemed to remember where he was and stepped away from the wall of tools he'd been leaning toward.

"Most halfers lead average human lives," he said. "Fae bodies are maintained by the energies that compose our magic, and we regenerate the same way. Halfers might have a limited amount of fae magic, but they have the mortal bodies of humans. Those bodies break down over time."

"So the—" I gestured to the tattoo spiraling up my arm. "Doesn't change that?"

"Even halfers with strong fae blood rarely pass a century without intervention."

I frowned. "Intervention?"

"The fact is, Alex, you cannot be immortal and remain human."

"The werewolves seem pretty immortal and they're still human."

"No, Alex, they're not. And you can't become a werewolf in any case. Neither can you become a vampire. Magics don't often mix, and when they do the results are unpredictable and dangerous. That's how we ended up with vampires and werewolves in the first place."

I reached for the glowing steel. "No one gets a guarantee on how long they have. It might be better to enjoy a handful of years than none at all."

"That's a very mortal sentiment," he said.

I set the orange metal against the anvil and lifted my hammer. "I am a mortal after all."

I RAN A SERIES of strikes along the red edge from hilt to tip, hammer-polishing the steel. The spine was straight, the shape was good. It had only taken three heats to shape the blade.

I smiled at Kai as the last words in our rounded chant fell from my lips. Then I set my hammer down and leaned against a counter. Forging was always tiring, but the magical component had sapped my strength in a way I couldn't believe.

"I don't know about the spell, but I'm feeling pretty good about the blade."

"The enchantment is working." Kai wiped a sweat-soaked sleeve across his forehead. "We won't know the potency until it's tested."

Forcing my exhausted muscles to engage once more, I reached for a saw. "I just have to form the tang and we can normalize the metal."

Kai waved a hand. "I'm not even going to pretend to know what—"

A knock at the door cut him short.

Hortense peeked around the corner, blanched, and pulled her head out of sight. "It's time for your lessons."

I gritted my teeth. "I wasn't aware we had a schedule."

"When I am present, you are in lessons."

A muscle under my eye twitched. "Then by all means, come on in."

"I—"

The rasp of my saw biting into steel cut her off. I left three inches for the tang. The remainder dropped to the floor with an echoing clang.

Kai yelped when the bar rolled toward him, but it stopped a foot away.

"Are you all right, Malakai?" Hortense peeked around the corner again, finding Kai with her gaze. "What could possibly possess you to enter such a place?" She gestured to walls bristling with steel and iron tools.

"This is where Alex does her imbuing." Kai straightened his shoulders. "A good teacher works in the place most conducive to learning."

Hortense's face clouded over. "Ms. Blackwood is nowhere near advanced enough for such a lesson yet. And even if she was, *you* are hardly a fit teacher."

I turned to Hortense, brandishing my new blade. "You think you can do better? Then get your ass in here and try."

She sniffed. "I was engaged to secure your court training. Magic education was *not* a requirement."

"Then back off." I plunged the unforged end of the knife into the coals.

Hortense pursed her lips. "When will your current exercise be done?"

"When it's done. You can't rush these things."

She lifted her chin. "I shall wait for you inside."

"You know," I spun toward the door, hands on hips, "I never said you could stay here."

She frowned, eyes narrowed.

A thought struck me. "You didn't list this place on your visa, did you?" I cut my eyes to Kai, who had the good grace to drop his gaze.

"I have no visa."

My eyes jerked back to Hortense's stony expression and my heart skipped a beat. If I was caught harboring an unregistered fae . . .

"The human authorities have no idea I am here, and it will remain so."

The sweat on my skin turned cold. Unregistered fae could be executed under PTF law, and O'Connell would love the chance to roll me into that sentence.

Swallowing the sour flavor in my mouth, I shook my head. "I get that Gramps sent you to supplement my training, but that doesn't mean you live here. Kai needs his bed back."

The steely gaze shifted over my shoulder, and I heard the scuff of Kai's feet as he backed away from the glare.

"It seems hospitality is another area in which you are lacking."

Kai cleared his throat, and I threw my own glare his way. "Technically, the laws of hospitality state that you must house and feed a visitor for three days and offer them no harm."

"Well, human law requires I report any unregistered fae."

Hortense crossed her arms. "Then report me."

I ground my teeth till I thought they might shatter. "Does the first visit count?"

Kai shook his head.

"Then this is day two." I pointed at Hortense. "You're out tomorrow."

"And nights." Kai cringed away from my glower, but continued. "Days and nights. She has until the following morning."

I tipped my chin, waiting, but he just stared at his shoes.

"I see." Hortense's voice was as chilly as the snow blowing around her ankles. Turning with the precision of a parade soldier, she disappeared.

Kai sighed. "You need to learn to control your temper. Insults like that won't be ignored once we get to court."

I rolled my neck and groaned. "I know, I know. But how can you be so"—I threw my hands wide—"grovelly to someone who just waltzes in and acts like they're in charge?"

"If you'd learned the court hierarchy, as you were instructed, you would know the answer to that."

I rubbed my temples, smearing my face with soot. "Just let me get through this stuff with James. Then I promise I'll focus on my studies."

"By the time you're satisfied with the situation, there might not be any time left."

I grimaced. "Don't remind me."

"It's my job."

"It's her job." I hooked a thumb toward the empty doorway. "One bitch is enough, thanks."

The tang was cherry red. "Do we need to continue the enchantment for this part, or can we stop now that the actual blade is done?"

Kai scratched his chin. "Hortense was not wrong about my lack of qualification in this area."

I rolled my eyes. "Better safe than sorry. Start the chant."

Chapter 19

I PULLED THE dull red blade from the forge and drove it into a bucket of sand. This was the last step, the last tempering, before the blade was done. I'd heated and cooled it three times since forging the tang, letting the evening air sap its heat, but this needed to be slower. The sand would insulate the metal from the night to prevent the rapid, uneven cooling that could create weaknesses in the blade.

Heat billowed into my face as I raked out the coals and sealed the vents, the last roar of a dying beast.

I turned a slow circle. Kai was long gone, talking about who knows what with Hortense while I cleaned up. The tools were back in their places. A soft breeze blew a dusting of snow across the floor that quickly became water and disappeared. I rubbed my exposed arms and reached for the hoodie draped over my stool. Now that the fire was out, night was taking over.

My eyelids drooped, my stomach growled. I'd burned more energy than I had to spare, and my tab had come due. I needed food and rest. With a last glance at the sand that hid my only hope of leveling the playing field, I flicked off the lights and made my way across the clearing. The sun was gone, the moon not yet up, but the snow glowed with an eerie radiance that reminded me of the moonlit rocks where I'd taken Sophie what seemed like a lifetime ago.

I shuddered and walked a little faster.

Hortense was sitting at the head of the kitchen table when I stepped inside, her face a neutral mask. Kai was bustling about the kitchen.

I smiled. "What's for dinner?"

"Spaghetti." Kai lifted a colander from the sink and a rain of starchy water dripped from the bottom.

I staggered to the bathroom to scrub the sweat and soot off my skin, threw on a fresh shirt, and called it good.

Hortense continued to stare impassively through dinner, chewing each delicately twisted bite of noodles for an eternity before lifting her fork again. Kai slurped dangling ends, leaving trails of sauce across his chin, and chased his side dish of peas around the edge of his plate.

I stifled a laugh and focused on shoveling food into my mouth until my stomach finally stopped rumbling—it took three servings and half a loaf of bread.

When the dishes were washed and put away, Hortense cleared her throat.

"We will begin with species classification." She folded her hands on the table. "I believe Kai has gone over some of this with you already."

I slumped in my seat. My body weighed a thousand pounds. I could barely keep my eyes open. Now that I was full, sleep was pulling me away from the waking world. But I only had a few weeks to learn enough fae facts to keep me alive at court, assuming I survived my assault on the vampire nest. Tired though I was, I didn't have time for sleep.

I yawned and propped my chin in my hands to keep from resting my head on the table. "We covered most of the sea, elemental, and enchantment fae."

She nodded. "Let's focus on those you're likely to meet in the Court of Enchantment."

I took a deep breath and recited, counting off on my fingers. "Pooka, nymph, eloko, sidhe, backoo, vaettir . . ." I rolled my eyes to the ceiling for inspiration. "Panotti, kitsune, um . . ."

Hortense pushed back from the table and rose in one fluid motion. "What would you call Malakai?"

I glanced at Kai's high cheekbones and steeply tapered ears. "Sidhe."

"And me?"

When I looked back, Hortense's glamour was gone. In place of the steely old lady was a nightmare designed to frighten children and adults alike. Stringy black hair hung to her waist. Long, thin fingers tapered to thick, black claws at the ends of arms that were little more than leathery skin the color of algae stretched over bones. Small, dark pupils stared from red-rimmed eyes and her lips parted over teeth like daggers.

I swallowed, hard. "Hag."

"River hag, to be precise. Also known as maras, fates, or bakhtak depending on where you find us."

"What do you prefer?"

One knobby, hunched shoulder lifted in a shrug. "They are human words. None are accurate."

I scowled. "Then why not teach me the fae words?"

"Because you have enough trouble remembering these, and they were made for your mouth." She sat back down, once more an old woman with pale, papery skin and white hair. "Besides, names have power, true names even more so."

I remembered the chill I'd felt when Malakai said my full name for the first time, and my stomach did a little flip.

"Has Malakai told you much about true names yet?"

I shook my head. "I know fae have names they don't share, and that if you know that name you can have power over the person."

"Not all fae have true names." She tucked a stray wisp of hair behind her glamoured ear. "It requires passing a . . . trial, of sorts. A rite of passage."

I cocked my head to one side. "Who takes it?"

"Those seeking power. Generally members of the court. It is not for the faint of heart, for not all who seek a true name will find one, and not all return from the search."

"Then why bother?"

She steepled her fingers. "Having a name makes you vulnerable, but it also makes you powerful, your magic stronger."

I glanced at my arm, fingers trailing over the fabric of my shirt. "Like the tattoo?"

Her head wobbled. "Yes and no." She placed both palms flat against the table. "Should you choose to take the test—"

"I won't."

A small smile curved at the edge of her lips. "We shall see."

"MMM, THREE-QUARTERS?" My eyes snapped open and scanned the darkness around my bed for Hortense's disapproving frown. Only shadows greeted me.

I rubbed one hand over my face and scraped my tongue on my teeth, trying to dislodge a flavor like something had crawled into the back of my throat and died. The blurry red numbers on the nightstand said it was 2:43 a.m.

What the hell? Hortense was a pain in my ass, but I wouldn't have thought she was startle-awake-nightmare-worthy. Especially considering how tired I was by the time my head hit the pillow. Then again, the image of her without glamour was—

I shuddered.

Something thumped, soft and distant, and a whisper drifted under my door.

My jaw tightened. It hadn't been the memory of Hortense's lessons that woke me. Every muscle in my body quivered as I strained to hear.

Another whisper, then soft footsteps in the hall. My door opened a fraction of an inch.

Rolling slowly to avoid the creak of springs, I set one foot on the floor.

"Alex?" Kai's voice was barely a breath, the half-imagined memory of a word until his face leaned past the door to give it substance. "Are you awake?"

His eyes met mine through gloom my mortal eyes should never have been able to pierce, and the tension left me with a sigh.

"I'll take that as a yes." He jerked his head toward the living room. "They're back."

I opened my mouth, and Kai's finger flew to his lips. Then he was pushed into the room with a grunt and Chase filled the doorway.

I stared for a full second, then folded over my knee to grip the bed as relief washed over me. They were all right. They—

My head jerked up. "Where's—"

A white leopard ducked through Chase's legs, a bright streak in the darkness. She leapt to the bed in a single bound. Her tongue was warm and wet against my cheek.

Laughing, I wrapped my arms around Jynx's neck and buried my face in spotted fur that smelled of dank and smoke.

"Where's my hug?" Chase settled at the end of the bed, starlight mapping his face in highlights and shadows.

Releasing Jynx, I leaned forward and punched Chase in the arm. "Where the hell have you been?"

He rubbed his arm with a scowl, and jerked his chin toward Jynx. "I've been chasing this little—"

"Shh." Kai glared around the room and pointed at the closed door. "She's still asleep."

The snow leopard shifted to a once more naked girl with bright eyes and hair that practically glowed. "Who?"

I tossed the edge of the blanket over her, and dropped a pillow in Chase's lap. "Hor—"

"Ah." Kai raised his hand to cut me off. "Don't."

"But—"

Kai shook his head. "She's a court tutor, here to oversee my training of Alex."

Chase's lips twisted as though he'd caught a taste of the flavor still contaminating my mouth. "Same one as before?"

Kai nodded.

Chase shifted his eyes to Jynx. "Keep it down."

Jynx crossed her arms over the comforter and stuck her lip out like a pouting two-year-old.

"So?" I leaned against the headboard and wrapped my arms around my knees. "How did it go?"

That brought a smile back to Jynx's face, and she leaned so close my eyes went out of focus trying to track her. "We found it." She bounced back to her side of the bed with a screech of springs and a giggle.

Chase rolled his eyes. "The nest wasn't missing."

"You made it inside?" I asked.

He gestured to Kai. "Probably the same way he did. Through the sewage drains and into the caverns past the cistern."

Kai nodded.

"There are a handful of ways in and out," Chase continued, "but that's the easiest." He frowned. "Or it used to be."

I stiffened. "Not anymore?"

Jynx shifted beside me, her chin tucked tight to her chest.

Chase crossed his arms. "Someone wasn't as quick as she thought."

"It's not my fault." She glared at Chase, then at Kai and me for good measure. "That guard shouldn't have been there."

Chase rolled his eyes. "Someone taking a smoke break found the same dark corner we did. They'll up security now that they've found the breach."

I winced, but kept my mouth shut.

Kai ran a hand through his hair. "You said there were a handful of ways."

"Most are out of the question. Either too far or too heavily guarded."

"So how do we get in?" I asked.

"*You* can take your pick, but I'd say the club is your best bet."

Cold tendrils spread through my chest. "You're not coming?"

Jynx's voice was barely a whisper. "Chase says we can't."

"I'll make you a map." Chase shook his head. "That's it."

"I thought—"

"The wolves aren't the only ones with other considerations." His eyes shifted to Jynx. "We can't go with you."

I looked at the teenager huddled on my bed, at the angry frown that creased her whole face and the eyes that wouldn't connect with anything.

"Okay." I pulled out the sketchbook I kept in my nightstand for recording stray creative thoughts and ideas that inevitably struck with the worst possible timing. "Let's get started on that map."

I YAWNED AND thumped my hand against the map on my knees. "That's really the most direct route?"

Chase shrugged. "If you want to avoid the sleeping chambers, that's your best bet."

"It's a labyrinth."

"It's designed to be."

I rubbed my temples and set the map aside. Pre-dawn light streaked my window, glinting off a thin layer of frost collected around the edges. Jynx was a ball of softly snoring fur, spots rising and falling with each breath.

"Did you actually *see* James?"

Chase shook his head. "We didn't risk the guard station, but there was talk. It seems James and one other person of note are being held in the lowest levels."

"Who?"

He shrugged. "I didn't ask."

"Aren't we getting a little ahead of ourselves?" Kai stretched, arching back until his spine popped. "I hate to be the damp blanket here, but—"

"Wet," I corrected.

He blinked. "What?"

"The phrase is wet blanket."

"That's what I said."

"You said damp."

"It means the same thing."

I shrugged. "But that's not how we say it."

He shook his head. "Fine. Not to be a *wet* blanket, but to even attempt this we need to get past the club's security system."

I turned to Chase. "Did you notice any magical alarms, or was it just the electronic kind?"

Chase looked at Kai. "The enchanter would know better than I."

"Vampires are illusionists," Kai said. "They don't have the skill to set up a barrier."

"What if they had a fae do it for them?"

Kai's head was already shaking. "They are abominations. No fae would help them."

I leaned back against the headboard. A thought had popped into my head, but it made my stomach churn.

"If it's just electronics, David might be able to bypass the system. He does run a security company after all." Even voicing the suggestion made me feel like a traitor. Could I really drag David into this, knowing what it might cost him? Could I risk one friend to save another?

"It'll be dangerous," Kai said. "Are you sure you want to include him?"

"No, but . . ." The flutter around my heart when I thought of James and what might be happening to him drowned out the sinking dread of what I was considering. "He's our best bet."

A muffled thump brought all our eyes to the door.

It was still closed.

"She's up." Kai's voice was even lower than the hushed tones we'd used all night.

Chase glanced at Jynx, then caught my eye.

"It would be best," he said, "if she did not know we were here."

"Agreed," Kai said. He stepped to the closed door and pressed an ear against it. "She's in the bathroom."

"Let me borrow your phone," I said. "I'm going to finish the knife this morning, so I'll call David from the studio, where Hortense won't overhear."

"And I'll head to town. There are a few things I need to pick up if we're going to pull this off." He pulled his phone out of a back pocket and tossed it on the bed, then slipped out the door and tugged it gently closed behind him.

Chase reached for Jynx, but I stopped him with a hand on his wrist. "Let her sleep."

He frowned. "We should leave until the house is clear."

"She'll be gone tomorrow. Just stay in my room until then."

With a fluid shrug, he melted into the familiar gray tabby and arched his back against my still extended hand. A deep purr resonated in his chest.

"You're welcome," I said, and slid off the bed.

Chapter 20

BRISK MORNING air froze my lungs, making each breath short and shallow as I trotted carefully across a layer of fresh frost. Kai's car was already gone. Lights sputtered to life in the studio as if the chill had seeped into the wires and slowed even the electricity. The forge slept in its scorched corner, coals cold and black in a bed of ash. The lingering smell of soot and smoke clung to the bricks and wafted around me when I passed, a lover's caress falling short. The bucket of sand sat undisturbed.

Licking my lips, I pressed my fingers into the cold grains. The sand was soft, and parted like water around my questing fingertips. My hand brushed something solid, and I gripped the steel tang.

Pulling the blade free, I brought it level with my face. The metal glowed a faint blue, like the light of a distant star barely discernible to the naked eye.

"I hope you're enough," I whispered.

Setting the knife on a workbench, I pulled out Kai's phone and huddled in the farthest corner of the one place I knew Hortense wouldn't venture.

"David? It's Alex."

A pause. "Whose phone is this?"

"Kai's. I . . . seem to have misplaced mine."

Another pause.

"David?"

"Are you in trouble?" His voice was tired, a little rough around the edges.

"Why would you ask that?"

"Because I know you."

I leaned one hip against a counter and tucked a strand of hair behind my ear. "I need help with a security system."

"Yours?"

"No."

He sighed. "What kind of security?"

"Cameras, locks, maybe an alarm. Probably an alarm. Hypothetically, could you turn those things off even if it wasn't your system?"

"Is this about James?"

My heart flip-flopped at his name. "Maybe."

"If you're asking if someone hacked his system, the answer is no. If you want to know if it *could* be done, then yeah. Hypothetically."

"Could you do it?"

Distant thumps like fingers drumming a hard surface. "Not me."

My hope plummeted. "Oh."

"If I needed a job like that, I'd go to the wizard."

I'd been hoping to keep Oz out of this. The last time I'd seen him, when he installed the security system on my property, he'd been acting weird. I liked Oz, I just wasn't one hundred percent sure I could trust him. But with David out of the picture, there was no other choice. "Do you know if the wizard's available today? Time's kind of a factor."

"I'll have him give you a call at this number."

"Thanks, David."

His sigh was so heavy I imagined I could feel the breeze against my cheek. "Be careful, Alex."

Dropping the phone in my pocket, I pulled down a piece of maple wood left over from a previous project and started sizing for a handle. I muttered while I worked, voicing the chant Kai and I repeated ad nauseam the day before. Probably overkill, but it couldn't hurt.

Three steel rivets pinned the handle in place, then it was on to the belt sander to smooth out the edges. Finally, I took the dull knife to the whetstone and worked it back and forth until it shone, reciting the whole time. Patches of sweat formed on my clothes while I worked, despite the cool of the room. When the cutting edge shimmered like light across an oil-slick, I smiled.

Wrapping the blade in a scrap of fabric, I placed it on the top shelf of my project cabinet and rested my forehead against the closed door, breathing in the sharp scent of metal dust.

This would work. It had to work.

Snapping the lights off, I headed back through the cold.

Hortense was sitting, stiff and straight, at the kitchen table, layers of impractical fabric cascading over the sides of her chair in a velvet waterfall. A white braid coiled around her head like a crown, or a sleeping snake. "If only you showed such diligence in your studies."

I kicked snow off the sneakers I wore in place of my ruined hiking boots and pulled the door shut behind me. "Good morning to you too."

"Morning was two hours ago." Hortense pointed to a pile of scrolls on the kitchen table. "Time to work."

I wrinkled my nose, but flopped into a chair on the far side of the table. I pushed the scrolls around like a child rearranging vegetables. "What's on the schedule today? Family history? Realm geography? Obscure trivia?"

Hortense lifted her chin. "Magic classification."

I propped my cheek on a fist. "Goody."

She smoothed a scroll between us as though I hadn't spoken. "I trust you know why the courts are divided?"

"They specialize in different kinds of magic." I waved a hand in the air. "Enchantment, and illusion, and such."

"That is correct."

I tried not to growl at the verbal pat on the head, but didn't quite manage it.

"The courts are the guardians of the schools of magic."

"So you can't learn magic without aligning with a court?"

"To borrow a phrase from your culture, why reinvent the wheel? The courts house all the accumulated magical knowledge of—"

Gangsta rap blared from the pocket of my hoodie, and we both jumped.

Pulling out Kai's phone, I retreated to the far side of the room and turned my back on Hortense's scowl. "Oz?"

"Hey Alex, David said to give you a call." His voice was strained.

Was it my imagination, or a holdover of the awkward way he avoided me the last time he was over? I bit my lip. Only one way to find out. "It's not really a phone conversation. Can you come over?"

"I'm doing an installation this morning, but I can stop by when it's done. Probably around three, maybe four."

"You can't get here any earlier? It's kind of an emergency."

"Sorry, but I'm already at the installation. I can't just cut and run."

I wanted to scream. It had taken James a day and a half to rescue me, and every second had felt like an eternity. He'd already been trapped twice that long. How long could a mind, even one as disciplined as James's, hold out?

"Fine," I gritted out. "But please hurry."

Hortense was still scowling when I turned back. "Your phone is a distraction. It should remain off during lessons."

I set the phone on the coffee table. "A friend is coming over this afternoon. You need not to be here when he arrives."

She bristled, eyes flashing like diamonds in the overhead light. "Does your rudeness know no bounds?"

"We're not at court yet. This is *my* house. Which means we play by *my* rules."

Long, thin fingers folded together on the table top. Her face was all hard lines and sharp edges draped with sagging skin. Her lips were tight and turned down at the corners. Somehow, her silence was worse than her scolding.

I returned to my seat, heat creeping up my cheeks. I was an angry teenager again, flapping my lips at authority.

"I shall endeavor to find alternate accommodations this afternoon. We will then establish a lesson schedule, which I expect you to adhere to."

I slouched under her steady gaze. Then the front door opened, and I cut my eyes to the promise of a distraction.

Kai stepped into the living room with a brown paper bag tucked under one arm. I wanted to jump up and interrogate him on what he'd managed to collect for our infiltration, but Hortense's scrutiny was heavy as her gaze shifted back and forth between us.

I gripped the sides of my seat and tried to keep my voice light. "Good shopping trip?"

He nodded. "Productive."

Hortense scowled and crossed her arms. "It's no wonder your pupil is lacking in education when her instructor is nowhere to be found."

Kai closed the door and bowed low. "I had business to attend to, and I knew Alex's educational needs would be well met while she was in your capable hands." He peeked up through the fall of his bangs, his eyes still glamoured to look human brown. "Did I miss something?"

"Alyssandra and I were just discussing arrangements for the future."

I cringed, and the little muscle under my eye jumped. "Please don't call me that."

Hortense leaned back in her chair. "Perhaps you understand more about names than I gave you credit for."

"I just don't like being called that. Everyone calls me Alex."

"Very well." She sniffed, and turned her attention back to Kai, around whose shoes the carpet was turning a darker shade thanks to the snow he'd tracked in. "This will be your last night on the couch. I will return regularly to assess and supplement your student's knowledge, but remember that it is upon *your* shoulders that her success or failure rests, not mine."

He bowed again, his face a solemn mask. "Understood."

"Now." She clapped her hands with the authority of a drill sergeant. "Back to work."

JYNX WAS A bouncing ball of energy, zipping from one end of the house to the other, hurdling furniture. Hortense's bag was still in Kai's room. She'd be back, but in the meantime the cats had the run of the place.

A lamp crashed to the floor.

"Do you mind?" I stooped to pick it up and a streak of speckled white flew over my back, the lightest brush of paws and razor claws skimming my neck.

"Your friend is here." Chase was stretched across the length of the couch, long limbs draping both ends. He yawned.

Straightening, I caught the crunch of gravel in the drive and smacked Chase's jean-clad leg. "Quick, change. Jynx, you need to hide again."

The snow leopard shifted to a girl mid-leap. "But I just got out!"

"And you'll be out again soon, but I can't explain a wild animal in my living room." I turned toward Kai's closed door and yelled, "Kai, Oz is here."

"I'll be out in a minute," he shouted back.

Jynx pointed an accusing finger at Chase. "He gets to stay."

"Go." I shooed her.

She stomped into my bedroom and slammed the door. An oil painting of a mountain meadow hanging in the hallway jumped, dipping to a wonky angle with the impact.

"You." I turned to Chase just as a knock sounded at the door and pitched my voice lower. "Change."

"Are you ashamed to be seen with me?"

"Now," I hissed.

Oz knocked again.

Chase smiled, but his eyes were emeralds, cold and hard. Rather than change, he rolled off the couch and sauntered down the hallway. He let himself into my room and closed the door, not quite as hard as Jynx had.

I shook my head. Chase's sense of humor was always a little odd, so I couldn't tell if his feelings were really hurt or if he was just teasing me. Even if he really was angry, sorting it out would have to wait.

I opened the door, and Oz stepped through with the gangling lope of someone whose body never grew out of its awkward teenage phase.

There was a smile on his lips, but too much tension in his face to pull it off. Short brown hair that matched the color of his eyes stuck off his head in fuzzy tufts.

I closed the door behind him. "How ya been, Oz?"

He scuffed his foot on the carpet, looking anywhere but at me. "Not bad."

The tightness in my chest ratcheted higher. Whatever had broken the easy association we'd had was still there, and I still had no clue what it was.

I swallowed the lump in my throat. "Want some water?"

"Yeah, thanks." He sat on the couch, long fingers dangling between his knees.

I trotted to the kitchen. This was a terrible idea. I couldn't tell him the truth, and we weren't good enough friends for him to do me a favor without question, if we were friends at all.

He rolled the glass I offered between his hands, staring into the swirl of ice and water.

Did he like ice? Guess I should have asked.

"So this security problem you've got?"

I chewed at a corner of my cheek. "It's . . . complicated."

Ice clinked in the glass when Oz set it down, still full. Condensation droplets had started to form, and the impact sent them racing toward the surface of the coffee table.

"I'm in."

I blinked, mesmerized by the swelling circle of moisture beading on the wood, then looked up. "What?"

"I'm in." His brown eyes stared into me with a focus that made me shift in my seat. The tension was still in his face, but the worried creases around his mouth and on his forehead had smoothed into tight lines of resolve.

It took three tries to get my voice to work. "You don't even know what—"

"Infiltrate a vampire nest to rescue your boyfriend."

My jaw dropped. The room faded out of focus, color leaching from the walls and furniture. Only Oz's eyes stayed clear, perfect pools of melted chocolate in a gray world.

"How did you—" I shook my head.

He leaned back with a sigh, pushing both hands along his scalp so his hair flattened and his already oversized ears seemed to stick out even more. "I haven't been entirely honest, Alex."

"About?"

"Me."

We stared at each other for the better part of a minute, statues carved in stone.

He blinked first.

"I'm a member of . . ." His gaze skittered across the floor, up the walls, and finally closed. "Marc's pack."

"Seriously?" I sank against the pillows like a deflated balloon. It was starting to feel like everyone I knew was some sort of paranatural or other. "That's why you were so weird the last time you were here. It was right after . . ."

"I'd never seen a survivor before, not one who didn't change."

It was my turn to avoid eye contact. "You know why?"

He nodded. "Small world, huh?"

"So it seems." We were silent for a moment. Then I smiled, and he smiled back. I gestured toward the back of the house. "I guess you know about the others then?"

His smile twisted into a self-satisfied smirk. "Two shifters, a sidhe, and a recently departed hag. Quite the rest stop you're running here. Soon you'll be able to give Crossroads a run for its money."

I tipped my head. "You know about Crossroads?"

"Sure. My band plays there from time to time."

"But it's a fae bar."

He shrugged. "So?"

"Don't werewolves," I waved a hand like I could catch the right words, "hate the fae?"

His smile turned sad, but didn't collapse entirely. "Most do. They claim the fae cursed us, but that's a pointless accusation. Just angry people looking for someone to blame for their pain. We are what we are. No changing that."

Kai stepped into the hall and came to stand beside the couch. He gave Oz a nod, then smiled at me. "This one's got a good head on his shoulders."

Chapter 21

JYNX STUCK HER head out of the bedroom wearing a simple white shift that shimmered like ocean waves under the sun. "If he knows we're here, I don't see why I have to stay locked up."

I waved her over. "No point now, I guess. Oz, this is Jynx. Jynx, Oz."

She plopped down next to him, shoulder to shoulder on the couch, and looked up with a smile. "I've seen you in Crossroads."

Oz nodded. "You're the one who's been hanging around Ava lately."

She blushed.

The door to my bedroom stayed open and empty. "Isn't Chase coming?" I asked.

Jynx wrinkled her nose. "He's pouting."

Lips pressed tight, I forced my eyes away from the empty doorway. Guess he hadn't been joking.

Kai rolled his eyes and took the remaining chair. "Now that we're all acquainted . . ." He caught my eye.

"Right," I said. "Down to business."

Jynx perked up, and Oz leaned forward over his knees. Everyone's eyes were on me with an intensity that made me want to squirm. I rubbed my hands over my thighs and focused on Oz, a new thought worming its way into my head. A thought that dropped the bottom out of my stomach, and my plan.

"You're a werewolf," I said dumbly.

Oz looked at the other two, then back at me. "I think we've covered that."

I shook my head. Oz being a werewolf simplified so many things. I didn't have to explain about James or the vampires, or even myself. But. . . . "You can't help."

Oz's expression crumpled, pinching around his eyes and mouth.

A growing pressure in my chest and throat made my voice thready. "Marc made it clear. The werewolves can't get involved."

Oz's knuckles turned white on his knees. "I'm here for myself." His voice was low and tight.

"But if the vampires find out a werewolf was involved, even if he wasn't acting on pack orders—"

"It'd be war," Kai finished.

Oz's jaw stiffened. His eyes grew distant. "What chance do you have without me?"

I shuddered at the echo of my own thoughts, and the hollow despair the answer brought. "None."

He nodded. "So I'm going."

The inside corner of my cheek was ragged from being gnawed, so I forced myself to stop. I couldn't get past the club security on my own. I didn't know anyone else capable of the job. With David out, there wasn't even anyone to ask. But Marc had made his stance clear.

A month ago, my head had been on the chopping block for learning the wolves' secret. Outsiders weren't tolerated, and it was Marc who argued my reprieve when we all still thought I was human. To act against his wishes, especially when the result could have such dire consequences for his pack. . . . Even if everything went well, my head would be back on that block.

No one moved while my emotions warred. Even Jynx sat stony-faced and silent. It was as though I'd stepped out of time.

Was James worth risking the wrath of the werewolves as well as the vampires? He'd lied to me. He was an immortal creature who fed on humans. He'd live forever while I grew old and died, and the whole time he'd be feeding off people like the dead escort in his apartment. He'd always be involved with people like Merak. . . . And if I didn't save him, he'd be at Merak's mercy forever. I shuddered and clamped a hand on the armrest as a wave of nausea washed over me. I knew all too well what Merak's tender mercies were like.

When I was able to pull in a full breath, I blinked, and moved my hand back to my lap.

James had sacrificed himself for me. However long his existence, he was willing to spend it as a prisoner to save me. He'd revealed his secret to protect me, even knowing what it could mean, knowing I might never forgive him. Whatever else happened between us, he was my friend.

"Just the club." I pinned Oz with my best "no-compromise" glare. "Once we've got access to the nest, you're out of there."

The corner of Oz's mouth rose in a half smile, but the crease in his forehead didn't ease. "I took the liberty of doing a little research. The club's security is on a closed network. I'll need to physically enter the building to hack it."

"I've got a nifty phase-shift patch that should do the trick." Kai grinned. "One of the baubles I picked up this morning."

Oz nodded. "Get us into the electrical closet of the club, and I can access security to the nest."

Jynx bounced in her seat. "And I can lead you to the dungeon."

I shook my head. "You're not going."

"But—" She gestured to Oz, marking the inequity.

My eyes cut to the empty bedroom doorway and darted away, but she caught it.

Her back straightened. "He's not in charge of me. And it's a maze down there. Even with the map, you'll have a hard time finding your way."

"That's a chance I'll have to take." I clenched my jaw and murmured, "I can't risk losing any more friends."

Jynx stiffened, then smiled.

I didn't bother to correct her. Whatever kept her out of harm's way.

Chase still hadn't come out of the bedroom.

"How long will it take to reach the cells?" Kai was slouched in his seat, legs stretched in front of him, ankles crossed.

"For you?" Jynx's lips pursed in a pretty pink pucker. "About an hour."

"And an hour out," I said. "Assuming we don't run into trouble. If we left right now, it would be full dark by the time we reached James."

"It would be suicide," Kai said.

I tapped my index finger against the armrest. "Can we get James's amulet back from Joe by tomorrow morning?"

"Doubtful."

"Then it has to be night anyway, for James's sake. No point in waiting."

I pushed to my feet, but Kai set a hand against my wrist.

"Night when we leave," he corrected. "We should go in during the day, when the club is empty and the vampires are asleep. We can time it so the sun is just setting when we come out."

I bunched my fists at the prospect of waiting through another night. If only we had one more hour of daylight. And who's to say an hour would make much difference in the lightless caves and dark hallways of Merak's nest anyway? Recalling the perpetual flicker of blue torches, I shivered and clamped my arms tight around a sudden chill. The dozens of semi-circles fading on my skin seemed to burn. "I think—"

Kai's phone rang. We all looked at it, vibrating across the coffee table like a lame wasp.

He picked it up, paled slightly, and handed it to me.

"We found Abernathy's housekeeper." Sarah's voice was stiff, and the edge of a growl crept into her words.

"Elsa? Where?"

She answered with a low rumble that made me want to curl into a ball to protect my vital organs. "Meet me in front of James's house. And bring your fae. Herrera's here too."

My mouth was open with unasked questions when she hung up. I wanted to get to James as soon as possible, but now I needed to know what had happened to Elsa, and what her fate might mean for James and me. I cut my eyes to Kai. "Fine, we'll go tomorrow.

"You need to shower." Oz was on his feet, pacing.

I blinked, handed Kai the phone, and stared at the agitated werewolf.

Oz's hair was plastered to the sides of his head by his grip. His eyes were wide. "I didn't think you'd see any other wolves so soon. Certainly not tonight."

Hands raised in a placating gesture, I stepped into his path. "Relax, Oz. I'm not gonna tell her you're helping me."

He shook his head. "Won't matter. She'll smell me on you. Then she'll tell Marc, and Marc will question me, and, and—"

"Take a breath." I rested my hand on his shoulder, but he jumped away as though my touch had burned. Realization settled in, and with it the familiar weight of keeping yet another secret.

"You need to take a shower," he repeated. "Scrub down with the strongest scented soap you have."

I pointed at Oz. "Meet us outside Abandon at two-thirty tomorrow." I hooked a thumb toward the door, and he followed it out.

"Kai, grab a bottle of cleaner from under the sink and wipe this place down. If Sarah or Marc stop by, I want their noses to burn with lemony freshness."

"What about me?" Jynx was on her feet.

I frowned. "Get your brother to stop sulking."

She collapsed back to the couch with a huff, and I headed for the shower. I didn't have time to stop for the gray tail lashing under my bed.

A BLACK SEDAN was parked across the street from James's curving drive. If the couple keeping watch behind its tinted windows were trying to keep a low profile, they were failing.

I swung my Jeep into the driveway and parked. "I'll keep their eyes on me. See what you can do about Herrera."

Kai nodded, slouching lower in his seat.

I stepped out of the Jeep and walked back to the waiting car.

Sarah stepped out of the passenger seat and closed her door.

Herrera came out of the driver's side and glared over the roof of the car. "What are you doing here?"

I cut my eyes to Sarah, standing bare-armed in a gray t-shirt and jeans, but at her slight head shake I folded my arms and focused on Herrera. "What are you?"

"Surveillance. Your turn."

Kai moved in the shadows behind Herrera.

I gestured to their car, the only one on the street. "Not exactly subtle."

"We weren't trying to be. Now answer the damn question."

Kai's hand settled on the side of Herrera's neck and the detective's eyes glazed over. His shoulders dropped two inches as the tension left them.

Sarah's nostrils flared, but she stepped around the car to help Kai maneuver Herrera back into his seat. Closing the door, they both joined me in the street. Sarah sniffed when she stepped up to me, and my heart surged. My sinuses stung with the mixture of soap and lotion I'd slathered on, burning out all other smells, but I didn't have the nose of a werewolf.

"We've got about half an hour," Kai said.

Sarah narrowed her eyes, but gestured to a flagstone path that led around the side of James's house. "Let's make the most of it."

I held in the sigh that tried to escape, and willed my heart to slow down. Smell wasn't the only thing that would tip Sarah off.

The bare branches of ash and birch trees reached between evergreen needles on the three acres behind James's house. Patches of crusted snow clung to the shadows, but most of the ground was clear, unable to hold its snowy blanket against the sun at this elevation. In another month it would look like the forest around my house, and my house would be buried in winter.

Twigs and needles snapped as I stepped off the path to follow Sarah. Kai brought up the rear. It took a moment to realize my footsteps were the only ones making noise. Sarah stalked forward, muscles tight, but nothing stirred at her passage. Behind me, Kai was a ghost gliding across undisturbed ground. I was a clumsy giant crashing along between them.

Sarah pulled up short and raised one fist, a combat leader directing her troops. "This is where we found the body."

Two feet away, a ribbon of thin yellow plastic whipped in the wind where it drooped between trees.

"How close do you have to be to do . . . whatever it is you do?"

Hugging myself against the cold both inside and out, I said, "Touching."

A muscle jumped in her jaw, but she nodded.

Without warning, she scooped me off my feet as though I weighed no more than a child.

"What are you—"

"Techs have already been through here. Can't have new footprints showing up if someone decides to do a second sweep."

Kai lifted the yellow barrier, and Sarah ducked under, holding me tight to her chest.

Even through the thick layers of my sweater and jacket, and the thin fabric of her shirt, heat radiated off Sarah like I was hugging a furnace. No wonder she didn't bother with a coat.

Sarah placed her feet with care, matching up to some map on the ground I couldn't see. Nothing stirred around us but wind in the pines and my own auburn waves.

A coppery scent pushed its way past the lavender and patchouli I'd doused myself with. I tipped my head away from Sarah and pulled in a deep breath. The rusty tang of blood slapped me in the face.

The woods were a patchwork of shadows, dark and darker, but I began to pick out pieces of the darkness that were out of place, deeper than a shadow should be. Streaks of pitch splattered the pale white of birch bark; scattered puddles reflected from matted leaves on the forest floor; the snow under a nearby fir was stained along one edge.

I shuddered, and huddled closer to Sarah's warmth.

"The body's gone. That gonna be a problem?"

Swallowing past the lump in my throat, I opened my mouth, then closed it and shook my head.

"What do you need?"

"What was she touching when she died?"

She tipped her chin to a nearby aspen tree. Four ragged streaks of dried blood ran down its trunk. There was an indent in the leaves at its base.

I took two shallow breaths and reached out a hand. Sarah stepped forward so my fingertips brushed against the matching streaks.

Focusing on my breath, I forgot about Sarah, and Kai, and the heat and cold pressed against me. I pushed James from my thoughts, though he clung to the fringes like a burr. When my mind was as clear as I could make it, I opened myself up to the emotions I'd been carefully keeping in check.

Fear poured through me. Fear that James was already dead. Fear that Sarah would discover Oz was helping me and put an end to the rescue mission before it even started. Fear of returning to that dark place where blue lights hid monsters in the shadows. Fear of having my freedom stripped away again. Fear of being helpless.

Tears trickled over my cheeks as my own cowardice washed over me. Then I licked my lips and shrank my world to the blood, and the bark, and the memories buried there.

Branches slapped my face, catching loose hair and fabric. My side ached, and I couldn't get more than a shallow breath, but still I ran. My ankle throbbed with every step, threatening to drop me into the frozen leaves that cut my bare feet like glass. Clouds of steam billowed from my nose and mouth, and every inhale froze my lungs for a split second.

Something moved to my right and slightly in front of me, curbing my flight. I might have been running in circles for all the progress I'd made toward safety.

I stumbled. My shoulder collided hard with a tree, but I rolled away and kept running, panting, living.

A cloud of something darker than the night brushed my side, and I clapped a shaking hand over fresh blood and a ragged tear in my nightgown. Something caught my hair, and I grabbed a nearby tree trunk as I turned to find bloody fingers twined in the graying brown strands I usually wore pinned up and out of the way.

A man stepped out of the shadows, but he wasn't a man. No one that fast could be. Two orbs of molten gold flashed in the light of a crescent moon. Fingers like blades streaked toward me, and fabric and flesh alike parted at their touch. Something warm and wet dribbled past my lips. My knees hit the frozen ground. Numbness spread through my stomach, my chest. The scent of bile and ruptured organs filled the still air.

Too long teeth glinted in the darkness, and something wrapped around my upper arm. A steel-toed boot connected with my sternum and pressed rough tree bark between my shoulder blades. Then he pulled, and the cold woods were washed out in white-hot pain.

Chapter 22

"YOU NEARLY suffocated her."

"She was screaming loud enough to wake the dead."

Something thudded, a car door maybe? And the voices cut off.

Vinyl creaked under my wet cheek, sticking when I tried to lift my head. I smelled pine, and metal, and the sickly-sweet scent of the raspberry slushy that soaked into my floor mats a month ago.

My joints flared with phantom pain when I sat up, and I patted myself down to confirm my limbs were intact.

I shook my head, mindful of the dizziness it caused. "That doesn't get any easier."

The Jeep's back door swung open, and Sarah's face filled the gap. A thin line of blood marred her lower lip and chin. "Back with us?"

"What happened to you?"

"You've got a mean right hook." She wiped the blood away with the back of her wrist, revealing whole, healthy skin, and stepped back from the door. Her super-fast werewolf healing had erased all evidence of the split lip I'd apparently given her.

Sliding to the opening, I huddled at the edge of the bench so I could include Kai in the conversation. He stood off to one side, hands thrust so deep in his pockets it seemed he'd split the seams.

"She wasn't just killed." My voice was raspy and dry, but images of Elsa's slim hand—the same one I'd shaken when I'd met her, the one she'd used to serve dinner and wave her feather duster—laying on the frozen ground too far to be a part of her, kept me talking. "She was torn apart." I mimed ripping, but my hands shook so hard I gave up and wrapped them around my middle, as though that closeness could make up for the image burned into my brain. "There was a man."

"Vampire," they said in unison.

Kai snorted. "A human couldn't tear someone apart, but a vampire could." He glanced to the side. "Or a werewolf."

"Or a fae," Sarah shot back, crossing her arms. "But the area smells of vampire. Did you see his face?"

I nodded. "It was dark, and Elsa couldn't see well, but yeah. He was taller than me . . . um, her." I recalled Elsa's gray eyes looking up at me from our relative heights. The petite woman couldn't have been more than five-foot-two. "Maybe five-seven, five-eight. Black or dark brown hair, yellowish skin, and—" I swallowed. "His eyes were gold."

Tight-lipped, the others absorbed my story, then looked at each other. Kai shook his head first.

Sarah followed suit with a sigh. "Not someone I've run across before, but I don't doubt he's one of Merak's."

Closing my eyes, I imagined the dull flicker of bluish torchlight in Merak's chamber. The pedestal was an island, but grinning faces peered from recesses around the room. A crescent burned on my arm, and I set a hand over it.

Bryce's teeth sank in, dark, bright eyes locked on mine the whole time. When he smiled, blood dribbled out the corners of his mouth.

I shivered like a junkie in withdrawal.

Moving my hand down to the softest part of my belly, I found another mark, and another memory. Polished bronze skin and straw-colored hair. That one hadn't watched me, just drank and drank until my limbs went numb. The next was Merak, no longer shrouded in illusion, but terrifying none the less. The echo of my desire to please the monster who hurt me twisted in my stomach and made me want to puke.

He was going to pay.

On my side, just above the last rib, I found Elsa's attacker, jaundiced and feral. He'd torn out a chunk of flesh the size of my thumb. Pinning my lower lip between my teeth, I ran my fingers over the thin scar that remained. Guess even faerie healing couldn't fill in the holes when someone took a bite out of me.

"He was there." My voice was a broken whisper. I wasn't even sure who I was talking to, me or them. I shook my head and raised my eyes. "He was with Merak in the nest."

Sarah's eyebrows rose and she looked me up and down, assessing. Her nostrils flared. I could only imagine what her werewolf nose was picking up. My magic? My fear? My anger? Wouldn't have to be a werewolf to notice those last two with the way I was shaking. I unclenched my fist and found four perfect, purple semicircles.

"You're really going after him?"

I dropped my eyes.

Sarah ran a hand over her tightly bound hair. "I can't help you."

"I know."

She shook her head. "You're crazy."

That made me smile.

"We need to go," Kai announced. "That partner of yours won't stay under much longer."

Sarah nodded. "Chances are we'll be knocking on your door tomorrow, and with the way she died . . ." She gestured over the roof of the car to the waiting woods.

"PTF's gonna get involved," I finished. "And O'Connell."

A grim nod and she walked away.

Kai climbed into the driver's seat, and I handed up the keys. Then I settled back on the worn fabric that smelled of me and metal and spilled slushy, and closed my eyes.

I WAS HALFWAY through my yoga routine when Kai stepped out of his bedroom in the morning.

He was wearing jeans, a t-shirt, and his human glamour. "They're here."

I emptied my lungs and straightened, feeling lightheaded. Then I grabbed a sweater off the hooks by the door and pulled it over my tank top. We'd anticipated this visit. We just needed to get through their questions and get them out as quickly as possible so we could focus on getting ready for our infiltration.

The doorbell rang.

I counted to five, then pulled the door open. Sarah was front and center on the porch, her skin glowing gold in the early morning sun. Herrera was beside her, and behind them both stood O'Connell, a smug smile on his thin lips. My jaw stiffened and my heart beat faster to keep up with my quicker breath.

"May we come in?" Sarah asked.

Nodding, I moved aside. The two officers stepped into my living room, followed by O'Connell. A muscle under my eye twitched. I closed the door gently behind him. I would have preferred to slam it in his face.

Sarah and Herrera took the chairs in the living room. O'Connell stood, spine rigid, just inside the door.

I strode through the room without making eye contact, and headed for the half-empty pot of black fuel in the kitchen. "You have more questions about James?"

"We found Elsa McNamara's body yesterday. She was ripped apart by some kind of creature." The smile on O'Connell's face didn't match his words.

Coffee sloshed as I gripped the mug and tried not to heave it at his misplaced grin. How could anyone be happy about—

Tearing flesh, ripping muscles, snapping bones. I slammed my mug on the counter and took a deep breath, hugging myself to make sure I was all there.

"Feeling guilty, Ms. Blackwood?"

Sarah growled, but it was a mostly human sound. "You just told her someone she knows has been torn to pieces. Who wouldn't find that upsetting?"

O'Connell snorted. "I'd think she'd be used to that kind of thing, considering the company she keeps."

My fingers turned to claws on the counter. I was glad we'd sent Chase and Jynx out of the house in anticipation of this visit. We'd also warned Hortense to steer clear today as we bundled her off with the first light of dawn, her three days of hospitality finally up. They were all far away, safe from the hunger in O'Connell's eyes. Kai, on the other hand, was leaning against the wall beside our little Christmas tree. His posture was relaxed, but the tension around his mouth and eyes made it a lie.

Pressing my temples, I rubbed small, soothing circles that did nothing to lessen the pressure behind my eyes and tried to imagine I'd just learned of Elsa's demise for the first time. "What do you mean creature? You don't know what did it?"

"Oh, I have my suspicions." O'Connell cut his eyes to Kai.

"We're still investigating," Herrera said. "But with the . . . unique circumstances of Ms. McNamara's death, the PTF will be taking the lead."

Pointing to O'Connell, I addressed Sarah and her partner. "Why him? He's hardly impartial. He flat-out said he was out to get me after what happened to his friend."

Herrera's hands went up in a placating gesture. "He's a senior PTF agent, and the one assigned to this case."

"But we're working it together," Sarah added. Her eyes were tight and fierce. She wasn't any happier being saddled with O'Connell than I was.

Scowling, I crossed my arms and sank into one corner of the couch. "Ask your questions."

O'Connell remained standing. "Where were you between midnight and three a.m. the night before last?"

"Here."

"Can anyone corroborate that?"

"Kai." And half a dozen other paranaturals O'Connell would love to get his hands on.

He snorted. "Anyone else?"

I shook my head.

"So no alibi."

Kai pushed off the wall. "Since when do fae not count as witnesses?"

"Since you're my prime suspect."

My teeth ached from clenching. "That's insane. He doesn't even have a motive."

"But you do," O'Connell said, nasal voice taunting. He pointed at me, "Motive," swung his finger to Kai, "means," and spread his hands to encompass us both, "opportunity."

My mouth dropped open and I stammered, "Why would I—" at the same time Sarah said, "That's going too far."

O'Connell shrugged. "There's an easy way to check."

My forehead puckered.

He turned to Kai. "Let me test your abilities."

I jumped to my feet, but Kai raised a hand to still me.

"My abilities were cataloged when I received my visa."

"Not thoroughly."

"I'm flattered you think so highly of me, but I assure you the abilities on my record are quite thorough. I haven't the strength to pull a woman limb from limb."

"Only one way to be certain."

Fists balled at my sides, I stepped in front of O'Connell to break his eye contact with Kai. "You're fishing. There's no reason to suspect Kai other than your personal dislike for me."

"He's not wrong." We all spun on Herrera, who flinched, but continued with a small shrug. "Testing would be the easiest way to clear him."

My mind flailed like a drowning swimmer. Hortense, Chase, and Jynx were unregistered. Bringing any of them into this would just make matters worse. The footage from my security cameras should prove Kai and I were at the house, but we wouldn't be the only ones on it. I clenched and unclenched my fists, weighing options.

There had to be footage with just us. If I could find it . . .

"My security cameras were recording the whole time. They can prove we were here."

O'Connell was already shaking his head. "Too easy to fake." He gestured to Kai. "Who's to say what I saw wasn't an illusion?"

"Kai doesn't do illusion magic. Even if he did, it doesn't—" I snapped my mouth shut. If O'Connell didn't know illusions didn't work on recording devices, I wasn't going to be the one to tell him.

O'Connell stepped around me so he was right in front of Kai. "One way or another, you're coming with me." He pulled a set of cuffs from his belt and dangled them from one finger. "If I have to come back with a warrant, you're gonna regret it."

Kai pursed his lips, eyes tracking the hypnotic swing of the steel bracelet. "I'll go."

I opened my mouth to argue, but Kai cut me off. "If I don't go now, he'll just come back later. Better to get it over with quickly." He gave me a meaningful look.

I gritted my teeth. If O'Connell came back later, we'd miss our window of opportunity to break into Abandon. And if we left before O'Connell got back, he could declare Kai a fugitive and revoke his visa.

I glared at O'Connell, wishing I could rip the smug smile off his face. "I'm going with him."

Sarah pushed to her feet. "We'll come too. To ensure there aren't any . . . irregularities in the testing."

Herrera shrugged and got to his feet. "I guess we'll meet you all at PTF headquarters."

PTF HEADQUARTERS was more modern-looking than I expected. It rose eight floors above us. Not a skyscraper to rival its towering neighbors in the heart of Denver, but enough to hold its own in LoDo at the edge of Confluence Park. Especially compared to the tents and shacks of the refugee shanty town stretched along the banks of the South Platte River.

A white metal façade waved over most of the PTF building's surface like giant sheets of corrugated tin, though I didn't doubt the metal was steel with a high iron content. Pretty and practical. Expertly trimmed hedges dotted river rock borders that ran along the paths, leading pedestrians in like the lights on a landing pad. Large, reflective windows encased the main entrance, funneling all inquiries into a two-story atrium. Walking toward the building felt like being pulled into a black hole.

O'Connell was waiting by the front door, having parked somewhere behind the building. Sarah and Herrera were nowhere to be seen, and the tightness in my chest increased, making it hard to breath. If they'd been called away . . .

I reached over and gripped Kai's hand. His stride was relaxed and even, but his fingers sang with tension. If we went in without backup, chances were he wasn't coming out.

"Didn't run off." O'Connell's hands were on his hips, and he raised his face to squint at the pale blue sky. "I'm surprised."

"I have nothing to hide from you," Kai said.

O'Connell spit to the side. "You people all got something to hide. All you do is hide, and lie, and scheme." He shook his head. "But that's gonna change. We've finally got someone who understands taking the reins."

The smile that spread across O'Connell's lips sent a shiver down my spine.

I pulled the collar of my jacket tighter. "Anderson may have won the election, but people won't let him—"

"The people have spoken. The fact that he won proves people don't want the fae around." He looked me up and down with a sneer. "Or the traitors who harbor them."

Sarah and Herrera parked beside my Jeep in the visitor lot and started up the sidewalk. The knots around my ribs loosened, if only just a little. I raised a hand to wave in greeting.

O'Connell leaned in so close a warm breath of coffee and gingivitis wafted past my face. "Come January, none of you will be safe."

My hand stuttered mid-wave, but I managed to complete the arc even as my blood first froze, then boiled. I lowered my arm in a stiff but controlled manner, careful to keep my fingers from curling. If I made a fist, it would be that much harder not to use it. I kept the tight smile on my face, and never took my eyes off Sarah.

"Everything okay here?" she asked as they stepped up.

"Of course," O'Connell said with a smooth smile as he pulled open one of the oversized glass doors. "Right this way."

The reception area was bright and airy. Modern chandeliers dangled on improbably long wires from a vaulted ceiling to supplement the cool morning light streaming through the glass enclosure. Utilitarian gray carpet speckled with maroon and indigo covered the floor, and blown-up abstract prints in matching colors hung from cream-colored walls. Overstuffed couches and chairs made clustered groups around polished wood tables topped with popular magazines. Only three seats were occupied.

A man with slim shoulders and slimmer fingers slouched behind a copy of *5280*—Denver's mile high magazine—in the farthest corner of the room. Closer, a heavy-set woman in a pink parka sat with her arm around the shoulders of a girl whose Hello Kitty snow boots dangled over the edge of her seat with the carefree swing of ignorance.

O'Connell stepped up to the curved white surface of the reception desk and flashed a badge at the pretty brunette behind it. "Three visitor badges and a testee bracelet.

The woman offered our group a warm smile, then turned to her computer and started typing. She wore scrubs in the same color scheme as the waiting room. A brass tag on her pocket said her name was Ruth. I sniffed, half expecting to catch the antiseptic smell of a hospital.

"Here you are." Three plastic lanyards slid across the countertop. Then Ruth held up a white plastic band between flame red nails. "Who's getting tested?"

Kai stepped forward. His stance was relaxed, the dishwater brown of his glamoured eyes half-lidded in disinterest, but sweat streaked his upper lip and his hand shook slightly when he held it out.

Ruth snapped the plastic band around his wrist. "Good luck," she said with a wink.

My fingers twitched with the desire to slap her. She probably assumed Kai was a potential halfer, and the only good luck would be to test negative for paranatural abilities.

O'Connell led our little group through a set of double doors to the right of the waiting room. Evenly spaced office doors lined the walls, each decorated with a plastic nameplate and a slim window that gave flashes of people pacing, talking on the phone, or, in one case, sleeping at her desk as we strolled past. A larger window offered up an oval conference table surrounded by tall black chairs. None of the seats were occupied.

The door at the far end of the hall was locked, and O'Connell swiped his ID to enter the new section. When the door fell closed behind us, it latched with the solid *thunk* of an iron bar sliding into place.

The air was noticeably cooler on this side of the door, and the wall-to-wall carpet was replaced by dark gray tiles that clicked and echoed with our passage. Doors continued to line the hall, all closed, but none of these bore placards and none had windows. The only distinctions were numbers on the frames. I rubbed my upper arms as we walked, our steps creating a staccato melody in the sterile corridor. How many of those doors had fae huddled behind them, waiting for testing, or deportation, or who knew what else. I was walking down death row with no idea if any of the cells held inmates.

Another locked door clanged open, but behind this one was a bank of elevators.

The five of us fit easily. The elevators were clearly designed to hold a gurney as well as people, and I wondered how many fae made this trip on their own two feet.

The elevator lurched into motion, dragging us down. I hadn't realized the building had a basement. It didn't seem prudent so close to a river, but the direction was undeniable. When the doors slid open, it was on white tiles and white walls. Overhead, lights alternated with black orbs that marked the ceiling tiles like cancerous lumps and recorded our every step. These halls seemed to have collected all the windows missing above.

Walls of glass broke the uniform white at even intervals, and behind each was a different nightmare. The first room was empty except for an operating table under a huge, adjustable lamp. Thick leather straps arced over the table where a person's waist, wrists, thighs, and ankles would be. One of the straps dangled loose, the end frayed as though someone had snapped the binding.

I'd heard stories of PTF tests, but never a first-hand account. People whispered about torture chambers and sound-proof rooms where no one could hear the screams. I'd tried not to think too much about it, but faced with the evidence, and the very real threat of being on the receiving side of those straps, I couldn't suppress the shudder that ripped through me.

Peace treaty or no, basic human rights didn't apply when the subjects weren't strictly human, and the situation would only get worse once Anderson took office. The rules regarding treatment of halfers were a little hazy, but I doubted being ninety percent human would save me from O'Connell if he found an excuse to test me.

A small glass tank sat on a pedestal in the middle of the second room. Inside, something that looked like a sea lion but was no larger than a chihuahua floated in greenish liquid. Electrodes, suctioned to the small creature, dangled colorful wires that draped the edge of the tank and snaked to a terminal where a woman with burnished red hair and skin that never saw the sun adjusted a set of dials.

A low rumble rolled out of Sarah's throat, and I set a hand on her shoulder. She bared teeth that were slightly too long for a human mouth, but I kept my hand in place and gave a small shake of my head. This was not the place for a werewolf to lose her temper.

She managed to seal her lips, but her muscles quivered under my hand.

Calming Sarah helped numb some of my own horror at our surroundings. So when O'Connell stopped in front of the door to the third room, I was able to meet his smile with a straight face.

"This is the advanced testing center," O'Connell explained. "We already know you're a fae. This will tell us what you can do."

He pushed the door open and motioned us inside, a butler welcoming us in.

Chapter 23

KAI STOOD ON A mat in the middle of the room wearing only the loose cotton pants O'Connell had provided. His feet were anchored to the ground with thick leather bands, like the one that had been snapped in the first room. Other bands held his wrists. He gripped padded handles attached to the enormous machine he was strapped into.

The woman from the second room joined us, introducing herself as a technician named Jen. She didn't offer the false smile of the receptionist, but her face held an easy calm that made me shudder. Who could keep their peace while hurting people?

Jen stuck electrodes to Kai's bare chest and back with practiced ease. She didn't even look him in the eye when she attached two pads to his temples. She moved as though she was handling a doll rather than a person.

"Jen's one of our best technicians," O'Connell said. "She's been doing this a long time."

O'Connell had shed his coat and was leaning against the mirrored window wall in his PTF uniform. Not the faerie riot gear with iron threads laced through the fabric, but something a cop might wear, with an emblem of authority embroidered on the breast. The fabric was thick and black, and a belt of anti-fae paraphernalia cinched his waist.

"Done." Jen plugged the last wire dangling from Kai into the back of a console, adjusted a dial, and stepped back.

O'Connell pushed off the wall. "We'll all need to step into the other room for the actual test."

He led the way through a side door set into another mirrored wall. Sarah and Herrera followed. They'd been tense but quiet through Kai's prep, huddling close as though waiting for an ambush. Sarah's nervousness made sense, but Herrera's surprised me.

I stepped up to Kai and set my hand on his bare shoulder. He was shaking.

I opened my mouth, but all that came to mind was, "It'll be okay." I wouldn't insult either of us with such a meaningless platitude. I squeezed his shoulder. "I won't let them hurt you."

The smile he forced was weak and wavered. "This test is designed to hurt." His eyes flicked up to the rubber-coated bars his hands were strapped to and the overhead tracks they would move along.

I licked dry lips.

"We won't do any permanent damage," Jen said. She lifted a clipboard and motioned me toward the open door.

I rested my forehead against Kai's and whispered, "I'm so sorry." Then I spun and trotted into the observation room.

Blinking in the sudden darkness of lights dimmed to the faintest glow, I went to stand beside Sarah. O'Connell was settled in one of the two seats. Jen shut the door and took the other. Through the window, we watched Kai, witnesses to his crucifixion.

Dark panels hummed under Jen's fingers and flared to life. A jagged line rose and fell on one monitor in what looked like the rhythm of a heart. Other lines jumped and dipped in no discernible pattern. More switches flipped, and the baselines looped on a monitor to one side.

Jen leaned toward a small microphone and pressed a button. "We're beginning the test."

The black and steel bars to which Kai's arms had been bound began to move, sliding along tracks in the ceiling. The dips and spikes of Kai's heart became more pronounced and crammed closer together, as though they could protect him by huddling in larger numbers.

I wiped sweaty palms on my jeans.

Kai gripped the wrapped handles to keep the pressure off his wrists as the bars pulled him to full extension and paused. Across the room and behind the glass, his chest rose and fell in too-fast breaths. Lines jumped on the monitors in the dim, cramped room.

Jen fiddled with more knobs, adjusted sliding switches, and pressed another button. The machine began to move again.

It was slower this time. So slow I couldn't see the difference until twenty seconds had passed. Kai's lips grew thin and pale. His eyes widened. His arms were taut lines to either side, and his knuckles were white on their grips. Then his heels lifted off the floor.

The monitors were frantic ribbons of colored lines bouncing across the screen.

I ground my teeth. "You're hurting him."

Jen glanced at the monitors. "He's within safe parameters."

I bunched my hands into the front of my jacket to keep them away from the hundreds of knobs, switches and buttons on the control panel.

I wouldn't know how to stop his pain even if I dared. I might accidentally kill him.

He was up on his tiptoes, chin tucked to his chest. His eyes were closed now, but his teeth were exposed, clenched to the breaking point. His body seemed to vibrate. Every muscle and tendon was visible beneath the smooth skin on his arms and torso, stretched thin and forced to the surface.

My own muscles strained with the need to act. To stop this. My jaw ached and my nostrils flared as I sucked air into my too-tight chest.

"Surely that's enough?" Herrera's voice seemed far away in the tiny space we shared, a cowardly whisper needing to escape but hoping not to draw attention.

"We have to push him to his limit," said O'Connell. He leaned back in his chair and laced his fingers behind his head. All that was missing was a bowl of popcorn. "Otherwise we won't know what he's truly capable of."

Kai's feet left the tiles. The monitors were nearly solid color, black spaces eaten by lines that strained to break their frame.

I hugged my shoulders and shivered, remembering Elsa, and how it felt to have my arm pulled from its socket.

When the straps around Kai's ankles pulled tight, he threw his head back and screamed. Galaxies of swirling pain opened wide and stared through the mirrored glass.

"Shut it off." The words slurred through my clenched teeth, but Jen nodded, wide eyes an inch from my own. I untangled my fist from the front of her shirt and she fell back into her chair. I didn't remember moving.

O'Connell was half out of his seat, but Sarah's hand on his shoulder kept him in place.

The machine relaxed, sliding back on its tracks until Kai's feet hit the ground.

I was out the door and halfway across the room when his knees buckled.

Sweat slicked his skin, thick and rank, but I tucked myself under his side and tried to take the weight off his still suspended arms.

"Get him out of this!"

Sarah and Jen each took a binding, Jen releasing the clasps with practiced ease while Sarah tore at the strap with a ferocity I feared might land her in a test of her own, but both restraints opened without incident.

Kai's weight settled fully on me, and I staggered.

Jen started pulling electrodes off his skin, leaving angry red welts in their place. Sarah attacked the straps still pinning Kai's feet to the floor.

When Kai was freed, Sarah and I lowered him onto his back. I cradled his head in my lap and grimaced at the rings of purple decorating the pale skin around his wrists. Tears burned behind my eyes.

O'Connell strolled out of the little control room and took up his earlier position, lounging against the mirrored wall with his arms and ankles crossed. His head was cocked to one side, as though he was working through a puzzle.

I glared until it felt like the pressure in my head might rupture something. How many tortures had he overseen? How many tests conducted just to satisfy his curiosity? How many excuses made to justify them?

Herrera finally emerged from the dark room behind the glass, pale as a bleached sheet and clutching the door frame for support.

I shifted my glare to Jen, who flinched. "Well? Did you get what you needed?"

She swallowed audibly, then dropped her eyes to the console Kai had been plugged into. "We know the limits of his strength." Her eyes cut to O'Connell, then dropped back to the panel. "Slightly above human, but—" She shook her head.

O'Connell's expression darkened, the victorious glint dying from his eyes. I breathed a sigh of relief.

Lowering my forehead to press it against the flushed, wet surface of Kai's, I whispered, "Let's go home."

Kai's lips twitched up at the corners, but he didn't open his eyes. "Please."

O'Connell pushed away from the wall. "He could have used a strengthening charm. Or had an accomplice."

"And if you find any evidence of that we'll bring him in again. Until then . . ." Sarah gently lifted one of Kai's arms and slid her own behind his back to lift him. "We're done here."

SLUSH AND GRAVEL skidded under the Jeep's wheels as we crawled back up the mountain. Kai was asleep in the passenger seat. He was back in his own clothes and slouched with his head rocking gently against the window, but lines of tension in his pale face made me wonder if his dreams had taken him back to that underground room.

I shook my head and pinned my eyes to the uneven road, pulling in a deep breath of the hot, static air blowing from the dash.

It had been a medieval dungeon down there, locking people away to be tortured for confessions. The Inquisition, the Salem witch trials, the McCarthy Communist scare. My knuckles turned white on the wheel. Humanity always fell into the same patterns of suspicion, fear, and violence.

Maybe becoming less human wasn't such a bad thing.

The area in front of my house was blissfully clear of vehicles save Kai's old Toyota. I pulled up as close to the porch as I could and sat for a moment, scanning the woods. Nothing moved but pine needles shaking in the breeze and a few winter birds scavenging for food.

I lifted my hand to Kai's shoulder, changed my mind, and gave his knee a shake until his eyelids fluttered open. "Home again, home again."

He murmured and wiped a hand over his face.

"How are you doing?"

He glanced down, and I followed his gaze to his wrist. The bruises were gone, healed by his fae blood. "Better."

"Will you—" I snapped my mouth closed and turned away, ashamed of my own selfishness.

"I'll be good to go. Just let me sleep till it's time to meet Oz."

I nodded and turned off the car. "Then let's get you to bed."

The air was a cold stab in my lungs when I opened the car door, and I hustled to unlock the house as Kai lowered himself carefully from the high seat. I was inside and kicking off my shoes before I looked up.

Hortense perched at the edge of one of my living room chairs, hands folded across her lap, eyes holding a calm disinterest.

Freezing with one shoe off and the other still on, I glanced around. No sign of Chase or Jynx. "I thought we agreed you'd stay away from the house today."

Kai cleared his throat behind me, and I stepped aside so he could shut out the cold.

"Put your shoe back on, Ms. Blackwood. We are going for a walk."

Shivering, I looked at Kai, then back to Hortense. "Kai needs—"

"He needs rest. Which is why you and I will hold our conversation out of his hearing." She shifted her gaze to Kai. "And beyond the range of temptation."

He raised both hands in surrender and slunk toward the hall. "Fine by me." His words were slightly slurred, as though he was already half-asleep. He cast one look at me over his shoulder, but I couldn't read his muddled expression. Then his door closed, and I was left alone with Hortense.

Smoothing the heavy fabric of her skirt, she rose and strode to the door, pausing beside me to put on an antique cloak of cream and crimson. As she spun the fabric over her shoulders I caught a whiff of cinnamon and the charged scent of ozone before a storm. She pulled open the door and stepped outside.

Sighing, I slipped my missing shoe back on and grabbed a scarf from the hooks by the door for a little extra warmth. Then I stepped onto the porch and pulled the gloves from my coat pocket, shivering as I tugged them into place over my fingers.

Hortense was halfway to the tree line when I stepped off the porch. I trotted to catch up, then fell in step with her easy stride.

Patches of brown needles and matted leaves peeked through the thin layer of winter. The snows had come late this year and hadn't hit critical mass yet. Soon, the frozen ground would disappear and I wouldn't see it again until spring.

"How do you get up here?" I gestured around us. "You don't have a car."

One corner of her mouth lifted. "I have my ways."

I curled my toes inside the thin protection of my sneakers to keep numbness at bay, and lamented again the loss of the boots now buried in the woods with the ashes of my gore-spattered clothes. "What did you want to talk about?"

"How do you feel about the fae?"

I pulled up short, but Hortense continued and I was forced to jog again. She took us through the trees as easily as strolling down a sidewalk, and it wasn't long before we reached a ridge that offered an overlook of the valley. We weren't high enough for a truly spectacular view, but we both pulled up in silent admiration.

"It's complicated." I kept my eyes on the distant horizon. "What do you think of humans?"

"You are not human."

"I'm not fae."

She sighed, and a cloud of breath billowed out to be snatched by a passing breeze. "You are . . . different."

I rubbed my gloved hands together, then dragged them up my arms and hugged myself tight. My own breath fogged the view in streams and bursts like a sputtering steam engine.

"Loyalty is an admirable trait," she said. "Though sometimes it makes us take foolish risks."

She spoke to the landscape, but her words made me tense like a deer blinded by headlights. Did she suspect what Kai and I were going to do? Would she try to stop us? I swallowed a dry lump in my throat.

She folded her gloved hands over her abdomen. "I need to make a report."

I tore my eyes from the horizon, focusing on the tutor's sharp profile. "About what?"

One eyebrow rose. "I will be back in three days, at which point I expect you to be more focused on your studies."

My cheeks warmed.

"In the meantime," she continued, "I have a practical assignment for you."

She reached beneath the folds of her cloak and pulled out a small, plain looking box.

I took a step back. "The last time I opened a box from a fae—" My thumb rubbed over the tattoo.

She smiled, a lifting of lips that didn't show her teeth but made her eyes spark in a way I hadn't thought them capable of. "This is not a gift. It's an assignment."

The box rested in the palm of one hand, and with the slim, gloved fingers of the other she lifted the lid. A leather cord pooled over black velvet, and from a simple bail hung the strangest pendant I'd ever seen. A variety of twigs bound together with green thread, or maybe tiny vines, dangled from the end of the necklace.

Pulling the odd jewelry out by the cord, Hortense tucked the box away and knelt, her knees crunching into snow at the base of a Douglas fir.

I crouched beside her, balancing on the balls of my feet.

"This is a charm for stealth. Something your fae blood doesn't seem to have given you."

My heart was racing. The timing was too perfect. She had to know what we were about to do. But how? We'd been so careful. Still, against all odds, it seemed she was actually going to *help*. Maybe we'd misjudged her.

She held out an empty hand, gesturing for one of mine. "To finish the charm, you must wrap it in silence."

"Silence?"

She set the twisted twigs in my hand and dropped the cord, then gestured to the snow beneath us. "Nothing coats the land in silence better than fresh snow."

I snorted. "This is hardly fresh."

"But it's what we have." Fingers clasped in her lap once more, she looked like she was waiting for someone to break out the picnic on a summer afternoon.

"What do you want me to do?"

"Finish the charm."

I rolled my eyes, but Hortense just smiled.

Brushing some snow away to reveal hard dirt, I plopped my butt on the ground and crossed my legs. Silence, huh?

I scooped up a handful of snow.

"You need connection for your magic to work."

I glanced at Hortense, at my gloved hands, at the snow, and let my hands fall with a groan. One at a time, I tugged the soft, warm gloves off my hands and tucked them back in my pocket.

The leather was cold, and I let it dangle over the side of my palm so I didn't have to hold it. The twigs were rough, catching my skin with invisible barbs.

Clenching my teeth, I drove my free hand into the snow and clapped the numbing scoop over the talisman.

Silence. Silence. Fields of fresh snow in the morning, unbroken by tracks, and the heavy weight of nothing in my ears.

I cupped and twisted my hands like I was making a snowball, the little bundle cocooned in its center.

Ice on a lake, so thick you could cross without a single creak. Big, fluffy snowflakes filling the sky, muffling the world. Silence. Silence.

"Now seal it." Hortense's voice was a whisper in my head that came from everywhere and nowhere. "Make it whole. Make it strong."

I pressed my hands together, thinking of the heat and pressure that made diamonds of simple carbon. Warmth bloomed against my palms. My fingers tingled as feeling returned, aching with each throb of my heart. The snow no longer gave under my hands, but I pressed harder, locking it all together until my palms felt bruised. Then I opened my eyes, unsure when I'd closed them.

In my palm sat a crystal egg. Dark streaks marked its milky white surface where the sticks buried at its heart came close to the surface. The silver bail was half-entombed, but the cord still slid freely.

"And now," Hortense lifted the necklace and reached around me to secure the clasp, "you will not trample through the forest like a wounded moose."

The egg thumped against my sternum, heavy and solid.

I traced the smooth shape with a once more numb finger. "This will keep me from being heard?"

She tipped her head and pursed her lips. "It will not make you invisible. It will not prevent someone from hearing you kick down a door." She sighed and pushed to her feet. "It may mask the sound of your racing heart and the smell of your fear."

I closed my fingers over the charm. "Why are you doing this?"

She sniffed, but I caught that twinkle in her eye again, just as she turned away. "You may be rude and rash, but you are a lady of the court. And as I said, loyalty is admirable . . . even if misplaced."

She twitched her skirts, shaking loose a shower of pine needles. "I will be back in three days. I expect to find you fit and ready to learn." Then she stepped between two trees and disappeared.

I blinked at the spot where she should have been, then let my eyes focus past it. The valley wound away below, a snaking path back to civilization. I smiled and cradled my new charm. The old bat wasn't so bad after all.

A breeze tugged my hair, twisting it in knots. I pulled my scarf tighter with hands that wouldn't close properly. I couldn't feel my feet.

"Hang on, James. I'm coming."

Chapter 24

GNAWING ON A ragged edge of fingernail, I stared through my windshield at the decrepit husk of worship crouched at the end of the street. My view was unobstructed, the club's nighttime traffic a distant memory in the light of day.

"I should call Maggie."

Kai twisted in his seat, wielding a half-devoured candy bar, his third since we'd parked. The ghostly pallor had faded, and his cheeks held a pinkish glow beneath the shadow of pain that still lingered in his eyes. He wasn't in top condition, but a few hours of rest and enough sugar to put me in a coma had made a world of difference.

"Why would you want to call your boss right now?"

"Not just my boss," I corrected. "My friend."

He shrugged, tracking a plastic bag as it danced across the empty street. "Why call her?"

"If things go south . . ." I let my head fall against the headrest. "I'm supposed to work tomorrow."

"You're going to tell her what we're doing?"

I slid my thumb along the not entirely smooth wood of my knife handle. I'd only had time for one coat of finish. I shook my head. "That would just worry her more."

"You should give up that job. It's an unnecessary complication."

I dropped my eyes to the leather scabbard Kai had lent me, tracing the tooling with a fingertip.

The bookstore was one of the only normal things left in my life. My house had been invaded by fae, my solitude a distant memory. My art had become another form of magic practice, and my boyfriend sucked the life out of people to survive. The bookstore was boring, and safe, and the last wholly human thing in my life. The bookstore . . . and Maggie.

Even my friendship with David had changed since October, since he'd caught even a glimpse of my new life—shooting lessons instead of movie nights, conversations about drugs and murder instead of fashion follies and bad jokes. Maggie was the only one I could still pretend with, and I needed that. I needed to believe I could still feel human.

"If I don't make it out—"

"You will."

I rolled my face toward the window to watch the fluffy white flakes just starting to fall from the slate gray sky and tried not to think about tomorrow, but I couldn't get Maggie out of my head. I'd kept her in the dark to protect her. And, if I was being honest, to protect myself, to preserve the illusion that I could still have a human life. But if something went wrong here . . .

I tipped my chin toward the glove box. "Hand me the notebook in there, would you?"

Stuffing the last bite of candy bar into his mouth, Kai rifled through crumpled napkins and old receipts, finally pulling free a small sketchpad with a yellow cover, a pencil shoved through the rings of its binding. He gave me a curious look, but handed it over.

I flipped past half-formed doodles and sketches of people and places until I found a blank page. Pulling the pencil free, I took a deep breath, and started writing.

Kai crossed his arms and stretched to see my paper. "A confession?"

"An explanation, in case I don't survive this."

"A dangerous thing. I can think of at least one PTF agent who dreams about that kind of evidence."

Folding the letter twice, I scrawled Maggie's name on the front and tucked it back into the notebook. "If I make it out, I can get rid of it. If I don't . . ." I shrugged. "It won't matter who has what evidence against me then." *And Maggie will have the truth.*

The hum of the heater and the gentle vibration of the idling Jeep blended with the thick silence of the afternoon. If not for the pins and needles of anticipation sparking my nerves, I might have closed my eyes. As it was, I drummed my fingers and flicked my gaze around the deserted club and surrounding area.

A cobalt blue Tesla Model S rounded the corner and parked across the street from us. The driver door opened and a man stepped out. He wore a calf-length wool coat, an olive green scarf wrapped around the lower half of his face, mirrored glasses, and a ski cap pulled down over his ears, but the gangly frame was all Oz.

Hefting a padded backpack over one shoulder, he trotted across the white-specked asphalt and slid into the back seat of my Jeep. "Sorry I'm late."

Twisting to face him, I asked, "Any trouble getting away?"

"Nah. Marc thinks I'm on a tech job," he shrugged, "which is sorta true."

Kai chuckled.

I frowned. The idea of going behind Marc's back still made me queasy, but if it got James out. . . . "Ready to go?"

The three of us strolled through the dilapidated neighborhood as though we belonged there. I was feeling particularly gangster thanks to the gun concealed illegally on the back of my belt. The extra weight made my cargo pants sag low on my hips, ragged bottoms obscuring the mud-encrusted sneakers I'd been wearing since I lost my hiking boots. The tip of my knife's scabbard peeked past the bottom edge of my jacket, and I pulled the hem to keep it covered. Kai slouched along with his hands in his pockets, chin burrowed in the collar of his coat. Oz must have been sweating under his layers, but he hunched his shoulders and stalked alongside me in grim silence. Every now and then he'd lift his nose from the knit scarf obscuring his face and take a quick sniff.

"Any vampires?" I whispered.

He shook his head.

We rounded the side of the church-turned-club and found an updated electrical box with enough juice flowing through it to support a small city. There was also a backup generator in a steel cage with a thick black cable snaking into the building. My first thought had been to cut the power, but Oz assured me that was an easy way to let the vampires know we were there. What we needed was finesse.

We continued past the tempting wires and around another corner. The bricks on the back section of wall sported graffiti in a wide array of colors and styles. Oz twitched his head toward a pole-mounted camera at one end of the building.

Taking a deep breath, Kai reached into his pocket and retrieved a tiny ball of white fluff. He held it behind his back while we walked, shielding it from view, and muttered a chant under his breath that mixed with the rising wind. The snow around us stopped falling, hung motionless for a split second, then whirled and whipped toward the camera in a concentrated blizzard.

Kai opened his hand and the white puff blew up and away to lodge in front of the camera's lens, just a drift of misplaced snow. Nothing to make a mortal suspicious.

Oz pulled a set of blueprints out of his bag, checked them against the wall we huddled beside, and stuffed them away again. Then he tapped a section of brick and took a step back.

Rubbing my gloved hands together, I shifted from foot to foot and prayed for luck from any god who'd listen.

Kai licked his lips, then wiped the chapped skin with the back of his wrist, dropped to his knees on the frozen ground in front of the indicated bricks, and pulled four clear patches of plastic from his back pocket. I still found it hard to believe those stickers could shift a section of reality partway into the rift between realms. Kai assured me solid objects, like us, would be able to pass through, but the wall would appear whole, an important detail since most illusions couldn't trick a security camera.

He pressed the patches to the wall about two feet apart to create a square. Then he bowed his head and started a new chant.

With his hood up and Latin-esque words tumbling from his lips, he reminded me of the chanting monks from a Monty Python skit I'd seen years ago. I started to giggle.

Oz shot me a strange look, so I clamped a hand over my mouth and shook my head to clear the thought.

Just nerves. Adrenaline looking for a way out.

Taking a deep breath, I brought my focus back to Kai.

The bricks between the stickers were dimmer than the others, like a shadow had fallen across the wall just in that space.

I glanced at the camera behind us. The fake snow was still in place. Kai had promised two minutes before it blew away with the evidence of our tampering. We had to be inside by then.

Oz shrugged his pack higher on his shoulder. "Tick tock, man."

Kai's voice wavered, but he continued his chant.

My fingers were itching to do more than drum my leg, so I shoved them in my pockets to keep them still.

The bricks were hazy around the edges, a photo out of focus. Then they flickered, and the solid beige bricks streaked with graffiti were back in place. Kai sat back on his heels with a sigh, arms loose at his sides.

"Well?" I asked.

He nodded.

Oz pushed past Kai, ducking to pass through the section of bricks framed by the phase patches. When he reached the wall, his torso, backpack, and finally legs disappeared through seemingly solid brick.

Smiling, I offered Kai a hand.

He waved it off and crawled through the hole. I followed after.

My nose bumped into Kai's leg, or maybe it was Oz's, impossible to tell in the tiny room we crammed into. I blinked a couple times in the dim interior and pushed to my feet. Light trickled in from the open ceiling to show wooden lattice encasing three sides of the confessional-turned-make-out-closet. Stale sweat and mingled perfumes burned my sinuses.

I'd wanted to phase straight into the electrical closet, but Oz was worried we might compromise something on the far side of the wall and trip an alarm. So we'd chosen the cover of the confessional as our point of entry.

I backed away from the walls and stepped on someone's foot. Then Oz pushed open the door to the club proper. I stepped out behind him and took a deep breath.

The stench of sweat was still there, but thinner. The strobing lights of the night were gone and only pale, colored streaks of stained glass broke the gloom. The bone-jarring beat was also absent. Silence filled the vaulted ceilings and transformed the enormous room back into the sacred space it once was, a thin veneer that would crack when the sun set.

Oz signaled us forward like the commander in a soldier movie and led the way down one of the shadowed aisles that lined the room. I hugged the wall well back from the arched openings that might expose me, and tried to ignore the prickly itch of the hairs on the back of my neck. There was hardly any distance between the confessional and the electrical closet, but every step felt like crossing an open field under the noon-day sun.

The air was barely warmer inside the club than it had been on the street. I hugged my torso and clenched my jaw tight to keep it from chattering. My shoes clomped softly on polished wood as we skulked forward, and I gripped Hortense's silence charm, praying it was working.

Oz picked the deadbolt to the closet. The door groaned open. I froze, holding my breath. Silence pressed against me, countered only by my pounding pulse. Nothing moved.

Oz swung the door wider and gave a soft whistle that rang like a freight train in my straining ears. Stepping into a space only slightly larger than the re-purposed confessional, I motioned Kai through and pulled the door closed.

Colored cables snaked over one wall. The organic odor of active bodies was replaced by the charged scent of static and insulating rubber. Oz dropped, cross-legged, to the floor and slid a laptop out of his bag. Plugging a thin black wire into the side of his computer, he hunted for a place to attach the other end. "Let's see what we're dealing with." He found an open port and stabbed the end of his cable into the enemy system.

Oz's fingers flew, a blur of motion, and strings of gibberish flowed across his screen, foreign words punctuated by brackets, slashes, stars, and symbols I'd never seen before. I leaned in, squinting, until my face hovered above his shoulder like a second head.

"This is gonna take a minute." He turned and our noses brushed.

I jerked straight and took a step back.

He smiled and turned back to his commands.

There wasn't space to pace. Kai slouched against the door, arms crossed, eyes half closed. The hilt of his katana peeked past the parted front of his long coat, an eight inch dagger was strapped to the opposite thigh, and leather bracers showed at his wrists.

How could he be so calm?

I bobbed on the balls of my feet, chewed my cuticles, tightened the bun that kept my hair from flying free, and picked at the edge of the chain mail choker Kai had insisted I wear.

I'd just crouched to tighten the laces on my shoe when Oz threw his hands in the air with a whoop.

"Done."

I looked from the impenetrable wall of code on the laptop screen to the wall of plugs and cables, and back. "Are you sure?"

He disconnected his laptop's umbilical and snapped the lid shut with a self-satisfied smile. "You can't tell the difference here, but in the security control room—" His smile got wider. "Actually, they can't tell the difference there either. That's kinda the point."

He stuffed the cord and laptop back in his bag and zipped it closed. "The door to the nest tunnels is unlocked and the security feed is on a loop. Whatever daytime desk-jockey they've got on security won't have any clue we're here."

I wrapped my arms around Oz's neck, startling a grunt out of him. "Thanks, Oz." I took a step back. "Now get out of here."

He pulled his backpack onto one shoulder and shook his head. "Not gonna happen."

I blinked, opened my mouth, blinked again.

"I'm coming with you."

"The hell you are." My voice, raised above the whispers we'd been using, bounced around the small room and slammed into me like a slap. I snapped my mouth closed.

We all waited a breath. Kai was off the wall now, hands hovering at the ready, watching the door he'd been using as a prop.

When nothing came through, he glared at me over his shoulder.

I turned back to Oz. "You can't come."

"It's my fault Sophie got out."

I shook my head. My mouth was a desert, my mind a storm.

"I was there the night she called you. I only overheard the last part of the conversation, but it was clear she was planning to sneak out." He shook his head and tightened his grip on the backpack strap until his knuckles turned white. "I should have stopped her."

"Why didn't you?" This time my whisper was a broken rasp, barely audible.

"Not dominant enough," guessed Kai.

Oz hunched his shoulders and nodded.

I frowned. I was going to have permanent wrinkles before I hit thirty.

"I'm pretty low in the pack," Oz said. "Never was much for physical confrontation, and well, that's pretty much all the hierarchy is based on."

"So you weren't strong enough to stop her," I said. "Why not go to Marc?"

"I did, as soon as I could, but——" He studied the worn sneakers on his feet. "When Marc found Sophie outside the club, you were already gone."

I stepped back until my hands found the wall behind me.

Big brown eyes like pools of melted chocolate peeked up past the lower edge of Oz's green ski cap. "I'm so sorry, Alex." The eyes closed. "It's all my fault."

I took a deep breath. "You screwed up."

Oz cringed, bracing for an impact.

"But what happened to me, and to James, isn't your fault."

His jaw tightened. "I'm still coming."

"Marc said no."

"Marc's not here. And you can't stop me."

"So much for submissive," Kai grumbled. "We're burning daylight here folks."

Oz and I faced off, eye to eye. He wasn't going to back down, and Kai was right, we were wasting time.

"Fine," I huffed, yanking the door open.

THE TUNNELS WERE just as dark as I remembered, until Kai summoned a dim ball of light to hover above his outstretched palm. The illumination barely reached the walls on either side and a few feet of path in front of us. It never touched the ceiling. Kai led the way, glowing orb in one hand, map in the other. I took the middle, Oz brought up the rear.

Much as I hated him being there and dreaded what Marc would do when we got out, assuming we got out, it was good to have a friend at my back as I slunk down the tunnels after Kai. Memories of my last trip into that darkness pressed against me, and I had to remind myself I was making the journey on my own two feet this time, not draped over Bryce's shoulder. Still, four points of pain dug into each of my palms, and my breath came in quick, shallow gulps.

The tunnel changed quickly from panels to concrete to raw rock braced with intermittent arches of thick, dark wood. The air grew colder with each step, and the scent of mildew and raw earth clung to everything. Every now and then I caught sight of a thin wire snaking along the wall or stringing over the splintered wood of a decaying arch.

Stones crunched under my feet, but the sound didn't travel. I squeezed the talisman dangling from my neck. Kai moved like a ghost in front of me, and Oz was a shadow behind.

Kai snuffed the light between his fingers without warning, and I stumbled into his back. He pressed me to the wall.

Holding my breath, I strained to hear anything past the rushing in my ears, to catch even a glimpse in the ink that pressed against my eyes and suffocated me. My hands started to shake and I clamped them against my thighs, digging fingers into flesh to anchor myself.

Something scuffed in the tunnels ahead, and I caught a faint whiff of decay that made my nose wrinkle.

Kai's arm remained stretched in front of me, a statue pinning me to the wall. I couldn't sense Oz at all.

Every hair on my body stood at high alert. My nerves twitched in anticipation. My skin itched. I pulled a thin stream of air in through my nose and forced it into lungs that had forgotten how to expand. Every passing second twisted my muscles tighter, like a spring about to snap.

Then Kai's arm fell away, and his dim light pierced the darkness once more.

I cringed away from the sudden light, blinking. When my vision adjusted, I turned to Kai, but he beat me to the punch.

"Just a low level grunt," he whispered.

Then we were moving again, down a set of slime-slick stairs that clung to the wall of a cavern without end—at least none that could be seen with our tiny sphere of light. At the bottom was a lake of smooth black glass. Two feet of shore hugged the edge, and we followed it around the room. Distant drips punctuated our progress with staccato splashes.

"I never imagined there were caves like this beneath the city," I whispered.

"There might not be." Kai held his light over the water, squinting into the distance. "Not everything we see down here will be real."

I shivered. "Can't you tell?"

He shook his head. "Not without wasting time we don't have."

At the far end of the cave, several dark arches broke the surface of the wall. Kai checked our map, then led us through the second from the right.

The tunnel was narrow. Dirt and rock pressed in above, and below, and on all sides until I felt like the earth was burying me alive. My skin grew slick and clammy. Kai's back hunched ahead of me, and I focused on his bobbing form as I ducked to keep from scraping my head on the encroaching ceiling. Jagged stones snagged my clothes and scraped my skin.

I folded into a half-crouched shuffle, and my back and knees began to ache. Surely this couldn't be the path? Then again, would a cat have noticed the too-close walls when scouting the place? I swallowed a thick wad that tasted like bile and prayed Jynx and Chase hadn't forgotten the size of a human when making our map.

My knees were nearly pressed to my chest when I reached for Kai's back with a shaking hand. "Maybe we should turn—"

But Kai wasn't there.

I pitched forward onto hands and knees, sharp rocks biting my palms. A pit of endless black yawned around me, and the sudden absence of walls made me shiver.

"Careful." Kai set a steadying hand on my shoulder and helped me to my feet.

Kicking a pebble over the edge of the thin shelf we crowded onto, I waited. . . . And waited.

"Where's the bottom?"

The light bounced when Kai shrugged. "Let's hope we don't find out."

"We have to cross that?" Oz was crouched on my right, pressed tight against my leg, and I followed his gaze to a strip of black rock that stretched over the gap like an obsidian thread.

My mouth went dry.

"That's what the map says," Kai confirmed.

I clenched my fists. "Remind me to kill Chase when we get home."

Oz looked up at me, a little green around the edges. Healing super-fast didn't make pain hurt any less, and a fall from that height . . .

I turned to Kai. "Let's get this over with."

He held the light high and started across the stone bridge.

The rock was hard and smooth, and barely the width of my foot. I shuffled forward in the wavering light, sliding my sneakers over the surface. Kai strode across like a tightrope walker, pausing every now and then to glance over his shoulder and wait for me to close the distance between us.

A low moan brought my attention around to Oz, a flickering shadow too far behind me. He was crouched on the beam, hands tight on the stone in front of him. His eyes were scrunched shut.

"Oz?" My whisper bounced crazily around the cave.

Holding a hand up for Kai to wait, I shuffled a few steps back the way I'd come. I was almost directly over the middle of the pit.

"Oz, what's the matter?"

He didn't move.

"Are you hurt?" I inched a little closer.

My shadow fell over him, erasing the path between us.

"Oz?"

"Sorry." His voice was a strained thread. "I . . ." He swallowed. "Heights."

I leaned closer, spreading my arms wide when my balance shifted. "You're afraid of heights?"

One pale hand shot out and gripped my wrist with bone-crushing strength. I cried out, pinwheeling my other arm. One foot came off the bridge.

The light bobbed behind me.

"Oz!" I braced against my trapped arm and got my foot back on the stone. "Pull it together."

Wide brown eyes flickered in the dancing light, bright with tears. "I'm sorry." He let go of my wrist. "I thought I could do it."

I glanced over my shoulder. Kai was trotting toward us, making the light bounce and sway. Then I turned back to the werewolf huddled at my feet, panting like there wasn't enough air in the world, and my foot slipped.

Oz's fingers clutched my sleeve and the sound of tearing fabric filled my ears. I opened my mouth, but I'd left my breath behind on the bridge. Fingers straining toward the shrinking light, I fell into darkness.

Chapter 25

PAIN EXPLODED along my ribs, and sandpaper rocks scraped my side where my shirt peeled up. Then I was rolling. The light disappeared, and with it any sense of direction. I tumbled up, down, sideways, ricocheting off walls, curling tighter and tighter as I barreled through a dizzying series of chutes, my senses as lost as my friends. One wrist banged against a jutting stone, and a fresh wave of pain washed through me. I scrunched my eyes tight against the darkness and held my breath, willing the hellish ride to end, terrified what that end might bring.

The chute fell away, and my stomach went with it. I was once more tumbling through space.

Something solid met me on an inhale and knocked the air from my battered body. Scrapes and bruises flared in a chorus of complaints while I writhed, helpless, on the cold, hard ground.

I strained to hear, to see, to feel anything besides pain and the press of gravel. My senses reeled, coming slowly back online like Magpie's old computer when it was forced to reboot.

No shouts. No hands grabbed me from the darkness. No running feet. Wherever I'd landed, I hadn't raised an alarm. Yet.

I took a shaky breath. How was I even alive? The initial drop should have—My jangled brain dredged up a snippet of conversation. *Not everything we see down here will be real.*

The abyss hadn't been real. At least, not entirely. I'd definitely fallen, but probably no more than ten feet before tumbling into the hole that separated me from the guys. And how long had that chute really been? Vampires couldn't work enchantments, they couldn't make a barrier, but they could trick the senses to hinder intruders in the labyrinth around their home.

The bruise on my lower back told me my gun was still in place, and I said a silent thank you that it hadn't gone off during the fall. I found the comforting hilt of my freshly forged knife, patted the bump of the LED flashlight in my pocket, then reached up to massage the bruised line around my neck where my choker had dug in before tearing free.

The tattered sleeve of another coat I'd have to throw away thanks to Oz's grip dangled from my elbow, and the shirt beneath was a collection of ragged strips down my right side. Heat and cold mingled where fresh blood oozed over raw skin. My ribs ached, but a deep breath told me nothing was broken.

Swallowing the sour flavor in my mouth, I tried to sit up, but fell back with a yelp as a wave of pain washed through my left wrist. My head hit the ground and snapped my teeth shut. Blood filled my mouth.

Somehow, biting my tongue chased all the other pains into the background. I sucked air through my nose for a minute, jaw clenched, then pushed myself up again, careful not to use my left arm.

Gently cradling the damaged wrist, I flexed my fingers. Still working. I rolled my hand to the point where the pain flared, then backed away. Sore, maybe sprained. I could use it in a pinch, but it would hurt like hell.

Tearing off one of the strips of fabric that used to be my sleeve, I wrapped my injured wrist to give it extra support and pushed to my feet.

Black in front, black behind, black to either side. I couldn't see the hole I'd fallen from or the ground beneath my feet. I couldn't even see my own body. I pushed my fingers into my pocket, but froze when they closed around the flashlight. I could chase away the black, but I'd be a beacon in the darkness, an easy target.

I bit my lip. If I could climb back up to Kai and Oz, or let them know where I'd fallen, it might be worth it.

Pulling out my flashlight, I pressed the switch. The hole I'd tumbled through was eight feet above me, right in the middle of the ceiling. The walls were rough rock that I could maybe climb, but the overhang around the hole was well beyond my skills. There was no going back.

I flashed my light around the hole, hoping to catch a glimpse of the bridge and my friends, but a sharp curve cut my vision off not far beyond where I'd fallen out.

"Kai?" I hissed, pitching my voice to a stage whisper. I glanced side to side along the rocky hall I'd landed in. My light faded to gloomy darkness in either direction. I raised my voice. "Kai?"

The word echoed back, followed by silence.

Clenching my teeth, I faced the looming hall to my left, switched off the light, and slid the plastic cylinder back into my pocket. No point giving away my position if there were enemies in these tunnels. I pushed aside the sensation of being a wraith without form or substance, stretched my hand out in front of me, and started walking.

A dozen shuffling steps took me right into the sticky gauze of a spiderweb. Clinging threads caught in my hair and eyelashes, tickled my skin, and dangled over my lips. Biting back a shriek, I flailed at the strands, ruffling my hair and wiping my skin, waiting for the bite of the unseen creature whose trap I'd stumbled into.

When no paralyzing venom entered my system, I stopped waving my arms like a madwoman and tried to breathe, but shudders wracked me with every tickle over my ultra-sensitive skin, and memories of Merak's insect army swarmed my mind as they'd swarmed my body.

"Get it together, Alex." I slapped my hands lightly on my cheeks and took a deep breath.

A handful more steps, blessedly web-free, brought me to a wall.

Right or left? Kai had the map, not that it would do any good with no idea where I was.

A soft breeze tickled my cheek, barely enough to stir the loose hairs around my forehead. Shrugging, I set my right hand against the wall as a guide and turned toward the promise of slightly fresher air.

MY PALM WAS raw from scraping along rough tunnel walls by the time I found the first light. I didn't notice the lessening of the darkness until I pulled my hand back from a close encounter with a jutting rock and realized I could see my torn nails and scraped knuckles. Twenty paces on, the natural stones were replaced by bricks and concrete.

My heart stuttered as my feet stopped. I'd found the inhabited section of the labyrinth.

A single bulb cast a circle of weak yellow light over the hall. To the right and left, a trail of glowing orbs connected by a cluster of black cables as thick as my forearm was strung along the ceiling, spheres of illumination barely brushing against each other so the light waxed and waned. Pillars, alcoves, and intersections broke the bricks at irregular intervals and scattered shadows along the path.

From what I remembered, the dungeons were north of the main nest, so I headed in what I hoped was that direction.

Noises echoed through the halls, every scuff and cough chilling my blood. I clung to the walls like a living shadow, darting under the blazing bulbs and into the intermittent shadows as though the light burned. The random alcoves that dipped into the walls were way stations in a hostile land where I paused for breath and listened for pursuit.

A quiet shuffle brought my head up. I shrank farther into the shadow of my sliver of safety, bricks pressed against my back. My fingers brushed the talisman around my neck, then drifted south to wrap the hilt of my knife. Crouching low, I held my breath.

A woman in the tattered remains of a faded, yellow sundress trudged into view, one leg dragging behind, the knee fused in place. Hair the color of a wheat field ready for harvest hung in clumps, dreadlocks of neglect more than fashion. Her pale skin still held the hint of a tan, the memory of pink clinging to her cheeks, but her eyes were glassy and unfocused.

I clamped down a shudder; every nerve thrumming.

That could have been me. . . . It very nearly was.

My lungs burned and pressure pricked behind my eyes. I coiled tighter around my cold center. I wouldn't let Merak take me again, no matter what.

The woman stared straight ahead as she limped—step, shuffle, step, shuffle—until she was past. She turned a corner, and I waited until the rhythmic tread faded to nothing. Then I waited some more.

Strain as I might, only the sound of my own racing heart greeted me.

I let out the stale air in my lungs, but its replacement wasn't much better. Mold and mildew, and under it all, decay. This was a place of dead things.

Turning after the departed woman, I picked up my pace, pausing at each corner to listen. Two intersections and no sign of her. She must have taken a different route. The tension in my shoulders slacked off a little. My chest wasn't quite so tight on my next breath. The hall after the third intersection was clear, and my heart surged with relief when I saw a well of stairs leading down at the far end.

I trotted down the corridor, holding my knife and talisman to keep from jingling.

In the shadow between lamps, a pool of light fell across the pale concrete, and I skidded to a stop inches from wide, glassy eyes the color of desert sand. The woman who'd passed me earlier stood frozen for a second, her expression slack. Then her hands came up.

So did mine, along with the knife.

Cracked nails and dry skin reached for my neck, and the smell of decay was overlaid by lavender and soap.

Without thinking, I gripped the solid wood of my hilt and twisted so the blade slid through the faded fabric of the sundress at the angle of the woman's ribs. The woman grunted, then gurgled, the sound oddly flat in the empty hall.

Clawed fingers scratched my neck and dragged over my torso, trailing down my jacket. I couldn't pull my eyes away, couldn't move.

The knife tugged, then slid free, rigid in my hand and heavy with thick, black blood that filled the corridor with a coppery tang.

She collapsed with a muffled thud, a dark stain eating up the pastel flowers on her dress. For a second, the glazed eyes sparked with life, and a tiny smile curved the edges of pale pink lips. Then the clouds came back, and she was gone.

I dropped to my knees, blood rushing in my ears. The world shrank to a pinpoint of lightless eyes and bleeding flowers.

It could have been me. . .

The blood on my hand grew cold, and I wiped it on the ruined dress with a shiver. I rubbed my blade until it gleamed, and shoved it back in its sheath. I couldn't get the stain out from under my nails.

Numb, body and soul, I stared at the dead woman, then down at my hands. Three people in as many weeks. What was I becoming?

It was my knees, cramped and aching, that reminded me of the passage of time. Someone could discover us at any moment. I couldn't afford to wallow.

Groaning, I straightened, and peeked into the room the woman had come out of. A set of industrial-sized washing machines stood against the back wall. She'd been doing laundry. Fuck.

I wiped a hand over my face, but cringed away from the metallic smell.

I looked down at the dead woman, back along the hall the way I'd come, up to the stairs that made me eager enough to get careless, back to the dead woman, and sighed.

Her chest was still warm when I wrapped my arm around it. My stomach cramped. Careful of my sore wrist, I braced my other arm under her armpit and heaved. She slid with a rough scrape across the floor. A streak of smeared blood marked her passage, brighter now that it was thinned out.

The coppery scent grew stronger, drowning out the sweat and lavender smell of her hair.

How long until the vampires woke up? If there were any nearby . . .

Once the woman's feet cleared the door, I lowered her as gently as I could to the blue and white tiles of the laundry room. Then I started opening cabinets above and below the sink that claimed one wall.

I found the bleach behind the third door.

SINUSES BURNING, I set my foot on the top step and started down. I was eighty percent sure where I was now. With a sniff, and one last spit to the side to clear the flavor from my mouth, I hurried on. James was waiting, and I'd already taken too long.

Concrete stairs folded back on themselves at small landings, and I paused at each to scan the lower flights and listen. The walls were the same dull gray as the floor, as the metal rail that ran along one side. Nothing stirred in the shaft, and I quickly dropped two levels. End of the line.

Ninety percent sure now. The dungeons weren't far.

The air was heavy with damp, and I shivered as the cold penetrated my shirt. My jacket had joined the blood- and bleached-soaked laundry in a washing machine. Hopefully the few stains remaining on my clothes wouldn't be enough to draw any unwanted attention.

The tunnel beyond the stairs returned to raw rock and dirt. The spaces between lights grew longer, islands of illumination along a river of darkness. I trotted to the first of those twilight spaces and crouched low in the shadows. My eyes flicked back and forth across the path. Nothing moved.

I crossed to the next pocket of shadow and scanned again.

My fingers twitched on the hilt of my knife. Had there been a sound, or was it just my mind playing tricks? My nerves hummed, stretched too far for too long. I licked my lips and the taste of old pennies flared.

Two more turns, maybe three, to the entrance of the dungeons. James would be there. Hopefully Kai and Oz too.

I crept forward in a crouch, hugging the wall to stay out of the light as long as possible. The bulb dangling from the ceiling of the next intersection cast rays down the four spokes like a child's drawing of the sun. Pebbles stood in high-relief along the floor, the deep shadows shrinking as I moved into that revealing light.

There was no sound, no movement, but something made the hairs on the back of my neck quiver. I slid the knife free.

The blade shook a little, eager to get to work, and the cold knot in my center twisted. I was not a killer. I was—

I licked my lips again, mingling the flavors of bleach and blood.

The corner ahead was rounded, and I stopped well back from it to take stock. My racing pulse and the slight electrical buzz of the light, stark shadows, the scent of bleach still burning in my sinuses. I tightened my grip. There would be nothing. I'd slash the open air, feel stupid, and move on.

Jaw clenched, I lunged around the corner, knife swinging.

Blade met blade with a clang that echoed off the walls and raced away into the black.

"Not bad."

My mouth gaped open and my knees went weak, then I threw my arms around Kai's neck. A sharp pain in my ribs flared and I withdrew with a groan, clutching my side. Jamming my blade into its sheath, I slugged Kai in the arm.

His smile faltered. "What was that for?"

I shook my head, dizzy with relief. "What took you so long?"

He quirked an eyebrow.

I tipped my head to see past him. The passage was empty. "Where's Oz?"

Kai's expression closed down. "He fell when you did. I'd hoped you were together."

I turned to search the adjoining halls, willing him to miraculously step out of the darkness and laugh off my concern.

"Don't worry. The wolf can take care of himself." Kai scanned me up and down and wrinkled his nose. "Which is more than I can say for you. Did you bathe in bleach?"

Eyes narrowed, I cross my arms. "It was necessary." Images of glassy eyes and a stained sundress pressed against my mind, but I pushed them aside. No time for nightmares. Not yet.

"Whatever you say." He hooked a thumb behind him. "Dungeons are this way. The vampires are waking up."

An icy shiver slid down my spine. With a nod, I followed him deeper into the tunnel.

Chapter 26

"THE GUARD STATION is here." Kai pointed to a spot on the map. "That's where we'll find the stairs between the upper and lower levels."

Shifting to ease the ache in my knees, I traced the line of sketched cells. "Nowhere to hide along here."

"As long as the guard's just a thrall, I can cloak us."

"And if the guard is a vampire?"

He shrugged and folded the map. "We were lucky to make it this far without fighting."

I swallowed the memory of a blood-soaked floral pattern and nodded.

"Stay close to me, and don't make a sound."

My left fingers closed over my silence charm. My right hovered over the hilt of my knife.

Kai's galaxy eyes found mine. "You ready?"

"As I'll ever be."

With a nod, he led the way around the last two corners of raw rock and into the dungeon.

Grooved concrete made a square tunnel straight to the guard station. The walls were broken at regular intervals by rusty iron doors with wheeled handles on the front like the doors in a submarine. The lonely lights of the labyrinth were replaced by blazing LEDs that washed the world in harsh white. At the far end of the cell block was a set of double-paned French doors right out of a *Better Homes and Gardens* catalog. Behind the glass sat a bored-looking man with greasy blond hair down to his shoulders and glassy eyes that looked right through us.

He slouched in the kind of cheap folding chair used for outdoor weddings and funerals, one jean-clad leg draped over the other, arms crossed over a Mickey Mouse sweatshirt. Behind him was a solid wall.

Afraid to raise my voice above the hum of a gnat, I whispered, "Where are the stairs?"

Kai bobbed one shoulder, continuing his slow, measured steps. Eyes fixed ahead, he walked directly through the center of the hall, hunched away from the offending iron of the cell doors. I stayed one pace behind, moving when he moved. The air felt thick, too thick to breathe. Sweat prickled my scalp. My skin itched.

Halfway down the hall I noticed tiny rectangles of glass set into each bulky door at eye level. The windows were hatched with wire, and brought to mind the windows in my ancient elementary school before the building was remodeled. A bright light shone in the ceiling of each room, illuminating walls of flaking rust. The cells were iron.

The back of Kai's neck was a river of sweat as he melted under the combined pressure of metal and lights. Over his shoulder, the guard station was still twenty feet away.

Something moved to my right, and I stumbled against Kai's rigid back. His muscles quivered, but he didn't look around.

"What?" His voice was a thready whisper, hoarse with strain.

Leaning toward the nearest door, I squinted through the little window where I'd caught the motion.

A shadow sat in the middle of the floor, a crumpled absence of light. Then it twitched, and two orbs of deep amber pierced the darkness. The shadow unfolded, growing to the height of a man.

I pressed close to Kai's ear. "There's someone in there."

"Doesn't matter." He took another step, and another.

I was rooted in place. "We have to help him."

"And lose our chance to save James?" Kai's hands were shaking now, his legs wobbling. The iron was taking its toll, and he hadn't been in top form to begin with thanks to O'Connell's test.

With one last look at the dark form encased in toxic metal, I stilled my itching fingers and caught up to Kai.

Five feet from the door to the guard station, Kai's knee buckled.

Fingertips pressed to the ground to keep from going all the way down, he stared at a space six inches from his nose with unblinking eyes.

"We'll have to rush it," he said between gritted teeth. "I can't . . . hold . . ."

"On three." I tucked one hand under his arm and pulled him up with a grunt.

"One." My knife slid free. "Two." I leaned onto the balls of my feet, ready to charge. "Three."

Kai flung out his hand, and the doors blew wide. My ears popped, not with the blare of an explosion, but like a sudden loss of cabin pressure at thirty thousand feet. Glass rained to the floor in a hail of tiny polygons that bounced off my head and back as I launched through the open space.

A steel baton deflected my overhead strike as the guard surged to his feet. Thrall or no, this wasn't some domestic caught off-guard while doing laundry.

The baton swung toward my bruised ribs and I jerked away, sacrificing balance for distance. Mid-swing the shaft spun in the guard's hand, arcing up to catch my extended wrist and yank the knife free. It clattered to the cheap linoleum that started just inside the ruined doors. He swept the knife aside with a kick.

Stumbling back, I groped for the gun at my waist. It pulled free with a tug, and I leveled it just as I had in practice with David. The guard was smaller than a mountain, but only three feet away.

I flipped the safety with my thumb.

A gunshot would draw attention. On the other hand, a vampire-zombie prison guard was about to club my skull in.

I set my finger against the trigger and took a breath.

"Wait for the exhale," David had said. *"Shoot in the space between breaths."*

Licking my lips, I let the air out of my lungs.

The guard was a foot away when the shining silver tip of Kai's katana erupted from his chest, right between Mickey's oversized ears. Warm, red droplets speckled my hands and arms. A few reached my face. A cough of black bubbles dribbled down the man's chin. Then the blade disappeared and he sank to his knees, folding backward over his legs, creating a sad parody of the chair he'd abandoned.

The gun shook in my locked arms. I took my finger off the trigger.

Wiping the blade clean, Kai slid his sword home and fell into the cheap plastic seat.

I lowered my gun.

"Does killing bother you?" I couldn't take my eyes off the hole in Mickey's head.

Kai tipped his head back and took a deep breath, stretching his lungs. He held it, then let it out in a long *whoosh*. "Does it bother *you?*"

Tucking the gun snugly back in its holster, I stepped around the corpse and retrieved my knife from the corner. "Not as much as it should."

"Why should the death of an enemy who was about to kill you be a problem?"

I shook my head and sheathed the knife.

It could have been me. . .

Pushing to his feet, Kai stretched his arms and nodded to a wooden panel in the avocado green linoleum. "Let's hope the cells down there aren't iron."

Together, we heaved the hatch up on greased hinges to reveal a six-foot drop to the top landing of a metal staircase.

I looked at Kai. "Maybe you should wait here."

THE LOWEST LEVEL of the dungeon was chiseled from rough, reddish rock. Moisture condensed on the ceiling and slicked the floor. Three lights burned above, illuminating six wooden doors with thick, weathered planks. The wood belonged in a medieval castle, but the knobs could have been picked up at any modern hardware store. There were no windows.

I leaned close to the first door and gave it a light knock. "James?"

I pressed my ear to the wood, hoping for a response, but only silence greeted me. Chase had said there were two prisoners in the dungeons. Since we'd passed one upstairs, hopefully that meant James was the only occupant down here and I wasn't about to open the door for a monster that might rip my throat out.

My fingers shook as I lifted the key ring we'd recovered from the dead guard. It held eight keys and a bent crank handle. I found a key roughly the color of the lock on the first cell door, and slipped it in. The bolt turned with a satisfying click. The hinges didn't make a sound.

The pool of light cast by the bulb in the hall ventured barely two feet into the room before it was pushed back by a darkness so thick it seemed to have form.

Swallowing the lump in my throat, and pushing aside the feral part of my mind screaming at me to run, I tucked the keys into my pocket and pulled out my small flashlight. White light swept the room in a thin beam, revealing dank walls, puddles of standing water, and a low rock ceiling. There was a dark box, about seven feet long, in the middle of the room.

Mouth suddenly dry, I stepped up to the casket. Heavy brass handles hung loose along the side and at either end, as if waiting for pallbearers.

Something clicked off to my right and I whirled, flashlight swinging wildly to track the noise, but there was nothing there. My breath came fast enough to make me lightheaded, and I made a conscious effort to slow it down. No good passing out six inches from my goal.

Turning back to the ominous box, I trailed my fingers over polished wood. A seam halfway down meant the lid lifted in two sections. I rapped my knuckles against the dark surface. The knock echoed through the chamber, and I held my breath.

No answer.

Was he already dead?

Shaking the thought loose, I bit down on the end of my flashlight to free both hands and set my palms against the lid. Heart hammering in my chest, I closed my eyes and pushed.

Sharp pain shot through my wrist, but the lid lifted on its hidden hinges.

Light glinted off the inside of the empty box.

Squinting, I leaned in close and touched thin sheets of silver riveted over the inner wood in place of lining. The open lid was dull white on the inside and didn't match the outer curve. I ran my fingers over thick, smooth plastic.

What the hell?

Shaking my head, I let the lid fall back in place and returned to the hall.

Five more doors.

I stepped across the hall and pushed keys into the lock until it clicked. Third try this time. The room beyond was another dank cave, but there was no box. Instead, thick manacles hung from the walls and dangled from the ceiling. Dried blood crusted the inner edge of one set.

The next room down the hall was the same as the second, and I barely glanced around the empty space before moving on. Room Four held another casket.

Stepping up quickly this time, I heaved against the lid. My wrist flared. The lid didn't budge.

Clutching my throbbing wrist, I stepped back, then grabbed my spit-covered flashlight and ran it over the obstinate box, walking a full circle around it. Like the other, the hinges were hidden inside where I couldn't get to them. Three brass handles ran down each side and there was one at either end. The lid was split into two sections. Maybe I'd just picked the wrong half?

I heaved against the second section, then repeated the effort on both halves on the other side.

"Dammit!" I kicked the side of the box.

When the echo died down, the box thumped back.

I jerked back. Then I took a tentative step toward the casket and leaned in.

It thumped again.

"James?" My mouth was inches from the polished surface and my breath bounced back, stale and acidic. "Is that you?"

A muffled voice mumbled something, and I pressed my ear to the wood.

"What?"

". . . ock . . . "

"What?" I yelled, pressing my cheek against the seam in the lid until it bruised. "I can't hear you."

"Lock," said the voice. It could have been James. It could have been anyone.

"Where?" My nails scraped into thick polyurethane.

"Foot."

Springing to my feet, I raced to the end of the casket. The light shook in my hand. Wood base, wood lid, brass handle and two wide brass screw covers. Biting my lip, I ran to the other end, just in case. Exactly the same.

Desperate, I pulled out the guard's key ring. One key had opened the first and fourth doors, another had opened the second and third, so one key for each side of the hall. Coffin rooms versus chain rooms. Two heavy iron keys seemed to match the thick doors of the floor above. Of the four remaining keys, one probably opened the glass doors Kai had blown through. That left three and the bent handle.

I turned the crank over in my hands. If I couldn't find anything that looked like a *lock*, maybe I needed something that didn't look like a *key*.

The end of the crank was a long, thin hexagon. It reminded me of an Allen wrench.

Fumbling the light, I ran my fingers over wood and metal, searching for a matching shape. The box itself was a dark hardwood, polished to within an inch of its life and smooth to the touch. The handle had a few scratches, but nothing intentional or useful. It was held on by four flush Phillips head screws. Just below the lid, two quarter-inch-thick brass circles stuck out from the wood.

Pinching one, I gave it a twist. It wasn't a screw cover. It hid a hole. . . .

A six-sided hole.

Heart hammering, I jammed the thin end of the crank into the hole and spun the handle. Round and round, faster and faster. Then it jerked still, and my hand lurched off, scraping my palm.

This time, when I pushed, the lid lifted.

Light spilled out around the seams, and I nearly dropped the lid in surprise. Warm, soft light flooded the room, shining from a panel in the lid and reflecting off silver sheets that lined the walls and base of the coffin.

I blinked in the brightness, and braced against the side of the coffin. "James."

Where the light touched his face, patches of skin charred black and fell to dust, only to be replaced by a new, pink layer.

Fingers flying, I searched the inner edges of the lid. At the top, near his head, was a simple black switch. I pressed it, and the room plunged into darkness.

My eyes rebelled against another abrupt shift, and it took a moment to focus on the thin beam of my flashlight. When I did, I brought it up to flecks of silver-blue ice set in bruised circles.

His eyelids fluttered closed until I moved the light away. Then he lifted one skeletal hand that fluttered like a leaf and trailed a chain of fine silver links that tinkled like chimes in the silence.

"Alex?" he whispered.

The world blurred as tears of horror and relief filled my eyes. I cupped his outstretched hand to my wet cheek. "I'm here."

"Get me . . . out." His words were slurred and stilted. His eyes rolled without focus.

Releasing his hand was like letting a lifeline slide through my fingers, but I turned to the bottom half of the casket and heaved.

James's arms and legs were thinner, his suit soiled and caved in below protruding ribs. How could he have lost so much weight in four days? He'd gone from a sexy, upper-class entrepreneur to a starving refugee from a war-torn country.

Setting the flashlight on the floor, I helped him sit up, then let him rest. His chest heaved. He swayed slightly from side to side. When he stopped shaking, I tucked myself under one emaciated arm, grabbed him around his waist and pulled. He tipped sideways, gripping the coffin edge to stop from falling.

"Keep going," he growled.

I pulled again.

James half slid, half fell out of the casket, sinking to the cold, wet stone. My knee hit hard with his weight bearing me down, but I cradled him as best I could, holding him as he panted into my hair, breath cool against my neck.

"James?"

He shivered, fingers digging in where he held on to me. His breaths were smoother, deeper, but he clung like a baby koala, making no effort to hold his own weight.

I shifted, easing some of the strain off my ribs, and his grip tightened, a boa constrictor squeezing its prey. Memories of teeth and claws against pale skin swam through my thoughts and drowned my vision. "James!"

He shoved me away so hard we both fell back.

Staring at the ceiling, rough stone pressed to my back, I licked my lips and tried to slam a lid on the terrified flutter filling my abdomen like a swarm of locusts. I was sweating despite the cold, and my breath came in short, ragged gasps.

"You shouldn't be here," he croaked.

As my panic attack passed, I tipped my head to see the sharp shadows of his face dance and sway as he rolled his head slowly from side to side as though denying a dream.

I took a deep breath and tried to smile. "You're welcome."

He shifted, and the fine chains pooled on his stomach slithered to one side. Groaning, he raised his arms and turned deep silvery eyes on me. "Could you?" He jingled the chains.

I was slow to go to him, staring at lips I'd once kissed now stretched over teeth that could tear the flesh from my bones. But pushing past the dread constricting my chest, I rolled to my knees and crawled across the space between us.

My hands shook as I unwound the chain. The metal was ice against my fingers. "I thought silver was a werewolf thing." My voice wasn't any steadier than my hands.

He looked away, jaw tight, and a curtain of lank black strands drifted over his face. "It's not the silver," he mumbled. "Just holds the magic better."

The chains fell away easily, tiny links slipping to pool on the floor.

He sat up and nodded at the chains. "Might want to hang on to that." His eyelids fluttered and he swayed. He looked like it was taking all his strength just to keep from passing out.

Bundling the chains into a small coil, I stuffed them in my pocket. Then I looked back at the coffin-turned-tanning bed and shuddered. "How did that not kill you?"

"Careful calculation. Merak wasn't trying to kill me." He closed his eyes. "Thank you for freeing me."

"We're not out yet."

Chapter 27

IT TOOK KAI pulling and me pushing to get James out of the hole. His muscles had wasted to practically nothing. The once well-tailored suit hung limp and baggy on his frame. His shoes were gone. Pale toes curled around the rungs of the ladder when he climbed. Kai grunted above us, shifting his grip lower to yank James over the lip by his jacket and slacks.

When I popped my head into the bright light of the guard room, James was sprawled on the green linoleum.

Kai leaned over him, braced against his knees. "You look like crap."

James grunted.

A streak of red marred the floor, shades of pink and crimson that marked a trail from where Mickey Mouse had been skewered to the folding plastic chair where the guard's corpse was now propped like a taxidermy doll. His arms were crossed over the hole in his chest, hiding it from view, but thick drips of viscous black clung to the bottom of the seat and dripped lazily to a small puddle beneath.

I quirked an eyebrow at Kai and jerked my head toward the corpse.

He shrugged. "Just in case."

The glass from our earlier entrance had all been swept into a corner, and the empty door frames realigned.

I chewed a piece of loose skin on my lower lip. "No sign of Oz?"

"He probably turned back when we got separated," Kai said. "Would've been the smart choice."

I nodded, but the cold, hard knot in my stomach tightened.

"We should get going." I reached for James's arm, but Kai grabbed my wrist.

"Allow me."

In the end, it took both of us to get James on his feet again, sagging between our shoulders. His head lolled from side to side. The blue had bled entirely from his eyes, leaving alien pools of silver, and his thin lips didn't fully cover the jagged fangs stretching his mouth.

I swallowed, and he swung toward the sound, or maybe he was

drawn by the rapid surge of blood through my veins.

Tightening my grip and gritting my teeth, I stared straight ahead and tried to pretend the man in my arms didn't feel like a stranger. I pictured James the way I remembered him—before I'd learned his secret—strong, and sure, and safe.

Thump.

I missed a step and we all stuttered to a halt halfway up the hall.

"What was—" I looked over at Kai, but swirling shadows drew my attention behind him to a tiny rectangle set in the nearest door. I'd completely forgotten about the other prisoner.

"No," Kai said. He hefted James's weight a little higher on his shoulders and took another step.

"We have to help him."

"We already have one invalid."

I slid out from under James's arm.

Growling in protest, Kai lowered James, and I eased him against the wall Kai couldn't approach. James's eyes fluttered. His mouth parted, but all that came out was a labored breath.

Kai gestured to the prison cell. "We have no idea who or what that is."

"It doesn't matter."

"Of course it does," he snapped.

I pulled the guard's keys from my pocket, glaring.

He spread his hands, pleading while blocking my path. "The vampires will be awake by now. No way we get through the nest dragging two dead weights."

"I have to help." I clenched my fists. Since learning I was part fae I'd committed a number of criminal acts. I'd killed three people. I'd become less human. But through it all, I'd tried to convince myself I was still me, still a decent person. I licked my lips and whispered, "I'm not a monster."

Kai flinched, and something flickered behind his eyes. Pain? Guilt? I pushed past him so I didn't have to see it.

The thick iron key perfectly matched the lock. I set my hands on either side of the wheel and turned. Hinged beams retracted along the edges of the door, clicking into place one by one. When the last bar released, I pushed. The door didn't move, and I worried it might be rusted in place. Pressing my shoulder to the metal, I planted my feet and leaned in. The door shifted, then swung open with a groan.

I caught my balance just before stumbling over the lower lip of the opening, hands braced against the frame, and looked up to find a cloud of shadow swarming toward me.

Snapping my mouth shut, I scrunched my eyes and held my breath. The dark cloud billowed over my skin, cold and damp. It flowed out of the room and pooled in the middle of the hall, coalescing into a six-foot-two man with grayish skin. He wore a long black trench coat, dark shirt, and black slacks that were starting to fray at the hem. Dark gray sneakers scuffed stone as he turned a slow circle, blinked amber eyes, and nodded.

Kai gasped and took a step away from the stranger, but there was nowhere to go in the iron-lined hall. "You're—"

"Grateful," said the stranger. "To the lady."

My mind raced. Gray skin and amber eyes. . . . Just like Morgan. My late night study session after our encounter in Crossroads had yielded several possibilities for what she could be. None were creatures I'd want to meet in a confined space.

He lifted a hand toward me. "Thank you."

Kai's back stiffened.

The stranger's hand hung unanswered in the air between us, so I reached out and took it.

A muscle jumped in Kai's jaw, but he held his tongue.

"You may call me Galen."

The name struck a chord in my memory.

"I am in your debt." Cradling my hand, he turned it to plant a cool, dry kiss on the back. "On my honor, I shall repay it."

"Alex," I said. "I couldn't leave anyone here to—" Memories of fangs, and fear, and wanting to please the monster that was hurting me swarmed my thoughts.

I pulled my hand away, hugging myself. "You're welcome."

Kai narrowed his eyes at the newcomer. "Will you open a road?"

Galen looked to the ceiling, as though considering, then shook his head. "I ask to join your group for the journey out of this pit under the wayfarer's clause."

Kai dragged a hand over his scalp, but nodded. "Well met."

My gaze jumped back and forth between the two fae, following their words like an invisible ball thrown between them. "What are you two talking about?"

"Galen will be joining in our escape from the nest," Kai said.

"Yeah, I figured."

One corner of Galen's mouth curved up. "This must be Enchantment's newest claim. We've all been dying to meet her."

"Standing right here, ya know." I gestured to myself.

The other side curved up. "Cute."

Kai stepped between us. "Shadow has no qualm with us right now."

"My father is always interested in the rare and unique."

Midnight swirls and amber orbs locked together.

I rolled my eyes. "We need to get out of here." I turned to Galen and planted my hands on my hips. "Can you walk?"

He blinked, his smile returning. "That should still be in my power."

"Good." Leaving the boys to their pissing contest, I crouched in front of James.

His skin was anemic, but smooth and solid, with no evidence of the damage it had sustained. His chest rose and fell with shallow breaths that were still too fast. His chin dipped almost to his chest, as though he'd fallen asleep, and the rapid flutter under his eyelids reinforced the image.

"No rest for the weary," I muttered, and leaned in to slide my arm behind his back.

James's eyes snapped open, but they were the mercury eyes of the monster inside him, and they looked right through me. He surged forward with strength I hadn't thought he still possessed and pinned me to the floor.

A tiny yelp escaped before the air was pressed from my lungs. Then I was gasping under the weight of a full-grown man. Sharp pain tore into the tissue between my neck and shoulder, and my already useless lungs froze in place as every muscle in my body cramped in response. Rivers of ice raced through my veins, and tears washed out the world. Distant voices echoed in my ears, but they were muffled; sounds under water.

James's weight shifted and the ache in my ribs clamored for attention, but I didn't have any to spare. Not when I was reliving the horrors of my last visit to this hell hole. Not when the world was fading. Not when the man I thought I might love was killing me on a dungeon floor.

". . . COULD HAVE . . ."

". . . never . . . She'll . . . just . . ."

". . . will. She . . . you."

Words drifted in and out of my head. Or maybe it was me who was doing the drifting. The voices were fast and muffled, a heated debate in whispers that couldn't hold my attention. My body was heavy, bones of granite with raw nerves stretched over the immovable frame. My chest struggled to rise. My throat was dry and raw, and stung like I'd been chugging glass. The fabric pressed to my back was damp and cold, and a rock jabbed uncomfortably into my kidney.

My eyelids slid open, curtains on a rusted track.

Kai and James were inches apart, hissing and spitting like cats after the same prize. Kai's sword was out, but dangled from his fist like the need for it had passed but he was still hoping for an excuse to use it. His skin was flushed almost purple, and his words scraped between bars of clenched teeth.

James was on his feet, tall and strong as ever. He had a healthy pink glow in his cheeks, and his bones no longer pressed to the surface as though trying to break free. His hair, still greasy and limp, flapped around his face when he gestured. His hands looked better too, ending in fingers rather than claws.

I relaxed a little, grunting when the annoying rock dug deeper into my side. James was going to be fine.

"Ahem."

I tipped my chin. Dark gray sneakers shifted next to my head, and I followed a line of black clothing to an unfamiliar face that plucked at the severed ends of my memory.

"Your princess has awakened," the stranger said. His eyes were deep amber set in the face of a soot-covered chimney sweep.

The memory of a dark booth in a faerie bar surged to the front of my thoughts. The hairs along my arms stood at attention.

"Morgan."

Amber eyes flashed.

"Alex!" Kai was at my side, cradling my hand. His grip tightened, and he glared above me at James as he knelt on my other side.

"What happened?" My voice rasped, a desert wind across scorched earth.

James looked away. His hands were loose at his sides, and while he crouched two inches from my lonely fingers, he made no move to touch me. "You don't remember?"

I frowned. "We got you out, into the guard room, and we were walking down the hall." Images formed behind my eyes. "There was a shadow . . ."

My eyes snapped to the man above me.

"It wasn't him," said Kai. His narrowed eyes hadn't left James.

I lifted my hand, and it shook with the effort. When my fingers brushed James's knee he pulled away.

"What did you—" I swallowed the lump in my throat, understanding dawning.

"I was half-mad with need." His voice was measured, a robot relaying facts.

I lifted my free hand to the side of my neck. My fingers brushed puckered flesh that flared like a wild fire at the touch. They came away damp.

"You could have killed her." Kai's accusation was flat, dulled from too much use.

James didn't deny it. He rose to his feet, towering above me. "I needed the strength."

"So you took it from me." I struggled through waves of anger and betrayal.

"We wouldn't have made it out as we were." He crossed his arms. "This way, we have a chance."

It made sense for James to take the energy he needed to walk out on his own two feet. He'd be more useful than me in a fight against vampires, and thanks to my fae healing I was feeling less lethargic by the second—though my head pounded with the promise of a colossal hangover. But that didn't make him right.

How was James any different from Merak if he just took what he wanted when he wanted it? How could I trust someone like that? Then it hit me. Trusting James wasn't just about opening myself up to another person. Trusting him meant trusting a vampire. I'd thought he was nothing like Bryce and Merak, but the cold calculation in his voice made me reconsider. Deep down, there was a part of him that was exactly the same, a part that always would be. He couldn't stop being a vampire any more than I could stop being fae.

Gritting my teeth, I tugged his pant leg. "James, look at me."

Sighing, his ice-chip eyes found mine. The silver swimming there since I'd lifted the lid on the coffin was gone.

"Why do your eyes change color?"

He blinked, a small pucker appearing on his forehead. "What?"

"Your eyes. Why were they silver?"

Kai sat back on his heels. "Alex, is this really the best time for—"

"I lost control." James's words were quiet but steady.

I took a breath, and the rock jabbed deeper into my back. "Are you back in control now?"

He nodded.

I looked into James's clear blue eyes, searching for silver. The vampire would always be there, inside him, but for the moment he was keeping it in check. "Then we need to go."

"Alex, I—"

"Later." There were enough hungry monsters between us and the exit; we needed to get out before the one by my side woke up again.

Kai draped my arm over his shoulder and helped me to my feet. James reached for my other side, but I flinched away. His hands fell to his sides.

Kai's arm was stiff. Sweat ran down his forehead and dripped off the end of his nose, but I didn't suggest a different crutch. My feelings toward James were too raw, and the man who'd stood silent during our exchange—

"What was your name?"

He frowned. "Galen."

"I think I met your sister."

His eyes widened.

"She was looking for you."

Panting with the effort to stay on my swaying feet despite Kai's assistance, I turned away from his obvious wish for more information and raised my chin toward the far end of the hall. "Let's get the hell out of here."

Chapter 28

MY BRUISES WERE a dull ache, forgotten in the numbness that spread through my body like a disease when James drained my blood. Exhaustion pulled at me, dulling my focus, but it was getting easier to move. My feet no longer scraped over the concrete floor, and I was supporting my own weight. Go, go fae healing. James had made the right call . . . I just wish he'd asked.

Kai was breathing easier now that the iron walls of the prison weren't looming over us. Galen also seemed more relaxed, strolling beside me as though unconcerned by the mile of vampire-infested tunnels between us and our exit.

James walked ahead, shoulders tight and straight under the loose fabric of his suit. When he came to an intersection, he would pause, and we'd all hold our breath while we waited. When the coast was clear, he'd wave us forward and set off again without a backward glance.

I hadn't seen his eyes since we started walking. I hoped they were still blue. The way I was feeling, I wouldn't survive another encounter with his hunger.

We approached another intersection. James pressed his back to the wall and motioned us to do the same. Voices drifted around the corner, growing louder. Kai pushed me back against rough bricks, leaving enough space between us that he could draw his sword. On my other side, Galen was a dark statue, nearly invisible in shadows that weren't deep enough to hide the rest of us.

". . . stupid enough to come here." The speaker had a rich baritone that echoed down the hall.

"Wolves aren't known for their brains," a nasal tenor replied.

I gripped Kai's forearm. "They have Oz."

Kai stiffened, and turned to look at me with a sad, slow swirl of galaxies as pitiless as the real thing. He shook his head. "We can't."

I bit off my first reply and took a breath through clenched teeth. "We have to."

"Are you *trying* to get caught?" Galen hissed in a barely audible whisper.

James was still frozen at the corner.

Footsteps ricocheted like gunshots off the bricks.

Pushing away from Kai, I stumbled forward.

Fear surged through me, but I slammed a lid on it and threw it into the furthest corner of my mind. I set one shaky hand on James's shoulder and looked for icy blue.

Silver swirled around the edges, and it was all I could do to keep from pulling back.

I licked dry lips and leaned as close as I dared to his ear. The familiar scent of him, buried though it was beneath dirt and sweat, made my stomach clench with something other than fear. That too, I pushed aside. "I need to talk to them."

His glacial stare pinned me in place. A muscle in his jaw twitched. Then he was gone.

A blur streaked around the corner, followed by one startled yelp and two thuds. Then silence.

Trembling hand pressed to the wall, I stepped into the intersection. Kai was at my shoulder before I cleared the corner.

Three feet up the intersecting passageway, a thin man with a hawk nose dangled from the fist twisted into his shirt. His eyes were saucers staring up at James. Another man, built like a bulldozer, lay at James's feet. His head was facing the wrong direction.

Bile burned at the back of my throat, and I clamped a hand over my mouth.

Blue and silver warred in the eyes that watched my approach. The silver flashed, then faded. James's gaze dropped to the side. "It's not for nothing that Merak fears me."

I couldn't tear my eyes away from the man's backward head. "I said *talk.*"

"And you will." His still-conscious captive pried at James's grip and scraped his feet over the floor, looking for purchase. James's eyes flared silver again and settled on the struggling man, who fell quiet with a whimper.

Dragging the man with him, James pressed his ear to the nearest door, then pushed it open. His eyes flitted over me, but settled on Kai. "Bring the other." He dragged his squirming victim into the room he'd opened.

Sheathing his sword, Kai wrapped both hands around the ankles of the man on the floor. The guy must have outweighed him by a hundred pounds, but Kai didn't even grunt. The man's head rocked sickeningly as his body followed Kai into the room.

Taking a deep breath, I moved to follow. Something crunched under my foot. I picked up a thin, black cell phone that must have fallen from a hand or pocket during the exchange. The screen was cracked, but a half-typed text message lit when I pressed the power button.

East passage se . . .

Eyes locked on the trailing words, I stepped through the door. "How does this even work down here? We're under—" I looked up, and froze. Galen bumped into my back.

The concrete floor stopped at the threshold, replaced by thick gray carpet. White, orange-peel walls took the place of dusty bricks, and modern, inset lights flooded the room. A king-sized bed sat against one wall, and a large desk with a sleek silver laptop took up the far corner. A black leather couch framed by polished oak end tables faced a screen wider than I was tall and a pair of standing speakers.

I whistled softly.

Galen pushed me into the room and pulled the door closed. "Just because Merak chooses to decorate his nest in the guise of a medieval castle, doesn't mean it *is* a medieval castle." He pointed to where a snaking cable disappeared into a little box with a thick antenna. "Repeaters." Then he slid past me to lurk in a corner.

The man with the backwards neck was sprawled on the carpet. James tossed the second man at my feet and nodded to Kai, who drew his sword and lowered the tip until it rested against the man's bobbing Adam's apple.

Silver was eating away the blue in James's eyes. "Do you have that chain?"

Reaching into my pocket, I pulled out the jingling mass of fine, silver links.

"Where did you get that?" Kai's question was strained, his voice too high.

"It was on James." I flicked my eyes between them, resisting the urge to drop the chain like a poisonous snake. "Why? What is it?"

"It's how we're going to keep these two from causing trouble," James said.

Kai just shook his head.

James took the chain from me and began wrapping the wrists of the larger man.

While James worked on his hands, the man's foot twitched.

Galen gave a choked warning.

Looping the chain through the frame of the bed, James stepped back to admire his handiwork.

The previously dead man pushed awkwardly to his knees, head hanging at an unnatural angle. Then he reached up and gripped his head with his bound hands, twisting until it faced forward on his neck. It settled in place with a chiropractic *pop* that made me cringe.

Gray eyes flickering with rage found me. "Do you have any idea how hard it is to repair spine damage?" The man had a slight Southern accent.

"Some." James stepped between us, crossing his arms.

"You won't get away with this," said the hawk-nosed man under Kai's sword, finally finding courage now that his friend was awake.

"Shut up, Tony." The larger man never took his eyes off James. "So you got out."

"Working on it," James said.

The man looked around and raised his palms as if to say, "Who's stopping you?"

James gestured to me. "The lady has a question."

I tried to still my hands. The man was large, even kneeling he came up to my chest. His eyes were solid granite beneath furrowed black bushes. Dark hair buzzed short and straight shoulders gave the impression of a soldier.

He looked at me. "I have nothing to say."

James smiled. "I figured as much."

With a sickening crack, the man's head snapped around so his eyes were replaced by a thinning patch of close-cropped hair.

I spun away, bracing one hand against the wall and the other on my stomach, and took shallow breaths.

"He isn't dead." James's voice was quiet.

I nodded and wiped my mouth with the back of my wrist. "I know."

"Even if he was—"

I raised a hand. "I know."

The hawk-nosed man stared between us with those saucer eyes, lank blond hair dangling over his forehead. His lower lip quivered.

James crouched, just out of reach. "You're new."

The man tried to nod, but the tip of Kai's sword dug into his neck, drawing a single crimson bead.

"Then you don't know how much that," James nodded to the larger man, "hurts yet."

His eyes got wider, wrinkling his forehead.

"Want to find out?"

He vibrated more than shook his head, but a few more drops of blood oozed out. "What do you want to know?"

Kai raised the silver blade so the tip danced in front of those wide eyes. "Where's the wolf?"

"Last I heard, they were taking him to the main chamber. Deek and I," he twitched a hand toward the man chained to the bed, "were sent to check—" His eyes locked on James and he licked his lips.

I rubbed my upper arms, pacing a small circle that mirrored my thoughts. First James traded his freedom for mine. Now Oz had lost his for James. Every time we tried to save someone, someone else took their place.

"What will Merak do?" I stopped, glaring at the whimpering vampire. "Will he risk war with the wolves?"

"I . . . I don't know. I only got promoted to guard duty last week."

I cut my eyes to James and gestured to the quaking hostage who seemed about to piss himself. "You sure he's a vampire?"

James lifted one shoulder. "Newly turned."

Running my hands through my hair until my scalp pulled tight, I gritted my teeth and tried to think of a plan that didn't involve some or all of us dying.

"We don't have the manpower for an impromptu rescue." Kai's voice slammed through my thoughts like a sledge hammer. "We should get out while we can and leave the rest to Marc and the pack."

"Oz could be dead by then. He—" Something vibrated in my pocket.

Pulling out the pilfered cell phone, I lit the shattered screen.

Well? The tag on the text message read *Bryce.*

An aching tightness spread through my chest and cut off my breath.

"What is it?" James was at my shoulder, hovering but not quite touching. "He's expecting an update."

I looked at the man who had yet to put himself together a second time.

"What should I say?"

James held out an open hand and I set the phone in it.

"What if he realizes it's not that guy?" I jerked my head toward the body.

"Deekon's speech patterns are predictable."

I stared. "You know him?"

"The world is not such a very large place for those of us crowded into its shadows." His fingers flew over the screen, and the phone disappeared into his pocket.

"That should buy us a little time." His eyes were mostly blue when he looked up. "Where are we heading?"

I looked at Kai.

He met my gaze, shook his head. "We can't."

Teeth and claws and tearing flesh. "I can't just leave him."

"We'll lose more than just Oz." Kai took a step toward me, but shifted his gaze to the man at our feet. "We aren't prepared for an assault."

"Just a look then." I hugged myself, fighting the shivers that wracked my frame with the memory of Marek's throne room. "So we can tell Marc what to expect."

Kai frowned, but didn't argue.

I turned to the quiet shadow lurking at the edge of our group. "What about you?"

Galen shrugged. "I'll stick around as long as you're heading in the right direction."

I rolled my eyes. "Swell."

FLICKERING BLUE torchlight made my skin crawl, and I raked ragged nails over the itch of remembered insect legs. The warm lights of the brick halls had disappeared, replaced by the watery illumination of my nightmares. Bricks turned to raw stone, then stone blocks and carved columns as we approached the heart of the nest. The one place we'd been trying to avoid. The last place I ever wanted to be again.

The four of us paused just outside Merak's throne room. Murmurs, and shuffling feet, and all the tiny sounds of people pressed together drifted to us from the main chamber. Beyond the arched hallway that wrapped the room, a line of silhouetted backs blocked our view of the central area. Mostly burly men with broad shoulders, muscles straining the fabric of their shirts. Merak definitely had a type.

James in the lead, we crept through the shadows at the edge of the chamber, hidden by the spectators of Merak's court.

The smell of burning hair drifted past the observers, and my nose itched with the need to scratch or sneeze. I cupped a hand over it.

The high-pitched wail of an animal in distress cut through the silence. I froze, my blood running cold. The witnesses leaned in.

"Why would a wolf be skulking around my domain?" Merak's voice sent shivers across my scalp and turned my legs to jelly.

James took two more steps, then turned with a frown.

Kai, one hand under my elbow for support, gave a gentle tug. My legs wouldn't move.

A nudge prodded me from behind, where Galen was a mere outline among deeper shadows.

I managed to shuffle one foot forward. I couldn't help anyone if I didn't move. My second foot responded, and we were walking again, tiptoeing behind the backs of Merak's captive audience.

My nerves were raw at the surface, screaming at every shift in the air or brush of stone. My heart hammered against my ribs like it was trying to get out, and I squeezed the charm Hortense had given me as though my life depended on it. James was only half-visible in front of me, and Kai glided as though he never touched the ground. Galen might as well have been a shadow himself. If anyone gave our party away, it would be me.

I bit hard on my lower lip.

The crowd thinned out as we moved to the far end of the chamber. I guess even Merak's circus of pain had VIP and nose-bleed seats. Two of the arches stood empty, giving us a view of the raised dais where Merak lounged on his dark leather throne. At the center of the space in front of that throne was a silver cage. A giant white wolf was inside.

The wolf swayed on its feet, yelping and shifting when its shoulder brushed the bars. Smoke curled around its paws, adding to the acrid stench. Patches of crimson stained its snowy fur.

"Is this some sort of power play by your alpha, or were you acting alone?" Merak twitched a finger, and two men standing on either side of the cage jabbed long, thin spears through the bars.

Another howl, and Oz collapsed, only to struggle to his feet again when the lower bars seared into his exposed underbelly.

Pressure built in my chest and behind my eyes until I thought I might pop.

"No. Wolves don't act without permission." Merak leaned forward, bracing elbows against his knees. "So what is Marcus up to?"

"We have to get him out of there." My voice cracked.

Kai was already shaking his head. "We're here to look, assess. There are too many. Even with James and Galen, we could never take them all."

"We have to try."

"We'll die, and Oz will be no better off."

"It's my fault he's here."

"The wolf made his own choice."

"His *name* is *Oz*."

"Shhh." James's thin, pale fingers settled on my shoulder, a matching hand on Kai's, and steered us into the mouth of the nearest tunnel. "If you get any louder, it won't matter."

Kai shifted his glare to James. "Tell her this is suicide."

James's eyes were blue ringed with silver. "The chances we all survive such an endeavor are . . . slim."

I hugged myself, frowning. "You won't help?"

James smiled and raised a hand as though he would stroke my face, but let it fall without touching me. "I would fight all the demons in the Rift for you, Alex. If you choose to fight for your friend, I will join you."

"Besides," he turned back to Kai, "Merak won't stop. He'll come after us again."

"After we've had time to recover," Kai growled. "None of us are at full strength."

"I cannot take on the room by myself, but I should be strong enough to hold Merak in check," James said.

"And I'm feeling a lot better thanks to my fae healing."

Kai snorted. "I doubt you'd stand much chance against a vampire even in peak condition."

I squared my shoulders. "Are you with us, or not?"

Tipping his head to the ceiling with a defeated sigh, Kai set his hands on his hips and said, "I've sworn my life to protect you. If you insist on throwing it away, we'll go down together."

Throwing my arms around his neck, I gave Kai a quick kiss on the cheek.

He looked down with a small smile that didn't come near the swirling galaxies of his eyes and said softly, "I'm not a monster either."

"Since you all seem set to die, this is where I'll leave you."

James, Kai, and I swung our attention to Galen.

"You owe a debt," Kai reminded.

Galen's back stiffened, but his expression didn't change. "Much as it pains me to admit it, I am weak from my stay here." His eyes shifted to me. "I shall not throw my life away on a fool's hope."

"So much for honor," I grumbled.

Galen's chest puffed out and he stood even taller. "I shall fulfill my debt when I deem it appropriate. This," he gestured toward the writhing werewolf, "is not worth my life. Nor yours."

I balled my fists. "What good is a debt I can't call in?"

"Let's hope you live long enough to find out." Galen melted into the dark cloud he'd been when we first met and faded into the shadows.

"Shadow-walkers," Kai spat.

I shook my head and tried to tune out the animal screams coming from the silver cage. Tears pricked my eyes. I was going to get us all killed.

Kai patted my shoulder. "We can still get out of here. If we call Marc, maybe . . ."

My head snapped up. Marc hadn't been willing to risk an all-out war with the vampires for James, but Oz was one of his. Even if Oz had disobeyed orders, surely Marc wouldn't just leave him to die?

I held out my hand. "Give me your phone."

"What?" Kai stepped back. "Why?"

I waved my open hand. "Just give me your phone."

Cradling the screen to keep its light contained, I searched for signal. Two bars, the second faded in and out when I moved. I guess even repeaters couldn't work miracles this far underground.

Kai didn't have Marc's number programmed in his phone, and I didn't know it by heart.

"Do either of you know Marc's number?"

They both shook their heads.

Sighing, I called Magpie.

"Magpie books," Maggie answered in her sing-song voice. "How can I help you?"

"Hey, Mags. No time to talk. Do you have Marcus Howard's info in the system?"

"Alex, is . . . you? You're breaking up."

"Marc Howard. I need his number."

". . . guy who's been . . . lately?" Her voice took on a mischievous edge. "Why?"

"Now, Mags."

There was muffled grumbling on the other end, so I assumed she'd set the phone down to access the store records. I crossed my fingers, praying Marc had requested a book at some point.

"Promise . . . tell me what . . . is about?" Maggie's question was sharp. She was dangling the information like a threat.

"Later, Maggie. What's the number?"

"Promise."

I bit my lip. Maggie was my last link to humanity, my last sanctuary.

An agonized howl tore through the room.

"What . . . hell was that?" Maggie shrilled.

"I promise. What's the number?"

"Alex, what . . . that noise?"

"Just give me the damn number, Maggie!" My hissed whisper rose in pitch, and I cupped the phone closer to my mouth. James was watching the backs of the crowd. He hadn't moved. Hopefully, that meant my outburst hadn't broken the trance of Oz's torture.

Kai shifted his weight from foot to foot, sword gripped tight in his hand.

"Three oh three, five five five, oh one seven two." Maggie's voice sounded flat and alien. "This . . . bullshit, Alex."

I opened my mouth, but there was nothing to say. It *was* bullshit. All of it.

A sad sigh echoed through the line, then the call cut off to sharp silence.

Grimacing, I stabbed Marc's number into the phone with numb fingers.

The line rang and rang, stretching each second into nerve-fraying agony. It clicked over on the fifth ring.

"Marc!"

"Alex? Whose phone is this?" Marc's connection was stronger.

"Merak has Oz. We're in the nest."

Silence rang through the line. I checked the screen to make sure the call hadn't dropped. "Marc?"

"How?" The word was more growl than voice.

"Not important right now." I sucked in a breath and held it. "Will you help me save him?"

Short, sharp breaths came over the line. "I'm in Lakewood. I'll grab who I can and meet you at Abandon in fifteen minutes."

I shook my head even though he couldn't see it. "I want to keep an eye on Oz . . . just in case."

"We don't know the nest. We'll waste time trying to find you."

I looked between Kai and James, then back up the hall where Oz was howling as another spear tore into his side. "Kai will guide you."

Kai's mouth opened and I lifted a hand to cover it, ignoring his glare.

"Fifteen minutes," Marc repeated.

The echo of Oz's scream was replaced by a howl of fresh pain.

I shuddered. "Hurry."

Chapter 29

"LIKE HELL I'M leaving you here."

I raised my palms. "The wolves need a guide."

"Send tall, dark, and brooding." Kai jerked his head towards James, whose scowl deepened.

I shook my head. "He's the only one who stands a chance against Merak."

"Then you're coming with me."

"I'd just slow you down."

Hands on hips, he planted his feet. "I'm not leaving you, Alex."

"You said it yourself, we all die if we fight them alone. If you want to save my life, bring the cavalry." I placed my hands on his shoulders. "It's the only option."

His eyes narrowed. "It's not, and you know it."

I let my arms fall. "I'm not leaving him."

Kai rubbed his temples. "This is suicide."

"Not if the wolves come through." We both turned to James. He'd kept his peace through most of the debate. The sunken cheeks and waxy complexion were gone, but a deep tiredness weighed down his eyes, and the corners of his mouth dipped as if they had anchors attached. He ran a hand over the sharp line of his smooth jaw. Guess having your flesh constantly burned off eliminated the need to shave.

"Merak will keep coming after us," his eyes flicked toward me, "all of us, as long as he's alive. This may by our best opportunity to take him down."

"One sip in four days and you think you have the strength to handle a master?" Kai snorted. "You're more arrogant than I remember."

"I won't be alone."

Kai crossed his arms and stared up at the cold stone blocking us off from the world above. Sighing, he shook his head, pinned James with a glare, and jabbed a finger at his chest. "You keep her safe."

I smiled, but he just ran his eyes over me once and muttered, "Lord's gonna kill me." Then he skulked off into the tunnels.

I wrapped shaking hands around my knotted abdomen. Arguing had been one thing, now it was time for action. Me, a reluctant knight, a man I wasn't sure I could trust, and the promise of help against a room full of deranged, psychopathic vampires who got their jollies from torture and pain. My breath caught, a physical lump in my throat, and I choked it down with a shudder.

James's fingers found my shoulder, and when I didn't pull away, gave a gentle squeeze. "I won't let anything happen to you."

"You can't promise that." Pushing aside the anger and betrayal, the lies and distance, I set my hand over his to take the sting out of my words, and because I needed the comfort. He wasn't perfect, but he'd come for me when I needed him, and he'd stayed when I asked. I couldn't trust him completely, but he'd proved more steadfast than many people I'd known. "We need to get in position."

One eyebrow arched above solid blue.

"The wolves will be coming from this end. You and I need to get closer to the throne. When the attack starts, all eyes will be on the wolves. I'll rush to Oz, see if I can get his cage open. You take that opportunity to get to Merak. If you catch him by surprise, you might be able to kill him before the battle even starts. Then we'll just have the lesser vampires to deal with."

He nodded. "Once Merak is dead, the other vampires should fall into line. There's no one else strong enough to challenge me here."

"One of those, 'cut the head off the snake,' situations?"

"Something like that."

"Then that's the plan. Once the fighting starts, you focus on Merak."

I inched toward the vampire backs lining the main room, and prayed their focus stayed fixed on my friend's pain while we slunk along the outer wall. Blue torches lit flashes of faces from across the room as they cheered Oz's pain like gamblers at a dog fight. Shadows danced across the nearest backs, half-in, half-out of the arches. Pools of watery blue light spilled from the tunnels that dotted the outer wall, beacons marking the breaches.

I clutched my charm and moved at the speed of an arthritic snail through the shadows despite screams and cheers that would have covered the noise of a cattle stampede. The lingering odor of bleach still burned in my sinuses, so I could only hope the blood on my clothes wouldn't pique any appetites. Then again, Oz was spilling enough blood to make even a sated vampire drool.

We passed a tunnel directly to the right of Merak's throne and I crossed the pool of blue with bated breath, searching the crowd for signs of alarm. Stepping into the darkness on the far side was like reaching the shade of a tree on a blazing summer day. The sweat on my back instantly cooled to leave me shivering.

Three steps into the shadows, I tugged James's sleeve to pull him up short.

"I'll wait here. You go past the next arch so you're right behind Merak." I pointed past the throne.

He frowned. "We should stay together until the wolves get here."

"We need to be ready when they do. I'm going to draw attention when I run for Oz. You've got a better chance of surprising Merak if we split up."

He looked like he wanted to argue more, but his jaw clamped tight on any response. With a stiff nod, he crept off to take his position.

I hunkered into the deepest shadow I could find. When the wolves came, Merak's back would be exposed. James would be ready. I fingered the handle of my knife, the dips and ridges of the grain were canyons against my skin. I just hoped the little bit of light I carried was enough to hold the monsters at bay.

MY LEGS WERE cramped, my knees ached, and the weight in my bladder was getting intolerable. Surely fifteen minutes must have passed by now? Merak's questions had grown fewer, the time between them stretching to infinity while his guards poked new holes with their silver-tipped spears. Oz's howls had grown hoarse and lost their volume. Now there was just a constant moan punctuated by grunts and an occasional yelp. The crowd around the macabre scene was starting to shift, attentions wandering as the torture lost its intensity.

"Enough of this." Merak's voice tore through the room on a cold wind, sending a fresh wave of shivers through me.

All the backs went still, faces snapping to the throne and the monstrosity sitting on it.

From my vantage, Merak was little more than a gesturing arm draped over the edge of his leather-bound chair and an occasional profile, the sharp angle of his nose and the cruel curve of his lips peeking past long, lank hair as he surveyed the room.

"If the dog can't bark, what good is he?" Skeletal fingers flicked the air in a dismissive gesture.

The faces turned back to the space in front of the throne, jostling, crowding tighter, standing on tiptoes for a better view. Low murmurs broke out as the crowd's anticipation mounted. They were going to kill Oz.

The far end of the room remained wolf-free. No alarms sounded. No half-shredded vampire thrall stumbled into the room to announce an army of vengeful werewolves descending on the nest. I chewed at my chapped lower lip and scanned the shadows behind the throne. James was crouched low near the wall, a barely visible outline.

I placed one hand on the cold stone wall for support and rose to the balls of my feet for a better look at the space in front of the throne.

Oz was huddled in the middle of his cage, curls of smoke rolling off his fur. The skin on his legs and stomach was charred, and chunks of sizzling flesh stuck to the bars in clumps. His ribs rose and fell in short, sharp breaths, his tongue lolling like a dog in August. Once-white fur was slicked down red, a few bare patches of raw pink skin showing through.

Blinking away the pressure in my eyes, I gagged, and thanked the bleach for burning out my sense of smell so the acrid scent of scorched meat was only a faint tickle.

On either side of the cage, men whose bare chests were spattered with blood lifted silver-tipped spears, thick muscles coiling.

I looked again at James. He was standing now, but he wasn't facing the throne. He was looking at me. When my gaze met his, he shook his head. I could feel his will pushing against me. *Not yet. Wait for the wolves.*

But we were out of time. The wolves hadn't come.

I turned back to those spears. The room was a freeze-frame of rapt faces waiting for the wash of group ecstasy at the climax of a porn show.

My hand left the wall.

The executioners inhaled, living statues stretching their molds.

I stepped to the edge of the shadows.

A few nearby faces turned in my direction.

The gun snagged on its holster when I pulled it free. My thumb flicked the safety.

The spears started to move.

I leveled the gun, exhaled, and pulled the trigger.

A crimson shower sprayed from the left shoulder of one of the spearmen and he stumbled back. His spear bounced off the floor, muted by the ringing in my ears. The second spearman froze mid-stab, tottered for balance, and reached one hand to steady himself on the nearest object—Oz's cage.

Oz's teeth sank into the man's hand and pulled it through the gap between the bars until his shoulder wedged.

The man's mouth was open, but I couldn't hear his scream.

Half the faces in the room were still staring at the split-second change in script, but the rest were starting to look around. I shivered under the pressure of a dozen hungry stares.

Six bullets left in my gun. I swung my weapon to the nearest enemies and emptied the clip. Motion burst out around me as vampires spun and tumbled to avoid the shots, knocking into their companions. A few meaty impacts sent men to the floor. I dropped the empty gun as soon as the last round left the barrel and sprinted for Oz's cage, pulling out my second weapon.

My knife barely cleared the sheath before the first clawed hand reached me, but my blade sliced into the vampire's forearm. The gash wasn't deep, but it sizzled and peeled back like paper crisping in a fire.

The vampire shrieked and stumbled away, one hand covering the light-infected wound. For a moment, we all stared, eyes jumping between the singed vampire and the knife in my hand.

Not enough to kill them, Kai had said, but enough to keep me alive. At least for a little while.

Before the group could do more than take a collective breath, I launched into the first man I'd shot, the one who'd been about to stab Oz. I slashed and stabbed, pressing him against Oz's cage.

Again Oz's jaws slipped between silver bars to sink into flesh. The vampire screamed and staggered as teeth tore through the muscles of his leg. I brought my knife down, piercing his chest. Black spread from the wound, a time-lapse video of rot seeping across a piece of fruit. His scream gained in volume, then petered out as he dropped to the floor. My knife pulled free with a wet squelch.

Time seemed to stop, frozen between one beat of my heart and the next as everyone nearby stared at the downed vampire. If Kai's stories were true, he wouldn't stay dead for long, but I'd surprised the circling vultures and earned a second of breathing room.

Then the universe seemed to exhale, and the vampires regrouped. They were wary of my weapon, but after I landed a few more blows it became apparent that my knife could only sting. Even as I whirled and slashed, the man on the floor took a shuddering breath and began to move. Still, these were creatures unused to taking damage, so even a small shock was an advantage. And I'd take all the advantage I could get.

The door to Oz's cage was held closed by three simple crossbar latches. Guess the vampires didn't have to worry so much when the prisoner didn't have human fingers. I had the first latch clear fast enough, then the vampires were pressing me, trying to maneuver me away from the cage.

Oz snapped at anyone who came in reach, which bought me enough space to pull the second latch, but once the vampires got over their initial surprise, their movements sped up. I was reacting more on instinct than input as a series of attacks prodded my defenses. Even with my fae evolution, vampires at full speed were little more than hazy streaks of vile intent.

On the far side of the throne, another fight had broken out. Blurs jerked into focus for milliseconds at a time in a series of still frames punctuated by grunts and snarls before smearing into motion again. James had entered the fray. Even without the wolves, he had my back.

A ridiculous smile tugged at my mouth. I wasn't alone. For all James's faults and failings, he was with me, and that meant the world. Even as clawed fingers slipped through my guard, turning the already stained and tattered fabric across my abdomen to ribbons, my heart soared.

But without the distraction the wolves would have provided, James hadn't had a clear path to Merak. Now there was an army between him and the throne, with more vampires running to intercept him every moment. We'd lost our chance for a quick victory.

Something impacted my side, and I rolled with the momentum. There was a loud thud, then another. Metal groaned. When I came up from my roll, Oz was three feet away straddling his second executioner, his muzzle wet and red. The door of his cage was twisted open. He'd managed to snap the last latch.

A group of vampires closed in around him.

I barely made it to one knee before streaks in shades of gray darted toward me. The attacks were accompanied by snarls and the scuff of stone as the ringing in my ears dissipated. My jeans tore, and hot, wet blood seeped into the heavy fabric on my thigh. An impact on my back sent me sprawling. Gasping, icy shards stabbed through my chest and sparks danced across my vision.

Beyond the swirling darkness, Merak stood in front of his throne, ashen face glaring from the recesses of his hooded robe. His whole body was turned to James with quivering intensity. One hand reached beneath dark folds. A long thin blade emerged, and he held it aloft like Excalibur freshly pulled from the stone.

Hot pain sliced through my shoulder and my knife fell from numb, blood-slick fingers.

I'd managed to hold out for maybe three minutes. Kai had been right. We were all going to die.

Chapter 30

A DISTANT HOWL filtered through my addled senses. Then another. Oz, muzzle glistening, raised his head in answer.

I twisted to see the far tunnel. Between the wavering flames of the blue torches poured a sea of fur. Pelts in shades of brown and gray flooded into the room, splitting off to tangle with the waiting vampires. A large wolf with dark gray fur barreled into a vampire on my right, massive jaws snapping inches from my ear. A spurt of metallic warmth splashed my cheek. The vampire fell back, clutching a hand with three missing fingers.

The solid muscle of the wolf's shoulder bumped me, and I burrowed my fingers in the furry side to convince myself it was real. Deep brown eyes turned to me.

Ignoring the gore and what might have been a finger dangling from teeth as long and thick as my thumb, I focused on those eyes. "Sarah?"

The wolf snorted, a hot breath of blood and decay that warmed my cheeks and fluttered my hair. Then she jumped back into the fray.

Pushing to my feet, I darted to my fallen knife and wrapped my fingers around the comforting weight. I couldn't straighten fully without pain arcing through my chest, so I hunched and hugged my ribs with my left hand. I swayed slightly. All around me, blurred shadows clashed with snarling fur; teeth and claws met swords and knives. Vampires and wolves went down with wounds, only to get up again a moment later as skin sealed and bones mended. Blood slicked the floor in evidence of wounds that no longer existed.

My heart sank. No wonder the wolves hadn't wanted a war. This fight would never end.

"Enough!" Merak raised his arms, silver sword flashing like a super-nova.

The world went black.

I blinked, reached out one hand. My groping fingers found only darkness.

Pressing back a wave of panic, I took a deep breath. The air was stale and cold, and carried the tang of blood. My exhale was a sonic boom in my ears, highlighting the eerie silence the darkness carried with it. More than when the gun had shattered my hearing, the world had been muted. Distant, muffled grunts, a far-off chime that might have been metal against metal. I turned toward each minute sound, straining, but there was nothing in the abyss but me and the invisible ground on which I stood.

My right arm itched and burned as though an army of fire ants was making a meal of it, and I scratched until I felt the skin give way beneath my nails and warm wet smeared my arm.

My knife was a cold, solid comfort in the darkness. Was it my imagination, or was there the slightest glimmer of imbued light pushing back the black?

Squinting, I pulled the blade closer.

Something bumped my arm, and I whirled, losing the flicker of light.

Hot lines of pain tore through my side.

I stumbled away with a gasp, clamping my arm over the fresh wound. The heavy scent of my own blood filled my nostrils. I spat bile into the pressing darkness and took a shuddering breath. Merak had taken back the advantage.

Thick, warm fur brushed my leg and I spun toward it, groping. I stumbled forward and tripped on . . . something. My knees hit stone with bruising force. I reached down to trace the flaccid flesh of an arm that stopped short of an elbow.

Yanking my hand back, I scurried away and crouched in the dark silence, the thin blade of my knife raised to shield me from all my straining eyes couldn't see.

All at once, the terrible itch in my arm subsided. Light flooded back into the world and blinded me a second time.

I blinked through tears that caught in my lashes and trickled down my cheeks, trying to make out the shapes swirling around me in a once more audible clash of blades and fangs. Kai was two steps to my right, his katana a blood-smeared blur tearing through shadows. Sarah's gray fur was spattered red, but she snapped and lunged on my left, holding back three bladeless vampires.

The vampires had lost all semblance of humanity. Jaws extended, unhinging, to reveal rows of jagged fangs. Waxy skin stretched over bones. Sunken eyes glowed in a spectrum of molten metal.

Up on the dais, in the swirling eye of the storm, James clashed with

Merak. He held a stolen sword, shorter and more battered than Merak's. The two were a series of still frames between bursts of motion. Blur, *clash*. Blur, *clash*. If it had been a movie, sparks would have flown off their blades. The friction in their glares was enough to light a fire.

A canine yelp snapped my attention back to Sarah, who hit the stones and slid a good three feet before losing the momentum of the backhand that sent her sprawling.

A small, tawny wolf jumped in front of her, jaws snapping at the vampires who rushed in to finish the job.

The hairs on the back of my exposed neck rose, and I rolled.

Steel sparked off the stones where I'd been crouched.

"You and I have unfinished business." Bryce's voice rolled over my skin like oil.

I shivered at the memory of his hands on my throat, his breath on my cheek. Even more than Merak, his was the face that haunted my dreams and stalked my nightmares.

The tip of his blade scraped stone as he trailed it lazily across the floor.

Kai threw a worried glance over his shoulder, but three vampires were pressing him and blood already soaked one of his sides. I was on my own.

Pulling in all the fear and disgust Bryce's presence brought to the surface, I pressed it into a cold, hard knot in my center, pushing until it turned hot, and a burning rage took its place. Setting my jaw, I steadied my blade and squared my feet.

Bryce lifted his sword with a flick, lips peeling back from a smile of too-long teeth.

I swallowed, and he lunged.

My knife connected with the sweep of his sword as it arced toward my head, but even as the metal touched, my arm started to bow. I didn't have the strength to flat-out block his attack. Probably wouldn't even if I wasn't scared, wounded, and about to pass out from exhaustion and an overused adrenal gland.

Shifting, I let the blade slide off the end of my knife. It sliced through the air an inch from my left arm.

Bryce blurred to the side, not fast enough to be invisible, but smeared, a painting left in the rain.

I dropped to a crouch, hoping I'd read his intention correctly, and pivoted to deflect the incoming blow.

His sword bounced off my knife a second time, hard enough to shake my bones with the impact. He didn't pause between strikes this time, but swept his sword back down. The long arc of his swing gave me plenty of warning, but my body was slow and heavy. I kicked off the ground with all my strength, pushing back and away.

The edge of Bryce's blade tore into my jeans before I was clear, and a fresh slice of wet pain ripped through the side of my calf and scraped my shin.

The leg folded when my weight came down and I went to a knee, rolling with the motion. Bryce's sword found stone again, close on my departing heel.

Lashing out as I emerged from the roll, I caught an edge of loose fabric with the tip of my knife, but Bryce was already moving, and the blade fell short of flesh.

Waves of pain rippled through my chest with every heaving breath, blood trickled from my calf, my thigh, my back, forming cooling stains that seeped and spread through my clothes and sapped my strength along with warmth. Shivering and gasping, I pushed to unsteady feet and raised the shaking knife between myself and death.

One side of Bryce's mouth lifted. "Playtime's over."

He blurred, but he wasn't as fast as James. Not fast enough to disappear. He was a series of afterimages strung together. I swung the knife where I thought those images would end, and Bryce jumped back.

His smile fell. Dark, waxy skin showed through a puckered gap in the maroon silk of his shirt. The skin beneath was smooth and solid, a rippling wall of unbroken muscle, but I'd gotten close.

Bryce narrowed his eyes.

Wolves and vampires still writhed and fought in clusters around the room, and somewhere behind me James was locked in battle with Merak, but I blocked it all out. Taking a deep breath, I let it fade until only Bryce remained.

He rolled his neck, loosened his broad shoulders, braced his feet, and lowered his center of gravity like a charging bull.

I shifted my stance a little wider . . . and watched.

The afterimages spread in several directions this time, possibilities for the future. Bryce was a big, scary thug, but he wasn't stupid. Shadowy blurs streaked to my left and right. One dove straight for me.

I raised my blade to block the rage-contorted expression barreling down on me, but something slipped around my wrist with bone-crushing strength and pulled the knife down. Spinning with the motion, I brought my elbow up, but it bounced harmlessly off the solid wall of Bryce's chest and a second arm came up to wrap my bandaged wrist.

A gasp escaped at the sensation of bone rubbing bone as my already sore wrist screamed under the pressure. My heartbeat threatened to burst through my eardrums with its cacophonous knocking and my lungs refused to expand, trapped by the steel bar of Bryce's forearm pressed against my chest. I couldn't breathe, couldn't move, couldn't think. . . . I was going to die.

"Don't think for a second this will end quickly for you." Bryce's cheek was cold against mine, but his breath was hot and carried with it the scent of blood and peppermint candy.

His arm squeezed, and fireworks exploded across my darkening vision.

I pushed and pushed, but he was a statue, carved in stone, immovable. My knife glinted menacingly two inches from my own face, clutched in fingers I could barely feel. Beyond it, James and Merak clashed, their blurs coming to rest for a split second of communion before breaking apart and repeating the process. Both were breathing hard. The next image showed James parrying Merak's thrust. The parry was sloppy, and the tip of Merak's blade kissed James's forearm.

A dozen patches of darker fabric decorated James's clothes. He was losing.

My heart seized, the constant thudding in my ears falling silent as the blood stopped dead in my veins. If James fell, it was all for nothing. Not only that—

My eyes roved the room. Kai was holding his own against three opponents, but his left arm cradled a dark stain on his side and he was favoring his right leg. An anxious glance flitted in my direction, but it cost him a moment of focus and the next attack raked claws across his upper arm. Pain and desperation pinched his features. He turned away from me.

Furry bodies still snapped at shadows, but they were slowing down, grouping together. There weren't as many as I'd first imagined in that initial rush. Maybe a dozen.

The reddish wolf I'd seen earlier was holding one paw curled off the ground, hobbling on the other three. Sarah was by its side, snapping and snarling. Blood soaked her fur, maybe hers, maybe someone else's. A smaller, lighter brown wolf lay on the ground twenty feet away, not moving. Two wolves stood guard over the still figure, fending off the circling vampires.

If James fell, there would be no one to hold back the darkness. If

James fell, we all fell.

I took a shallow, shuddering breath and swallowed, blinking away tears.

I'd done this. Me. We were all going to die here, in a place I'd promised myself I'd never be again, and it was my fault.

"What's the matter, girly? No witty comeback? No show of strength?" Bryce's tongue flicked out, licking the salty sweat off my neck. "Don't tell me you've broken already."

The cage of Bryce's thick arms squeezed tighter. Push as I might I couldn't budge them.

It's not about strength. Ryan-sensei's voice echoed in my head. Sun warmed the mats under my folded legs, making me want to curl up below the window and nap like Chase on a cold day. Ryan-sensei's knees bumped mine. He lifted his hands, and I reached for his wrists. *Aikido isn't about fighting your opponent.* He twisted, and my body followed. I rolled to the warm mat. *It's about feeling them.*

I stopped struggling against the crushing weight of Bryce's constricting muscles. I let every shift in his posture move me, ripple through me, until I was shifting with him. *Come on, Alex. Find the weakness.*

His weight shifted slightly to the right, freeing his left foot to move. The world seemed to slow down, each second stretching to infinity.

I moved with him, using the shift to open a space between us. It was barely wide enough to slip two fingers between our pressed bodies, but it was a breath, a hope. Continuing the motion, I carried Bryce's shift farther, overbalancing his right leg.

The gap between us grew.

Dropping my weight, I started to turn, pushing into Bryce to fill the space growing between us.

One of his hands released for balance, and I spun. Time snapped back into place.

As I spun, I turned the knife. The blade met resistance, and a howl of pain and rage erupted from Bryce to mingle with my own victorious cry as I stumbled away, crouching.

My gaze rose first, preceding my body by fractions of a second. Enough time to see my handiwork.

A ragged line of sizzling flesh crossed the left side of Bryce's face, starting near his close-cropped hair and tapering out on his cheek. The eyelid between was sealed tight. The edges of the wound hissed and peeled, reacting to the light in my blade.

I'd seen this before, when I'd struck a fae with iron. Then, it had turned my stomach. Now, I smiled. I really was becoming a monster, but it was worth it. I'd hurt one of my nightmares.

Bryce bellowed.

I tore my eyes away from the damage I'd done in time to see the blur of his arm arcing toward me, but not in time to move.

The smile dropped off my face, following my heart to cower somewhere in the region of my bowels as I braced for impact.

The back of Bryce's fist was a cinder block on contact. My head snapped to the side, but not before the bone in my cheek collapsed. Pressure burst inside my skull, exploding behind my eye and lancing across my nose. The world spun and tumbled, vampires and werewolves flashing through my scattered, hazy vision. Blood filled my mouth, and I had a brief moment of weightlessness to wonder if I still had all my teeth. Then the ground came up to say hello.

It wasn't happy to see me.

I rolled three times before something hard and sharp dug into my back. My arms and legs lay limp, the limbs of a rag doll dropped down the stairs. My ruined cheek was pressed to the cold ground, and the concrete drew out my pain to leave me blessedly numb. The knife was gone, lost to the world that skipped by while I flew. My right eye wouldn't open.

An eye for an eye.

The thought made my rebelling mind giggle, but I choked on the inhale and coughed. Blood sprayed across stone.

Above me, the clash of metal sounded again and again, and I rolled my one working eye to find the source. Blurred shadows, then James and Merak, posed like dark gods in combat.

Bryce's hit had fetched me up against the dais.

James's arms were raised to brace his block. They shook under the force of Merak's downward arc. His knees bent a little more, sinking him lower. His teeth were a white wall of clenched fangs framed by peeled lips. Sweat dripped off his brow.

James was at the end of his strength. The wolves were barely holding their own against the vampires. There was no way I could beat Bryce.

We were going to lose.

No. I gave myself a mental shake. *No way. Not now. Not to these monsters.*

Pressure exploded behind my eye when I rolled to my elbows and knees, and I took a moment to let the throbbing pain subside. Ragged breaths tore through my chest, igniting my ribs. I wasn't going to die. Not here. Not like this.

Dust and gravel stuck to my damp palms, and I wiped them along my thighs. My left hand ran over a lump in my side pocket. I froze.

Not much of a weapon, but maybe . . . just maybe . . .

James and Merak hadn't spared me more than a glance, locked as they were in the cycle of *clash*, blur, *clash*, blur, *clash*. Kai had managed to move his battle between Bryce and the dais, buying me time.

I pushed to my feet, hands splayed for balance as darkness swam behind my eyes and swirled through my brain like snow on the winter wind.

Bracing one hand on my thigh, I reached the other into my pocket, groping for the solid weight of my last, desperate hope.

My fingers closed around smooth plastic.

It was suicide, a fool's gambit, but I'd led my friends to this slaughter. If I could give them even the slimmest chance. . . . I had to try.

Licking my lips, I planted my feet, took a deep breath, and waited for the clashing titans to come to rest. As soon as Merak came into focus, I shouted, "Hey, Merak."

Lifting my hand, I thrust it at his exposed ribs and pressed the rubbery button on my flashlight. Light exploded from the end of the tube, bright and warm in the cold flicker of blue torches.

Merak's eyes went wide, but couldn't focus on the object in my hand. Couldn't see it for the bluff it was.

He spun, thrusting past the shorter reach of my attack.

James's blade came up, a streak of silver that matched his wild eyes.

Hot pain pierced my abdomen, followed by a wave of numbing cold.

The flashlight dropped from my fingers, cracking against the stone dais. It rocked back and forth, spraying scattered light through its fractured lens.

James's sword completed its arc, bursting through Merak's neck in a spray of warm, wet droplets that sparkled as they fell, a shower of liquid rubies.

Merak's head landed a foot from my flashlight with a wet squelch. His mouth hung partly open, his eyes wide, like an actor who'd forgotten his lines and been caught in an unforgiving spotlight.

Silence fell.

Vampires froze in every corner of the room, eyes wide and empty, as though they were looking inside themselves. Then their faces turned as one to the dais. Kai and the wolves turned too, more warily, to see what had stopped their adversaries dead in their tracks.

Merak's robes fluttered as gravity claimed his body, pulling it down to join his lolling head.

I sighed, coughed, and a stream of coppery bubbles dribbled down my chin.

Tearing my eyes away from Merak's empty stare, I looked down at the sword embedded in my gut.

Then gravity claimed me too.

Chapter 31

I NEVER HIT the ground.

James's arm slipped behind my shoulders in the space between breaths. The fingers of his other hand flitted over my cheek. My head lolled against his chest, and I breathed in the spice of him mingled with sweat and blood. A heavy numbness spread through my abdomen, stretching, expanding to fill my chest, my limbs. All the aches and pains I'd been carrying disappeared. James's fingers continued to stroke my cheek, but the sensation was distant. We were prisoners pressing our palms to the glass.

"Alex!" Kai dropped to his knees beside me.

I tried to turn my head, to reply. A thick stream of cooling bubbles trickled from the corner of my mouth and dribbled a sticky line down my neck.

Kai's hands hovered over the hilt sticking out of my abdomen. His cheeks were wet.

"She's too far gone." James's reedy voice drifted to me, a distant whisper, a secret carried on the wind.

Kai shook his head, eyes scrunched closed, jaw clenched. Shimmering drops streaked his cheeks and fell from his chin. Each tear flared Mediterranean blue with reflected light before shattering against the growing darkness spreading across the tattered remains of my shirt.

James's arm tightened, his free hand cupping my numb face.

I tried to find his eyes, but the world rolled in and out of focus. My mouth was open—I could tell by the thick, foul flavor drying on my lips—but it wouldn't form words. My systems were shutting down one by one, refusing to respond to my commands. I couldn't even say goodbye, couldn't tell James I forgave him.

I willed my arm to move, to find his hand one last time, but my fingers just twitched like a suffocating fish and fell limp. I was a prisoner in my dying body, trapped just out of reach while the world faded around me.

"Pull it out." James's words were a low rumble that reached my ears some time after his lips had moved. He was staring at Kai.

"That will only kill her faster." Kai reached down and lifted a limp piece of pale flesh. His fingers twined with mine, but I was watching a movie screen while I melted into the darkness of the theater.

"I can save her." Quiet words, barely spoken, as though nervous to leave the safety of James's mouth and face the big scary world outside.

A flicker of hope deep inside me stirred groggily, but didn't have the energy to surface.

Kai's empty, streaming eyes lifted, cloudy with confusion. Then they narrowed. The lines around his frown grew more pronounced. "No."

"She'll die."

"I won't allow it."

"It's not your decision to make."

The floppy hand Kai had been holding hit the floor, knuckles slamming the stone with the force of an unarrested fall. It should have hurt.

"You would defile her?" Kai spat the words in James's face, his fist buried in James's collar so the two were inches apart above me.

James's Adam's apple bobbed, his nostrils flared. "You would let her die?"

They stared at each other for a long time. Long enough that my attention wandered and I forgot the statues posed above me were actual living people deciding my fate.

When Kai released James, I jumped, at least in my head. My body didn't move. He threw himself back against the stone floor with a growl, face hidden behind blood-streaked hands.

"Just enough to save her." James's words were stronger, yet they seemed even quieter than before.

"It might kill her anyway." The mumbled voice must have been Kai's, but it carried a strange, tinny quality. A bad connection on a cheap cell phone.

James's eyes slid closed then opened, a slow motion blink. No, a regular blink, I was just out of sync. Dark curtains shrank the world to slits. James's face loomed close to mine, filling my vision, flooding me with regrets I couldn't quite remember as my cares and worries faded.

His mouth moved in silence, forming shapes without words.

The world faded into nothing, swallowing James with it.

"Alex." His voice tickled my mind. "Drink."

IT BURNED.

I writhed and flopped as flames licked up my bones and melted my nerves in a cascade of spreading, searing pain. Flesh that had been numb a moment before burst into agonizing existence. Every scrape, every bruise sang to the world of its rebirth and slammed into me with the force of a runaway semi.

Distantly, I could feel hands, arms, pressed against me, restraining as I thrashed against pain and stone.

My mind unraveled, shrieking, shrinking from the inescapable. It was inside me, clawing through my veins, my muscles, tearing me apart and putting me back together. Dying had been the better option. Dying was quiet, peaceful. It was cold and empty and over. This was a raging conflagration that swelled and grew and never stopped. The threads of my sanity snapped one by one as the agony tore through me again and again. My muscles seized, rigor mortis without the release of death. Nails ripped against stone as my clawed fingers scratched and tore, searching for something, anything, that would end my misery. My jaw ached, teeth locked together over a guttural scream that found its way out through my nose.

"Breathe, Alex!"

My eyes snapped open to find Kai's panicked face, eyes wide above me. The galaxies spun like children on a merry-go-round. My stomach joined them, cramping in a full-body heave. Kai shoved my shoulder, rolling me onto my side as the first wave of bile and blood spewed forth, splattering stones and dribbling down my cheek with the sharp scent of sick that brought another wave up in response.

I heaved and gasped until nothing remained. My stomach was empty, my muscles were slack. I didn't even bother to lift my head from the sticky puddle gluing cheek to stone.

Kai's hand rubbed a steady circle on my back until the shuddering spasms stopped. Until my chest rose and fell in even increments. Until my heart returned to its steady rhythm. Then he tucked his hands under my armpits and lifted.

My cheek peeled off the floor with a wet squelch, the edges of the slime itching and flaking where it had started to dry. Kai's arms were a life-preserver in the ocean, and I clung to him until my butt came down on solid ground.

Perched at the edge of the dais, I blinked a few times, trying to focus. People were moving all around me, but not in the super-fast, fighting-for-your-life way I remembered. Clumps of men and women dragged away broken weapons and severed limbs. Buckets of soapy water sloshed as mops plunged in and out of pink liquid and slapped against stone.

Kai squeezed my shoulder. "You okay?"

Was I?

My eyes snapped down, fingers groping at the blood-stained hole in my shirt. The skin beneath was slick but smooth. "How—"

He gestured to the largest group, clustered near the now empty cage where Oz had been. James's back was to me, his hands moving in animated conversation with the other members of his group. Marc stood beside him in a pair of gray sweatpants several inches too short. His arms were crossed over his bare chest, shoulders knotted around his neck. He wasn't happy. That apology was going to be a bitch.

Beside him, Sarah was shaking her head. She wore an oversized t-shirt that hung to her thighs, commemorating a heavy metal concert. A tall, thin man with reddish-brown hair, the billowing shirt of a pirate, and sagging khaki shorts was tucked under her arm. Around the room, I noted other people wearing mismatched, off-sized clothes in a range of styles from modern vagabond to Victorian gutter snipe, probably pilfered from the vampires so they didn't have to stand around in the buff after shifting back to human.

On James's other side, as far from the others as possible while still being included, stood Bryce. An angry red line stood out against his skin. His eye was still closed.

My heart and breathing picked up a notch. My muscles tensed.

"They're sorting out the details," Kai said. "Merak is dead."

It took everything I had to tear my eyes away from Bryce and focus on the blood-stained dais beside me. Thick, black pools smeared its surface, and a large, wet splat marked the spot where Merak's head had landed, but there were no remains.

I tipped my head to one side. "Where—"

"The body was disposed of." Kai's hand thudded my shoulder, rocking me. "You did well, Alex."

"I was afraid." James's voice came to me, blurred around the edges.

I smiled, eyes still locked on the stain on the floor. "Me too."

"What?" Kai pulled his hand away.

I looked up. Kai studied me with a frown, his eyebrows drawn together so they nearly touched above his nose.

James was still twenty feet away in conference with the others, hand lifted as though it had frozen mid-gesture.

"Sorry. I thought I heard—" I shook my head. "It doesn't matter."

James's arm fell to his side. He turned until his eyes met mine. A flood of relief slammed into me, and I gripped the edge of the dais with both hands to keep from being washed away.

A giddy smile broke out on my face as warmth seeped into every cell of my body. My heart swelled and jumped like an excited puppy. Then something hotter and wilder began to stir, a hungry ache that reached for the man walking toward me with a life of its own.

What the hell? Am I drunk?

Something like that. James's lips hadn't moved, but I'd heard him, loud and clear. Then a cold wall slammed into place between us, severing the connection.

No, not severing. Muting. He was still there, thoughts and emotions swirling on the other side, pushing to get through. The force of my desire dulled to a steady throb that surged with the beats of my heart.

"A side effect." This time his lips did move, forming the words in the space between us for all to hear. After the intimate connection, it felt distant, empty, and I mourned the loss.

Kai looked between us, shook his head, and stalked off to replace James in the group.

"It should be temporary," James continued. He stood two feet from the dais, rigid and unyielding.

"A side effect of what?"

His eyes, clear blue, shifted to the side. I followed them to the blood smears that were all that was left of Merak.

"You were dying."

A phantom blade of cold steel lodged in my gut, piercing me with the memory of its physical counterpart. I shuddered, pressing my hands over the missing wound. "How am I still alive?"

"Vampires heal fast. Faster than fae. Faster than werewolves." He raised one hand, looked at his fingers, turned it over to see his wrist. "The magic is in our blood."

"Your—" I swallowed hard. My hand flew to my throat, tracing the gulp to my chest, where it disappeared into my body. "I drank . . ." I shook my head. "Vampires have demon magic."

My mind reeled, grasping at facts drilled into me during hours-long tutoring sessions with Kai and Hortense. Demons and fae were antithetical. Their magic didn't mix. *You can't become a vampire any more than you could become a werewolf.* Kai's words, sharp and clear in my memory. I couldn't, I *wouldn't* become a vampire.

The corner of James's mouth twitched. "Kai is not the end all of knowledge. The fae have been wrong before."

"Then—"

He raised a hand. "You will not turn. Your fae blood burned the magic out almost as fast as I could put it in. Almost, but a little vampire blood goes a long way."

My eyes lost focus as I tried to recall those final moments. My body had felt like it was tearing itself apart. "That's why it hurt so much."

"Your body was rejecting my gift, fighting the demon for supremacy." His expression tightened. "I'm sorry, Alex."

"Don't be." I shook my head. "I'm alive. I wouldn't be if not for you."

"Nor I, if not for you."

A lopsided smile pulled at my lips. "Guess that makes us even."

James took a tentative step through no man's land. He dropped to one knee an arm's length in front of me. "Alex, I . . ." He lifted his hand.

"James." Marc's word was a whip, slicing the moment. "Time to move."

James's hand fell on an exhale, never quite connecting. I pounded at the mental wall between us, searching for the words, the emotions, that would give us our happy ending, but the barrier kept me at bay.

"I have to go." He pushed to his feet. "We can continue this—"

"Another time," I finished.

His smile was bitter when he turned away.

Marc met James's eyes for one tense moment, then took the space in front of me. The thin man with reddish-brown hair stood behind him, eyes on his feet.

"Alex," Marc said.

I shrank from my name like a kid who knew she'd done something wrong. My gaze flicked to the empty cage in the center of the room. "Is Oz—"

"Why didn't you wait for us?"

"They were going to kill him."

"He shouldn't have been here in the first place."

I ducked my head, ceding the point.

Marc ran a hand through his hair with a sigh. "He and the other injured are on their way to Luke."

Tears stung my eyes. Happy that Oz would be okay, or upset I'd gotten others hurt? Maybe both. I wiped them away.

Marc set a hand on his companion's shoulder. "Gil will take you home."

"What about Kai?"

"He's needed for cleanup." Marc looked back over his shoulder where Kai, James, Sarah, and Bryce were still talking. "We've got a lot of loose ends to tie up."

That was an understatement. There were a handful of dead thralls scattered around the chamber, a nest of leaderless vampires, and a truckload of injured werewolves trying to stay under the PTF's radar. James was still on the line for murder and drug trafficking, and O'Connell was still a royal pain in my ass. Merak was gone, but that was a far cry from solving all my problems.

"It's my mess." I set my jaw. "I should stay."

"You'd only be a distraction." The words slammed into me, a fist to the gut. "One we can't afford if we're going to pull this off."

I narrowed my eyes. "Pull *what* off?"

"Gil can fill you in." Marc turned to the man at his side. "Get her out of here." Then he stalked back to the group.

"Come on." Gil's voice was light and soothing. He offered me a smile and set a hand on my shoulder. "We should go."

Clenching my jaw until it ached, I pushed to my feet. "Like hell I will."

I marched after Marc, glaring for all I was worth at the group of men who thought they could shuffle me off while they handled things.

Kai was first to notice my approach. He shook his head, lips pressed thin. Marc crossed his arms and frowned. Bryce stood slightly to one side, but his one working eye bore into me like a poison dagger. Sarah was talking to James, gesturing as she spoke. James had his back to me, but stiffened at my approach. The press of emotions beating at the wall between us grew stronger.

"I'm seeing this through to the end," I said

James sighed. "You already did."

"Then what are you talking about over here?"

He turned to face me. His eyes were blue, free of silver, but tired. He reached out as though to grab my shoulder, but pulled back at the last moment and gestured with his other hand instead, back toward the dais. "Please."

I planted my hands on my hips and stood my ground.

He closed his eyes. "Fine. Our battle with Merak is over." He tipped his head toward Bryce, but I didn't follow the gesture. I'd be happy to never see that bastard again. "Bryce is strong enough to keep the others in line, but too weak to challenge me. Together, we will hold the nest until another comes to claim it."

"Wait." I held up a hand. "You're gonna let *him*," I jabbed a finger in Bryce's direction, still not making eye contact, "run the nest?"

"For now. The vacuum left by Merak's passing won't last long."

"He's a monster," I snapped.

"He's the only lieutenant strong enough to hold the nest."

"Why can't you do it?" I jammed a finger against James's chest.

A wave of frustration crashed into me, and I stumbled back, barely keeping my feet. "What the hell?"

"Contact makes the connection stronger." James crossed his arms and turned so I was watching his profile. "I don't have time for this right now, Alex. And I don't have the energy to keep shielding you. The nest is a matter for the vampires, and Sarah and Bryce are going to help with my legal troubles. There's nothing left for you to do here."

I opened my mouth before I realized I had nothing to say, no argument to give beyond that of a petulant child angry at being sent to bed while the grownups stayed awake.

"Marc." A short, Asian woman with a long gray braid trailing to her butt stepped up to the group. Marc glanced in my direction, then turned to the woman with a nod.

"Luke reports two of the injured wolves are critical, the others will be released by morning."

Marc nodded again.

Steely black eyes found me for a moment before the woman turned and marched off.

"I need to go." Marc clapped a hand on Sarah's shoulder. "See me when it's done."

"Alex." My attention swung back to James. "Go home."

Chapter 32

"ALEX, ALEX, YOU have to see what's on the TV!" Jynx's voice grew louder as she spoke. The bed jolted on the last word, springs creaking under her added weight.

My eyelids fluttered, and I scraped my tongue over fuzzy teeth, cringing at the flavor.

Beside me, Chase groaned and rolled over, pulling a pillow over his head. "No one cares about your cartoons, Jynx." His muffled voice was barely audible through the pillow.

Jynx stuck out her tongue. "It just so happens, I'm watching the *news.*" She stretched the word like it was from a foreign language.

"Come on!" She grabbed my arm and pulled until I fell off the bed, barely getting my legs under me before I hit the floor. I cut my eyes to the clock. 4:36 p.m. My mouth went dry.

Work. Maggie. I'd missed my entire shift.

Mind spiraling, I ran a hand through my snarled hair. Maggie was gonna be so pissed that I didn't— Another thought hit me and I groped for the discarded cargo pants next to my bed. The fabric was dark and stiff. Another outfit I'd need to burn.

Jynx bounced on the balls of her feet. "You don't need to get dressed, Alex."

Ignoring her, I closed my hand around the folded paper I'd stuffed in the pocket last night and pulled out the crumpled note. I'd survived, the letter was dangerous.

I went to tear it, the thick paper stretched between my hands, but stopped. The way my life was going, what if something happened before I got the chance to come clean face to face? Maggie still deserved an explanation.

Jynx glanced over her shoulder. "*Hurry*, Alex." She grabbed my arm and tugged.

Pulling open the nightstand drawer, I dropped the note inside and slammed it shut. Then I let her pull me into the hall. "All right, all right, I'm coming. What's—" The words died on my lips.

James's face filled the TV screen. Blood coated one side, cascading from a gash in his forehead and over a swollen purple knot that hid one eye. As the camera angle widened, I saw he was strapped to a gurney. His shirtless torso was a camouflage of green and purple bruises lit by the strobing lights of a waiting ambulance.

My breath caught. Invisible ropes squeezed my throat shut. Bryce had betrayed him. Of course he had.

My mind flashed to another body, another person I loved being carted away. Mom never woke up after that ambulance ride.

But the world wasn't black and white anymore. James wasn't human. He could recover. . . . But why hadn't he already? Was he protecting his secret from the prying eyes of the human media? Or was he out of energy? Bryce must have been stronger than James thought.

The camera panned to another gurney being wheeled out the front door of a single story house with stucco walls and a blue front door. A hole the size of a small car was punched through the front wall, and a mangled refrigerator lay on the lawn.

The occupant of the second gurney was encased in a thick black bag.

My heart stuttered, stopped, then slammed into overdrive. I braced against the back of the couch. Who had died? Kai? Sarah? My knuckles cracked. I never should have let Bryce live.

A pouty-lipped reporter with bleach-blond hair stepped into the frame. "That was the scene just moments ago after an anonymous tip led police to a fatal shootout. The suspect, identified as Raymond Kamryn, was shot and killed after throwing a *refrigerator* through the front window."

The image of a middle-aged man with thick black hair and eyes the color of autumn wheat filled the screen. I caught my breath. I'd seen those eyes before . . . somewhere.

The image shrank to a thumbnail to hover in one corner while the reporter continued. "Local PTF agent Benjamin O'Connell is here on the scene."

The shot widened to include O'Connell's pinched features. Even on TV, the guy made my skin crawl.

"Police say that despite his strength, the culprit here was not a faerie but a human using some sort of drug. Can you confirm that?" She shoved the microphone under his nose.

O'Connell looked like he wanted to spit. "The PTF has been

investigating reports of an enhancement drug that gives humans fae-like abilities."

"Does the PTF have any idea where this new drug is coming from?"

"Not yet, but we believe it to be of fae origin."

"Why would the fae produce a drug to make humans stronger?"

"No further comments." O'Connell pushed the microphone aside and stalked out of the frame.

"Also taken from the building was James Abernathy," the reporter continued without missing a beat, "a person of interest in the death of a young woman found in the apartment above his Boulder art gallery. Mr. Abernathy was found chained in Kamryn's basement, where he seems to have been a prisoner for the past several days. Whether this has any connection to the previous crime, or allegations of Mr. Abernathy's involvement in the drug trade, has yet to be confirmed."

Ice and gravel crunched.

Muting the TV, I stepped up to the window and pushed the curtain back for a peek. The sky was a deep amber that shrank the shadows of the forest and made the world flat. Pink clouds dotted the sky above snow-speckled trees.

James's black Lexus rolled to a stop beside my Jeep.

A rushing warmth flooded my system and made my limbs turn to rubber.

"Jynx, could you—"

She raised both hands. "Say no more." Melting into the furry white leopard, she bounded down the hall and disappeared into the storage room at the end. A streak of gray darted from my bedroom to follow her.

James stepped out of the SUV. The collar of his coat was turned up, obscuring his face, and a thick, maroon scarf wrapped his neck. A brimmed hat shaded his eyes.

Letting the curtain fall back into place, I took a step toward the door, and froze. My hands traced the long t-shirt I'd thrown on to replace my shredded, blood-soaked clothes. My fingers fluttered past a mouth the flavor of roadkill and the area around my puffy, dry eyes, and touched snarled strands of unbrushed hair.

I flicked my eyes to the bathroom, sighed, and grabbed a sweater hanging near the door. My bare feet slipped into a pair of muddy galoshes.

Taking a deep breath, I straightened my shoulders and pulled the door open.

James was standing in the middle of the porch, hands clasped behind his back. His suit still hung a little loose under the folds of his long, gray coat, but his hair was a dark gloss that swallowed the sunset colors like a black hole, every strand perfectly in place. The swollen bruise that marred his cheek made my eyes sting, but the blood was gone. His skin was pale and clean.

As soon as I saw him, a push of muted thoughts and emotions slammed into me. I gasped and grabbed the door frame.

"Could you turn off your security?" His voice was strong and steady.

Nodding, I reached for the panel by the door and punched in a code.

"Thank you." He swept off the hat and scarf in a single motion. The bruise faded from his face and the swelling disappeared, leaving him with two perfect blue eyes. "That's much better."

"Your face . . ." I lifted a hand, but stopped short of touching his perfect skin. "Of course." I snorted at my own stupidity. "You'd be healed by now."

His eyebrows drew together. "Alex, I was never injured."

I shook my head. "But . . . the news. Illusions don't work on cameras, and I saw—"

"Makeup, applied to match the illusion I used on the humans present. Nothing more." His frown deepened. "Didn't Gilbert tell you?"

"I . . ." Heat crept up my neck as I recalled the soothing voice of my tawny-haired chauffeur. "Fell asleep."

The frown flipped, turning into a smile.

I tugged the sweater tighter and rubbed the back of one goosebumped leg on the other. "Guess almost dying really took it out of me."

It had been nearly four a.m. when I made it to the car, thirteen hours after entering the nest. I shook my head. The giddy, invincible feeling I'd had when I woke up had started to fade almost immediately. Then came the aches and fatigue. My skin was whole and smooth, but beneath the surface, everything hurt. Not broken bones and shredded muscles kind of hurt, but a dull throb that sapped the strength from my body and wore at my mind. I'd passed out two blocks from Abandon.

Something smashed into the invisible wall between us, and I clutched the door frame tighter. Tears burned in my eyes. My chest constricted as though someone was sitting on it, pressing the air from my lungs.

"What—" I gasped.

The wall thickened, pushing back the feeling so I could breathe again.

"I'm sorry. The closer we are, the stronger the connection."

I rubbed my chest, easing air back into my lungs. "I thought the connection was supposed to fade along with the energy you gave me."

"The fae in you *will* burn out the demon." He frowned. "But it seems it'll take longer than I expected."

"How much longer?"

He shrugged. "This is uncharted territory for me as well. So long as even a drop of my demon soul remains, we will be connected."

Recalling all the warring emotions I'd been trying to keep in check lately, I cringed. The thought of having an audience to my inner turmoil was like salt in an open wound. "Can you hear me too, or is this a one way street?"

"The link goes in both directions, but the wall I've erected protects us."

I mentally prodded that wall, pushing against it, imagining I was placing my hands against bricks. "How?"

"Years of practice."

"I've had plenty of occasions to wall off my emotions, but this . . ." I shook my head.

A shadow flitted through his eyes and something dark brushed the wall like a creature seen through the depths.

I shivered.

James shifted, and I caught sight of something clutched behind his back. Something small and dark with a braided cord strap.

"Is that my purse?"

His smile returned. "I found it in the nest. Thought you might want it back." He held out the small clutch I'd carried on my first trip to Abandon.

Wrenching it open, I found my wallet and keys. My fingers closed on my cell phone.

Dead battery. Of course.

I dropped the useless phone back in the bag.

A breeze flowed over crusted ice and kissed my skin with frost, sending a shiver through me. "Want to come in?"

James's jaw tightened. He glanced behind him, looking at the Lexus as if he wanted to run. Invisible fingers tightened around my heart. Then he nodded and slipped past me.

I hadn't moved out of the way, but somehow he got by without so much as brushing me.

A lump lodged in my throat. He didn't want to touch me. He was barely looking at me. Had I saved James only to lose him anyway?

My eyes widened at the thought. Did I want him back? Had I forgiven him? I hadn't had time for conscious thought since the rescue.

Shit! Was he listening to all this? I searched his face for any sign he'd been eavesdropping on my thoughts, but his expression hadn't changed.

I mentally prodded the wall between us again, wondering if I could trust it. . . . trust him.

The news still scrolled silently on the TV, now covering local sports. I gestured to the screen. "So you set it up to look like that guy abducted you. I take it that's what you and the others were discussing when you shooed me out of the nest."

"Not just that. Your friend Oz did a brilliant job giving Kamryn a background in drug trafficking, and an obsessive history with the girl from my apartment."

I breathed a sigh of relief. If Oz was healthy enough to work his techno-magic, he'd be fine.

"Sarah made sure she and her partner were closest when the call came in. She also made sure the shots were fatal."

My thoughts circled to the black bag being wheeled out in front of the cameras. Not Kai or Sarah, but . . . . "You sacrificed him to clear your name."

A flash of heat hit the wall in my mind, followed by a cold so deep it made the winter evening seem like a summer day.

"No one was sacrificed. Though if he had been, it would have been well deserved."

The man's eyes flashed in my memory, and I remembered where I'd seen them before. "Elsa."

I gripped my upper arms, shuddering. His eyes had been gold in the forest that night. "He was a vampire." I frowned. "But the news said he was killed at the scene."

"And the news never lies." He snorted. "Kamryn is old enough to play dead convincingly."

"So he was—"

"Shot through the heart and the head, zipped in a light-proof body bag before he was wheeled out in front of the cameras, and autopsied at the morgue."

I swallowed. "Autopsied?"

James shrugged. "The police and PTF needed evidence to explain Elsa being ripped apart. The new enhancer drug was the perfect cover."

"But," I waved a hand in front of my torso. "How could he let them cut him up if he wasn't dead."

"He didn't. Have you forgotten how potent an illusion can be?"

The memory of a million biting insects swarming my skin rose in my mind. I'd felt the bones beneath me, heard them crunch.

"So it's over?"

James tipped his head back and forth. "I'm sure the police will have more questions, and I'm going to have my hands full keeping Bryce and the nest in line until a new master comes, but. . . . Yes. For now, it's over."

I nodded, chewing my lip. No more big bad coming to kill us. No more interruptions. No more excuses. Crossing my arms, I braced against the back of the couch and took a steadying breath.

"We need to talk." I shook my head. "I'm just not sure where to begin."

He stepped up so we were toe to toe. "Allow me."

The wall between us fell away.

At first, I fought against the crash of thoughts and emotions. I was floating in an ocean with no land in sight, the more I struggled, the faster I drowned. Pain and guilt swirled through me, and loneliness settled around my heart like an anchor.

Even as I fought not to be overwhelmed by the inrush of feelings, I strained to hold on to my own. Every hope, every fear was laid bare between us. I gathered them up like dirty laundry, but there was too much. I couldn't hide it all.

"Let it go." James's hands cradled either side of my face. Piercing blue stared into me. Then I saw myself through his eyes, pale skin and sleep-matted hair, dark bags drooping under eyes that looked more gray than blue.

I swayed, disoriented. Then my face was overlaid with others, hazy images painted over a used canvas. My features were the most clear, but mixed in with them were the features of a middle-aged woman, a raven-haired child, a boy on the cusp of becoming a man, a blond woman with sharp features and cold eyes. . . . The faces blurred until I couldn't distinguish one from another.

"People you remind me of," he whispered.

"Ghosts," I corrected. "Of the people you've loved."

He nodded. "And I love you, Alyssandra Katherine Blackwood."

The words shivered through me. They carried the weight of truth, but I pushed past them looking for the lie, the trap.

Burrowing beyond the thoughts and emotions he'd laid open to me, I found a cold dark knot huddled inside him; a place I could feel but couldn't see. He was still blocking me, letting me in so far but no farther.

You don't trust me. The words were an echo with no origin. Was it my thought, or his?

My consciousness brushed against that hole, an emptiness without form or texture. This was where the monster slept. The silver-eyed demon.

"I cannot change who I am," he whispered.

"I know." I pulled back from the void inside him. The demon was there, a dark, dangerous part of him, but his feelings were a vibrant counterbalance. He believed he loved me. But what about that dark spot in his soul, the part of him that was like Merak? What happened when the vampire took control? "I don't know if I can trust you."

"Give me a chance." His hands slid down my arms to clasp mine. "I may miss a few dates, but I'll always be there for the moments that matter."

I frowned. Was that the perspective of an ageless being? If a person lived long enough, did the little things in life stop being important? I pulled my hands free. "They all matter."

Ripples spread across the wall in my mind.

"I don't want to lose you, Alex."

I smiled. "I'm not going anywhere."

"You know what I mean."

"I appreciate you saving me from Merak, but if my life has to be in danger just to make your priority list . . ." I shook my head. "You've got a vampire nest to run now. You won't have time for me." He opened his mouth, but I lifted a hand to cut him off. "And you're not the only one with a full plate. I need to focus on preparing for court. I lost a lot of study time this week, and there isn't much left."

I set my hand against the side of James's cheek, and the connection between us grew stronger. I let him see my doubt, my hope, and all the confusion I needed to sort out before I could even begin to make a decision about the future of our relationship. "I'm not saying never. I'm saying not right now."

Warmth poured through my hand, along with a wave of resolve. "Do what you must. I can wait."

James pulled my hand away from his cheek and kissed my palm. Then he walked to the front door and pulled it open. He glanced back with a smile. "Another time."

I smiled back, finding comfort in the words I'd cringed to hear a week ago.

As the door closed behind him, I cradled the warmth he'd left on my palm and in my mind. Then I flicked off the television and turned toward the dining room with a sigh. Stacks of books and papers from my last lesson were still on the table. I pursed my lips and turned on the coffee maker. Time to study like my life depended on it.

Want more?

Continue the series with

FAERIE FORGED
Book 3 of The Magicsmith series.

About the Author

L.R. Braden is a bestselling, multi-award-winning author of dark-yet-hopeful urban fantasy stories. Her published works include the *Magicsmith* series, the *Rifter* series, and several works of shorter fiction. A bit of a recluse, she enjoys collecting skills that may (or may not) prove useful in the event that she is suddenly transported to an inhospitable alternate reality. Since that hasn't happened yet, she mostly spends her days weaving fantastic tales, playing with her family, and getting lost on purpose. Her writing has won many awards, including the Eric Hoffer Book Award for Sci-fi/Fantasy, the Next Generation Indie Book Award for Paranormal Fiction, and the Imadjinn Award for Best Urban Fantasy.

Connect with her online at lrbraden.com

www.ingramcontent.com/pod-product-compliance
Lightning Source LLC
Chambersburg PA
CBHW022033240626
47154CB00007B/2391